Perseid Press
P.O. Box 584
Centerville MA 02632

Hell Gate

Cover art and cover design by Roy Mauritsen.

Book design by Christopher Morris

Cover design © Perseid Press
A Perseid Press Original

First Perseid Press Kindle edition May 2019
First Perseid Press Trade edition May 2019

Kindle version, ISBN-13: 978-1-948602-24-2
Trade edition ISBN-13: 978-1-948602-25-9

Published in the United States of America

10 9 8 7 6 5 4 3 2 1

Acknowledgement

Once again, it is with a profound sense of gratitude that I say "thank you" to Janet for allowing me to step through the looking glass to play.

Dedication

"…Where is the wonder, where's the awe

Where's dear Alice knocking on the door...

Where is the trapdoor that takes me there

Where the real is shattered by a mad March Hare…"

Nightwish – From the album – Imaginarium

Dedicated to all those who see through the smoke and mirrors into the shadowland that waits for us all.

Contents

Hell Gate

The gateway to the city of Doom. Through me
The entrance to the Everlasting Pain.
The Gateway of the Lost. The Eternal Three
Justice impelled to build me. Here ye see
Wisdom Supreme at work, and Primal Power,
And Love Supernal in their dawnless day.
Ere from their thought creation rose in flower
Eternal first were all things fixed as they.
Of Increate Power infinite formed am I
That deathless as themselves I do not die.
Justice divine has weighed: the doom is clear.
All hope renounce, ye lost, who enter here.

—Dante Alighieri 1265—1321, *The Divine Comedy*

HELL GATE

Prologue

The reality of Skull Isle was vastly different to the picture I'd painted in my mind.

On a prior sortie here, I'd headed a team of pirates on a mission that led to the recovery of two of my Hell Hounds—Yamato Takeru and Champ Ferguson—from a Sibitti holding cell deep in the bowels of the clustered peaks once again before me. On that visit, a verdant ring of menace had encompassed a snowcapped cordillera, providing a taste of what lay in wait at the center of the island: the mother of all obstacle courses. An apt analogy, for rivers of molten metal, booby-trapped bridges, and lethal labyrinths riddled with hidden snares protected their prison.

But of course, that was before a monster tsunami pulverized the encircling heights and dragged the whole island beneath the waves.

I cast my senses down through the curtain of hydrothermal gasses. Fluids rippled up from the depths. I watched, mesmerized, as a veil of silver-gray mystery turned the murky waters of the Bitter Sea into an effervescent wash of contradictions.

The faint tang of fading thaumaturgy still lingered, a timely reminder of the potency that once dominated this whole region. Even better, that echo was a surefire sign my suspicions about this place might be correct.

And if they are, I'll have a nice selection of bargaining chips to take back to the Kigali homeland.

Albeit most of the mountains had toppled, the exterior of the catacombs remained remarkably intact. The visage of one of Erra's enforcers—the Sixth, to be precise—with jaws wide open, marked the main entrance to the waiting maze, adding a menacing overtone to a locale that didn't need any help exuding a heartfelt *fuck off* vibe. A gentle surge of energy propelled me toward that access point. Igniting the gem adorning the tip of my scythe, I surveyed the interior to find things much changed from my previous visit. While the atrium had survived most of the destruction and still displayed an impressive array of stalagmites and stalactites, there any similarity ended.

Now a forest of petrified megaliths and jagged stumps had replaced the glittery splendor of diamond-encrusted limestone. Stained black by an all-pervading discharge oozing from a fretwork of fissures lining floors and walls, those ranked columns filed off into the distance, obsidian clad sentinels waiting to frogmarch miscreants to certain doom.

Far from muting the former glory of the grotto, the mineral-laden soup had transformed it into a nightmarish tribute to the inexplicable and macabre.

Here ghostly eyeless fish gulped for breath, their albino feelers constantly testing the inky darkness about them for microbes and other tasty tidbits. There all manner of gothically-armored crustaceans vied with territorial starfish of outrageous size and color. Obviously wary, both soon put their differences aside to scuttle for shared cover the moment my staff illuminated them.

The only creatures unperturbed by my presence were the new colonies of hell-worms infesting the rocks around each freshly opened vent. And it soon became apparent why.

Wreathed by a halo of whiskery tendrils waving invitations to all and sundry, the hell-worms provided a calm and languid counterpoint to the frantic game of survival playing out all around them . . . until a careless shrimp or crab happened along. No sooner did those welcoming tentacles detect prey nearby than vicious looking barbs shot out to snare the unwary and reel them into a central maw lined with razor-sharp teeth.

Every so often shrill cries from another hapless critter that strayed too close punctuated the percolating backdrop, followed by a resounding *crunch* cutting short its protestations.

I smiled.

No matter where you venture in our many-layered under-verse, it's a constant cycle of eat or be eaten. Exactly the way it should be.

Shaking free of this pleasurable interlude, I decided it best to crack on with the business at hand: I'd come to catch what game was afoot, not to sightsee.

Examining the gloom, I noticed the rear gallery had escaped much of the damage evident elsewhere. The exit porch still boasted the same message, inscribed in ancient Hellanese, across its lintel: "*Fá entrig a-mhàile a' cothreh-tah* (Only the balanced may enter)," providing a subtle reference to the logic puzzle waiting beyond its threshold, where the pressure-activated floor-trap would consign reckless explorers to a lingering death.

A contending tide issued from within, resisting my progress. Working my way forward, I held tight to the doorjambs while I peered inside. Not until then did the cause of the outflow become obvious:

Four months previously, I had ruptured the wards emplaced by the Sibitti, Erra's seven personified weapons, to keep my captive Hounds incommunicado. In so doing, I triggered the chain reaction that caused the island to sink. Given free rein, the encroaching sea worked its way along myriad passages. Conduits crisscrossing the massif in a pulmonary network of fiery capillaries led down into the lava chambers, precipitating a further series of volatile events that spawned the current conditions.

This cell contained one such channel, and the flue connecting its two main levels must have remained open. Scalding eddies redolent with the heady aroma of sulfur had boiled up from below so fast that one corner of the puzzle room's tilting platform was forced against its roof.

Excellent. A surge of affirmation emboldened me. *The Sibitti's machinations were more thorough than I'd realized, effectively protecting the primary route to the oubliette from the worst of the damage. So I should be able to access the spire with minimal fuss. But first—*

Summoning my strength, I encompassed myself within a gleaming sphere of power, and then directed a bolt of kinetic energy through my scythe and into the raised section of flooring. Solid granite slabs exploded as if no more than but brittle plaster. The resultant cloud of hydrous dust and larger particles swirled around a common center before being swept away with the rest of the outflux in a race for the surface.

Inspired by their eagerness, I extended the front of my shield until it morphed into an elongated teardrop and shot forward into the opening. Piercing the opposing riptide like a marlin cutting the waves, I made speedy progress and soon sensed the end of the tunnel.

Painful memories intruded. During my last foray into this terminus I had been projected at high speed into a buffering wall and dropped through a narrow annulus onto the top of a solitary pinnacle above a cauldron of lava.

Forewarned, I reduced velocity. But I needn't have worried. This time I encountered no bulwark or accompanying exit.

Hmmm, no doubt blasted to smithereens during the cataclysm that tore the guts out of this place.

Sailing free of the connective artery, I entered the principal magma chamber and circled its circumference several times to get my bearings. Although ravaged by the colossal thermodynamic energies released when the ocean had breached its confining enchantments, the heart of the mountain yet maintained its core integrity. Swamped by a blanket of cauliflower pillars, billowing noxious steam and poisonous vapors, the intact bore resembled an upended cylinder a hundred yards across. Free of the undulating pall, its upper levels sparkled through all the colors of the visible spectrum. The invading aquatic confluence only complimented its stark beauty.

Flooding or no, the spirit of this once-mighty peak prevailed. Time and again, the ruddy glow of its flowing lifeblood ignited the brume's interior in rose-gold glory. Each flare served as a precursor to a new eruption whose pyroclastic fury hurtled toward the vault's roof in a bid for freedom, only to fall back, spent and impotent, into the forge's raging hearth.

Relief swept over me as I realized I needn't face that furnace head on, for it promised to be a swine to navigate, even for one with my rare talents.

Refining my probe, I hastily pierced the frenzied stream of luminescent bubbles around me while searching for my next target: an isolated archway cut high into the chamber's far wall.

A slender bridge had once connected that doorway to a splinter of rock at the exact center of the vault. But like everything else in this hellhole-in-hell, now it proved only a memory, another casualty in a war not of its choosing.

I willed myself toward and through that exit without hesitation. A sharp contrast in outlook and a familiar tingle like insects on skin confirmed the portico still active.

Lowering my shield, I descended into a small and silent antechamber. It was pitch-black, for no hint of the havoc wrought on the other side of the esodesic plane intruded on this, the inner sanctum of repeated Sibitti atrocities.

I bridled at the thought of what the Seven had done. *And here I am again, undoing yet more of their mischief.*

Once I adjusted my perspective to the changed environment, everything sprang into crystal-clear clarity:

Telltale signs of my earlier mission lay scattered here and there about the hall: scuffmarks and footprints; discarded items from where Captain Charles Vane and the scumbag, Low, had rearranged the contents of their backpacks; deeper scratches nearer the fountain where Griffin poisoned himself and died in agony.

The shallow pool at the rear of the antechamber also remained, but its source had run dry or been diverted by the tectonic stresses brought to bear during the island's demise. The water was stagnant and coated in a thick film of scummy dross.

An ancient stairwell beckoned in the vestibule. Relaxing, I sent out my seeker-sense and followed the shaft's course with my mind's eye through a giddy series of descending landings and switchbacks, until its steps ended at a wide gallery, dominated by a bottomless pit.

Beyond that pit, a further tunnel gave onto a spiraling passage that wound down for over a mile into the roots of the mountain. Its outlet formed a small gorge with a precariously narrow ledge following the right-hand side of the scarp.

At last. Time to pick up the pace.

My curiosity satisfied, I saw no further reason to linger. Gathering my potential, I envisioned myself standing on the sill leading out into the chasm, and in less time than it takes to blink, I'd phased . . .

. . . and stood there.

A churning river of lava mumbled past, forty feet beneath me, only a shadow of its former self. Shocked, I spoke aloud: "The tributary's much lower than before. And it feels cooler...?" On impulse, I tested the air: "A balmy hundred and ten degrees . . . maybe a hundred and fifteen, at most."

I sent my farsight skimming along the bed of the trench. It detected multiple fractures running the length of its course. Some had scabbed over, fused shut by igneous caps.

"Bugger me. The magma's gradually draining away. If I hadn't hit on the notion of coming here, the *talle-bhést* would have been screwed."

More determined to succeed than ever, I strode forward for about thirty yards before turning to face the wall. The molten flow's lurid light cast puppets on the walls; flickering shadows and frenzied flares danced before my eyes, making every nook and cranny of the bluff pulse and quiver like a gravelly amoebic sac.

But the shadow play was mere illusion. Nothing but lava moved here. As keen as my augmented senses were, I could distinguish jack shit. *The talle-bhést must have discerned the dropping temperature and reduced their autonomous functions in order to hibernate.*

No doubt, the talle-bhést were here; and when they emerged, they would recognize me. Therefore, I decided to adopt the dignity of my station: the Phage.

Yes, I was here to render the talle-bhést aid. But they wouldn't know that, and the last time we'd met I dispatched two of their number with extreme prejudice. And so far as I knew, the only other entities they'd ever met were the Sibitti, who spirited them away from their home to dump them here, where they faced a withering death.

They'll be pissed, wary of strangers and, once they've gained their bearings, ready to fight. So I'll have to convince them we're on the same side.

I resorted to the eternal flame within me.

In an instant, the Bãlefire responded to my call. A corona of sparkling ebony and silver light glazed the atmosphere; purple and yellow streamers charged my soul-well to full capacity; a crown of gold and scarlet stars burst to life above my head, anointing me in unyielding dominion.

Holding the full measure of my might in abeyance, I raised my palm and trickled steady heat directly into the cliff. Soon, the entire escarpment glowed red. As the temperature rose, I reverted to ancient Hellanese and called out, both mentally and verbally, "*Se* áis *Daûmen Grÿrmm, Satanase Thanatos* (I am Daemon Grim, Satan's Reaper). *Prìoàrd mathas ruag etom cuirch measg iadcho* òrdaich *Ilfrinn Cuúgar* (Chief bounty hunter and master of those appointed as Hell Hounds). *Se ten seo caraíth bhure* (I am here as your friend)."

A keening shriek, strident and piercing, cut the air like an eagle's cry. The cliff trembled. Stones and other loose fragments broke free and slithered downslope. Abruptly, more than a dozen talle-bhést detached themselves from the rock face to either side me. They lumbered forward, their clublike arms held high. Their thoughts were jumbled and hard to fathom. Nevertheless, a storm of disquieting emotions betrayed their confusion.

It's only natural they're reacting this way, I suppose. Let's see what I can do.

Calm and deliberate, I opened my arms wide to show I meant no harm. Then I lowered my personal shield and repeated my message, so they could taste the nuance of my feelings.

Now they know I'm telling the truth.

I also took the precaution of uttering a single phrase in the Kigali language. "*Siothellnath* (Peace)."

So suddenly did the talle-bhést halt their advance, I was momentarily at a loss for words. Thankfully, instinct took over. Acting on the unexpected opportunity, I inched my hand toward my scythe and slid it from its holster. Leaving it folded, I then visualized a specific destination and depressed the second stud from the bottom.

A sizzling amber iris more than twenty feet in diameter manifested on the lip of the precipice overlooking the lava flow, its event horizon no more than a dappled gray void. *Not good enough, I have to make an impression.*

Channeling my considerable strength into a nub of focused intent, I molded the energies flowing into the quantum medium until a noval flare blanched the surrounding nimbus white. The geodesic plane shimmered and clarified, showing a picture of the exact coordinates I'd chosen: Kí-gal.

Surprised at the ease by which I'd circumvented the instabilities currently wreaking havoc on the hydraspace lanes, I snorted. *Well, well, well. Would you look at that? Satan's changes continue to manifest?*

Such a realization made me contemplate my growing list of private enemies who would one day face the consequences of their duplicity. For a fleeting instant, my mien darkened, causing a number of the talle-bhést to bark in dismay.

"For fuck sake, Daemon," I grumbled to myself, "get a grip."

Forced to dismiss such thoughts of revenge—for now—I sought to make amends.

Perhaps this *might work?*

Softening my countenance, I gestured to the vista displayed through the eye of the gateway, and tried communicating in the Kigali dialect, a tongue I had only recently learned.

"*Thig a-miŝ* (Come along). *Air fen cámad, tekt dión tau etu dûbit-e tau da-hel hí-gal* (I am a friend, sent here to protect you and take you home)."

I pointed for a second time. "*Argûs, aite sin ifé, Chí-ghâl* (Look, there it is, Kí-gal). *Chí-ven tok. S'gaul táir* (Hurry up. Let's go)."

Standing to one side, I reined back my aura so the lure of something familiar could take center stage and waited patiently for the talle-bhést to respond.

And respond they did. Whatever means they used to communicate was still beyond me. Even so, they arrived at a unanimous decision simultaneously. Shuffling forward from both sides, the ogres formed an orderly line and took turns stepping through.

Watching them go, I breathed an overdue sigh of relief.

Thank Satan for that. I've tippy-toed around Kigali etiquette for long enough. Well no more. The return of these boys is bound to win Kur's favor, or at the least force his hand to grant concessions. By this time tomorrow, I'll have a spook team and state-of-the-art surveillance inside the soul sapphire crèche, or my name's not Daemon Grim. I rubbed my hands together in anticipation. *I can only hope I'm there to see the look on Chopin and Tesla's faces when their whole underworld comes crashing down on them.*

And with that, I let the portal collapse in on itself and joined the talle-bhést on the far side.

Chapter 1: Picking up the Threads

Ferocious heat beset Frédéric Chopin from every quarter. The assault on his person raged, relentless, despite soothing salve applied generously to his face and neck. Sweat ran in rivulets down his temples and along his spine, staining his white shirt a filthy gray. His clothes stuck to his form like a glued-on second skin. Desperately thirsty, he tried to swallow, but received naught for his efforts but an overwhelming urge to gag.

Chopin refused to be distracted. He continued, devoted to the task at hand, which was downloading his most recent experiences into the glittering amber jewel wedged amongst the rocks at his feet.

Measuring three feet wide and twice that long, this soul sapphire (in the Kigali language a *trúllefeng*, or in everyday terms, a *stone of remembrance*) was among the biggest of its kind. Imbued with special mimicking properties, such sapphires occurred naturally, growing in an isolated cave deep in the heart of Kí-gal's greatest volcano. What was more; the first tribe of hell actually used such stones extensively to chronicle their accomplishments, and the distinguished history of their race.

During the course of their travels, Chopin and Tesla had found the larger sapphires capable of more, much more, than recording dry facts. Ever the opportunists, the two refractory damned sought to exploit the superior imprinting capabilities of those specimens by cloning copies of themselves as insurance against capture, torture, inevitable death and reassignment . . . or even obliteration.

Chopin stared at the serene countenance of his mirror image, sleeping soundly within the stable environment of its prismatic world. Fully formed, its epidermis appeared pale but healthy, with no signs of the waxy vernix goo that had coated it from head to foot during its early development.

Its eyes roved from side to side beneath its lids, signaling that the current memory packet had triggered an onrush of dreams.

"Not too long now, my fine fellow," Chopin murmured. He pressed his forehead against the cool exterior of the gem and savored a scant respite. "Hopefully, I'll never get to use you, in which case you'll slumber for all eternity. But if I do, it'll be satisfying to know the Undertaker won't be able to spoil the benefits of all the extra knowledge I've gained, or the fabulous feats I've achieved despite his insufferable machinations."

Someone grunted, and Chopin broke the connection with the clone to find his partner in crime, Nikola Tesla, staring at him, an open cooler to one side, two goblets of chilled wine at the ready.

"You were linked for an unusually long time," Tesla chided, "so I thought you might need *this* when you finished." He teased the sweaty composer with the largest of the drinks.

Hell's bells. Do I ever. Chopin stood, snatched the proffered beverage from Tesla's grasp and drained it in one gulp. His thirst only partly assuaged, Chopin tossed the glass over his shoulder and paused to listen as it shattered with a gratifying *crunch*. Satisfied, he made haste to work the kinks out of his back.

And now? Warily, he extended his arms and flexed his fingers back and forth. A hollow pulsing ache, similar to the discomfort of arthritics, radiated along Chopin's limbs. He breathed a welcome sigh of relief. *That's it?*

As Chopin had been delighted to discover recently, his own particular curse—that of a cruelly amplified form of temporal-lobe epilepsy that cramped his muscles, snapped his ligaments, and shattered his bones whenever he attempted to surmount a personal challenge—receded in those realms not among the latterday circles of hell.

In a contemplative mood, Chopin stared about the alien environment and marveled at its harshness.

*It's a pity conditions within this Gate are so barren. It rules out any chance of a permanent move, but—*inspiration struck—*but if I'm careful, it needn't preclude my coming here to compose and rehearse. After all, our enemies haven't the faintest idea this place exists, and those who have stumbled upon it by chance . . .* Chopin thought of those poor unfortunates who had blundered into this land by accident, and chuckled. *Well, they don't last very long. Yes, I think I should explore the . . . eh?*

Only at that moment did Chopin realized his daydreams had run away with him again. Well accustomed to lapses in his companion's concentration, Tesla had been forced to wait patiently for Chopin to pull his act back together.

"Ah, forgive me," Chopin apologized. "Yes, I took rather a long time, didn't I? Do excuse the inconvenience. I wanted to ensure I'd transferred the full extent of my musical repertoire for posterity, especially as several of my latest compositions—the Devil's Trull included—were dedicated to my dearest Amantine. Having gone to all that trouble, I'd rather not score them all over again should we run afoul of the Reaper at the last hurdle." He paused to salute his clone. "However, with these extra precautions in place, even the warped vagaries of the Undertaker's twisted perversions won't prevent the sweet joy of our sacred reunion. And once Amantine witnesses firsthand the obstacles I've overcome to show my devotion, I'm sure she'll be only too happy to forsake some placid heavenly existence and stay here with me."

Tesla didn't seem all that convinced by the reference to Chopin's long lost sweetheart, Amantine Lucile Aurore Dupin—aka George Sands—or her willingness to endure perpetual suffering for a man she'd secretly despised. Ill at ease, Tesla mumbled, "Well, it won't be for the lack of trying, that's for sure." He dropped to one knee to scoop some of their gear into a carryall and continued, "So in two weeks, when the Winter Soulstice is upon us, you'll get the chance to see Miss Dupin again. Tell me, how do you think it best to expend our energies meanwhile?"

Chopin gave the question serious consideration before replying: "In view of the escalating situation, I say we keep our heads down, enjoy the subtle delights offered by Hell's Kitchen, and trust in misdirection both subtle and foul to keep the Reaper's apes of wrath at bay."

"In other words, do nothing to attract attention?"

"Out of sight, out of mind." Chopin grimaced. "Not the best comparison, I know, but our remaining moles amongst Satan's hierarchy will give us fair warning—or unfair warning, if all hell starts breaking loose."

"Are you sure we're wise," Tesla pressed, "to trust our safety to their judgment?"

"Of course. They have given sterling service till now, blissfully unaware that their conditioning will spur them to even greater deceptions as we approach apogee. Though such subterfuge may result in their apprehension, their aptitudes ensure they'll remain silent . . . at least until it's too late to foil our plan."

"And if you're wrong about them?"

"Then we turn to our brutes. Their personal vendetta with Nettesheim aside, Castile and Guiteau are making enough noise to wake the devil himself. And with the additional mayhem of these latest riots? We couldn't have arranged things better ourselves—What?"

Throaty snarls rumbled across the open, blistering-hot plain.

"Do you hear that? Someone chases another party of slaves this way. Best not to press our luck," Tesla advised.

Picking up their equipment bag, he scuttled to his compatriot and removed a small silver-gray orb from one of his pockets. "Shall we?"

"Let's," Chopin replied, mopping his brow. "How about a brief stop at Niflheim first? I really do need to cool down properly before doing anything else."

The air warped, shimmered, and all that remained of the interlopers' existence was a spiraling pair of dust devils, dancing around a common center.

Nearby, the facsimiles yet slept, oblivious to the deadly game they might one day play.

*

At a small pavement table outside Cullognes's finest bistro—*Der Letzte Biss* (The Last Bite), safe behind Tesla's identity-masking profile inhibitor, sat Isabella Castile, once queen and instigator of the fifteenth-century Spanish Inquisition. She who once blighted the lives of thousands of innocents had long since perfected an air of aloof confidence. Dressed in a steel wool Killvin Klein pant suit, Isabella drew admiring glances from most passing by.

Her colleague, Charles Guiteau, relaxing opposite, pretended to read a newspaper. Similarly attired in business ensemble, he appeared even more elegant than his stunning companion, for his neatly trimmed beard and mustache and the gold rimmed spectacles perched upon his generous nose added a touch of sophistication to his demeanor that set him apart from most other patrons.

Outwardly, both appeared at ease and unconcerned by the boisterous antics of the revelers filling the city's central piazza around them. However, a more discerning observer would have noted the way they dissected each face in the crowd with unwavering vigilance. Closer inspection might also have revealed the distinctive bulges spoiling the outline of their tailored jackets.

Isabella leaned forward and sipped of latte from a delicate porcelain skull cup, her movements economical and feline. She swallowed, and her top lip peeled back like a panther's, in a moue of disgust.

Dishwater. But what else to expect from the peasants of New Hell's murder capital. She smiled disdainfully. *They try so hard to hide their coarseness behind the illusion of class, but constantly fail.*

An insightful observation, for Cullogne was the New Dead's simulacrum of "a tale of two cities."

While homes in the outer districts crowded together in jumbles that put most topside shantytown slums to shame, those located closer to the cathedral and twin palaces situated on opposite banks of the River Rhime gleamed, spacious and flamboyant. Châteauesque townhouses and rambling villas vied with miniature castles and sprawling mansions for dominance, their Byzantine inspiration highlighted by superfluous arches, imposing towers, and crenelated walkways overhead that lent frosty streets an opulent veneer.

Isabella marked the progress of several rape gangs and kill squads stalking the outer square's perimeter, their inbred aggression underlined by the way each crew evaluated their prospective victims and one another.

No wonder this place breeds violence for violence sake, Isabella reasoned to herself. *With nowhere else to go, the majority of its citizenry have little to do but vent their frustrations upon those foolish enough to flaunt success—as I do believe I'm about to witness.*

One young dandy braved the press with impunity, believing his wealth and two hired bravos sufficient to keep him safe.

At first glance his bodyguards also appeared as souls of substance. Strutting like roosters in designer combats and equipment harnesses, they made a great show of bullying other denizens into giving their client a wide berth. Where that failed, they shoved people out of their way or applied a bullet to the back of thick head.

But for good reason was Isabella Castile one of hell's preeminent femme fatales. "It's all in the details," she sang softly, unafraid.

And in this case, those details spoke volumes: unkempt hair and grubby fingernails; permanent nine o'clock shadows and dirty clothes; scuffed, ill-worn boots and counterfeit labels; frayed straps and filthy weapons. She noted the repeated glances exchanged by the *would be/ should be* protectors and the ruffians waiting patiently on the steps of the Low Court of Injustice who made a play of being out for a breath of sulfurous air, in the hope a spot of trouble might come their way.

Riffraff, she mused, *sent as backup should our intrepid guardians here prove ineffective.*

Anticipation sparked a fight-or-flight response in the queen, along with a corresponding flicker of arousal deep in her stomach, a sensation delicious and feral. Spurning the rest of her coffee, she turned instead to a bottle of Ty Rant spring water to slake her thirst and watched as the cuckoos herded their charge toward an alley running between the courthouse and adjacent uncivic center. The same alley, coincidentally, which the band of thugs also at this very moment chose to investigate.

Sure enough, a commotion ensued in which the unlucky dupe—minus his bodyguards—was pounced on and dragged away to certain reassignment.

Seconds later, a shriek split the ether, demanding retribution and freezing everybody in their tracks. Time resumed as the cry died and triggered a roar that erupted toward veiled Paradise, while a vast assortment of concealed pistols, knives, axes and cudgels appeared as the damned souls turned on their neighbors.

Isolated shots barked in quick succession, followed by yelps of pain, hissed curses and dissipating corpses. On the far side of the plaza, a machine-gun opened fire, thinning the crowd.

Those unarmed were few and far between. These swiftly resorted to other means, smashing furniture at hand to brandish broken table legs and chair backs or glass from shattered windows. Armed thus, they flung themselves into the fray with savage aplomb, beating, bludgeoning and slashing any soul in reach.

In some cases, bare knuckles sufficed. Townsfolk possessing a degree of finesse then snapped wrists, broke teeth, and popped eyeballs. Those unskilled resorted to choking the unlife from one another.

Anarchy ensued.

Combatants slipped in gore and other appendages that had no business paving the thoroughfare.

Although their particular establishment seemed immune from the unfurling rampage, Isabella herself most certainly was not. Pulse pounding, she felt the knot in her belly tighten. The hunger for slaughter rose in her throat in time to her accelerating heartbeat.

Then came an unexpected explosion that threw combatants across sidewalks and noncombatants into a panic.

Did some fool let off a grenade? Isabella licked dry lips with an unwieldy tongue.

A huge gap manifested in the midst of the throng fighting outside the uncivic center, extending the effect of the blast. Regardless, the brawl resumed almost immediately, but as it did so, Isabella's finely-tuned senses discerned an odd change in tempo. *Is the synergy of this conflict mutating in some way?*

Evidence supporting her suspicions soon surfaced: those rolling around on the pavement stopped struggling; they began to embrace; then kiss. Whereas before their fingers and nails had been deadly weapons, they now passionately tore at clothing, buttons and other loose fastenings.

Comprehension jarred her spine. "Oh no," she gasped, "the plague! It's happening again."

"Just look at them, Isabella," Guiteau snarled. He coughed, taking care to discreetly mop the ruby stains glazing his chin with a napkin from the table. "Some of the shortest fuses in the underverse reduced to pathetic, stuttering candles."

He surveyed the worsening debacle before them, his cheeks blushed red. "Hell and damnation, nothing goes right for us these days. This little shindig is devolving into another one of those cursed orgies that keep breaking out in one place after another. I tell you, if Nettesheim *is* here, it'll spook him. And if he's using his mystic abilities to watch events closely, our nonparticipation will earn his further scrutiny. Mark my words: Tesla's identity-diffusers or not, he'll be onto us and we'll have wasted—Eh? I don't believe it!"

Following the direction of his gaze, Isabella espied a number of former antagonists who'd thrown caution to the wind and were now ravishing each other in full view of all, and with wanton abandon.

"Oh lordy me," Guiteau spluttered, spraying blood across the tablecloth. Addressing the copulating couples, he yelled, "Don't spoil the fighting by fucking. What in Hades' name do you hope to achieve? You'll never escape the consequences, you know."

It was no good: nobody listened, although Isabella did spot several couples who hurried, perhaps inspired by her partner's admonishment.

Multitasking, eh? How the other half lives . . . or not, as the case may be.

Her judgment proved unerringly accurate: rhythmic movements became frantic; eyes screwed shut and mouths gaped wide; spines arched and then fell limp; moans of ecstasy turned to mewling groans of pain; stomachs distended; bodies doubled over and teeth clenched in agony. A ripping sound filled the air as flesh tore.

In seconds, the mall disappeared beneath a quivering, twitching blanket of biting fangs and darting stingers as a mass of hideous spiders and grotesque scorpions burst into view. Without hesitation, the arachnids set about devouring their hosts first, and then promptly set their jaws and venom on everyone else within reach with a commendable dedication to duty.

Isabella found herself aroused to the point of climax by the rampant butchery. *I don't suppose it would hurt to play along, if only for a little while? After all, the only lusts my associate and I covet tend toward the mortal.*

Reaching beneath her jacket, she slipped her Hell-Brass 6.66 Magnum from its holster, took aim, and blew the brains out of their waiter, the maître d' and two other customers in quick succession.

"What the devil . . . ?" Guiteau gasped.

"You're right," Isabella explained, "If Nettesheim is here, we can't risk that he'll recognize us and realize we've been tracking him these past months."

"Are you sure?"

Isabella shrugged. "It would have been gratifying to catch our target at last. If only to teach him the error of his ways as we slowly flay him over an open fire. But it matters not. For some reason, he's drawn to Cullogne as to nowhere else. Don't worry. We'll bide our time and pick up the threads on his next visit."

"And until then?"

"I'd have thought that was obvious, my lovely." Isabella's husky voice took a steely edge to match the stiletto blade she expertly extracted from her ankle sheath. "We let off some steam."

Without a further word, she hurled herself into the madness, and the screaming reached fever pitch.

*

Acclaimed throughout hell, the Bridge was an orphic structure of versatile scope, a sentient entity, capable of transporting passengers throughout the length and breadth of the underverse without those strictures usually imposed during multidimensionhell travel.

And Heinrich von Nettesheim was one denizen who was pleased it could.

Over the past several months, he had employed the Bridge's inimitable functions to further his quest for knowledge. His was a quest that had taken him through stygian landscapes, shrouded in perpetual midnight; across heaving oceans of acid, teeming with continually dissolving aquatic unlife forms; up mountain ranges erected from the bones of long forgotten titans; and through entire continents where endless fields of supplicants screamed for mercy.

On each occasion, the Bridge had adopted a modus best suited for navigating the obstacles it encountered. Sometimes it would materialize as an exact representation of its namesake—the Brooklyn Bridge—from fabled New York, topside. At others, it embraced the characteristics of an ingenious array of conveyances; carriages as diverse in appearance and operation as a pirate's galleon, a steam locomotive, even a 1920's Cadillac—or, as on this day's journey, a hot air balloon.

Despite the varying manifestations of the Bridge, all had one thing in common: they were capable of negotiating the instabilities wrought upon the Sheolspace continuum by the Sibitti. For this blessing, Nettesheim was especially grateful.

A bell sounded, followed by the hiss of gas venting from the top of the blood red envelope overhead.

Ah, we're almost there.

Nettesheim decided it might be prudent to mentally review his itinerary for the next few days, and his eyes glazed over as he summonsed a visible representation of his assigned work schedule.

Very well. So far, I've completed an examination of the archives from eleven of Cullogne's thirteen High Churches. The only two remaining— the Abbey of the Blessed Heretic, and the Chapel of the Epistle of Judas Iscariot, within the Grand Church of Profanity—should provide me with the details I need to complete my final preparations. Just as well. The Soulstice is upon us and the current unrest has caused me—?

"Next stop, Cullogne," announced a disembodied voice. The burners whistled as the flames keeping the balloon aloft extinguished. Nettesheim's stomach lurched as his rate of descent increased. "Please collect all your belongings prior to vacating your seat, and mind the gap when disembarking."

The seams around the edge of the gondola's floor space blazed, in an effect similar to that seen when a welder uses an oxyacetylene torch. Then the bottom of the basket faded into a thin transparent film, revealing a view familiar to Nettesheim: his usual arrival point here in Cullogne, the highest of the buttressed walkways connecting the gleaming spires of the cathedral itself.

"Thank you, my friend," Nettesheim whispered, as much from habit as courtesy. "Don't forget, I have a return ticket, so I'll be in touch as soon as my research is concluded."

As always, the Bridge declined conversation. But a tickling sensation across the top of his scalp signified that it understood him. Nettesheim smiled, stepped forward and dropped through the portal.

The subdued glow of Paradise filtered through the clouds, adding a jaundiced tinge to the verglas-coated rooftops stretching into the distance. Nettesheim reveled in the grandeur of his hometown from this vantage point, where the sheer presence of the imposing public monuments and stately homes surrounding the cathedral gradually gave way to the tightly packed maze of the farther slums. The mephitic breath of the River Rhime coated everything in a chilling haar, as if the entire city had been dipped in frigid gossamer and left to congeal inside a gigantic permafrost cobweb.

Taking a deep breath, Nettesheim inhaled the invigorating stench of carrion. The acrid odor reminded him how deadly this place could be. Forewarned, he reached into the subatomic medium binding the varied levels of hell together, creating a pocket of reality slightly out of sync with the normal flow of time.

"That's better," he muttered aloud. "Now I'll remain hidden from direct line of sight and telepathic observation. If my shadows aren't already here, they'll soon follow. And while I'm sure Guiteau wouldn't present too much of an obstacle, only a fool would underestimate that Mata Hari, Castile." He whistled low. "There's a woman who kno–?"

Hello? An earsplitting shriek lanced up from the milling throng nearly six hundred feet below, a battle-cry of aggression. Sensing it, people charged one another, clearly intent on violence. From Nettesheim's perspective, the townsfolk resembled ants swarming to defend against an attack on their nest.

"Ah, home sweet home. It doesn't take much to spark a blaze. Odds bodkins! What now?" A glittering net of diffuse energy materialized within the fabric of the esoteric backdrop. Nettesheim caught his breath, recognizing the onset of the mystery infection running riot through most of the latter-day hells."

He adjusted his scanning frequency to better apprehend the purpose of the pathogen now spreading its influence through the air. "It's like a virus," he mused aloud. "Yes, it attaches itself to the nucleus of any predominant emotion, and mutates it into something atypical. Something unnatural." His blood ran cold. *Is that lust? Adoration? Wait a minute.*

One facet of the contagion's character struck a familiar chord.

"It's mystical in origin, and designed to target a specific behavioral response. No wonder we're seeing so many orgies." Incensed, Nettesheim undertook a further review. "I need a closer look. This underhanded attack against hell's unsocial instability must not stand, We can't have unrestrained . . . *Scheisse!"*

Down below, the crowd's mood had changed.

Here we go. Things will turn real messy, real soon.

As if by his command, they did.

An unstoppable tide of scorpions and spiders of ghoulish variety burst from the bellies of those unable to curb their deviant desires. No sooner had they surfaced, than the rampaging arthropods set about consuming their lustful progenitors. Afterward, they went to work on those too stupid or distracted to flee.

Nettesheim noted how a small number of combatants seemed immune to the effects of the insidious catalyst in their midst. The scientist in him wondered, *What makes* them *resistant while so many others succumb*?

He zoomed in to take a closer look and was nonplussed to discover two individuals in particular—a male and female, dressed similarly in business suits—whose faces he couldn't properly distinguish.

Trying again, Nettesheim saw his mental probe dissolve while the features of his targets remained unresolved.

They're shielded somehow? Okay, got something to hide, have you?

While watching the scene unfold, Nettesheim inscribed a series of glowing pictographs in the air before him. Each glyph flared in turn, allowing him to draw on the latent potential saturating the infirmament with devilish power. Adding its potential to the mix, his next attempt successfully pierced the veil around his two targets.

What he saw came as no surprise.

So, my stalkers were already here and waiting. Nettesheim pondered his recent movements and realized what had happened. *Ah, my research has brought me to this city so often that they easily tracked me: an avoidable mistake I should have corrected much sooner.* He shrugged. *Still, it couldn't be helped. The convergence is almost upon us, and Grim's power grows exponentially. If the occult restraints shackling his mind fail before we are ready, everything we hope to achieve may be lost. And* that *just won't do.*

Nettesheim studied his would-be antagonists as they vented their pent-up frustrations, and his pulse surged at the prospect of eventually facing them.

"Your time will come, my friends," he muttered, as if vocalizing his thoughts would validate the promise he now made. "But not yet. Alas, my personal satisfaction must await the master's pleasure. Once my obligations are fulfilled, though, I shall see about you."

Chapter 2: The Sound of Silence

The trees ringing the hills around my present location didn't merely brood, they exuded maleficence so profound that the rank and file of damned souls would be under no illusions that they weren't welcome here. In case some didn't get the hint, mists of foreboding and ghostly vapor trails squeezed between the close-packed boles of the forest during every hour of every day. The wood and its ambience formed a first line of defense for one of Satan's most prestigious seats of power: the Palace of Verse and Sighs.

Not one to leave things to chance, His Infernal Majesty had put a second defensive contingent in place. In recent months, the demon and reaver patrols of old had been bolstered by a squadron of Dread-Locks, phantoms from another dimension, granted free rein to drain the unliving essence from anyone or anything naïve enough to think they could encroach on our dark father's privacy with impunity.

The encircling region around the palace itself boasted checkerboard parklands, neatly manicured lawns and walled enclosures containing arboreal and sculptural displays. Although the mere mention of this place evoked bad memories, I'd come here quite often of late. It was rare I got time to myself, and the gardens called *Sentinels Square* exuded a rare vibe that allowed me to do something even rarer, which I desperately needed at the moment: the chance to clear my mind and see things more clearly.

Gravel crunched beneath my boots as I walked toward the square's west gate. Approaching from this direction allowed me an unobstructed view of the shattered remains of the Colonnade of Eternal Reflections, a half mile beyond and to the east. At this distance the missing roof offered scant testimony to the cataclysm unleashed nearly four months ago when I'd destroyed the cherub, Gaz-árdiel, aka the Angel Grislington.

Not so eternal *now, is it?*

Despite my jibe, the magnificence of the Colonnade was memorable. A testimony to Satan's pride, thirteen great onyx pillars gilded in liquid fire had blazed opposite an equal number of arcaded windows that spanned the length of the six hundred and sixty-six-foot room with ease. The floor, its huge marble slabs smoldering like molten ice, had formed a perfect medium to intensify the light of a thousand candles and more than a hundred crystal chandeliers. And the mirrors . . .

Even this fleeting consideration brought that conflict flooding back:

The thrill of imminent satisfaction as the pursuit of one of the underworld's most dangerous fugitives finishes; anticipation of imminent death as I close on him; triumph as I obliterate my enemy. Elysian energies surrounding me. Filling me. Burning me. Suffusing every pore of my being as a heavenly backlash renders me senseless.

My recollection jumps to events some hours later. Greasy vapors ascend from great rents in the earth. All around me, the stench and stain of a hard-won battle assails the senses. A smoke blackened regnal mound takes center stage. The devil himself sits there, cold, proud and aloof, an island of calm amid a storm-wreck of ruined walls, fractured columns, shattered glass and pulverized fixtures.

My Hell Hounds and Chief Inquisitor are close by, come to celebrate the victory with me. Only then do I realize Satan's fallen angels gather opposite. Armed. Waiting. Eager to act. Bristling with indignation and barely veiled malice.

The dark lord speaks directly to me. I remember his words as if spoken only yesterday:

"In a moment, I'm going to give you a simple command. I expect you to obey that command instantly and without question. My directive will allow you a certain degree of latitude. I look forward to witnessing *how* you interpret it. Will you extol my sovereignty or not? We shall see where your heart truly lies."

This cannot be happening, I think, confused that such a test of my integrity should be necessary after my great conquest on His Infernal Majesty's behalf.

A flare of alarm courses through my gathered Hounds. Seasoned killers all, they teeter on the verge of arming themselves and fighting back. But dare they fight and face the consequences? Doing my best to forestall catastrophe, I intercede: "Tell me. *What* do you want me to do?"

Assuming his most dreadful fire-flaming aspect, Satan points toward my closest, most precious companions, and passes judgment. "A head is nowhere near enough compensation for this debacle. One must suffer obliteration, a soul effaced from existence. Now!"

From Abbadon's mouth comes a decree for full extinction. Its resonance burns with a siren's call I cannot resist. The lives of those for whom I am responsible flash before my eyes:

Strawberry: a kindred soul whose damnation and depravity balance my own; Nimrod, the closest thing I've ever had to a friend; Yamato. Uncompromising, noble, steadfast; Champ, stolid and unflinching, as down and dirty as they come; and Gemini, my newest recruit who shows such great potential.

For all their qualities, my loyalty to Satan is absolute and merciless.

I am the Reaper. I am Death personified, constrained by my creed to respond.

Faster than thought, I react. My blade stretches into an altar upon which I offer my oblation. A body falls, severed from crown to crotch, its anima consumed. A rumbling fanfare rends the heavens. Lightnings etch the sky with lurid threats.

Nimrod, my closest confidant, remains reduced to sand, to dust, to naught. More than dead, he no longer exists—and never did.

I feel my fondest memories of him torn away, expunged.

Turning, I kneel before my king. "It is done. I trust you find the value of such an offering sufficient?"

Approval pulses through the air . . . along with something else.

Fear?

"Do you see, Samael?" Satan croons, "Did I not deem your suspicions unfounded? My Reaper's ruthlessness extends even to his most intimate associates."

Samael? My chest heaves; my eyes flare in comprehension. *So he . . . ?* Thunder plays across my brow.

I almost look up from the floor, but the Angel of Death speaks:

"That you did, Sire," mumbled Samael the coward, "that you did." His acknowledgement comes grudgingly. Not surprising, for thus he reveals his duplicity.

There and then, I mark him in my secret heart; I allow the veneer over my mind to turn opaque. *I'll remember this day, you motherfucker. You and I will have an accounting—accounting—accounting—*

The certitude underlying my threat hadn't diminished with time. Blinking, I found my place in the present: fists clenched, shaking with rage, and on the verge of my own combustion. Every flashback I suffer feels the same, as if I picked at a festering wound and opened it, bit by bit. *And perdition has an endless supply of salt for those who need vigorous rubbing.*

Fortunately, I'd continued walking through my *déjà vécu*—or, as I felt was more appropriate, déjà fuck you—and discovered I'd already reached my destination. Pausing just within the entrance, I took a deep breath and surveyed the only place that guaranteed me some measure of solitude.

I could gain access by any one of the trellised arches sited midway along the north-, south-, east-, and west-facing prospects of the main wall. A wide shingle walkway circumnavigated that wall, while four narrow aisles led straight from each toward a central grass island protected by a low stone bailey. There, in pride of place, grew a solitary glowing Wyrd tree, its silver-white bark and ruby leaves dwarfing all lesser flora.

Sentinels Square hosted a total of thirteen sculptures positioned so that they dominated all four corners of the court. For some reason, the uniformity of the arrangement had been offset in the southwest quadrant, for while the gardener had grouped the other figures by threes, that corner possessed one additional guardian.

Positioned upon individual plinths, those statues arrested the eye.

Every one stood over seven-foot tall; each was an armored knight, carved from a single block of arcane stone. Coated as they were in effluvium from the nearby forest, they might have been fashioned from stardust-encrusted jet. Winged, hooded, and with gauntleted fists wrapped tightly about the jeweled pommels of inhumanly long swords, the warrior gods stood silent, contemplating the glowing Wyrd tree for all eternity.

Turning left, I made my way along the track and halted before the first three monuments. I studied them awhile, trying to spy anything that differentiated one from the others. But it was no use. No matter how I tried, I could detect no detail—be it a minute difference in their finely carved features or a variance in their impressive dimensions—that set one of them apart from its fellows.

Undeterred, I worked my way around the square and repeated the process before the next two groups in turn.

Nothing. Not a goddam thing.

Continuing along the path, I finally arrived at the mystery quartet. As usual, the second effigy from the right fascinated me.

So, what makes you *so special? And why do you haunt my dreams?*

On impulse, I stepped up onto the platform and ran my fingers along the cross-guard of his weapon, a crystalline representation of a Vidium Sword. It didn't surprise me in the least when I found myself becoming lightheaded and, an instant later, floating free of my physical form.

On an astral plane I witnessed events from an entirely different era; an age when infernity stretched before me, laid bare, young, and uncluttered. And less substantial . . .

The only evidence that the square exists there are its foundations. And apart from the Wyrd tree, not a single plant grows. In fact, an endless waste surrounds me as far as the eye can see. Witnessing desolation on such a scale, I am convinced a colossal battle raged here recently.

Bittersweet triumph and sorrow pervade the ether.

Yet all is not lost. A rose-gold warmth radiates like a beacon of hope from the Wyrd tree, infusing the area with beneficence. Under its influence, the ruined, ashen soil freshens, darkens, and pushes forth tender shoots.

A captive in this time thread, my mind reels under the assault of too many thoughts from too many viewpoints all at once, so that in the end, nothing remains except the certainty of confusion and isolation.

I sense another entity nearby and am moved to venture a question.

"Where . . . where am I?"

"Fear not," a commanding voice intones, "all will be well again . . . eventually."

"Again?"

"Trust me. We will refashion you, blend and forge you anew into something better."

"Better?"

"You'll see."

Hands turn me so that I face the glowing Wyrd tree squarely. Its leaves chime and dance to the caress of an unfelt breeze. The sound of a distant choir recedes; closer, a harsher chorus rises in unison. The weight of their words fall upon my neck, and the desire for slumber becomes irresistible.

I sag forward, exhausted. My palms fall upon the hilt of a great sword. "Who . . . whose is this?"

"No more questions. Sleep now. Though it takes an eternity, you will be mine."

A shroud descends to filter out the glorious light still visible from on high. As it does so, it releases a bane of stunning complexity that weaves itself through the bedrock of this new and terrifying plane. Detached, I am yet aware that seasons come and seasons go in a flickering cycle of baleful embers and somber darkness.

Memories of a life lived aforetime now fade.

Time marches on and new ones are introduced.

Eventually everything, everywhere, twists into its most debased form.

As do I.

My perspective jumps forward to an unknown space and time. In it, a lucent full moon fills a cloudless magenta sky. Resonant with purpose, lunar purity focuses the night like a lens, and fills the now lush square with an expectant hush. Here lies snow; a virgin glaze that powders the garden in a crystal white cocoon as cold and brittle as the heart that no longer beats within my obsidian chest.

From the edge of that sanctuary I maintain my silent vigil, patient, knowing that the day will come when I mature and am ready to be unleashed upon an unknown enemy. But for now, I wait . . .

The soft *crump* of feet upon icy flakes intrudes as a lonely figure walks the unblemished snowy path. Hooded in black, her footfalls are light, and leave indented scores along its length.

Without a word, she approaches and stands before me. Pale fingers draw back the cowl, and burnished raven-blue hair that blazes like a plasma storm in the moonlight cascades around her shoulders. A livid scar divides her countenance in two. One side retains its natural vivacity; the other is ravaged, reducing her complexion into dried out parchment.

For all that, she remains beautiful, glowing with an inner strength that signifies she is at one with her surrounds.

I feel that I should know her from somewhere, for this woman bears a familiarity as appealing as it is instinctual. She climbs the pedestal on which I stand and stretches up toward my ear.

Cupping her hands, she whispers, "Though the Divide has been established, beware the convergence. The Veil is imperiled, and only you have the power to stand between both worlds. It's time to wake up. Wake up! Wake up! Wake up!"

I staggered and flailed my arms; only a pair of guiding hands pressed firmly against my ass prevented me from falling. *Phew! What a rush.*

Gaining substance, the interceding voice became more insistent: "Daemon, can you hear me? Daemon?" Firm fingers gave my butt cheeks a quick pinch before letting go.

Ow! I turned on the spot and looked down. *Gemini?* "My apologies. I was a million miles away for a moment there, and then the return journey caught me by surp—?"

Still disorientated by the sudden change in circumstances, it finally registered that she was actually here, in person. "Hang on; aren't you supposed to be with Champ and Yamato down in Kí-gal, overseeing the instillation of our spyware? Don't tell me we've run into unexpected hitches?"

"Relax; everything's fine. Six different forms of covert surveillance now ring the trúllefeng crèche including infrared; motion detector, and thermal imaging. Oh, and I thought to add an additional esoteric I.D. tracker into the Kigali world's geodesic boundary." In answer to my surprise expression, Gemini reached out, squeezed my hand, and explained, "It's been camouflaged to appear as a completely natural byproduct of Erra's meddling, so don't worry. We'll tag those trying to sneak in by unfair means or foul. I also spliced it to our team's mental signatures so we know immediately who's closest and best able to respond."

Smart girl. Returning her embrace, I replied, "I take it you've had no hassle from Kur or his petulant eromenos?"

"On the contrary, both Kur and Eshi have gone out of their way to help. You know how insular their race is. I think they're rather put out that someone would dare to intrude upon their borders, and value how determined we are to punish transgressors."

The Sibitti included, I thought to myself. Jumping down, I queried, "What are Champ and Yamato up to now?"

"Yamato wanted to get straight back to Perish. Pascal Fléau has finished vetting the latest batch of GDSI recruits for our Inquisitor snatch squads, and I think Yamato's keen to ensure they know our standard operating procedures and are properly introduced to the raft council's representatives before they're let loose on the city's scum. Both Champ and Yamato are cooling their heels, waiting for the council's ambassador, Brown-Tail, to ferret out the next bit of actionable intelligence."

"And how's that going?"

Gemini pursed her lips. "Slow. Don't get me wrong, it's not for lack of trying. The damned tend to forget the thousands of miles of subterranean pipes and tunnels beneath Perish. I tell you, there's nowhere our targets can hide. What's more, the hell-rats have been a devilsend, unearthing most of Chopin and Tesla's known associates, no matter how tenuous the link."

"But?"

"But even when we arrest and interrogate likely candidates, no one seems to know anything. The sound of silence is deafening. Pascal's patrols have coordinated their operations to include innocents and suspects alike, so the panic's spreading. And the fact that we're dragging most of them all the way back to the Black Tower in Juxtapose, has ramped up the fear factor of noncompliance beyond our wildest dreams. Prisoners yet await Sparky and his Inquisitors, but they're literally up to their nuts in blood n' guts. The Brutish Broadcasting Company airs hourly bulletins on the fatality rate of those being needlessly tortured and reassigned."

Gemini's reference to *Sparky*—aka, Dr. David Livingstone—our new Chief Inquisitor, prompted my next question. "How's David managing our flood of customers? It can't be easy, being thrown in at the deep end while fresh to the job."

"He's taken to the role like the proverbial duck to water. I think his time as warden of Cadavers Lunatic Asylum prepared him to handle responsibility without complaint. And after seeing what he can do with a simple set of jump leads, the team's glad to have him."

"Good to hear. So since we've established a rhythm and assessed the results, what's the overall consensus?"

"The evidence tends to confirm your earlier theory that Chopin and Tesla have packed their bags and gone to ground elsewhere." Gemini smiled, eyes gleaming with savage delight, "An inconvenience we can easily counter if you give us permission to expand the net into other circles of hell."

A twinge of pleasure rippled upward from my gut at the prospect. "Any suggestions as to where we should start?"

Gemini shrugged, and her grin became more ferine. "Why limit our efforts to one realm at a time? News of our actions has spread far and wide, so let's add indiscriminate and random incursions across the board."

"Oh, I do like the way you think. Ask Yamato to liaise with all of our contacts within The Devil's Children and kick-start things. I know he's busy, so have him delegate to Pascal on this side of the pond, and Bella and Donna Nightshade over in New Hell. The wider our web extends the more flies we'll catch."

"I'll get right on it, once . . . er . . . once you've sorted something else out."

Gemini's statement reminded me that she wouldn't have come so far merely to exchange pleasantries, burgeoning romance or not. Suddenly suspicious, I growled, "Not that it isn't nice to see you, but why are you *really* here?"

"Ah yes, that . . ." She stepped closer and gave me a quick peck on the cheek. "The Undertaker's been on my back since yesterday afternoon, demanding your assistance on an urgent matter."

"Demanding?" My tattoos flared hot.

"You know the way he is, Daemon. I get the impression he desperately needs your help and is posturing for his minions, hoping to save face."

Now I was confused. "If he's so desperate, why didn't he whine to me directly as usual?"

"He's been trying"—Gemini pointed to the enclosure surrounding us—"but something about this place mutes telepathic communication."

I stared at the walls. *Sheolanite, that's what it is. Satan's been using that stuff more and more.* Gemini's words tweaked a nerve: "Wait a minute; you say the Undertaker's been on your back since yesterday? How? Why? I haven't been incommunicado that long. I only got here what, twenty, twenty-five minutes ago?"

Now it was Gemini's turn to look perplexed. Placing her hand on my shoulder, she lowered her voice and whispered, "I'm sorry, Daemon, but you're mistaken. We lost contact with you"—she checked her watch—"more than fifteen hours ago. That's why I came here in person."

"Fifteen hours?" Echoes of my mysterious vision trilled through my mind. I turned in place, a slow full circle, searching for clues that might explain the discrepancy. *There's more here than meets the eye.* Aloud, I continued: "And what is it, exactly, that Old Rotten Breath deems so urgent?"

Gemini snorted. "Hey, I may be a fully-fledged Hell Hound, but to him, I'm one of your underlings. You think he bothered to explain himself to me?"

"Buggering hell and damnation!" I spat, "why does that twat continue to be so difficult, even when—Eh?" I glimpsed something I'd never noticed before: a faint mark etched into the stone parallel to my favorite statue's sword tip. *What in Hades name is that?*

Intrigued, I stooped down and rubbed my fingers across the indentation. Then I glanced along the rest of the line. *There are more of them?*

Altering the resolution of my astral sight, I enlarged each character and projected them into the air. Only then did I realize I was looking at a series of archaic celestial glyphs. The two furthest away on my left—*Ƀ* and *₵*—had been rendered in an obsolete form of Hellanese, a language whose syntax and grammatical formation was so close to the divine tongue that its use was now forbidden. Nevertheless, here I noticed seals representing my favored boy and his friend, inscribed in that same vernacular, *ꝟ* and *ꝛ₷*, although those symbols retained their original clarity.

The marks were inestimably old. Even so, I instinctually connected to them on the basest level. Scanning from left to right, I read aloud, "*sèiadah* (storm), *cógath* (war), *eysh-éh* (burning flame), *shamár-as* (annihilation)."

As I plangently intoned the musical score, a phosphorous scarlet light distinguished the occult characters from the blue-white glare of their angelic counterparts.

Something stirred deep within me. "I can—I can almost —"

"*Merde*! Where did they spring from?" Gemini spluttered. "I could have sworn they weren't there before?"

"You and me both," I grumbled, "and knowing how keen your sight is, I've no doubt they've manifested only this second." Cocking my thumb toward this new enigma, I declared, "These are elohgraphs, antiquated even by heaven and hell's standards, and now the latest pieces in a jigsaw that represents my ongoing struggle to understand what the fuck is going on in my life. You'll see, the longer you're with me, the more crap like this keeps on—?"

Reaper? Are you there?

This time, I heard the Undertaker's plea as if he were standing beside me.

Jesus, does that halitosis-spewing dick-on-a-stick have a crystal ball that automatically alerts him to the most inconvenient time to call? Projecting my thoughts toward the netherworlds' most unsavory skid mark, I amplified his signal so that Gemini could eavesdrop and snarled, "I'm here. What do you want?"

About time, the Undertaker complained. *Where in Satan's name have you be —?*

"Don't ever imagine I'll explain myself to you," I interrupted. "That's never gonna happen. I asked what you wanted."

What do I want? The Undertaker seethed.

Even at this distance, I could taste Bad Breath's ire lacing the ether. He verged apoplectic from helplessness in the face of repeated sleights against his station and person.

I nearly hemorrhaged from staying my laughter.

What do I want? I . . . I want action, of course. I am still the Undertaker, so I want screaming, merciless injustice!

I imagined the blood vessels in his temples palpitating like a retard's on the receiving end of a stun gun.

Not content with stealing the reanimating unlife force of our society's dregs, some blithering bastard of an idiot is now siphoning the sin out from under my nose. I want it stopped, Reaper, and I want you to deliver the culprit or culprits to my slab so I can work my most heinous arts upon them.

Siphoning the sin . . . ? The diablo dropped. "Are you telling me," I asked him calmly, "that a Trojan virus has infiltrated the Hub itself?"

Yes. Why else would I be so distraught? You have to do something. Satan will have our heads served up on platters . . . go further than that and twist . . . roasting over . . . pitchfork shoved so far up my . . .

Filtering the Undertaker's constant barrage of complaints, I turned to Gemini. "I'm afraid he's right. Reassignment is one of the bastions of His Dark Majesty's misrule. Without it, Satan can't extend the misery of eternal suffering beyond a single unlifetime. We have to respond."

"I agree. Hopefully you'll know how?"

I recalled a startling discovery made on a previous visit to the Mortuary, and from there took a leap of faith: "As a matter of fact, yes I do. You're coming with me. I suspect that your heightened senses will come in handy."

Nodding toward the distant simulacrum of our gray-faced acquaintance, Gemini asked, "Are you going to tell him we're on the way, or not?"

I listened as the Undertaker vented his spleen for a moment or two longer and then turned to regard the still-glimmering sigils.

Dammit! Their secrets will wait a little while longer . . . as will someone else.

The look on my face wordlessly conveyed my retort.

Chapter 3: Idle Hands

Poised on the balls of his feet, Yamato Takeru needed only a fraction of a second to select his next target. Spinning lightly on his toes, he jumped into the air and struck with serpentine speed and grace. So keen was his fabled katana, the *Sword of the Gathering Clouds of Heaven* and so sure its action that the blade barely registered the shock of the unwilling tissue through which it passed.

Maintaining his form, Yamato wheeled around to survey the results of his attack.

His victim, one of dozens plucked at random from the streets of Perish, whimpered forlornly. Delirious, she was only partially aware of the dank chamber imprisoning her here below the capital's Palais de L'Injustice. But that was understandable: over the past two hours she'd been bound to a wooden frame and subjected to a litany of physical and mental abuse that, so far, had cost all her fingers and toes, along with a considerable amount of flesh from limbs and torso.

The pallor of her rapidly blenching skin stood in stark contrast to the crimson stain pooling at what remained of her feet.

Yamato noted how her blood trickled, inch by inch, toward the drain in the middle of the floor, as if seeking escape

Lingchi—the death by a thousand cuts—was both a torture and execution common throughout the Orient for more than two thousand years before its abolition in the early twentieth century. The punisher used a razor-sharp instrument to methodically remove portions of a person's body over an extended period—sometimes many days—to extend their captive's suffering and humiliation. Yamato Takeru was a past-master of the art whose experience spanned millennia.

He studied his patsy closely and smiled. While not a vindictive soul, Yamato remained a formidable assassin and a man dedicated to the integrity of his profession. As he watched, a string of tiny beads appeared on the woman's face, sanguine pearls which commenced tracing their way down her jaw to her neck, followed by a meaty flap of cheek.

Splat!

No sooner had the hunk of fresh raw meat landed in the scarlet puddle at the base of the post than it dissolved, joining the many other chunks, appendages, and digits already in transit to the Undertaker's slab.

On the far side of the room, a hollow *thuck,* followed by a stifled moan of pain, indicated that Yamato's fellow Hell Hound and partner in misdeeds, the infamous Champ Ferguson, practiced with his new set of throwing stilettos on another helpless victim.

Although he hadn't been keeping count, Yamato estimated that Champ had disposed of a score of their prisoners in this manner. Fortunately, the number of captives didn't matter. Quality did. The day's catch lacked actionable information, but possessed a silver lining: their latest batch of fall guys and girls, unworthy of processing back at the Den, allowed Yamato, as Lead Hound, to use them for a spot of stress relief.

Ignoring Ferguson, Yamato circled his prey, reversed his grip, and leaped high once more. This time he used the flat of his blade to deliver a ringing blow to the side of his quarry's head before slashing downward.

Like a fragile leaf before a stiff autumnal breeze, a delicate ear flopped to the flagstones, lay there in a fizzling brew of vapors for a second or two, before joining its counterparts in spare bits n' bobs limbo.

The quivering handle of a dagger suddenly sprouted from the woman's ruined breast like an alien bursting free of its parasitic womb. Then she faded.

"Champ!" Yamato rounded on his partner, the extent of his ire conveyed in that single bark.

Before Yamato could say another word, Champ rushed to defend himself. "Jumpin' Jehoshaphat, brother. Relax. I only wanted to hurry thing up a bit. My spine is growing roots. How much longer are we gonna be stuck here, anyway?"

"As long as it takes," Yamato snapped. "The raft council has been exemplary in their support so far. If they say they're onto something, then I trust them enough to wait and see what they turn up."

"Onto somethin'? Shoot, you've seen for yourself how well Chopin and Tesla cover their tracks. The search for them has been grindin' to a halt for a few months now."

"That's as may be, but we can't rush. We have all infernity. Anyway, you should count your curses. Once we've completed this particular phase of the assignment, Daemon hinted we might get a day or two off."

"Really?" Champ visibly brightened. "That'd be great timin'. Word on the street is that Edward Low is about ready to debut his performance at the Cirque du Freak. If what I've heard is right, they're gonna pair him with a freshly mutated Thomas Cream in a fight to the reanimation armed with nothin' but cheese graters. Can you imagine?" Champ paused to fling another knife at the vacant torture stake. "I mean, how long would it take to sever someone's jugular or saw through their neck with somethin' like that?" His face a picture of delight, Champ shook his head and cackled, gleefully.

Champ's mirth wasn't lost on Yamato, since the entire infernal law and disorder fraternity despised both Cream and Low.

Dr. Thomas Neill Cream first attracted notice after stealing a prohibited article from Satan himself. Not content to have committed such an audacious crime, Cream then used that artifact to spirit himself topside—a near impossibility—where he planned to further his ambitions by committing a string of atrocities to increase his standing amongst the elite of Hellonian society.

With a damned soul topside, His Infernal Majesty had been obliged to dispatch his Reaper. Only after Grim tracked and slaughtered the wayward doctor—thereby condemning him to reassignment with extreme prejudice—did the Reaper discover that Cream was in league with two of infernity's most notorious rebels: Frédéric Chopin and Nikola Tesla.

Pursuing the malefactors throughout the many latterday levels of hell, Grim had finally cornered the troublesome trio within the maximum security penitentiary on Cog Isle. While Chopin and Tesla managed to escape, Cream had met his grizzly end at the hands and blade of a furious Reaper.

Edward Low, a different kind of deviant, was a manipulator who tried to hide his collusion with Chopin and Tesla under the pretense of comradeship and mutual support.

Joining Grim on a mission to rescue Champ and Yamato from a Sibitti holding cell on Skull Isle, Low showed his true colors by trying to double-cross and kill the Reaper. A foolish thing to do and one that resulted in a one-way trip to the Mortuary for Low and his reassignment as a permanent member of the grotesque troupe inhabiting Icepiccadilly Circus.

News of Low and Cream and the duos' respective fates had spread, perdition wide. Their just deserts captured the imagination of the damned public, for few find anyone in hell unquestionably worse off than the next fellow.

And knowing my dark father like I do, their degradation promises a welcome distraction for centuries to come.

That thought warmed Yamato's heart more than he would have deemed it possible, and he was moved to declare, "Now that you've mention it, I think you're onto something. I might even commandeer a block of front row seats for our entire department at this weekend's matinee performance. I'd relish the opportunity of watching them suffer, and I know others would too, especially if the ringmaster allows a little *celebrity* audience participation to make things a little more interesting."

"Seriously?" Champ sat bolt upright. "You think you could manage that?"

"I don't see why not. After all, with the number of Hounds, Inquisitors and Devil's Children who'll attend, it . . ."

A scrabbling noise issuing from the main drain caught Yamato's attention. "Heads up, someone's coming."

Quick as death, both Hounds dropped to their hands and knees, trying to prize one corner of the heavy trellis away from its casement. Slick with gore, progress was slow and arduous, but eventually they managed to lift the lid free.

Beady black eyes stared up out of the gloom. Glittering fiercely, they seemed to regard the hulking great figures looming over the cover with professional curiosity before edging into the light to reveal a wiry profile with a long twitching nose, gray whiskers, and well-groomed fur.

"Brown-Tail," Yamato cooed. Conscious of the fact he didn't possess Gemini's inter-species communication skills and keen not to scare away the ambassador, Yamato struggled to calm his mind and present a friendly demeanor. "Good to see you. Please don't hang around down there in the dark, c'mon up and say hello."

The little hell-rat responded immediately. Squeaking loudly, she scuttled out onto the bloodstained floor, whereupon Champ and Yamato allowed the heavy grating to fall back into place with a loud *clang*. Only then did Yamato realize Brown-Tail carried something in her front paws.

Unable to commune with animals in the way Gemini could, the Hounds had devised a simple means for the raft council to convey the import of what they uncovered on each of their forays into the labyrinthine depths of Perish's sewers: tokens of varying color. Green to denote there were no concerns or all was clear; orange for those denizens or locations suspected to have infrequent or unsubstantiated connections to Chopin and Tesla; and finally, red, where evidence of prolonged interaction with the fugitives was beyond doubt.

And as Yamato had come to appreciate, the rats were never wrong in their evaluations.

"Red," Champ gasped, "after all these months, a red disc."

The two Hounds stared at each other.

"You know what this means, don't you?" Champ continued.

Yamato was already on his feet and heading toward the door. "Of course I do." He glanced back and noticed his partner still crouched beside their visitor. "What are you waiting for? Pay the ambassador for her troubles and let's move. We need everyone in on this. Hounds, GDSI . . . and get Pascal, too. His local knowledge will prove invaluable."

"That many?"

"We take no chances. This is the first break we've had in a long time, and I want to ensure we make the most of it. And think about it: Would *you* like Daemon to go Lingchi on our asses if we screw things up?"

*

Erra rarely walked the outer wards of Emeslam, his palatial cathedra of plague and putrefaction, for he seldom had need, content to consecrate himself wholeheartedly to his sacred calling: judgment of the damned and their castigation under the all-consuming jaws and swords of the Seven.

All damned souls measured, guilty or not, were treated thus, for his motivation wasn't spurred by vengeance or lust for satisfaction at seeing punishment rendered. No, Erra's whole existence revolved around fulfilling his purpose with unquestionable reverence.

Even so, today was one of those rare occasions when circumstance demanded his attention elsewhere; he would interview someone whom he'd been surprised to find had earned his respect in recent months.

The subject of Erra's interest had been a devout Christian in life, Teresa Sánchez de Cepeda y Ahumada, otherwise known as Saint Teresa of Ávila. She had been pious, chaste, and (due to lingering periods of debilitating sickness since childhood) prone to episodes of religious ecstasy. Her visions were so intense that Teresa claimed she could rise from the lowest form of devotions to the highest: one of perfect union with God, wherein she'd experience the rich blessings of tears.

Many skeptics believed her knowledge diabolical in nature. Dismayed by such rumors, Teresa began to doubt. Doubting, she inflicted grievous injury upon her person. This gave Satan the opening to claim her as a great prize. Needless to say, upon her death, the saint had been shocked to learn the harsh truth.

In spite of this, Teresa had never bewailed her condemnation to hell. Far from it. Buckling down, she'd dedicated herself to winning the hearts and minds of those who heard her simple but profoundly powerful message: no matter what a person may have done in life, love could heal any scar and give worth to all things.

And the denizens of infernity oft responded.

Outraged at his miscalculation of how dangerous was this saintly woman, Satan reacted swiftly. To reduce the impact of her ministry he locked her away in one of perdition's many prisons. And there she stayed for centuries, until two of Erra's deacons of destruction set her free to continue her work unmolested.

Evidence of the saint's intervention now bloomed everywhere, for the plague currently sweeping the latterday levels of hell was a conjugation of her own devising. Even more remarkable, its reactive agent bore the same curse that had so alarmed His Infernal Majesty in the first place: love. And love could instigate unrest and confusion as easily as it inspired unity and respect.

Yes, Erra thought to himself as he traversed the manifold galleries of his abode, *Teresa's approach differs vastly to my own. Yet I must admit she gets results . . . and exceptional ones at that.*

Turning a final corner, he grinned as he entered the corridor leading to Teresa's suite. Even if no one realized the true nature of his visitor, the sheer number of flowers arranged in chains suspended between groined windows and hanging in fantail sprays from baskets and braziers alike provided an extravagant hint of a gentle feminine presence . . . Until you looked closer, that is. For these bouquets were comprised of monkshood, red-berry and white-snake; poisoned ivy, Amazon lily and oleander. Colorful, yes, but deadly.

And the fragrance: something about the smell of death—no matter how subtle or sweet—always put Erra in a reflective mood. *Typical of my saintly lodger to find beauty in the midst of so much danger. Speaking of which . . .*

Reaching the terminus of the passage, Erra took a moment to change his startling visage into one less frightful to the human condition. Only then did he knock upon one of the golden panels adorning each of four floor-to-ceiling double doors.

Two great leaves swung inward of their own volition almost immediately, revealing his charge, deep in conversation with the First of Seven.

". . . said before, don't you see?" Teresa's face betrayed the stoic demeanor adopted by teachers when explaining something straightforward to a pupil who should already know it. "Although it has taken many weeks for my invocation to mesh fully with the composition of the Sheolspace continuum, it now spreads exactly as anticipated."

"Yes, I understand that aspect," the First replied, "and we Sibitti watch with interest as your sorcery runs its course upon the vermin of this . . . ?" Erra's principle champion noticed his master's presence. "My Liege?"

"Forgive the intrusion." Erra inclined his great head. "Have I disturbed you in the midst of something important?"

"No apology is necessary, and your interruption is most fortuitous." The First turned to the fallen saint and extended an invitation: "Teresa, please. Repeat the gist of what you

just said, especially your conclusions. I'm sure Lord Erra
will find it most enthralling."

Teresa sauntered forward, gaze raised to the plague god
towering above her. Regardless of the difference in their size,
Erra found the fragile woman before him no longer overawed
in his company. That fact irked him more than it should.

She bowed formally. "My Lord Erra, how are you today.
Well, I trust?"

At least she's still polite. "All things considered, well
enough, though I'm not one to sit on my hands when work
waits."

Teresa's face broke into a self-satisfied smile. "Then take
heed. I was explaining to the First that we now enter a crucial stage of the operation, one on which you will wish to
capitalize."

"How so?" Erra took a seat without waiting to be invited,
a privilege of rank.

His host carried on: "Now that the seeds of love have
been implanted into the matrix linking Satan's realms together, we at last begin to see its fruits manifest. As I emphasized
from the start; in those precious few who are truly remorse-
ful, my enchantment has kindled a desire for repentance.
Such ones should be ripe for harvest under your mandate, for
they will face their fates with resolution and hope."

"And the rest?"

"No doubt you already noted how the majority of hell-
kind are too far gone; too self-centered; too quick to take advantage of weaknesses in others to benefit from the cathartic
effects of my gift. In them, the saplings of unity soon withered and died, allowing the weeds of sin to choke what goodness remained in their hearts. In some, rejection and abandonment leads to isolation and suicide; in most, to hatred and

violence. And once inflamed, the damned become enslaved to the deviances sown by their own lusts."

"A negative result, wouldn't you say?" Erra replied, still slightly puzzled by Teresa's earlier assertion. "How will I capitalize on this?"

"Isn't it obvious? It works to your favor when sinners' habitual actions continually condemn them. Wouldn't you say these are ideal for auditing?"

A surge of pleasure coursed Erra's illusionary form; sparks crackled in his beard and along his exposed arms. "So you feel that *now* is the time to let the Seven off their leashes?"

"I do, Lord Erra. Good news, I suspect, for while I don't possess the constitution of a demigod, even I can see they chafe to be about their divine commission."

Erra glanced toward his First, and their eyes blazed in unison like stars. Nevertheless, a note of caution caused Erra to lower his voice and lean forward in his chair. "And what of Grim?"

Teresa took a seat close to the glowing titan. "Grim? He is a creature of infinite quality. He acts with no restraint or re-morse. Since the loss of Strawberry and Nimrod, he's grown harsher—if that's possible for Satan's Reaper—and darker, too. Thousands have fallen to his blade, thousands more to his unbridled fury. Yet, for all the peril he represents, there's purity to his service. Outside influence cannot sway him. Such piety I have only witnessed in rapture, a long, long time ago . . ." Teresa's voice trailed away.

To Erra, she appeared caught in a current of memories from another time and place.

Then she remembered where she was, for she jumped and breezed on as if nothing had happened: "That's why I say without doubt that his capacity for true love knows no bounds.

"True love? The Reaper? And that flaw makes him vulnerable, you think?"

"Possibly. But be wary, Lord Erra. Evidence of my labors resounds throughout the underverse: hatred; violence; unprecedented wrath. Bedlam ensues, and things get worse. Now imagine such unbridled passion in the hands of the Reaper. Those most sorely wounded often commit the greatest atrocities, and Daemon Grim has been hurt more than any other. It—It goes far beyond what happened to his lover and friend. I can feel it, sense it. Nevertheless, where he is concerned, my second sight is confounded, so I am unable to further clarify the matter . . ."

Once again, Teresa fell silent, succumbing to her personal tides of reflection.

It mattered not, for Erra had heard enough.

Maintaining an outer calm, he sent a shielded order thundering toward his primary enforcer: *Notify your brothers. We begin afresh on the morrow.*

Our parameters? the First enquired without moving a muscle.

As before the enforced hiatus: strike everywhere, but stick to the previously agreed strategy of fighting in pairs. This configuration will expand our range and increase the expectation of terror among the masses.

What about the Reaper?

We will test his resolve. If it transpires he can be distracted, then we bait him and lure him into a trap at a time and place of our choosing. He will pay for the insults heaped upon us, mark my words.

It shall be done. The slightest flicker of reticence on the First's face betrayed a lingering doubt. *Teresa won't be happy you're ignoring her counsel.*

Erra's countenance flushed, and for the merest fraction of a second a horrific entity occupied his chair, in dread repose. *She has almost served her purpose. Mystic or not, the day will come when she too must answer for her actions. Then we will feast and taste the truth and depth of her penitence.*

Chapter 4: Blades of the Left-Hand Path

Hoping to make up for the fifteen hours lost in Sentinels Square, I'd decided to jump Gemini and myself directly from the gardens surrounding the Palace of Verse and Sighs to the vicinity of the Mortuary itself. No easy task, seeing as travelling from one circle of hell to another had always been problematic. Even under the best of circumstances, each of the realms existed at times and in places that did not blend smoothly into that of their immediate neighbors.

Sometimes, the variance would amount to nothing more than a few minutes. At others, it might extend beyond a day, or for an entire season. For a random few realities, like Juxtapose, a whole host of alternative eras and dimensions came out to play, all crowding the same geophasic location and all struggling to seep into one another in any way they could. Consequently, the result was a patchwork quilt of temporal confusion. And ever since the Sibitti had poked their noses in, that confusion had become much worse.

Mercifully, my growing power and heightened state of awareness helped me compensate instinctually. And lately, I could cut through the multidimensionhell tangle now scrambling the hydraspace lanes into a Picasso rendering of spaghetti Armageddon, like a well-oiled javelin through a baby's skull.

Once again, those targeting skills were spot on, and the exit portal of my interspatial conduit dumped us exactly where I wanted to be: slap bang in the middle of the street outside the Undertaker's lair.

Horns blared, brakes screeched, and irate motorists and jaywalkers yelled. It made no difference. Rubber squealed, metal shrieked, glass smashed, and the barks of anger and alarm swiftly turned to cries of dismay as vehicles concertinaed into one another in a gradually expanding accordion ripple that undulated off for hundreds of yards in each direction.

Ah, it's like a melody to my ears.

Those drivers and pedestrians who'd managed to avoid the initial ruckus kicked off, waving their fists and shouting in indignation. Until they spotted who it was that had caused the commotion. For that, I had my latest wraparound Ray-Burns to thank. They must have made me look coolly intimidating, because no sooner had I thrown back my cowl than everyone fell silent simultaneously. Everyone, that is, except for one bright spark who'd been sat in the back of a blacked out Humvee.

Clutching a mashed nose, he stormed from the rear hatch in his very own personal tornado of testosterone, spitting threats and the contents of his ruptured nasal membranes. "Are you blind, you blithering idiot. Don't you know who I am?"

Poor thing, I chuckled, *he must have slammed into the back of one of the front headrests.*

Mr. Self-important was still on his first lungful of air. "Stay right there, I'll have your lungs ripped out and strung…?" Too late, it registered who it was he was threatening. "Oh shit a brick."

The smile I pitched his way contained no hint of empathy or cordiality. *And just like that, life in hell presents a large slice of corrupted karma with a side order of fries, and slaps my new friend in the face.*

Lightning played across my brows, and those tattoos that were visible steamed their vile mélange. I didn't bother to draw my scythe. Instead, I inhaled, and the underworld's most wondrous spirit rushed to fulfill my desire, infusing me from head to toe in dark potency. Tongues of fire danced through my hair and tendrils of plasma licked their way along the back of my hands.

I exhaled, and the conflagration that erupted from my fingertips melted asphalt, liquefied steel, vaporized organs, and burst tires, fuel tanks and bodies as if they were nothing but overinflated balloons.

Moments later, a gentle rain of blood and guts, interspersed with engine parts, pattered down around me. *That should do it, yet another little demonstration to keep our ever ungrateful flock of black sheep in line.* Clenching my fists, I swallowed my ire and extinguished the Bălefire. Only then did I think to inspect the damage.

Burnt-out shells and calcified skeletons littered the road for more than a quarter of a mile, north and south of my position. On the sidewalk, shocked bystanders looked on, too petrified to move or speak for fear of attracting my attention. *Bugger me. That was unexpected?*

Grinning from ear to ear, I turned toward Gemini to see what she thought about my outburst. For some reason, she was staring at me intently. An odd look clouded her eyes, and I could see her chest heaving, as if she was finding it difficult to breathe.

"Are you okay?" Cocking a thumb to the carnage, I murmured, "That didn't upset you, did it?"

"No…not at all," she giggled, but the sound came from deeper down in her throat. Ignoring those still looking on, she leaned in, and growled, "I can't tell you how turned on I am right now. Let's get this business done and dusted so I can get you alone for a while. I'd like to see what else you can do…if you're willing?"

Gemini was literally shaking with desire, so I thought it only fair to give her suggestion serious consideration. This was a big step for us, after all, and would take our *frowned upon* relationship to the next level.

It took all of a nanosecond.

"I can work with that." Grabbing Gemini by the elbow, I began steering her through the blackened vehicular and human bone yard and up toward the one place I'd have preferred to avoid, but which—for some reason—kept featuring ever more prominently in my affairs. "Let's see what this shite is all about, then we'll take a suite across the road at the Hexcalibur while we mull over the exact details of what I might be willing to do to you."

"Mulling?" The way Gemini purred the word out, it sounded far more sensual than any verb should. "I like… *mulling*. I can *mull* all day if given the right incentive."

Now that's *food for thought?* After the sabbatical I'd been forced to endure, Gemini's statement proved rather hard to ignore. Thankfully, I was distracted from the temptation of instant gratification by the hulking great turd of a monstrosity filling the entire city block in front of us.

Constructed from blood-veined Black Widow marble, surrounded on all sides by imposing columns, and adorned with an impressive portico, the Mortuary seemed able to generate its own personal shroud of gloom; a veil so dense, that not even the rays of Paradise welling down through the clouds overhead could penetrate it fully. It also seemed capable of dampening whatever amorous feelings I might be enjoying at this moment.

Rather fortuitous under the circumstances?

The legend emblazoned in sizzling magma across the pediment, *Abandon Hope, All Ye Who Enter Here*, was a fitting proclamation, as this was the only place in the underworld feared as much as my own base of operations: The Den of Iniquity. Unlike the Den, however, every doomed citizen had passed through the Mortuary's doors at least once.

That realization made me think of hell's most hated celebrity. The Undertaker. An oily, chit of a slimy asswipe who rarely made the effort to get his hands dirty, and someone who—in my opinion—got too much of a hard-on from the aberrations he was allowed to create under his charter as, RDR—Reanimator to the Dark Regent.

Sweeping up the steps, we passed an invisible filter and the smell of charred flesh and burning oil abruptly gave way to the fetid stench of four week old sweat that had been strained through the shredded underwear of incontinent geriatrics prone to excessive flatulence.

I was momentarily taken aback. *It's not as bad as usual?* Then a bombshell hit me. *Christ! Has the Undertaker been using mouthwash?*

If he had, the news was unprecedented and the entire underverse would owe Astarte a debt of gratitude impossible to pay...even if she was spectacularly off the mark where dressing her man was concerned.

Pushing our way through the smoked-glass revolving doors, my nostrils were assailed by the additional, but familiar brew of cheesy feet (stilton variety) and stale toe jam.

Ah, that's more like the home-from-home I've come to know.

More sensitive to the nuances of olfactory assault than I was, Gemini gagged violently, prompting her to slow her respiratory system right down. Knowing I could suspend mine entirely, she grimaced and glared at me with pure envy.

Deciding it best for my health not to poke fun, I prompted her forward again. A main arterial corridor led off into the shadows, punctuated at regular intervals by the gaping jaws of smaller passages and hallways. Offices lined either side. Fronted by wide opaque windows, none carried signs, and I'd never learned what actually transpired behind any of the frosted doors frowning silently back at me. Enfolded by an all-pervading hush, we adopted an easy pace and enjoyed the chance to simply catch our breaths.

The slightest breeze announced the prompt arrival of our escort. With slicked back hair, a greasy candle wax complexion, dour expression, and wearing an ill-fitting lab coat that must have been borrowed from a basketball player, he needed no introduction.

"Buttkiss," I boomed, warmly, "how the devil are you? And how's the chest, no permanent scars I hope?"

My reference to the incident in which the Undertaker had shot Buttkiss twice in the heart for failing to prevent Champ from taking a leak in one of the ground floor cubicles, produced not one shred of embarrassment. But I wasn't surprised. So far as I was aware, this creature was only capable of one emotion: unhelpful counter clerk gloomy.

"Why, thank you for asking, Mister Grim," Buttkiss replied, solemnly, "you'll be ecstatic to hear my injuries produced no long-term consequences…" *Was that an attempt at humor?* "…though my master *did* take the liberty of grafting several sets of crocodile teeth nipple clamps onto various parts of my anatomy as an incentive to never forget my previous oversight." He sighed, so deeply I thought he might deflate. "I am assured that if I improve my game, they might be removed after a century or two."

His admission invoked all sorts of scenarios in my mind. *Unholy shit, I'd love to see that. But how do I ask without sounding like a complete perv?*

I let the matter drop, reluctantly, and stood to one side. "Then you'd better lead the way. I've heard he's rather keen we speak?"

"That he is, sir. That he is." Buttkiss bowed, formally, and about turned without moving his legs. Then he was off, demonstrating his *Brides of Dracula* glide with a panache I could see was impressing the socks of my fellow Hound.

As Buttkiss led us past the usual parade of vacant interview rooms, storage cupboards and empty waiting areas, Gemini's gaze never left the hem of his whites. On one occasion, she even crawled on her hands and knees in an effort to get a better view of what lay beneath. To no avail. Eventually, she was moved to express her amazement, telepathically. *Daemon, have you seen this? It's incredible. I've never...He can't...I don't think he's actually walking. So how...?*

I know. I've never dared to ask, as I think it'll somehow destroy the magic of this place. Just watch, enjoy, and keep using your imagination.

Suitably entertained, we soon arrived at the latest upgrade the Undertaker had thought to install in his continuing drive to make the Mortuary one of the most efficient departments in New Hell: an all singing, all dancing, spiral escalator fitted with an additional baggage chute and miniature speakers for piped music.

It was with a profound sense of relief I discovered the Undertaker had decided to forgo his usual muzak, jazz-funk style mix that I'd always found so infuriating. Unfortunately, he'd replaced it with what sounded like a mixed bag of kittens and peacocks being slowly roasted to death over an open fire. It was only by concentrating that I was able to discern the screaming montage was a caterwauling medley of *alternative* reed trills—scratch that—noise.

We made our descent in a fugue of numbed sensibilities and jarred spines. I couldn't help but imagine the amount of bagpipes that had been murdered by the psychopath chosen to record this particular playlist.

Eventually—after I'd cringed so hard and for so long that I was sure I'd lost a couple of inches in height—we arrived at the bottom, and the explanation for the unmelodic mind fuck became apparent. The Undertaker wasn't just yanking my chain, he'd invited friend around to swing on it. *Bastard!*

Resplendent in full plaid, high-buttoned style doublet and kilt, with wing collar white shirt and black bowtie beneath, the Undertaker looked like a William Wallace wannabe in search of freedom from the debilitating effects of a major wardrobe malfunction.

Entirely ridiculous, I was nevertheless forced to concede that Astarte's attention to detail was astounding. The kilt was snugly fitted and of proper length with the sporran worn as it should be: high. His hose and gaiters were turned with due precision, above the calf and below the bottom of the knee. The Undertaker's version of a sgian dhubh—a black handled meat cleaver—was likewise worn correctly in the top of his right stocking. Buckle brogues and a floppy beret rounded off his ensemble so completely that I was lost for words.

"What?" the Undertaker quipped, "No opening banter? No twisting the knife at my expense in this hour of need to make me feel even worse than I already do?"

"I'm sorry," I mumbled, recovering swiftly, "I'm a little taken aback. I didn't have a clue the *Total Wankers Clan* had an official tartan...or that you we're its chief?"

I peered over his shoulder, half expecting to see herds of rutting highland haggis—thistly ears erect, proud horns bared—engaging in the ancient offal mating rituals, as passed down by migrants from the Outer Hebrides thousands of years before.

"Touché," the Undertaker countered, wearily, "the Reaper's wit at its cutting best. But if you're quite finished, I'd really like to address the emergency at hand? Keeping to theme, mine are not the only guts His Satanic Majesty will wear for garters if we don't sort this mess out, pronto. Even then, I might not get to live that long. Astarte went to a lot of trouble to get us tickets for this evening's performance of Shakespeare and Marlow's latest rendering of Macdeath. If I miss it, she'll kill me for sure. You know what hell's women are like if you let them down."

Do I ever. I thought about the *performance* I hoped to give once I'd finished here, and glanced Gemini's way. She must have been thinking the exact same thing, for her gaze bored into mine with an intensity that had lost none of its earlier passion. *Oh boy...*

Addressing the prince of plaid prick's himself, I replied, "You make a valid point. Let's cut the crap and get straight down to business."

Now it was the Undertaker's turn to appear flummoxed. He pursed his lips as if considering something for a second or two, then said, "Buttkiss, you are dismissed."

And with that, he spun on his patent heels and marched off without looking back.

Buttkiss? I didn't realize he was still here? He wasn't. When I turned to see what our guide was doing, the

Undertaker's meet-and-greet specialist had already vanished, back into whatever cupboard he hid in until needed again. *Bloody fast, too. Makes me wonder how Champ managed to get one over on him?*

When I peered back the other way, the Undertaker was already twenty yards ahead of us, and we had to rush to catch up. He must have heard us approaching, for as we neared, he called out over his shoulder, "We'll make a quick stop on the way. I have a little something that should emphasize how deep the rot has set, and I'm keen to get your opinion on it."

That sounded rather businesslike, and ominous?

My interest piqued, I picked up the pace and allowed the rhythms and sounds of the underground environment to pull me in.

A hive of activity, the Mortuary was a weird combination of what topsiders might expect to see if a pathology lab was left under the management of Hannibal Lecter and Victor Frankenstein. We passed rooms where saws whirred, drills shrieked and files rasped to the ululating accompaniment of those on the receiving end of their own personal catalogue of horror, for all the stiffs here were still alive...ish. An atmosphere I found morbidly intoxicating due to the casual approach of the Undertaker's lackeys. Busy to a munchkin, they chatted quite happily about all sorts of banal everyday things as they carried out their gruesome chores, heaving buckets or dragging nets laden with body parts and still steaming visceral remains to wherever they needed to go.

Without warning, a spiderlike apparition came scuttling through one of the open doorways, forcing me to check my step. Whoever this wretched soul was, the Undertaker had obviously gone to great lengths to vent his frustrations upon her. From what I could see, her entire head had been blowtorched free of the top layers of skin, and spliced onto what seemed to be a particularly hairy octopus—or what an octopus might look like if its tentacles had been replaced by the limbs of a gorilla. In turn, the ends of each arm had been lopped off, and a baffling array of knitting needles, kitchen knives, and butcher's skewers had been screwed into the still raw stumps.

Mesmerized, I watched her growing panic. Round and round she went, skidding and skittering, bumping into walls, careening off surgical trolleys, climbing mountains of soiled bandages, until she caught sight of the exit. A wail of anguished relief split the air, and then she was off, slithering and clicking her way toward it in a wash of ink that left an oily blue-black slick in its wake.

"That'll be murder on the carpets," I offered, absentmindedly.

I'd obviously lingered too long, for Gemini yanked me into motion, and kept prodding and pushing me in the back until the spell was broken.

Luckily, there were no further distractions to slow us down, and we soon branched off from the main passage toward an entrance with a highly polished brass plaque affixed to the wall beside it, which read: *Collections*.

The Undertaker barely slowed as he barreled his way inside. Gemini and I followed, hot on his heels, to find the "Inhuman Resources and Collation Center" of the Mortuary to be a bustling retreat of orderliness in comparison to the madness unfolding only a short distance away down the hall.

A half-dozen minions sat behind a cluster of heavily laden desks, studiously recording the names and symbols scrolling down their screens in a seemingly endless procession of information overload. Every now and then, one line or another would flash amber, and an alarm would sound, instigating a brief flurry of activity.

Referring to a particularly concentrated spate of such incidents, the Undertaker snapped, "Those *hiccups* are why I was so insistent you attend promptly, Reaper." He clicked his fingers sharply. "Oswald? Provide Mister Grim with a copy of the report you complied fifteen minutes ago, regarding our findings so far today."

Fifteen minutes ago? That's about the time we entered the Mortuary.

Although everyone working here would have looked right at home at a MENSA gathering convened to discuss the benefits of calculating Pi to the millionth decimal point, Oswald appeared especially cerebral. I don't know if that was due to his bottle bottom spectacles, the shiny silver badge sewn to his forehead that said, *Chief Clerk*, or the stray wisps of hair sprouting from the crown of his head that had been greased and meticulously parted down the middle.

Whatever the reason, Oswald exuded a comical aura of self-importance. Pushing himself away from his console, he selected a single sheet of paper from the top of one of his many trays. Adopting a suitably solicitous air, he then paraded toward me as if he were a VID at the Geek Awards about to present one of the underworld's most celebrated sons with a certificate in recognition of an outstanding contribution to never-ending fear and terror.

Feeling unexpectedly flattered, I accepted the offering graciously and waited until Oswald had traipsed his way back to his workstation before running my eye over the pertinent details. They read:

TOP SECRET

From: The Office of Acquisitions

To: His most despicable High Sheriff, the Grim Reaper

Subject: Suspected Treasonous Activity

Activity Report Dated:
December 17—ADT 13006 —18:43hrs.

Fatalities
Running Mortality Rate: 185,003

Condemned: 118,391

Fresh Souls Received: 117,267

Assigned: 113,849

Reassignments

Denizens Expired: 229,841

Essences Received: 189,933

Reassigned: 153,387

TOP SECRET

Despite its classification, the list was surprisingly concise. I scanned its contents several times to ensure I had the figures right, then sought some much needed clarification.

"I'm not at all familiar with the volume of customers you usually have to handle. What points do you need me to concentrate on?"

Bad mistake. The Undertaker came to stand beside me and my eyes instantly watered. *Hellfire! I must have started my lungs again by mistake.* Through a thick blur of tears, I could have sworn one or two of my tattoos were peeling away from my skin and heading for the door.

Inured to the effect he had on others, the Undertaker referred to the statistics, and explained, "The numbers speak for themselves. The upper portion of the report relates to the running total of deaths incurred by mortals living topside as of six forty-three this afternoon. The subheading below that shows the number of those fatalities damned to hell.

"As I've explained before, it takes a while to transfer all the deeds accrued by an individual during their lifetime, so we're sent a WET—a Writ of Expected Tenure—in advance. Think of it as a little token of what's to come, an esoteric data package containing the fresher's personal details and an overview of the reasons for their condemnation. I'm sure you'll remember from your previous visits, the WET matrices are encompassed within the swirling bands you've seen skimming across the surface of the Hub. Once a soul arrives in its entirety, its mass condenses into a concentrated blob of sin that looks like a tiny black hole. Then, when we've had a chance to process that information and deem them ready for allocation, their psyche gets swallowed by one of the many cyclones raging across the transition zone, and is transferred to the Slab. Are you with me so far?"

"Yes, I follow."

"Good. While the timing between each aspect of the process is variable, we've usually received sufficient tincture by this time of the day for more than a score of dark constellations to have formed across the plane of the Hub. Look at the figures again and tell me what you think."

Doing as he asked, I studied the list one more time and immediately noticed what the Undertaker was alluding to. "While I'd expect some degree of variance, these scores don't seem to tally?"

"No they don't," the Undertaker snarled, "especially when you compare the first list to those underneath..." he poked at the sheet in my hand, "because as you can plainly see, the discrepancy for those already damned and who should be due for reassignment is huge."

It was. A vast sea of souls was unaccounted for, almost forty thousand by my quick reckoning. "What the hell?"

"I know. Perhaps you begin to appreciate why I'm so pissed. It was aggravating enough when the divergence ran into the hundreds. Now it's into the tens of thousands its beginning to feel personal…and means *we* have to do something about it."

No shit Sherlock? "Who are they, these missing sheep? Where are they going? Is this a random thing or are certain groups being targeted?"

The Undertaker lifted his beret and scratched his head. "From what I've been able to ascertain, there's no distinct pattern. All I can say is that the rate of infection—for want of a better word—has increased dramatically over the past week or two. So much so, that further anomalies are now manifesting within the Hub itself."

"Further anomalies? How? In what way?"

The Undertaker was already moving toward the open stairwell at the back of the room. "It'd be easier if I just showed you."

Taking his comment as an invitation, Gemini and I set off after him, and were soon lost to the dizzying decent involved in reaching the heart of his now tainted kingdom.

Ten minutes later, we were there. As the Undertaker completed the prerequisites for dropping the force field and triggering the entrance, I wracked my brains in an effort to determine who might be responsible for one of the biggest upsets ever to grab Satan's system by the balls.

My suspicions naturally fell on Chopin and Tesla. But try as I might, I couldn't make sense of what they would gain by stirring up a hornet's nest, not after going to so much trouble to disappear off the face of the underworld. *Unless, of course, they're seeking to do nothing more than keep us distracted while they prepare for their endgame? If so, they'll be sorely disappointed. Champ and Yamato are relentless, and once we're free of all this crap, Gemini and I will be joining the hunt.*

Thinking laterally, the only bugbear that kept coming back to niggle me was that I'd overlooked something on Kígal, and that current events were in some way connected to the soul sapphires.

Further deliberation was forestalled as a deep *clunk* reverberated through the rock beneath my feet. The fifty ton blast doors cracked open and commenced sliding into the walls on either side. Then the hairs on the back of my neck stood to attention and my skin prickled as I was hit by a wave of cabbalistic might so powerful, the Bãlefire in my veins surged in response.

An impressive chasm more than two hundred yard wide stood revealed, filled almost in its entirety by an orb of scintillating plasma. *The Hub.* A metal walkway curved away, left and right, to encircle the Hub in a ring of girders and steel.

Service stations, positioned at random intervals about the suspended platform, created focal points of mechanical complexity. I'd always speculated at what their function might be, for while many possessed numerous ducts and conduits that ran—as you would expect—along the walls and substructure to intersect with corresponding junction boxes and circuit breakers, others had no purpose I could discern. Some pipes appeared and disappeared at whim from thin air or from within the ionized cloud itself, making it seem as if a magician had wound up his routine, mid act, and forgotten to take his props with him.

To my mind, the Hub always reminded me of a to-scale representation of Jupiter. Except, our version generated hurricanes in deepest midnight hues of purple, blue and black instead of the red and white ones the king of the solar system was known for.

Something caught my eye. *Is it me, or are some of the storms missing? I could have sworn it used to look bigger too?* I refined my analysis even further. *And what's that? A diffuse cloud of atoms seems to be condensing separately, away from the central body?* I caught my breath. *I'm right. It's gathering in a higher orbit and looks like a ring system.*

"I've no need to tell you about the various features of the Hub, Reaper," the Undertaker intoned, "however, I do wish to emphasize something." He pointed toward the darker currents swirling through the mass. "*That* represents the sum totality of those awaiting first reanimation or reassignment. Remember, this is unadulterated tincture I'm talking about; a living history of who they were and what they did while alive or since their arrival in hell. It distends the longer they've been here. Think of it as an ectoplasmic personification of their exploits. An irrefutable record I use to make my judgments. It shouldn't be possible for anyone to tamper with it, so how in Satan's name has...poke their...my business... and..."

He's right. The Undertaker's exasperation was well founded. Even so, his complaints faded into the background. *No matter how much I hate his guts, he has a job to do. An irreplaceable function that serves the needs of injustice...as have I. We both represent the highest, most abominable level of authority in existence. And any attack on us or the office of our station is an attack on His Infernal Majesty. That's something I can't allow.*

I studied the waning marvel before me and tried to think of a simple way of explaining what I was seeing.

Perhaps I shouldn't think of the Hub as a planet? That might be a start, especially as it contains many of the characteristics of a star. I looked again. *Yes, a star whose corona is being eroded by solar winds...?* I took that concept one step further. *Or better still, perhaps its distillate isn't being blown anywhere so much, as it's being sucked by...* I zeroed in on the other voids dotted about the Hub chamber. *Something acting like a singularity?*

Suddenly, I was very grateful for Gemini's presence. For all my might, her senses were more acute in unfathomable ways I still couldn't begin to understand.

"...know what we're going to do about...? Reaper? Are you listening?"

"Huh?"

The Undertaker sounded indignant. "I asked if you've been listening to a bloody word I've said."

"Partially...But don't worry, I wasn't trying to wind you up for a change. It's just that I had a hunch before I came here what might be causing this...this...*whatever* it is. And from what I've seen, I think I'm on the right track."

"What?" Hope bloomed across the Undertaker's face, "what hunch?"

Holding up my hand, I continued, "I'd rather not say. Not until I've had a chance to test something out. For that, I need you to take us to the Grumbles grotto."

"The Grumbles?"

"Yes, I'd like Gemini to get a taste of the distinctive resonance it gives off."

The Undertaker's eyebrows flared in comprehension. Tripping over his own feet, he almost allowed us to see if he wore his kilt traditionally. Not a sight I would have quickly forgotten, nor one I would ever want to admit having seen.

Recovering swiftly, he leaped out onto the gantry, and yelled, "This way."

Hastening along the path to the right, he made his way around to a metal ladder cut into the outer edge of the walkway itself. Waving for us to join him, he climbed down. Following, we soon ended up on a sub catwalk that led back toward the rock face situated beneath the site of the main doors. Except, I knew that cliff was just an illusion, a glamour masking a concealed entrance.

Sure enough, the Undertaker headed right for it without slowing. Gemini watched with evident interest as our host passed an invisible plane and vanished from sight.

"It's like my chameleon mesh," she murmured, "only much more powerful."

We crossed the threshold ourselves and I felt the familiar tingle of snowflakes on skin. My breath began to fog the air and the atmosphere chimed with a crystal-clear clarity at odds to the ambiance found in the rest of the Mortuary. If I had to use one word to describe it, I'd have said, *exhilarating*.

The chamber we entered was similar in many respects to the one above us, but far smaller. Fifty yards away, on the far side, wide stairs had been cut into the rock of a naturally occurring alcove. Even at this distance I could see they had been worn by the passage of many feet over time. Curling upward, they faded into the gloom of unknown destinations.

To our left, an area had been set apart on the rough stone floor of the cavern and marked out by a low circle of small white pebbles. Adjacent to them, a number of glowing power conduits hummed quietly in the background.

As Gemini had never been to this part of the Hub before, the Undertaker couldn't resist presenting a little factoid to her about the extent of his domain. "Lady Gemini. New to your position, as you are, you might not be aware that the presence of so much necromantic puissance in one place attracts a great deal of dark energy. That energy creates kinks in the Sheolspace continuum, pockets of nullity that tend to gravitate toward the mother lode." he spread his arms wide with a wave that released a sickening wash of body odor, "here is one such rift, a door left ajar into the world of my special servants…the Grumbles."

Everybody in hell had heard of the Grumbles. Ogres of mutant regard, they were a foulmouthed, bad tempered blend of piranha cum trashcan, that once unleashed would swarm and consume everyone and everything in sight. Flesh and fabric, mineral and metal, it mattered not. The Grumbles were equally happy stuffing their faces on things that crunched as much as those that screamed. And if their meal did both, then even better. And this, the only known portal into their world, was always open.

I turned to find Gemini sniffing the air and scanning for all she was worth.

Excellent, I must be on the right track.

Edging as close as I dare to the Undertaker, I whispered to him, "Do you remember the translocation orb variant that Chopin and Tesla managed to plant to draw Cream's essence here after he first came to my attention?"

"You mean the incident where he'd managed to steal…?" he knew better than to utter such things out loud, even in front of one of my Hell Hounds. "Er, yes, I most certainly do. Why?"

"Well, when you mentioned someone had managed to slip a Trojan into the Hub, I immediately thought of Chopin and Tesla. And then I gave thought to how many denizens now have access to their insufferable devices."

"Go on?"

"The thing is, despite our mutual loathing, I know for a fact your security is top notch. Like mine, it has to be, due to that nature of the work carried out here. I also know we went to great lengths to scour this place from top to bottom following the generator's discovery, in a search for anything else that might present a hazard. Neither of us found anything, did we?"

"No we didn't."

"And I'm sure that rankled you no end. So, I'm betting that after I left, you went over the place again. Am I right?"

The Undertaker seemed genuinely embarrassed at getting caught out. "Well…yes. Yes I did. This facility is *my* responsibility and I wanted to make sure the darn place was truly sanitized by sulforensic examiners before installing further upgrades."

"*Further* upgrades?

He shrugged, "Once bitten, twice shy, and all that."

"I'd expect no less," I returned the gesture, and the Undertaker positively glowed at my unexpected compliment. Then I played my ace. "Even so, we've been playing catch-up to that pair for some time now, and it's taught me to expect the unexpected and to look for things that aren't readily apparent. Now, I'm not saying Chopin and Tesla aren't involved, directly…but what if we missed something? What if, for all our considerable talents, there were other factors at play that escaped our notice?"

"What factors?" by the look on his face, I could see I had the Undertaker's complete attention.

"I don't know," I admitted, "because I missed them the first time as well…" then I pointed toward Gemini, "but I'm betting my companion can do a better job."

We fell silent and turned to watch as Gemini became acquainted with the confines of the cave. An odd experience, for although rapt in otherworldly concentration, she shuffled about like a slow motion sleepwalker having a bad dream. Every so often, she would pause and retrace her steps, where-upon she would reach out to feel the texture of the air be-tween her fingertips.

It was obvious something about the subtle nuances of our vicinity had caught her interest. Eventually, I couldn't stand the suspense any longer. "Gemini? Have you found —?"

"One second!" Gemini held up her hand to prevent me breaking her meditation, and rasped, "This place. There's more to it than being permanently active…" Her head kinked to one side. "It's saturated in a rarified form of esoteric ener-gy that…that's…" Then her eyes flared and came into abrupt focus. "Daemon, I've been sounding the environs of the cav-ity in which the Hub originally coalesced. Both the Hub and its satellite fractures are similar in nature, related you might say to the choral tones created by so much power in one geo-desic spot. But the sub-harmonics given off by one of those asperities are completely…?"

"Go on?"

"I'd like to say *unique*, but that wouldn't be right."

"What does your gut tell you?"

"It reeks of antiquity so adamant, so obtuse; it's alien to anything I've ever encountered before, except maybe, for the odd sonority I've run into here and there in the deeper parts of Kí-gal?"

Bingo! "Why don't you track it for us?"

"I'll try, but it's incredibly faint. I can only get a handle on it from here because I'm absorbing the constant emissions from the Grumbles homeworld."

Like a shot, Gemini sprinted from the cavern. By the time the Undertaker and I had recovered from our surprise and thought to follow, Gemini had already clambered back up to the main platform and had initiated her observations.

As before she moved deliberately, waving her hands to and fro, as if eager to unravel the structure of the quantum processes taking place all around us. It was painstaking to watch, but eventually, she worked her way back around to an area just past the main entrance and ten feet below our current location. Then her head locked into position as if she were staring into the abyss.

"There!" She opened her eyes. "Oh, isn't that...?"

"Yes," I replied, "that's the infamous Dead Zone, though it seems pretty lively for something that's supposed to be inert and anti-unlife."

Bringing the Undertaker in on the conversation, I asked, "Have you detected anything else coming from that thing since we heard pseudo-Strawberry's cries for help several months ago?"

I was amazed how mentioning her name didn't seem to hurt as much anymore.

"No, not really," the Undertaker replied. "The music that came with it—the Devil's Trull—continued for another day or two, and the voices for about a week after that. But by the time I'd managed to set up my covert surveillance posts in order to record quantifiable data, the bloody things had faded away."

"Oh really? A spooky coincidence if ever there was one?"

The Undertaker expressed my unspoken suspicions rather nicely. "Or evidence of something more sinister."

The beginnings of a plan began to formulate in the back of my mind. Fixing Gemini in my sights, I asked, "You mentioned you were able to detect this incongruity from the Grumbles grotto because you were absorbing the emissions given off by the gate there. Yes?"

"That's right."

"I was just thinking. If I used the Bãlefire to enhance the strength of your natural abilities, do you think you might be able to analyze the Dead Zone sufficiently to tell us more about it?"

"I've never tried such a thing before," Gemini acknowledged. She reached up to touch the ravaged side of her face, "but as long as you promise not to turn the rest of me into crispy bacon, I'm willing to give it a shot."

"Good girl..." Everyone crowded forward onto the edge of the balcony, and together, we faced the spiraling helix hovering in midair. "I'll do my best."

Gemini threw me a dirty look, so I whispered into her ear to reassure her, "Place your hands on the railing and hold on tight. As I blend to you, you'll probably feel an initial rush of euphoria. Don't worry, that'll be the Bãlefire infusing your nervous system. I'll be regulating the flow, so relax and let it rage through you unhindered."

A steely spike of intent pierced my defenses. *Stop being a jerk and get on with it.*

That's me told then. I thought to myself, *I'd better do as she says.*

Pressing my fingers against Gemini's shoulders, I allowed my astral sight to sink beneath the layers of her corporeal form until her base ego came into view. In this frame of reference, her anima appeared as a black and silver cord of vibrant power, connected by a series of seven sizzling balls of different colors. I took a moment to attune the Bãlefire to her identity, and then I held the floodgates ready.

"Gemini, once this process kicks off it'll take on a life of its own. So, I'm going to start at your root chakra and gradually work my way upward. That way, your spirit will have time to adjust to my presence without being overwhelmed. Are you ready?"

"As ready as I'll ever be."

"Here we go, I'll count you in: three—two—one—*now!*"

Given free reign the Bãlefire raged, immediately seeking to ravage, eager to destroy. The base of Gemini's spine flared and began to spin; rich, vibrant, and red. Within a heartbeat, a pulse of excess vitality had whirled upward and into her sacral nexus. The center of her creativity, it was a powder keg waiting to go off. It did. Condensing like a collapsing star into a screaming nub of supercharged potency, it boosted her latencies beyond measure and detonated in a meteoric concussion that cascaded into her solar plexus, heart, throat and third eye chakra points in blinding succession. Solar discharges followed, one after the other, as bands of astral matter were thrown into the ether in expanding rings of orange, yellow, green, blue and indigo light.

I could taste the lure of Gemini's fear and elation via our psychic link. A temptation I knew only too well, for the thin line between survival and obliteration was as intoxicating to walk as it was deadly. Not wanting to lose only the second person in existence I had ever developed feelings for, I reigned back a little.

Addressing her soul directly, I cautioned, *Gemini? This last stage will inflate your acuity beyond anything you've ever imagined. Stay calm, stay focused. I won't let it sweep you away. Once you've had a chance to adapt, use its efficacy to seek out the information we need.*

Just do it, she gasped, *I feel like I'm hyperventilating in here.*

Understood. Here we go. I squeezed her arm to send a little message of physical comfort, and then merged fully to her mentality. Only then did I open the dam.

From Gemini's perspective, it felt as if we were on a roll-ercoaster ride that had just crested the apex of the world's highest arch. Somehow, we were still accelerating over the curve. Then the vertical drop loomed before us...and we were lost to insane g-forces that lifted her crown chakra from its root in an astral supernova, cosmic in scope.

The tangible world seemed to vaporize. Seconds later, even the residual dust particles had dissipated into an insub-stantial elemental mist that ceased to bear any meaning. Gaz-ing about us, I was amazed by what Gemini's perspicacity had added, for everything had been transposed into a glitter-ing photonegative representation of what it once was.

A translucent orb of untold potential, the Hub was mag-nificent. From this standpoint, it really did look like a giant plasma ball, one that drew the substance of the underverse to its core via a network of ultrafine filaments beyond our ken.

In turn, smaller granules of light buzzed like sparks from within the brightest patches swirling through the Hub's chro-mosphere and off toward a warren of opaque cells, arranged like a giant darkened honeycomb to our right.

I was shocked, and momentarily broke contact. *Look at that, Gemini, do you see? We're catching a glimpse of the reanimation process. And what about some of those larger strands? They go far beyond the limits of the underworld, or even the land of the living. If I'm seeing this right, the Hub connects to...to...? Bugger me! I never knew?*

Shut up! Gemini's curt admonition was well deserved. We were here for a reason, and waxing lyrical was distract-ing her from her task. Fortunately, Gemini hadn't allowed the spectacular vista to sidetrack her.

Tuning into her senses once more, I could see she was already examining a steady stream of gossamer fibers that were being strained from the outer layers of the Hub's cabalistic atmosphere and sucked toward an iridescent breach in reality.

The Dead Zone.

In this new context, the inlet rotated gently in a sea of diaphanous gauze, an opulent fog that nevertheless retained sufficient substance to support the presence of a celestial rainbow. Except this rainbow didn't have a crock of gold waiting at the end of it. Far from it.

Forming a needle of conjoined intent, I sent out our challenge. No sooner had our scope penetrated the event horizon than the opening flexed like an elastic band, and our query was bounced back toward us with an additional component added to its context.

Reacting instantly, I intercepted the leading filament of the tracer and yanked Gemini's consciousness away from danger and back into normal helltime. Her psyche slammed into her body and she staggered, forcing me to sweep her into my arms to prevent her from falling.

Tougher than she looked, Gemini was instantly alert and struggled to stand unaided. I was happy to let her, for I had something I urgently needed to do.

Summoning my full potential, I turned and raised both hands. *"Troh a' lùreshe ain mi sealbġh, bi nagülle* (By the glory invested in me, be denied)."

Dual bolts of arcane lighting screamed from my fingertips. Meeting in a ringing thunderclap, they fractured to form a potent skein of forbidding that coiled itself around the entrance into the Dead Zone. Once in place, I then bound it with my strongest seal.

Not privy to what had just occurred, the Undertaker was understandably agitated. "What's going on? Why did you just generate a barrier around the opening?"

"I'm about to find out. Care to join me?"

Opening my mind, I magnified the view of what was left of our scan, and Gemini and the Undertaker huddled round to take a look.

The construct was incredibly complex. Not only did it radiate with intense heat, but it reeked of disquieting contrasts. Sampling them, I received a cascade of startling impressions, images that included shattered continents, stark and barren; clouds of ash, dark and brooding; skies like an inferno that scorched the earth below; oceans that boiled ceaselessly yet never evaporated. And flames. Flames everywhere that burned without end.

"That thing would set the Pyro-Forests of Hades alight," Gemini whistled, then she gave me a quick dig in the ribs, "just as well you're empowered by the Bãlefire, otherwise we'd have had our synapses fried to a cinder...hang on?" Sharing her concerns mentally, Gemini homed in on a fizzling ember orbiting the probe like a white-hot firefly. "Is that some kind of tag?"

It was. Opening it, I activated a hidden communication. The words were in a dialect I'd never heard before, and sounded like a complex blend of ancient Hellanese and old Arabic. I was stunned to realize I could interpret their meaning.

As the message repeated itself, I translated it for my companions:

"*Elmôh at fell janhîm rah e'ile* (Intrude upon our sovereign affairs again), âgus *cog to-gar nich set fêagk id set Ha'rthao id set Drig'vn Se-mol* (and you will face the wrath of the Blades of the Left-Hand Path)."

"A threat...?" The Undertaker was livid, and had turned an ugly shade of purple to match one of the tones interwoven through his plaid, "here, in my domain?"

I read the missive aloud for a second time, on this occasion using its full inflection.

"No. Brash confidence. *This* is a very blunt statement of intent from whoever it is that controls the Dead Zone."

"Confidence?" Now he was almost frothing at the mouth. "Open hostility more like. Is that why everyone we sent through never came back? They were incinerated, or died at the hands of these...these upstarts? His voice rose until it became a harsh croak. "What are you going to do?"

"*We* are going to go about our business as usual. Satan's system comes first, and now that I've isolated that sinkhole, the flow of sin toward it already appears to be easing...see? Something positive to put in your report to our dark father, eh? As we catch our breaths, it'll also give me time to develop an appropriate strategy."

"Strategy?" This time it was Gemini's turn to speak out. "You don't mean to say you're thinking we ought to go through, do you?"

"You're game for anything, aren't you?" I shucked her under the chin, "Alas, *we* won't be going anywhere...except across to the Hexcalibur. We have an appointment, remember?" Her eyes flashed and she grinned to show she hadn't forgotten. "But seeing as I'm the only one to have Bālefire running through my veins, it looks like it's down to me to find out who these creatures of the Left-Hand Path are and what hazard they represent."

"And then?"

"And then I'll establish once and for all if this is a huge misunderstanding or a prelude to war..." *Because the Fates obviously think my unlife isn't complicated enough.*

Chapter 5: Wheels within Wheels

Concealed within the gloom engendered by the press of narrow streets, awnings and pavement parasols, Heinrich von Nettesheim surveyed the crowds before him. He was confident that he'd shed his tails long ago, but it was best to be sure, especially when the stakes were so high.

His destination, the High Church of Lucifer of Cullogne, was a shrine second in importance only to the cathedral itself, and a fitting venue to wind up his business here.

Many people didn't realize the church was almost as high as their most famous landmark, but that was due to the fact that its foundations had been set within the depression of a huge glass sided crater, one hundred yards deep and more than four times that in circumference. Forged during the Time of Sundering, its surface shone like polished coal, and was thought to have been fashioned by the fall of a colossus from heaven, millennia ago.

Preserved for uncultured heritage, the region surrounding the impact site had been desecrated soon after, and was the perfect place on which to build a permanent testimony to one of Satan's greatest victories. And the High Church of Lucifer was certainly that.

Built in a Teutonic style from the still-glowing detritus of the original explosion, its blocks of amber and black stone gave the impression that the entire façade had been gilded in tarnished bronze, creating an effect that made it look as if the ghost of Atlantis was rising from the bowels of the underworld.

Huge, sprawling, and ethereal, its ornate belfries and ziggurat towers resembled the electrodes of some outlandish dynamo belonging to a mad scientist, for rabid electrical discharges danced from pinnacle to pinnacle, twenty-four seven, in a never-ending display that generated a permanent cloud mass above its thirteen great spires.

Nettesheim's gaze swept the width of the bowl for as far as the eye could see. For those areas he couldn't reach, he resorted to astral projection. *Good, it's all clear.*

Employing his arts, he conjured several doppelgangers and sent them off into the crowds in different directions. *If Guiteau and Castile are here, the mere sight of my good self, ambling along without a care in the world will flush them out. Then I'll be on them and —?* Power flourished nearby, only to cut off abruptly. Expecting word from his contact at any moment, Nettesheim knew he had to respond immediately. *Until then...*

A brief exercise of will sent his invisible form skimming across the edge of the marketplace and down one of the long flights of steps leading toward the bottom of the crater. There, burning braziers lined the perimeter of a plaza surrounding the church, adding an ominous chill to the heavy pall already saturating the atmosphere.

Reaching the Porch of Perdition, Nettesheim lingered to study those denizens attending the evening's dark mass. *Priests, acolytes, Blue Suits, and an unhealthy smattering of the impenitent. Excellent, all is as it should be.* Picking his moment, he tagged on behind the smallest group, slipped inside and manifested.

Having witnessed the hearthlike splendor of the High Church from afar, the interior was always something of a surprise, for the ruddy glow engendered by the rufous exterior gave way to an emerald green intensity so rank, so bitterly cold, that ice steamed in constant vapors through the very substance of the blocks lining the floors and walls.

Wide and spacious, the isle leading toward the Altar of Avarice had been arranged like a central basilica. Lined on both sides by long benches, the pew ends had been decorated by alternating telamons and caryatids, miniature representations of the giants masterfully incorporated into the pillars supporting the vaulted roof more than six hundred feet above him.

Encapsulated in onyx and jasper, and tourmaline and jet, the faces of each titan were bared in a rictus of pain, expressions that accurately reflected the staggering weight of rock and sin they carried upon the capitals of their shoulders. A burden made all the more forceful, due to the constant dirge in the background, a monotone cadence both sonorous and mournful, from a choir of throats that stirred the heart and enticed the unfaithful to prayers.

Selecting a blood red taper from the stand just inside the entrance lobby, Nettesheim made his way forward like any other supplicant. Only once he was sure nobody was watching did he veer off into a narthex cut into the western colonnade. Protected by a door bounded and studded in iron, the entrance opened as he approached, and closed behind him with a resounding, *clunk.*

Nettesheim found himself inside a darkened, ascetically furnished office. Gable-style windows, high and pointed, graced the wall to his left. A writing bureau had been positioned directly beneath it to catch the scant light creeping in through its heavily leaded panes of glass. Bookshelves, crammed with dusty tomes, flanked the desk on either side. At the far end of the room, an open fire burned warmly and the smell of brimstone filled the air.

A female figure stood silhouetted against the flames, hands clasped and with her back turned toward Nettesheim. The cut of her robes identified that person as a deacon, though her frosty aura and the fingers of black smoke curling indolently around her head suggested otherwise. She didn't bother to turn at the sound of the door closing and locking by itself, and Nettesheim knew better than to try and make small talk. That wasn't the way things worked. Instead, he leaned back against the edge of the bureau and waited patiently, content to let his contact initiate the conversation.

When she did, her first question was as open as they come.

"Well?"

Presented with something of a conundrum, Nettesheim decided to cut to the chase and began with what would be most important to his master. "I have completed an examination of all thirteen high churches, and can confirm that any and all references to the Unveiling have been expunged."

"What about other obscure texts or sources?"

"Unknown, and practically speaking, we simply don't have the time. The Soulstice is only twelve days away. Regardless, I am fairly confident the truth of the Reaper's origins will remain hidden until it is too late for him to do anything about it."

"*Fairly* confident?"

Nettesheim's voice betrayed his concerns. "As anticipated, Grim's evolution continues apace. While I am doing my best to prepare appropriate contingencies, we must be aware his burgeoning power will eventually overwhelm the shackles previously put in place. Once the safeguards fall, a storm of memories will resurface and the embodiment of his remaining persona will emerge."

The brume about the deacon's head grew thicker and more pungent. "And you still feel the Soulstice will prove pivotal in this respect?"

"I do." Nettesheim considered his considerable knowledge of what lie ahead. "From what I can deduce, Chopin and Tesla have all the tools they need to make their move. Their recent behavior confirms this. In the past, they have gone out of their way to taunt Grim; to bait him into making a mistake; even telling him where they will strike next in an effort to lure and manipulate him. And now? Their silence speaks for itself. They fear to be exposed at the last as they await the conjunction, the only time in a thousand centuries when conditions will be ripe for bringing their long laid plans to fruition. But, if we can maneuver events to ensure both parties clash, the environment in which such a confrontation takes place will work to our advantage. Remember, Grim's inherent nature will always drive him to fulfill his duty, tipping the scales in our favor."

The deacon swayed backward and forward on her toes, as if weighing the evidence. Eventually, she murmured, "Then it would appear we have a strategy on which to build. Prepare well, mind you. All involved in this little scheme are tenacious in their own way. It would be a pity if anything prevented us from maximizing our profits...speaking of which. What have you been able to determine regarding the current unrest and missing souls? Are Chopin and Tesla involved?"

"Regarding the unrest, we are dealing with a weapon in the form of a contagion. It acts like a virus by splicing itself to the prevailing emotion of any given situation, and once attached, it invades the host, introducing a catalyzing agent so those feelings replicate out of hand. Hell is no convent. Even so, the vehemence of the riots and the suddenness by which such violence erupts proves an unnatural element is at play. Despite their ingenuity, Chopin and Tesla are not to blame."

"How can you be so sure?"

"It is telestic in nature, and for all their acumen, neither Chopin nor Tesla possesses mystical ability."

"And what of our other concern? The problem is expanding without sign of remedy. Although the Undertaker has not yet reported matters officially, he has demanded the assistance of the Reaper. If your assessment of the current situation is correct and the timing of the Soulstice remains a crucial factor, we cannot allow such a diversion at so delicate a stage of events."

"So far, I have scant information on which to base a hypothesis. The mere fact that so much animus is missing does lean toward our rebels. After all, they have always sought ways to avoid injustice, and this fits their pattern. But...?"

"But?"

"The timing of such manipulations goes against the grain. As I mentioned, Chopin and Tesla have been conspicuous by their absence. Such maneuvering, now, will attract a great deal of attention. Exactly the thing they are trying to avoid."

The deacon fell silent once more. When she spoke again, it sounded as if the issue had already been decided and she merely sought Nettesheim's view.

"Options?"

A man of action, Nettesheim decided to be blunt. "That's easy. Prioritize and ignore the unrest. For now it serves a purpose, and can easily be addressed at a later date. I would have said the same regarding our missing denizens...however, now the Reaper has been involved, we have to get him back on track."

"And how will you accomplish that?"

"We need someone inside, someone who can influence matters directly..." Nettesheim took a deep breath, "So, I was thinking that perhaps I ought to offer my services?"

The deacon's tone betrayed her skepticism. "You think he'd accept?"

"Given my resume, I don't see why not. The Hounds have already run into me on several occasions where my skills have proven their worth. So, to gain further favor, I deem it might be best to contrive events in such a way that the Reaper thinks the idea to recruit me is his."

Amazingly, the deacon seemed to consider that part of the proposal seriously, "A masterful stratagem. But tell me, how the devil would you be able to arrange such a thing without raising suspicion?"

Nettesheim smiled to himself and thought back over his past few days in Cullogne. "Let's just say, I have one or two people in mind who will help more than they realize."

*

Undetectable behind the fine ivory gauze of floor to ceiling net drapes, Yamato looked down from his vantage point and out across the huge public square before him.

At seven hundred feet in length and more than four hundred wide, Place Venôme was a finger in every pie, palatial overload on the senses of lavish indulgence, served up in a huge slice to the elite of Hellonian society; a many-layered cake of townhouses and apartments, consulates, up-market hotels and other commercial establishments, all extravagantly arrayed behind a gaudy fascia of Corinthian pilasters, classical abutments and porticos.

The overall impression was designed to send a message to the vast majority of Perish's embittered, hardhearted residents: "you're clearly not good enough. Oh, and by the way, *joie de la souffrance*."

In case the city's parasites failed to appreciate the gist of such a cleverly composed subliminal message, the Venôme Column dominating the center of the court was happy to ram it right up where Paradise never shone.

Originally built to commemorate Napoleon's greatest victory in Austerlitz in 1805, the one hundred and thirty-foot high obelisk now gave testimony to the extent of Satan's influence, for a sickening variety of some of the most exquisite forms of torture to be found in each of the capitals of latter-day hell had been clearly depicted in all four hundred and twenty-five of the bas-relief bronze plates adorning the exterior shaft in serpentine display. Tortures that most denizens had been forced to endure far too often.

And there, crowning the monument and surveying the extent of his domain, stood a representation of His Satanic Majesty himself. Resplendent in his "Great Dragon of Revelation" guise, he reared up on powerful hind legs—defiant and awful—with wings spread wide, spitting real flames toward the clouds and the hateful reminder of divine purity taking shelter behind them.

Though if anyone dares to emulate his contempt, Yamato thought to himself, *especially in his own back yard, our Dark Father turns to us to ensure correctional therapy is swiftly and mercilessly applied. And we are glad to serve.*

He scanned the plaza one last time. The initial crowds of morning workers had thinned considerably, leaving only sightseers and beggars behind, and tardier individuals who obviously liked to cut things fine. *Good, our prey should be preoccupied by now.*

Thankful that everyone he was working with today was capable of telepathic communication, Yamato expanded his awareness until he had attuned to the predetermined psychic bandwidth, and called, "GDSI squads, report."

Mutt one here, we're stationary south of your location in rue de Castration.

This is Mutt two. We're likewise stationary to the north in rue de Pox.

Mongrel one, we're now in place.

Mongrel two, ready.

From Mongrel three, in position.

Mongrel four here, standing by.

Mongrel five, ready to go.

From Furball, we're mobile in the main boulevard. The pups are in the basket.

"Squeeee."

Yamato grinned at the enthusiastic response from the smallest member of the enterprise, and glanced out through the window toward a large nearby downspout where Brown-Tail waited with several representatives of the local hell-rat colony, the import of the event reflected by the fact that their party included the meister for this particular shire.

How quickly things change, he mused.

The last time he'd been at this address, just over a year ago, had been in the days following a raid led by Daemon Grim and Nimrod—the former Lead Hound—in their hunt for the renegade, Dr. Thomas Neill Cream.

Cream had been instrumental in subverting the minds of others by the use of a wide variety of deadly potions and cocktails, and Chopin and Tesla hadn't been shy in putting his talents to use. Their net had been cast much wider than anticipated, and went on to include lawyers, and other members of the Blue Suit and infernal intelligence community.

Infiltrating the establishment had been a stroke of fiendish genius, for along with the time bending elements produced by Tesla's translocation generators, the rebels used Cream's elixirs to stay one step ahead of injustice. A source of constant irritation to the Hounds in particular.

As Yamato's gaze came to rest on the local office of the Palais de L'Injustice across the street, his smile grew broader. *Such a target right on their doorstep was impossible to resists and went on to cause untold damage. Still, we weren't to know. At least we're slowly leveling the playing field.*

On either side of him, Champ Ferguson and Pascal Fléau began to fidget. Noting their impatience, Yamato decided it best to get everything underway and addressed the waiting units.

"All mobile and static teams, this is Pack Leader. We are about to advance on target. As we enter, Mongrels one through four, you are to move out from your OPs and cut all vehicular and pedestrian access to Place Venôme. You will be supported by your own contingent of rats in the sewers should our suspects attempt to evade us using the tunnels. Mongrel five? You are to follow us to the precincts of the Department of Injustice and establish a cordon around the perimeter. Furball, you are to close on our objective and secure the interior of the building and all exit points. Mutts one and two? Stand by until called forward to commence your sulforensic sweeps. After we start, nobody goes in or out until I give the all clear.

"These are the characters we are after." Yamato paused to project three images through the ether, "Castor Bean, Rosary Pea and Cherry Choke. All are employees of the Local Intelligence Office of the Unsûreté, and all of them are authorized to carry firearms. Don't be fooled by appearances. Remember, there may be residual commands buried deep in their subconscious minds waiting to be triggered, so stay sharp. If they do manage to bolt, take them down instantly and take them down hard. Don't give them an opportunity to activate any hidden devices. All that I ask is that you do your best to leave their brains intact for examination by our Inquisitors. Is that clear?"

Nine affirmations trilled back.

"Brown-Tail?" Yamato made an effort to create word pictures in his head, as Gemini had suggested, so that their rodent helpers would understand him more clearly, "I want your people underground where they'll be able to move unhindered and with speed. Be alert to any unusual activity, and make sure there aren't any hidden surprises down there that might cause unexpected problems. If you discover anything that looks out of place, I want to know immediately. Use the colored tokens we've provided to indicate the urgency of what you need to say...is that okay?"

"Squeeeek!"

That'll do.

Finally, Yamato turned to his lead GDSI investigator on scene, Pascal—the Scourge—Fléau. "Okay Pascal, do your thing."

All three headed for the door and swiftly made their way downstairs toward the main entrance. Passing a large hallway mirror, Yamato noted how their disguise for the occasion—blue pinstripe suits and executive attaché cases—didn't really look all that convincing. For one thing, Yamato's jacket was rather baggy. But it had to be, seeing as how he had tantō combat knives strapped to the insides of his forearms, and a ko-wakizashi short sword slung along his spine.

And Champ? Yamato snorted softly. Champ looked like he always did; a disheveled bag of shit in anything other than his usual Hell Hound combat fatigues and cowl. It had been an uphill struggle to persuade him not to wear his Hell-Brass 6.66 Magnums "gunslinger style" over his waistcoat, as was his custom.

Teleporting was a no-no, as any attempt to enter restricted buildings in such a manner would trigger inbuilt security protocols, frying them in their tracks. So, the only viable option to approach without raising any alarm was to do so by foot.

As luck would have it, they didn't have too far to go. And, as Pascal had pointed out, the Blue Suit persona didn't have to stand up to scrutiny, it was merely a spot of window-dressing to allow them to blend in with other commuters running late for work.

Pascal himself was a natural; casual, unperturbed, chatting about all sorts of mundane crap as they closed on the armored doors and windows of the bureau. Nonetheless, Yamato didn't miss the way the seasoned specialist's eyes played the open ground and other passers-by—over and over—until they were right on top of their target.

Stepping up to the automated sentry post, Pascal displayed his badge and submitted himself to a retinal scan. "Pascal Xavier Fléau, infernal serial number: Six, three, six, omega. Zero, one, three, zero. I'm here on official GDSI business with two inspectors from the ministry."

Confidence won the day. A bell chimed and the steel screen clicked open. Pascal whistled and gaggle of furry heads popped up from a nearby storm drain vent and immediately scurried forward.

Yamato made sure to hold the door ajar as everyone piled inside, much to the dismay of the female counter clerk and nearby security officer who appeared nonplussed that so many plague carriers had been allowed access to their sterile environs.

Once again, Pascal revealed how adept he was at dealing with awkward situations. "Don't worry; we're here to implement a new initiative from the classified wastes department, and this flea-bitten gaggle is with us. Evidently, these little guys have been trained to eat shredded paper..." he smirked. "Could you imagine an infiltrator trying to reconstruct a secret memo made from rat turds?" Then he pointed at Champ and Yamato, "That's what these schmucks have to do...and you think *you* have a shitty job?"

Playing along, Yamato shrugged and pulled a face. He was gratified to see the receptionist sneer down her nose, while the security guard burst out laughing and waved them through.

Another door buzzed open, and before they knew it, they'd gained the inner sanctum without the slightest sign of a hitch.

Lingering only to signal their progress to the units waiting outside, Yamato brought up a mental picture of the floor plans they'd studied in preparation for the raid. Highlighting a rear room on the first floor, he shared the image with everyone around him. "*That's* where we're going. Take a right at the top of the stairs and head toward the back of the building."

The team started up, studiously avoiding the rush of furry bodies swarming about their feet and a smattering of inquisitive staff, eager to see what the growing commotion was all about.

Yamato continued issuing instructions, "Pascal, block local radio and mobile phone networks. Champ, stay in the main corridor and cover the fire exit."

Both operators opened their bags as they ran, and dropped them to the floor almost immediately, Pascal having removed his jammer, and Champ his guns. Yamato lifted his own briefcase and depressed a small tab next to the combination lock. A gentle hum distinguished itself, which rapidly rose in pitch. Spotting the Unsûreté office door was halfway open; Yamato adjusted his pace and lobbed the entire case through the gap.

All three men dropped to one knee and covered their ears.

A bright flash lit up the back of Yamato's eyelids. It was followed in quick succession by a loud bang, a sharp change in pressure that reverberated through the walls, and the sound of tinkling glass and screaming. "Go—go—go!"

Surging forward, Yamato flexed his wrists, activating the spring release mechanism for his knives. Now armed, he kicked the remains of the door open and surveyed the scene within.

Four desks had been arranged around the edge of the room in an inverted *U* shape, facing inward. Three had been in use, and their former occupants now rolled about on the floor, clearly distressed. At a glance, Yamato ascertained two of them were women, bleeding from their ears. The other person, a taller, older male built like a weightlifter, must have caught the brunt of the explosion, for he suddenly stopped writhing and lay still, face down, groaning.

The site of the detonation was marked by shredded leather and a large black scorch mark on the carpet. And though the device had only been designed to stun, the blast had been sufficient to shred the blinds, shatter computers screens, and blow out three of the windows.

Moving inside, Yamato queried, "Pascal?"

Pascal responded by typing a brief message into the keypad on the scrambler. Once complete, he placed it on a nearby table and drew his gun. "I've just sent a coded blip to the Mutt teams. Sulforensics will be with us in less than two minutes. So..." he studied the disheveled group with interest, "what little fishes have we caught?"

Yamato chuckled. "Let's haul in the net and take a look."

Both ladies were still disoriented. Even so, Yamato exercised caution as he checked their profiles against a portable ID chip reader. "Special Agent Fléau, say hello to Rosary Pea and Cherry Choke..."

Yamato deftly removed twos set of blandcuffs from inside his jacket and fitted them about each suspect's wrists. Activating them, he gritted his teeth as they went to work. Within seconds, both prisoners' eyes went blank. As an added precaution, Yamato slipped a blackout hood over their heads. "That's two for two. So, this must be our friend Castor Bean...?" he leaned across and turned the unconscious man onto his back. "Shit! It's not him?"

A shock coursed through Yamato's system and his neck craned from side to side as he endeavored to take in the rest of the room and any hidey holes he might have missed. As a precaution, he also began to range for the missing fugitive with his astral vision.

Pascal reacted immediately, "All units, be advised, one of our targets is still at large. I say again, Castor Bean is still —?"

Yamato!

Champ's mental hail was loud enough to blister paint.

Yamato froze and concentrated on his partner's aura. *What have you got?*

The moment we entered this place, I activated our Tesla orb, just in case. Well guess what? The darn thing just pinged. Some yella-bellied coward just slipped into one of the bathrooms and jumped away. I'm checkin' the cubicle area now.

On my way. Yamato spun to face Pascal. "Can you tie things up here? If we can zero in on the esoteric footprint of the other generator, we'll catch our absconder with his pants down."

The GDSI veteran took the unexpected turn of events in his stride. "All in a day's work. Leave it to me; I'll have this place locked down and everyone in custody whether they're guilty or not within thirty minutes. You go and have fun."

The Lead Hound didn't need to be told twice.

Bounding from the Unsûreté office at a run, Yamato headed down an adjacent corridor and almost bowled into his partner as he exited the male shower room.

Skidding to a halt, Yamato grabbed Champ by the shoulders, and gasped, "Anything?"

Champ's expression said it all. "Nope. The lily-livered swine hightailed it outta here before I could draw a bead on him."

"Then quickly," Yamato began shoving Champ back inside, "let's get after him before the footprint fades."

Brandishing the orb, Champ rotated the top and the control slide came into view. Pressing the uppermost of three buttons, he held it down until a low-frequency whine became apparent. Then, holding the generator in front of him, he wove it to and fro in the air and retraced his steps. All of a sudden, the unit beeped and started emitting a steady two-tone warble. "Got the fucker."

Yamato slotted his knives back into their sheaths and drew his sword. "Well, what are you waiting for? We can't give him too much of a head start." To himself, he complained, *I wish we knew how to activate the temporal aspect; we'd have him for sure.*

Champ shuffled closer and the air before them corkscrewed inward. Everything went gray, and Yamato lost all sense of balance. Then reality sprung back into place. Except that now, instead of rows and rows of neatly arranged lockers, he found himself on a wide and spacious boulevard outside the Assemblée Diabolique et Niveaux, Inter-Circles of Hell travel terminal.

The people there were in uproar.

Why is everyone so...?

Crack!

Reacting instinctively, Champ and Yamato gamboled away from each other and took shelter. In Yamato's case, he scrabbled behind a group of citizens lying on the floor, each of who were nursing an assortment of injuries.

Yamato needn't have worried; the Hell Hounds didn't appear to be the target. Thirty yards in front of him, another victim fell, blood spraying across the pavement from a gaping neck wound. *He's one for the Slab.*

Beyond that unfortunate denizen, Yamato spotted the back of someone in a dark suit running flat-out toward the gateway. *Bean!* The shimmering field between the focusing collars started to sparkle. Cursing himself for stashing his knives, Yamato yelled, "Champ, he's getting away."

"I can fewkin' well see that," Champ retorted, dryly, "There's too many people in the way. Hang on a tic while I clear a path."

More shots rang out. Once. Twice. Thrice. Four times.

Struck in the head, a quartet of Perish's worst found themselves prospective guests of the Undertaker.

Champ stood and took careful aim. Yamato's gaze flicked between his partner and the fleeing traitor. He held his breath...then several things happened at once:

A glaring yellow-white light blinded him; the Hell-Brass magnums barked again; a louder roar drowned out the sound of gunfire; then the world span as Yamato was swatted to the ground by an invisible shockwave.

Blending to the impact, Yamato rolled and came to his feet almost instantly. Dust filled the air, clogging his lungs, obscuring his vision. A resonating tenor, as if from a loud gong, worried his sensibilities.

"Champ, report? Are you alright?" His own voice seemed muffled though he was sure he'd shouted. "Champ?"

"Bright an... fresh...daisy. Did you...must have...shitfest. Just look at...Those nearer the gate are goners for sure."

The travel junction? Peering through a cloud of yellow grime, all Yamato could see was a pile of twisted metal and shattered blocks of stone. Nothing remained of the terminus itself except for the ruined stumps of the restraining brackets.

Spitting out a mouthful of gritty residue, Yamato croaked, "Are you tracking where he went?"

"Nah, he didn't use his orb. Now we'll have to waste time interrogatin' the hub's travel logs."

And in the meantime, the trail will go cold. Yamato could barely contain his frustration. "C'mon, before I tell Daemon what happened, I'd at least like to have something useful that will soften the blow."

Disappointment made Yamato feel somewhat spiteful. "What say we go and help Pascal chew off some fingers and toes before we send the girls across to Juxtapose? I'm feeling a mite peckish, and eating people alive always works wonders in loosening their tongues."

Chapter 6: *Auld Lang Syne*

Devoted to the task at hand, Dr. David Livingstone was nevertheless thankful for the muting effects of the dampening panels lining the walls of the interrogation rooms, here, at the Inquisitors headquarters in Blood Tower, the Den of Iniquity. While he'd been aware of the existence of such contrivances for a while, it was an incredible experience to see them in action, for they not only prevented the pseudobodies of wayward miscreants from dissipating before he'd finished with them, but allowed him to stretch his skills to the limits—limits that had produced such remarkable results.

Livingstone leaned forward, leads in hand, and an ardent blue-white intensity threw back the gloom of the cell's darkened interior. The snapping discharge that accompanied that jolt of electricity cut a shrill scream in half. But the mind venting its pain? Ah, the mind continued to spout secrets in a veritable waterfall of insightful delights.

A flock of hell-ravens looking on through the window bars flapped their wings in applause. Some hopped from foot to foot squawking their approval and begging for scraps from the growing pile of intestinal silt lying about the doctor's feet.

Playing to his audience, Livingstone ran the end of a bare wire along the stomach of the latest test subject with one hand, and bent to scoop up a fistful of discarded strips of flesh and sinew with the other. Judging the distance, he then tossed the bloody offering toward his cackling entourage. Cawing with glee, ruddy beaks proceeded to stab and tease their way through each fatty morsel, before selecting the choices bits to dine on.

Livingstone stepped back, and the pathetic figure tied naked to the table before him slumped down, exhausted.

Interesting? Miss Choke's memories also contain a number of random passages to what must be a riddle? He glanced across to the other side of the chamber where a second subject, strapped to an adjacent metal frame, hung unconscious from her restraints. *Though they differ to what Miss Pea had stored away.*

The scholar in Livingstone spent a while comparing the cleverly concealed examples both women had accumulated.

"Okay, the first set of sentences said, 'for the valley of the shadow serves naught but a cup/sprinkled liberally upon open wounds/that gulf betwixt the silent spaces of now and then/curl like lazy fingers around your heart.' Then Miss Choke's selection made reference to, 'do not go gently into death/this perfect condiment to preserve your pain/existing in shadow and flame/tendrils of smoke, as fragile as a sudden intake of breath.'"

Absorbed, Livingstone skipped between the opposing phrases for some time.

"Hmmm. That's just a lot of nonsense. But didn't I...?" Something he'd seen, documented in the unwelcome pack introducing him to his new position, jogged at a memory. "I remember reading about all those incidents where Chopin and Tesla would goad Daemon in an effort to trip him up and get him to act rashly?" Livingstone gasped. "Of course, when the Reaper attended Cadaver's to assist in the disappearance of Charles Guiteau, Tesla had left that cryptic brainteaser pointing to Limes Square."

He glanced back to the expressions he already had. "What if I interrogated the women in the wrong order? It would be a simple matter to split everything up and change it round."

No sooner had he finished doing that, than a little thrill of excitement ran through him. Aloud, he read:

"Do not go gently into death,
For the valley of the shadow serves naught but a cup...
This perfect condiment to preserve your pain,
Sprinkled liberally upon open wounds...
Existing in shadow and flame,
That gulf betwixt the silent spaces of now and then...
Tendrils of smoke, as fragile as a sudden intake of breath
Curl like lazy fingers around your heart..."

Livingstone smiled. *That almost begins to make sense. I obviously have two-thirds of a series of stanzas. And I don't imagine for one minute the clue—for that's what is—will really make sense until I have the elusive Mister Bean in my custody? Such a clever way to hide information. I can't wait to see what further digging might reveal?*

Feeling suddenly thirsty, Livingstone helped himself to a fresh glass of bile, drained only that morning from the latest set of stooges from Perish.

As he partook of his refreshment, he congratulated fate on his fortuitous change in circumstances. "Most of my work as warden of Cadaver's Lunatic Asylum was devoted to indoctrination and nonlethal punishment. Even so, it was a professionally rewarding and productive tenure. I've no doubt about that. But here...?" He took a long pull on his drink. "Here at the Den of Iniquity I am allowed—no, expected—to inflict misery and suffering on a scale that puts the Undertaker to shame.

"And my fellow Inquisitors? Though I am their newest member, placed in a position of responsibility over them, they have welcomed me into the fold as if I've always belonged here. Such professionalism. Such dedication to duty. From the moment I arrived, I felt an affinity I've not experienced since my early days in the cotton mills of Scotland. It is a bond I never expected in hell and one I will always endeavor to earn..."

Livingstone's attention focused once more on his helpless stooges. "So, while I've always striven to be a gentleman, I really must apologize, ladies, for I intend to live up to my title as Chief Inquisitor without question. By the time I've finished with you, any old acquaintances you think you've forgotten will be bright and shiny and new."

He drained his cup and selected a thicker, more robust set of cables, these ones attached to the mains supply via a voltmeter. Touching the ends together with a loud *snap*, sparks flew, and the dial on the casing jumped.

His shadow fell across the women once more. Though delirious, they recoiled in horror and began writhing in their restraints.

Of course, that only increased his anticipation all the more.

*

Reality quivered, and two primeval entities manifested high above the smelting pot that was District S16—otherwise known as Sulfurous Sands—Dark Cairo. It had been a while since either of them had reason to visit this ancient edifice, for their last journey to the brooding metropolis to ambush a seriously depleted Daemon Grim had gone drastically wrong. But they'd learned a thing or two since then, and tonight, the Second and Sixth of Seven were here to wreak death and destruction upon the city of a thousand minarets itself.

Both enforcers made haste to scan their objective, ripe and overflowing with sinners, in spite of the lateness of the hour.

"I have looked forward to venting retribution upon the vermin crowding those streets," the Sixth hissed. "Too long they have escaped our wrath. Well, no more. But where to start? The Geyser Pyramids are an obvious choice, as are the souks. If we destroy their main attractions and rob them of their ability to trade, complaint and chaos will ensue. Perhaps it might also trigger a riot, and we will witness for ourselves the full extent of the saint's machinations." His spectral signature flared white. "What about the Sphincter? Would that not afford the perfect medium through which their morale might —?"

"No, we'll leave that place well alone," the Second interjected. "Don't forget, of all our company, I have some form of affinity with our foe that grants me a better understanding of his temperament. While Grim might ignore our presence here this evening—and even count it a blessing—a direct attack on one of Lucifer's greatest repositories of knowledge would prove a grave error on our part. For now, we will stick to the agreed upon strategy and make our presence felt by stirring up revolt and uncivil unrest."

The Sixth's essence paled, indicating he was considering the weight of the Second's advice. Eventually, he was moved to admit, "Your restraint grants you wisdom. There are, after all, but two of us present. So, what would you recommend?"

"We seek to spread mayhem, in this, one of the most unstable territories, do we not? How better to achieve that aim, then, than by making the very nature of the realm work against itself." The Second pointed to the close-ranked citadels and marketplaces on the far side of the River Vile where residents and visitors alike were crammed together like sardines, "especially if we can flood those streets in a way they have never experienced before?" He hovered closer to his brother. "My restraint in no way precludes my resolve for justice...as you will see."

On this occasion, the Sixth's aura glittered with aquamarine highlights. "Then it is agreed. Let us proceed with all haste."

Together, the demigods descended upon the northern causeway skimming the perimeter of Queen Hatepheres' tomb, and manifested in all their splendor, swords drawn and robes fluttering under the influence of unseen vortices.

At first, startled bystanders looked on in bemused ignorance. Then, realizing who the glowing titans were and what their presence meant, panic set it. People screamed and started running.

Feeding on the ensuing alarm, the Second raised his palm toward the firmament. Clouds answered his call, condensing from the constitution of the atmosphere in a hammer-headed fist of fulgurous intent. Thickening, they distended toward the city as if poured from a cauldron, Jovian in scope.

The Second felt his capacity swell to bursting point. Satisfied, he selected his target and leveled his weapon toward the Benben stone crowning Kung-fu's pyramid in golden glory. His eyes crackled with energy, potential that overflowed down his form and along his blade. A sizzling nucleus coalesced at the tip, and jagged fronds of lightning lashed out to obliterate the top of the northeastern corner of the monument in a ball of expanding light.

A rumbling sensation stirred in the substrata. Radical and resonant, that grumbling grew louder and more pronounced with alarming avidity. Small surface rocks and pebbles commenced dancing along the ground.

Boom!

The top of the pyramid blew out in a convulsion of orange and yellow fury that expulsed incendiary material high into the night sky. Great gouts of magma followed, hot on its heels, spewing from the breach like blood from a severed artery. So great was the outrush, that nearby cemeteries and burial mounds were subsumed in seconds.

The flow increased, widening and accelerating into a viscid torrent that effaced the village of Nazlet el-Shaman in less than a minute.

And still the molten river advanced, suppurating like the weeping excretion of an obscene boil, until the banks of the Vile itself and the island district of Za-molek were under siege.

Fire and water. The two elements met in a sizzling, hissing standoff, venting steam in such quantities that the heavens were obscured behind a veil of silver-gray mists.

Zzzt—thud. Zzzt—thud. Whump. Zzzzzt—thud.

Forgotten ejectiles rained down, striking old town and modern skyscrapers alike, and leaving scant time for anyone to react to the disaster approaching at more than three hundred miles per hour.

The evaluators took to the air to better follow the unfolding tragedy.

"See how quickly the Vile and its island are overwhelmed," the Sixth declared, "for as the lava cools, it solidifies to form a bridge over which the alluvial volatiles can flow more freely."

"Then prepare yourself," the Second advised, "for soon you must use your aptitude to recreate this effect, but on a much grander scale. Observe the far side of the river."

Down below, the narrow streets and myriad alleys were rapidly filling with an ever expanding tide of flickering flames. Wherever the igneous brew swirled, wood and fabric combusted; stone blackened and fractured; metal liquefied, oozing down like wet clay to join a deepening pool of bubbling slag. It wasn't long before the entire city was ablaze, and the sound of complaint had built to a crescendo.

"Quickly brother," the Second pressed, "before they are all consumed and we have nobody left to measure."

The Sixth slashed his sword across the underbelly of the sky, as if attempting to inflict a mortal wound upon an enemy. Subject to his elemental command, the boiling vapors saturating the air obeyed, and congealed into one liquefied mass. Then it dropped with the force of tsunami.

Crushed by the unbelievable weight of countless tons of water in such a confined area, the ruined shells of buildings shattered, monuments crumbled, and those people who weren't killed outright, were knocked unconscious, encased within a frigid crust of flash-cooled pumice. The power went out, fires were extinguished, and everything went dark.

"You see?" the Second proclaimed, triumphantly, his eyes aglow with purple and yellow streamers, "Simplicity in itself. Dark Cairo lies vanquished without the slightest response to our trespass. Come, let us pour out our cup of unkindness on the survivors and taste the extent of their wretchedness. I tell you, this will be a night the denizens of hell will rue for decades...if not longer."

Moments later, fresh wails of woe split the night.

*

Though the scene about him was merely illusional, the heat it generated was anything but. Everywhere he looked, Chopin was besieged by flames, sharp and penetrating. Flames in the sky above; flames in the air; Even the ground beneath his feet appeared to be comprised of millions of molten tongues of living fire. No matter how hard he tried, the embattled composer couldn't get his vision to clarify beyond the inferno in front of him.

"This is the fourth time in as many months I've tried to solve the secret of Grim's potency," he complained to himself, "and every time it ends in the same way."

Well used to traversing the esoteric medium between time and space, Chopin altered his acuity to include a representation of the totem grasped firmly in his corporeal hands, back in the safety and comfort of his living room. An image of the *Sword of Uncovered Secrets* materialized in the air before him, and he bent to inspect the composition of the glaive itself and the spectacular jewel adorning its pommel.

Vibrant power teased the hairs of his skin. Meshing to that vitality, Chopin became aware of a divergent current that was somehow at odds to the natural flow of supercharged energies surrounding him.

"It seems to be working just fine, but that feedback loop feels as if it's blocking the gem's capacity in some way."

Baffled, Chopin relaxed his efforts and reviewed what he knew about his expanding Vidium armory.

"Zion-forged, they are holy weapons, granted to the Chosen to combat Satan and his fallen angels during the Time of Sundering. Empowered by shards taken from the heavenly throne, each one amplifies a facet of God's Grace: power; strength; speed; wisdom; knowledge, and so forth. Now, while Satan was able to subvert the nature of their divine counterparts, the Daggers of Damocles—a feat he also managed, to some degree, by the fabrication of the Bãlefire from the infected extract of Holy Spirit—the Vidium Swords remained pure and untainted by corruption. That means no amount of deviltry can interfere with their operation. So, there must be an element to my query that's forbidden in some way, something that would account for the brick wall I hit every time I try and delve into Grim's past. But what? This is the Reaper we're talking about, for pity's sake...?" A troubling notion began to gnaw at his resolve. "Unless, of course, Satan managed to wrangle an extra component into his assassin's makeup that prevents snooping? But to do *that*, he'd have needed access to God's Grace. Impossible, once he had debased himself he no long...?"

Chopin caught his ethereal breath.

"There's more here than meets the eye. Grim bested the angel with ease. And no matter how twisted he'd become, Grislington was a cherub, a creature only Satan himself should have been able to manage."

Of course, that reminder only raised a storm of other questions.

"So how does the Prince of Lies maintain control of his beast? And if Grim *is* that powerful, and by all accounts, he's getting stronger, why does he endure being told what to do by an upstart?"

It was only by a supreme effort of will that Chopin was able to reign his frustrations in. "Ah, repeated castigation is getting me nowhere fast. And really, all this will soon be a moot point."

Releasing his mental grip, Chopin perceived his descent toward the land of the unliving begin almost immediately. As a matter of course, he braced himself for the ordeal ahead.

When it came, the pain was excruciating, and burned the fibers of his muscles so badly, that Chopin thought his ligaments would tear and his joints explode from their sockets.

The first vindictive comber radiated from fingertips to shoulders, breaking every bone, one after the other, in quick succession. The second threatened to do the same to the vertebrae along his spine.

No, not my back, not my back. I won't allow this thing to cripple me anymore.

Gritting his teeth, Chopin howled silently and rode the agony until white spots danced before his eyes.

The wave crested. Not expecting the release so soon, he moaned aloud and slumped to the floor, sweating profusely and gulping like a stranded fish. Slowly, his wits returned.

"Another unsuccessful attempt?" Nikola Tesla sat waiting at one end of a large couch, two glasses of chilled *Démon Bleu Cuvée* at the ready.

"I'm afraid so." Chopin groaned again, "Whatever it is that blocks the authority of the sword is unprecedented. And it's getting stronger." He struggled to sit up.

"Need a hand there?" Placing their refreshments on a side table, Tesla leaned forward, grasped his companion by the wrists, and pulled hard.

Crack!

Resetting, everything snapped back into place all at once, sending white-hot needles shooting along Chopin's nerves in every direction. *It doesn't get any easier, no matter how well I focus or prepare. When this is all over, I'm going to make a serious case for moving, lock, stock, and barrel into one of the older realms. I'll not go to all this trouble of freeing Amantine, just to put her in a position where she's forced to nurse me all over again.*

Tesla must have thought Chopin still needed help, for he stooped to retrieve the *Sword of Uncovered Secrets*, and offered the crook of his elbow for support, "Come on, up you get."

Chopin accepted the proffered elbow graciously, and once on his feet, took a moment to straighten his clothing and compose himself, before selecting one of the drinks and strolling across to the window. Looking down at the never-ending flow of nose-to-tail traffic crawling its way like an amoeba along 9th Avenue, did nothing to ease his melancholy.

Hell's Kitchen, one of the worst festering sores in existence... His heart skipped a beat. *I miss Perish so much. This cesspit lacks the style and sophistication I've become accustomed to. Gladly, it won't be for much longer. I have —?*

"Penny for your thoughts?" Tesla had come to stand beside him.

Chopin drained his glass before replying. "It's only this moment hit me how much I need to be away from here, Nikola. Eleven days. That's all we've got, eleven more days and then we'll see the culmination of everything we've worked so hard to achieve. But have you given any thought to what we'll do after? I'm not for staying here, where the Undertaker's perversions continue to plague me. So I was thinking...why not go for something completely different to see the New Year in?"

"Different?"

"We have the signets. The orbs too, if we want to move in numbers, so we can visit any realm we desire. But why not settle down in one of the deeper circles of hell where we don't have to worry so much about expressing our genius, or simply living?"

"That's certainly food for thought," Tesla appeared drawn to the proposal, "especially as it will be rather difficult to show our faces for a while after we bring the curtain down."

"I know. And the marvelous thing is, we've still got a little time to consider the perfect setting."

"A *little* time? Why, when were you thinking of moving to the staging area?"

Chopin set his glass down on the windowsill "I thought it might be prudent to move across to Madhatten by this time next week. It's rather cosmopolitan in comparison to this dump, and it'll give us several days to get settled before the conjunction is upon us. Best of all, it'll give us line of sight to our target. And then..."

"And then all our dreams come true."

"I do hope so, old friend. I do hope so." Chopin sighed. "In the meantime, we need only be discreet and allow our lapdogs to keep the Reaper and his minions occupied."

"They're certainly doing that," Tesla snorted. Expanding on his statement, he explained, "While you were off on your vision quest, I received word that all three of our Unsûreté moles in Perish were flushed out of their office yesterday, during a raid led by none other than Yamato Takeru and Pascal Fléau. From what I hear, at least two are already undergoing *processing* in Blood Tower."

"It is of no concern." Chopin shrugged and began walking back toward the center of the room, "the subliminal implants we thought to place in their minds should divert our foe sufficiently until it's too late to stop us. If Grim takes the bait, he will find himself up to his neck in a situation even *he* might find too hot to handle..." For a moment, images of a firestorm returned to haunt him. *At least, I hope it will.*

Tesla was insistent. "And if they don't?"

Chopin smiled, warmly. That's what he liked about Tesla, a man who tried to anticipate every eventuality. "Then we have several fallback options to put into play. Our brightest and best have been kept in reserve, well hidden in plain sight. They are beyond reproach and trusted without question. But I loathe resorting to them unless it becomes absolutely necessary. Remember, if all goes well, we'll need help in dropping off the radar until we're properly ensconced in our new home. Keeping us safe is their prime function. In the meantime, we can always task Guiteau and Corday to become more disruptive."

"Then it seems we have nothing to do but wait?"

"If you're content to sit idly and let time drag, then yes, feel free to torture yourself. Me? I hanker for the need to keep busy. What say we complete a final set of rounds on the soul sapphires to ensure the memories our clones retain are the latest and most up-to-date? That way, if the unthinkable happens, we'll still be in a prime position to enact the Soulstice intact?" Chopin's confidence was inspiring. "I tell you Nikola, nothing is going to stand in our way this time."

"A good idea. When were you thinking of going?"

Chopin retrieved his friend's glass and placed it on the table. "As I always say, there's no time like the present."

*

Having checked the site from end to end, Nettesheim could see that the reconstruction project at one of New Hell's most prestigious landmarks had almost been completed.

Only five months previously, a deranged angel using the guise of one of Erra's Sibitti had lain waste to the area surrounding the Statue of Lost Liberty, an attack that had split the 66,666 square-yard island in two, and which had reduced the three hundred and five-foot monument to rubble.

Topside, the Liberty figurine had been a gift to the United States from the people of France, an icon celebrating freedom, and a welcoming sight to immigrants arriving from abroad that had been especially inscribed with the date of the American Declaration of Independence: *July 4, 1776.*

Here in the underworld, this newly refurbished beacon of despair carried a reference to an entirely different kind of independence. The date of the original rebellion in heaven: *Cho-Stór 13, ADT171849.* What was more; the broken chains about the sculpture's feet had been replaced with heavy shackles to represent the bondage to which every denizen was sure to be subjected.

"My, my," Nettesheim mumbled quietly, "Satan's underlings *have* been busy. But I'd expect no less. This effigy is supposed to represent his authority, after all, and we can't have the masses being anything less than thoroughly impressed."

As much as Nettesheim was genuinely enthralled by the spectacle himself, he wasn't here to sightsee. In fact, the focus of his interest was currently doing his incompetent best to tag along, unnoticed, at the rear of a small group of tourists taking photographs and pointing out the various features of the pentagram-shaped fortified base upon which Lost Liberty had been positioned, Fort Blood.

"Castor Bean, you are a naughty boy. Not content to ally yourself with the anarchists attempting to undermine our most sacrilegious way of life, you make the catastrophic mistake of blowing Perish's premier inter-level travel hub all the way to heaven and back, putting a price on your head that everyone will be only too happy to collect. Except for me..." Nettesheim grinned, and his green eyes festered with a glacial tinge, "for Guiteau and Corday would have proved rather difficult to subdue. But *you*, my friend, will be my ticket to a one on one audience with the Reaper."

Safe behind a glamour granting him the appearance of an elderly woman forced to rely on a walking stick for balance, Nettesheim made his move.

Here we go, ten yards and closing. Get in close. A little stumble to distract his...eh?

A shift in the subtle balance of the all-encompassing es-oteric medium drew Nettesheim's gaze to a fold in reality, high in the sky, where two glowing apparitions had just ap-peared. Radiating power, their magnificence was neverthe-less muted by dusty raiment's that enfolded them in decep-tion and gloom.

Enforcers! Casting his own illusion aside, Nettesheim decided a simple snatch and grab would be the most advis-able course to follow. After sheathing himself within a pro-tective barrier, he closed on his prey without the slightest pretense at stealth.

In the meantime, other people had spotted the commo-tion taking place above them, and a shock of recognition suddenly rippled through the crowd.

"Fuck me. Are those Sibitti?"

"Sibitti? Where?"

"Up there...look."

"Oh shit, he's right. It's the Sibitti for real. We're gonna get audited."

"Audited my ass," someone else called out, "we're going to be eaten alive. Run!"

That sentiment was soon picked up by everyone nearby, and before Nettesheim had a chance to capture his prize, the gathered throng scattered.

As if the mere acknowledgement of their presence spurred them to action, the personified weapons threw off their cloaks to reveal their full glory. Then they drew their blades, and unadulterated power agitated the atmosphere.

One of the enforcers waved his shining sword and more than half of those cowering in fear started to cough, harshly. The coughing rapidly worsened. Denizens began falling to their knees, hacking and choking, and clawing at their throats. So slowly, that everybody appeared as actors playing their part, they folded to the ground, writhing and kicking; faces blanched; blackened, swollen tongues protruding from blood and foam-flecked mouths.

Nettesheim felt his defenses thrumming under a sustained assault.

"That's the Fourth of Seven. Foul pestilence is his weapon of choice. Thank badness I thought to generate protection; the air will be saturated in plague-riddled microbes."

Maintaining disciple, he scanned the rapidly thinning press, and spotted Bean as the fugitive scrambled beneath a clump of nearby hawthorn bushes. "I've got to get him out of here before his luck runs out..." Nettesheim's shield throbbed again, on this occasion for a much longer period. "Or mine, come to that."

More screams rang out. Glancing back over his shoulder, Nettesheim saw the other enforcer dropping like a stone from the sky, his form dancing and morphing into a whirling gyre of razor-sharp death. *The Fifth of Seven. This will get messy.*

It did. Limbs, heads and entrails sprayed into the air in a chrysanthemum burst of scarlet gore as the Fifth landed amongst the largest group of survivors. *Nobody's going to survive this. Time I wasn't here. But first...?*

Chapter 7: Phantom Menace

Following my visit to the Mortuary, I'd realized my impending mission into the Dead Zone presented a number of high-risk obstacles. For one thing, it was a totally alien environment. The only snippet I had to help me understand what might be lurking on the other side were those scant details retrieved from the remains of the probe I'd sent through.

The heat felt searing—far hotter than Hades during summer drought season by all accounts—and whoever the *Blades of the Left-Hand Path* were, it was fair to assume from the flavor of their response that they were aggressive and willing to resort to hostilities at the drop of a hat. My kinda guys.

Regardless of shared temperament, that meant I now faced a conundrum. Normally, I'd respond to such a challenge with a blunt show of force of my own. Hounds aside, those selected to serve on my staff in any capacity, and especially those on the security detail—collectively known as, *The Pack*—we're amongst some of the most physically adept and combat skilled individuals you would ever find in hell. I'd lost count of the times the mere presence of my teams at a scene of unrest or uncivil disorder would cause dissenters to: (a) turn and run immediately, or (b) piss themselves silly and surrender, begging for mercy that they knew would never come.

It was rare indeed, when we ever needed to take things further than to show up.

However, that option was unavailable on this occasion, for while my palladinium armor and the Bãlefire coursing through my veins would protect me from any amount of UV, Humvee, and hostile LZs we might find in the pyretic world awaiting us, the same couldn't be said for those under my command. So, it meant I'd be flying solo.

Usually, I'd be quite happy to play things by ear and go it alone. My power seemed to be increasing exponentially, and the polymorphic nature of my primary weapon was a joy to behold, as it allowed me to adapt to a wide variety of situations. Nevertheless, I wasn't all brawn and no brains. Something about the Blades message gave me the impression my scythe might not be enough. As such, I'd been experimenting to see just how far I could improvise.

I'd been stunned to discover that the flexibility of the staff's polymimetic milieu allowed the alloy to assume templates as diverse as a scimitar or baton; axe or spear; even a javelin or studded mace. Even so, any time I tried to split my budding arsenal in two, the section of the pairing furthest from the energy source would slowly lose cohesion and eventually dissipate. Not a complication I wanted to run into in the heat of battle.

Contemplating the problem overnight, I'd come up with the perfect solution. I needed a secondary power cell, one capable of channeling the vast potential at my disposal. And I knew just the place to get it, seeing as how the asshole in charge was living on borrowed time.

Needless to say, Samael hadn't been happy to see me when I'd turned up out of the blue across in New Hell first thing this morning. The Pentagram was his baby, and he didn't like having his toes stomped on. Not only did he throw his teddy out of the pram; his pacifier, rattle and blanket went with it.

I couldn't have cared less. His betrayal during the Grislington incident across at the Palace of Verse and Sighs, in Perish, had turned a cause for celebration into one of mourning. I'd never forgive him for causing the events that led to the eradication of Nimrod and Strawberry. And I'd made sure he knew that.

Giving him a taste of his own brinkmanship was rather gratifying, for he'd stood there, simmering like a volcano, as I took my time skimming the prohibited articles list, shopping for the item I needed—the crystal to a Vidium Sword. Eventually, I'd decided on the *Sword of Dauntless Strength*, for I felt it would be the perfect accompaniment for what I had in mind.

Of course, Samael had complained bitterly all the way down to sublevel five—which officially, didn't exist—until I pointed out to him how far I was willing to go to answer his attempt to screw me over: that one way or another, threat of punishment or not, he and I were going to enjoy a private tête-à-tête, where things would be *ironed out* once and for all.

That had done the trick. Samael was one of the few denizens of hell to know the full gory details of what I'd done to a heavenly cherub, and just after noon, GMT-J today—Gehenna Mean Time, Juxtapose—I'd arrived back at the Den and locked myself away in the main sparring court with orders not to be disturbed.

It had taken a couple of hours of fiddling and tinkering, but eventually, I'd found the plum location to embed the new gem: at the point a few inches below the control stud manifold along the main shaft of my scythe. Now, I could split the stem into two smaller weapons, and had chosen to permanently set the matrix to that of a twin set of ninjatō straight swords, reminiscent of those used by the ancient Shinobi of Japan. Such a configuration suited my fluidic fighting style and would allow me the flexibility of engaging multiple targets simultaneously.

That done, I'd spent the remainder of the day drilling, and familiarizing myself with the expected variance in relation to weight distribution, reach, and balance. Eleven hours later, I was confident that I could wield my weapons instinctively. But handling myself physically was only part of the issue. I still needed to assess how the ninjaken would manage the raw essence of hell's lifeblood, the Bãlefire. And for that, I needed volunteers.

We're here. Having to navigate the warping effects of the arena's esoteric defenses, Ferenc Nádasdy's telepathic greeting sounded muffled. Nonetheless, he was right on time.

The Den of Iniquity operated under a *meat-grinder* policy. It might well have been long past midnight, but excelling at hunting vermin down, then torturing the stuffing out of them was a twenty-four hours a day, seven days a week business which tended to play havoc with your unsocial calendar. The upside to this was there were always enough of the team available to offer their assistance at short notice. And from what I could see through the shielded walls, the Red Baron had brought a little company with him.

Triggering the doors, I took a well-earned break from my exertions and took stock of those who had come to assist me.

An old warhorse and a superb warrior in his own right, Ferenc had donned his armor for the occasion. I was looking forward to sparring with him, for it had been a while since we'd crossed swords.

Gemini slunk in behind him, silent and alert. Privately, I was glad she could make it. As everyone had gone on to discover, the trouncing she'd so skillfully dished out during her Houndship trials had been no fluke. If anything, she was even more lethal now she'd had the chance to adapt and settle into her power. I had no doubt that if she lived long enough; I was looking at a future Lead Hound.

Bringing up the rear was Ferenc's wife, our very own Blood Countess, Elizabeth Báthory. As unhinged as the city gates of Sodom and Gomorrah, she had chosen to decorate her nakedness with luminous body paint that only served to emphasize the erogenous zones of her elfin figure in lurid neon pink highlights. Some might have found her presence sensual. Me, I wasn't so sure, especially as she was waltzing and gyrating to an inaudible tune that—if her movements were anything to go by—couldn't possibly have been a hit, not even in a galaxy far, far away.

What made her entrance even more surreal was the fact she headed a small procession of six prisoners who had obviously been instructed to emulate her moves. A hopeless quest, seeing as how Elizabeth was triple jointed, and her impromptu troupe had been bound together at the neck, and kept bumping into each other.

Every so often, she would interrupt the erratic flow of her dance and express her displeasure by tugging harshly on their chains, causing them to fall to the floor.

Ah, the joy that is hell.

I cast my gaze along the line of misfits. One had shit himself; one looked to have wet her pants first, before soiling herself; and the two in the middle were blubbering uncontrollably. The final duo stared back defiantly. I could see in their eyes they knew their number was up—this time around at least—and were determined to meet their end resolutely.

I admire your spunk. Both exploded in miniature gold and scarlet mushroom clouds. *Not that it'll do you any good.*

The remaining sacrificial lambs froze, and even my Inquisitors and Gemini stopped what they were doing, struggling to come to terms with how swiftly I'd been able to draw the swords from my back harness and release two thunderbolts of energy.

Screw me, but I could get used to this.

Gemini studied me closely. "That was rather impressive? Even I had trouble following what you just did. I'm glad you're not so *expeditious* in private, where it counts?" She raised an eyebrow—the one on her good side—and cast a knowing glance my way.

"What can I say," I replied, struggling, of all things, not to blush, "lead by example, and all that."

Nodding toward the now vacant restraints, she continued, "So, how strong was that?"

"How strong?"

"Yes, on a rating of one to ten. What would you say you used?"

A fair point. I hadn't given any thought to the amount of energy I'd expended. "It's hard to say, really, but it felt miniscule in comparison to the reserve waiting inside."

"I see?" Gemini glanced at Ferenc. "Try quantifying it for us, so we know what we're dealing with here. If it makes it any easier, use a scale of one to a hundred instead."

"My gut tells me that was a fraction of half a percent."

Gemini let out a low whistle. "And how does that make you feel?

That was easy. "Alive, truly and unequivocally alive."

A fit of childlike giggling indicated Elizabeth wanted in on the conversation. Her eyes flashed, and she flipped from 'distant and lobotomized' to 'feral and rabid' in less time than it takes for a twelve gauge to fuck rabbits.

"Do it again," she breathed, "but this time, show some refinement. Anyone can wield a sledgehammer..." she reached out to snag the crybabies and pushed them forward. "See if you can use the Bãlefire to do two things at once. Prune the arms and legs off the idiot on the right and turn the other one into a colander."

This was exactly the kind of stimulus I needed.

Without even pausing to think about the specifics of the challenge, I drew my weapons for a second time, rolled to one side, and with a final flourish, lashed out. As the blades cut dazzling arcs through the air, I formed an impression in my mind. In it, the guy on the left was staggering backward, desperately trying to use his fingers to plug the flow of blood from a million and one perforations dotted across the front of his body. Next to him, his friend was already a corpse, his head rolling around on the floor within a circular boundary comprised of his neatly severed limbs. By the time I'd completed my movement, my thoughts had become a reality, and their ruined remains were beginning to fade.

Unholy shit. This is better than I ever imagined. That I would get a response from the jewel already incorporated into my scythe is one thing, but to get the same reaction from the Vidium crystal is...well, it's unprecedented. It accepts my mental commands without hesitation.

I hadn't realized it, but I must have been daydreaming. The next thing I knew, Elizabeth was flick-flacking toward me, head over heels, whilst somehow managing to drag the last of our terrified detainees with her. Stopping only inches away, she dropped their lead to the deck with a ringing chime, and leaned in close to run the back of her nails along the length of each glowing ninjatō. Then she whispered, "Oh,

I do like your new toys, Daemon. They're so shiny and bright and sharp. So deliciously powerful. So very, very deadly…" she pouted, struck a Tinkerbell pose, and blew me a kiss. "You must tell us your secret. How *do* you manage to balance the best of both worlds?"

Her pupils shrieked with inhuman delirium.

"I'm buggered if I know," I confessed, captivated by the intensity of her request, "it's something I've always been able to do." *Yeah, but why? Have you ever asked that?*

Deep inside the bottomless well of my soul, a single flame burned, hotter and brighter than ever before.

Further deliberation was stalled when the two defecators made a break for the still open door. A silly mistake, but one so many had made before them.

I smiled, and all at once I could see myself, as if witnessing events from the perspective of a dream observer.

Standing stock still, the real me stared into Elizabeth's eyes, my face a death's-head visage as implacable and unforgiving as stone. Somewhere, a terrible howling sound tried to gain dominance, but I couldn't be bothered to pay it much heed. Instead, my ethereal self was drawn to a swarm of spiraling leaves in human form, for they writhed within a tornado of fire, a seething envelopment of energy that had transformed flesh into a mass of tumbling bones, and then a scattering of ash, before the fools had taken more than a dozen paces.

Elizabeth blinked, and for once appeared to be completely lucid. "I'm watching you, Mister Reaper." She stood on phosphorous tiptoes and planted a rubescent kiss on the end of my nose. "There's more to you than I'd ever imagined…" Then she was gone again, surfing the tides of whatever sea her sanity had decided to wash her up on.

So matter-of-factly that I wasn't quite sure I heard her, she added, "I see you, sometimes, you know, in my dreams when you're in your other form. It's beautiful and quite, quite...breathtaking."

An elastic band effect snapped me wide awake. "Wait a minute, what's this about me being in a different form?"

"Daemon?"

Another bloody distraction. I turned to find my new Chief Inquisitor standing at the threshold, in the company of three prisoners of woe who had clearly been on the receiving end of his particular brand of injustice. "David? If you've brought us some new stooges to play with, I've got to say, your timing is impeccable."

My attempt at humor crashed like a lead balloon. Dr. L had other things on his mind. Ushering the mystery trio forward, he started babbling, "Sorry Daemon, but you really need to listen to what these subjects have to say. It...It's..."

"Let's slow this down a bit, shall we. Who are they?"

Seemingly distracted by what he'd uncovered, it took the doctor a few moments to register what—or in this case, who—I was alluding to. "Oh these? Yes...yes of course. Er, while you've been otherwise *engaged* over the last few days, Yamato and Champ have also managed to stay gainfully employed across in Perish..."

Oh Jesus, has the word spread about Gemini and me already?

"...anyway, the latest intel package we received from the raft council relating to high value targets was spot on. Cutting a long story short, Yamato, Champ and Pascal led a combined raid on the Unsûreté offices within the Palais de L'Injustice yesterday morning, and apprehended these women..." He placed a hand on two sets of badly mutilated shoulders in turn. "Daemon Grim, may I present former intelligence officers, Rosary Pea and Cherry Choke. Caught outright, they quickly surrendered priceless, if somewhat puzzling information that had to wait for the arrest of the gentleman you see here with us—one Castor Bean—to clarify."

"I'm sorry, why did you have to wait for this Bean character to clarify things?"

"Ah, you obviously haven't heard yet. Initially, Bean was able to evade capture, destroying the Assemblée Diabolique et Niveaux, Inter-Circles of Hell travel terminal in the process. As luck would have it, he made his way over to New Hell where he almost became a casualty in one of the latest incursions by Erra's enforcers who —?"

"The Sibitti have started their games again? When? And why wasn't I informed about this immediately?"

The doctor took my outburst in his stride.

"In light of recent events at the Mortuary and across the road from there at—*ahem*—elsewhere, you left specific instructions not to be disturbed, yes…?"

They do *know about Gemini and me. Sneaky bastards.*

"…As such, I believe relevant report crystals highlighting details of the attacks have already been left for you to peruse when you have the time. Now is *not* the time, as I need to bring something of greater urgency to your attention."

"Greater in urgency than the Sibitti? This I've got to hear. Please, do go on."

"Once we had the aforementioned Bean in custody, the reason for the compartmentalized intelligence their minds contain became clear. Each prisoner retains a segment of a single message, a clue if you like, that won't make any sense unless all three of them are together. Even then you have to replay it in the right order. I've brought them here, because that message invokes a rather unusual response."

"Unusual?"

"Yes, observe…"

Livingstone turned to his captives and sent a powerful, subliminal command. Under compulsion to reply, each of them began to speak. It quickly became apparent they had been conditioned to deliver separate phrases in a certain sequence. On every occasion they opened their mouths, Choke would begin, Pea followed, and Bean would conclude the sentence. What they had to say confirmed my suspicions that the latest game of cosmic chess between Chopin, Tesla and myself was about to begin:

"Do not go gently into death,
For the valley of the shadow serves naught but a cup,
Filled to the brim in bitter tears of salt.
This perfect condiment to preserve your pain,
Sprinkled liberally upon open wounds
By those whose black hearts practice darker arts.
Existing in shadow and flame,
That gulf betwixt the silent spaces of now and then
They reap a windfall harvest of fallen Souls.
Tendrils of smoke, as fragile as a sudden intake of breath
Curl like lazy fingers around your heart,
Only to squeeze…and prevent what's left from saving you.*"

The words of the clue stirred the embers of long forgotten memories that couldn't possibly belong to me; for they contained fragmented images of a place I'd never been before. A place I was shocked to recognize. *But how?*

A river, wide and deep, boiled its way across a parched and barren landscape, only to be swallowed by a sinkhole drilled through the rock scant yards from the edge of a monstrous canyon. The cleft itself was colossal, a wound upon the planet's surface that gouged its way off in the opposite direction like an immense scar.

The air reverberated to the sound of a hidden tumult, and I could just make out the suggestion of needlelike spans crossing the abyss through a thick curtain of spray, far, far below. Carried on thermals, phantoms spiraled up from the depths; whispering, taunting, enticing.

"Ruin—ruin—ruin…"

"Blades—Blades—Blades—Blades…"

"Tears—tears—tears—tears—tears…"

"Death—death—death—death—death—death…"

My blood ran cold. *I know this place?*

Everything took on an unusual solidity, and I found myself back within the arena with no doubt in my mind as to where I needed to go. Addressing my team, I said, "Guys? We're going to have to reschedule this for tomorrow. For now, wrap everything up down here and meet me in my study in thirty minutes. We need to discuss this latest revelation with clear heads."

Turning to Livingstone, I concluded, "And David, send a message to Yamato and his merry band in Perish. Tell them, 'well done' from me in bagging our latest brace of spies. They may not realize it yet, but this development ties into the matter I was dealing with at the Mortuary. I'll update you all on what that is when we get upstairs and…?"

My Chief Inquisitor held himself awkwardly, as if he was reticent to say something. Whatever it was roused my suspicions.

"David? Is there anything you'd like to add?"

"Actually, there was one more thing I needed to tell you," he admitted, "I just haven't had the chance."

"Go on?"

"Yamato and Champ weren't the ones who brought Bean in. They were tied up in the ensuing riots over in Perish, and didn't have a clue where he'd spirited off to."

"Then who did? I'd like to thank them personally."

"An acquaintance I believe you and your Hounds have already met on several occasions, Heinrich von Nettesheim? He's waiting for you outside your ground level office suite at this moment."

Chapter 8: Clouds on the Horizon

Perched on the apex of an impressive pile of skulls, Garôk, First Palm of the Third Link, Incendia Blade, stood tall, and surveyed the scene before her.

Flame orange skies peeped out from behind an obscuring veil of smoldering, rust colored clouds. The gloom added an unwelcome pall to the suffering below where the air itself labored, already heavy with dejection and pain.

Overseers snarled and firewhips cracked. Guttural and sharp, their tones blended to form a constant backdrop laden with criticism and threats. Though it made little difference, slaves grimaced and bent their backs to greater efforts lest their heads become another trophy adorning the punishment mound upon which their mistress kept a close watch on proceedings.

Garôk's gaze fell upon the rippling plane of the methân portal, and she spent some time inspecting its features. What she discovered caused her to voice her concerns aloud. "I knew I was right? It would appear the windfall of damned souls is drying up. But that should be impossible. Satan's system is ripe with a never-ending supply of fresh fodder. So...?"

She enlarged the aperture in her mind's eye. After studying it in greater detail for a while, she turned to the calode stones drawing the tincture through the rent. "It shows all the signs of having been tampered with. *El'hêd*! I knew we shouldn't have responded so aggressively to the probe they sent through. The creatures on the far side have obviously countered by erecting a forbidding. A cause of great concern, for anyone capable of such a contrivance must be a formidable foe indeed."

That factor troubled Garôk deeply. She ground her tusks and stared off toward the distant horizon, where belts of acid rain lashed the carbon peaks of the Paradân Massif.

"*Fenôm Salàk*," she cured under her breath, "why did this have to happen on my watch? As much as the power behind this act demands respect, it also demands rebuttal, and I am duty bound to ensure my superiors are notified. But who to entrust with such disturbing and sensitive intelligence?"

Garôk considered the character of those captains serving within her Chain. "Jotûn would be the best choice. Only a Fist of the Faith may approach the Gauntlet without fear of censure, and of all my commanders, he is less prone to conjecture and overreaction." She stared into the waning aperture of the gateway again. "Though I fear in my heart, *this* will require the strength of our entire Blade to counter."

Resigned to the backlash her report was bound to generate, Garôk glanced across to where the el-aha'del spirit jars had been stockpiled before their onward journey to the Lamp processing facilities at Sá-eer central. "At least this cycle's quota has been met."

That thought brightened her mood considerably. "And in all truth, no fault can be laid at my clan's feet. The circumstances leading to this development originated on the other side of the bridge, and we are free of blame. Even so...?"

Once again, Garôk's attention was drawn to the fading inflection of the methân rift and of the might needed to block it, "I dread to think how Gauntlet Nishôgh might react if the king sanctions him to put on a show of strength. He's always been an old firebrand, and if he is as blunt as he was with the message, things will only escalate...

"...In which case, it might be best to prepare ahead of time."

Jumping from the top of the skull mound, Garôk's spurred feet landed on the hard baked ground in a cloud of dust and ash. A nearby overseer paused, lash held high. "First Palm?" His voice sounded like wounded gravel.

"Derîn, spread the word. All slaves are to be rested, fed and watered. Work is to recommence at flame-down, but we won't be collecting the elixir of life anymore..."

"We won't?"

"No. Until instructed otherwise, I want a series of overlapping lava trenches and fortifications constructed from the site of the calode stones outward, to a distance of fifty cubits."

"Yes Mistress."

"I know its spur of the moment, so, if you need to requisition extra supplies and equipment, send to nearby Ladthâa for anything you need. Tell them it's for Blade business on the authority of First Fist Jotûn."

"It will be done. I'll inform everybody immediately."

As will I. Nodding once, Garôk spun on her heels and swiftly made her way toward her tent. *I'd better notify Jotûn straight away. He'll need time to prepare before everyone starts beating a path to his door.*

*

Erra relaxed, content in the knowledge his sons of heaven and earth were once again focused upon what they did best: auditing, and spreading havoc and fear in the process, a process that—so far—had managed to harvest over a hundred thousand souls without answer. Because of this, a sense of purpose now pervaded the halls of Emeslam that lately had been sorely lacking.

And not before time, either.

Unperturbed as he was, Erra dozed, and absentmindedly ran his fingers along the interlaced ribcages that had been fashioned into the cushions of his throne. A bricolage of foul vapors curled up from the gaps between the bones, bringing with it a welcoming stench of disease and decay.

An unexpected tickling sensation caused Erra to raise his hand and examine it. He was surprised to find a solitary rock-coach staring back at him. The tiny creature waved its antennae and vigorously turned from side to side, no doubt trying to make sense of its transition from the putrid warmth generated by the mountain of rotting flesh that served as Erra's footstool, into the cooler environs of the outside world.

So, an intrepid explorer craves the adventure of fresh hunting grounds? Let's see?

Erra splayed his fingers and watched, absorbed, as the rockcoach climbed round and around, and up and over its new living obstacle course in an effort to find its bearings.

The slightest impulse issued from the god's mind, sending the little insect scurrying along Erra's sleeve, across his broad chest, and up onto his neck. Straight as a die, the unsuspecting rockcoach scurried through jaws held wide in anticipation.

Crunch!

Erra bit down, savoring the contrast between dry flakey shell and acidic pus. After swilling the mush around in his mouth for a moment, he swallowed his snack whole. Closing his eyes, he leaned back across his divan, and sighed, "Ah, delightful. All is as it should be."

"As it should be?"

"Teresa?" The disapproving tone of the sudden voice caused Erra to start. *How did she manage to approach without my sensing her?*

"Oh, there are lots of things mystics can do that you obviously don't appreciate," Teresa snapped, in reply to Erra's unspoken concerns, "as you're just finding out."

Like reading my mind? His shields slammed into place.

Instantly composed, Erra decided to be gracious and overlook the insult of the saint's transgression. "How may I help you?"

Teresa narrowed her eyes and regarded the plague god warily. Erra found the experience unnerving, for the human possessed a degree of intuition bettered only by her courageous spirit.

When she eventually spoke, her opening questions caught him off guard. "Lord Erra. When we first met, did I come crawling to you on hands and knees, begging to be liberated from my unjust confinement? And once free, did I plead for an opportunity to hit back at my oppressors through the grand office of the Sibitti?"

"No, you didn't."

"Indeed, I did not." The dainty woman drew herself up to her full height—all five feet of it—and continued, "The fact of the matter is, you needed me. *You* made the opening move and did your best to make your offer as attractive as possible because you wanted to utilize the skills at my disposal. Yes?"

Erra made no attempt to apologize or hide the truth of the matter, for he was intrigued as to where this confrontation might lead. "Yes, that's right. But remember, it is my sacred function—my purpose—to appraise these latterday levels of hell with a vengeance. I must continue to do so until every foul deed ever considered in secret, concealed from sight, or committed openly, is extracted from the memories of those souls responsible and held up for scrutiny. Of late, my commission stalled due to...*extenuating* circumstances." *One I tend to eradicate.* "You, dear lady, are a means to fulfill my obligations."

To Erra's amazement, the saint wasn't in the least bit offended by his statement. "To be entrusted with such a charge is a privilege, is it not, and something that must weigh heavily on your shoulders?"

"It does. And that is why I cannot rest in my duty until all that is expected of me has been discharged appropriately."

"Appropriately," Teresa countered, "how can you hope to do that while you resort to deceit? Don't deny it. You went ahead with these latest raids thinking I would disavow your methods because you still wish to claim the greatest prize of all, Satan's Reaper."

"I do. And I doubt that will ever change, for everyone must be measured. I only wished to spare you the burden such knowledge would cause and the dilemma it —?"

"Poppycock!"

When Erra didn't respond immediately to Teresa's outburst, she pressed ahead, "I am a mystic, Lord Erra. Did you think I couldn't taste your frustration and that of your enforcers? You have been keen to placate your voyeurs of death for some time now, haven't you?"

"They are instruments of principle. When I choose to wield them, I know they will act according to the tenets of their nature."

"You see? That is exactly my point."

"Your point?" Erra was confused.

"I am not some tool that you can lock away in a cupboard until you come across a situation requiring my expertise. I am an individual with my own mind and my own destiny. And yes, I was tricked into hell by the fragility of my own faith, a failing I openly confess." Teresa took a step closer and brandished a pint-sized fist. Her eyes glittered fiercely. "Though condemned, I am still sure of who I am in my secret heart and do not fear the audit that will one day surely come…"

A slow smile played across Erra's face. *Well, well.*

"…Oh yes. I know about your plans, Lord Erra. And I do not fear to face the Seven. Why? Because they will set me—and those pitiful few like me who are truly contrite—free from this place…"

Yet again, this human woman confounds me.

"…Until that day, I am happy to work with you, for though I am motivated by love, we are more allied than you think."

Astonished by that admission, Erra was moved to ask, "How so?"

"Because the truly penitent, few though they be, must be found. That will not happen unless we are thorough in what we do, and ruthless. None can be exempted from the attention of your evaluators…not even Daemon grim, for how else can we be sure every single deserving one is found. Heaven stands ready, Lord Erra, and we must not be kept it waiting."

I don't believe it? She's far cannier than I realized. And when tales are told in future, history will laud her for her actions. Stifling his mirth, Erra grunted. "And this has been your goal all along?"

"It has."

Erra slapped his thigh, threw back his head, and laughed out loud. "If only I had known. What you say possesses a certain balance, a certain *rightness* that appeals...and all because of love? It must be a fickle thing indeed."

"Do not be fooled," Teresa replied with all solemnity. "Holy scripture tells us that love is the most powerful attribute there is, for it can exist in many forms and is capable of a wide variety of expressions. As patient and kind as it is firm and resolved when the need arises. Above all, whatever the situation, love never fails. And it will not fail us when your arbiters do their work, for there is no fooling their judgment."

"No there isn't, good lady, no there isn't." Suddenly serious, Erra leaned forward in his seat, "But tell me, how would you go about snaring the Reaper?"

Unruffled, Teresa explained, "Well, if you'd have just looked at the evidence instead of sending the Seven gallivanting off, you'd have discerned the seeds have already been sown. Would you like me to explain?"

Accepting the saint's offer, the god of plague and mayhem descended from his throne and walked with her through courts of hallowed stone. Listening attentively, he came to a slow realization about the innocent looking being before him. *This woman is one of the most dangerous creatures in the whole of hell...and I don't think she actually realizes it.*

*

The quixotic tempest moved so deliberately that the woman waiting at its core had time to imagine a whole catalogue of petrifying scenarios. Trapped, she looked on in horror as the eye squeezed inward, condensing ever smaller, until eventually, it had formed a nub of opposing impressions: hope and fear; rage and despair, incertitude and ice-cold clarity.

Charged with potential, the storm behaved exactly as its natural counterpart would, and struck with a vengeance. Assailed from every side, the woman was swallowed whole and soon became just another shard, lost to the churning bore filling her world with fragmented recollections…none of them useful.

Who am I? What am I? Where am I from? Each question chimed off into the ether with the shattered impotence of breaking glass.

The squall refracting her perceptions hit a lull, and for a moment, the mists drew back and she found herself in another time and place within a cavern:

I know this grotto? I've been here…?

Cold and mysterious, it is festooned in stalagmites and stalactites, all of which are riddled with fragments that glitter like stars in the night sky. Three huge gates allow access. Two are dark and foreboding, outlined in magma. The other is as pale as virgin wool.

The woman is not alone. A celestial entity glides toward her, flawless and unblemished, a living flame so clean and so perfect, that his radiance is beyond anything that could be described as 'white.'

Paired warriors stand to one side. Tall, proud and deadly, they are both predators, homing in for the kill. Opposite them, their prey cowers. Fugitives from injustice, they cling to prohibited artifacts of power, totems by which they hope to evade capture.

The woman's finely honed instincts scream at her to act. But she cannot, for her mind is an empty pit and she is a prisoner, robbed of free will.

A thought intrudes. She fights against it, for it prompts her to do something unnatural. Even when the thought builds into an impulse, the woman continues to contest its dominance over her. Finally, that impulse becomes a command, and like a puppet subject to its master's direction, she explodes into action. Now devoid of compunction, she attacks one of the warriors from behind with a savagery that defies belief.

A name filters through the layers of temporal silt and dissolution: *Nimrod.*

Nimrod is gravely wounded. Regardless, he reacts with a speed and strength that is frightening to behold. Before she realizes it, Nimrod's counter has fractured half of the discs along her spine and broken most of her ribs, rupturing organs and tearing sinews alike.

She coughs, spraying blood through the air. The action triggers a terrible scorching sensation that sets her chest on fire and sends lightning sizzling along her nerves.

No!

Yes…get up and fight again.

The woman struggles to obey, only to become a pawn in a standoff, helpless in the grip of a coward who hides behind her while holding a blade to her throat. The angel intervenes. His gaze bores into her, deeper, brighter, hotter, until the abyss claims her…

Everything was still once more.

She held her breath, expectant of another torrent of tumbling images, until she realized she was truly awake and could see and hear and feel, albeit she still couldn't move. *Where* is *this place?*

Everything resounded with ringing, tinkling echoes. Reverberations that seemed to chide her numbed sensibilities, daring her to recall who she was and all the things she'd ever done. *Why can't I remember?*

The woman tried to take stock of where she might be, but the amber crystalline background confused her sight as it confounded her ability to think. Any time she tried to concentrate on one thing, her attention was drawn along a variegated corridor of offset mirrors, prisms in such numbers; they quickly bent her focus away from reality.

Someone called out, the appeal as poignant as it was grief-stricken, "Oh, Strawberry. Not you—you—you—you..."

That was the dark hunter? Has he lost someone precious? It sounds as if he needs comfort? I must go to...?

The moment she stumbled toward that one act capable of anchoring her soul to reason, the effort became too much and she was forced to let go. Exhausted, she reasoned, *I'll try again later when things aren't so hectic.*

It didn't take long for the jingling harmonies of the woman's strange environment to lull her back toward sleep. As her troubled psyche sank slowly into oblivion, submerged desires began welling to the surface. Circling on plangent tides of need, those feelings gained strength and coherence, and sought to express themselves in the only way possible.

Filtering up through layer after pellucid layer of the gem's substance, they congregated at the conjunction of three multifaceted planes where they steadily accumulated sufficient resonance to mitigate interdimensionhell tidal fading. And when they did, the signal conveyed an appeal that—so far—hadn't been answered:

"Daaaaemon! Daaaaemon, heeelp meeeee."

Chapter 9: The Lion's Den

Having dismissed everyone, I rushed from the training area and motioned for Gemini to join me on the jog along the tunnels back toward Black Tower. As she drew alongside, I expressed my concerns. "I've got to be honest with you, I don't like coincidences."

"Coincidences?"

"Yeah. That message the three stooges played out for us has deeper implications than merely reminding us Chopin and Tesla are still at large. You'll see, especially if my hunch is right. And what better time for our friend Nettesheim to turn up? Like I said, *coincidences*. Or blind luck. Either way, I don't like unknown factors, and Nettesheim is definitely that. You may not know this, but when we were all on that mission at the Brass Steel several months back—you know, the one where Isabella Castile was helped to escape by our pain in the ass renegades—I managed to question Nettesheim quite closely before Pascal took him away for further interrogation. He made no bones about the fact he'd deliberately gotten himself incarcerated, just so he could experience the full ambience of what one of hell's harshest prisons had to offer."

"No shit?" Gemini's eyes popped at the news, "Being new, I never got round to reading the full debrief."

"Well, I shit you not." I opened my mind so that Gemini could share my recollection of that part of the conversation. "His exact words were, and I quote, '…this is hell. It's not supposed to be a picnic, but since my condemnation, I've so often found the opposite to be the case. I find that disappointing. So, if I can avoid eradication for long enough, I'm determined to savor the underworld's eternal torments to the full. And I do mean every deviance, every vile inducement, and every foul chastisement there is…' How about that for commitment?"

"Commitment?" Gemini struggled not to laugh. "Sounds like he's crazy enough to be commit*ted*? I hate to say this, but I like his style."

"He certainly has that," I agreed, "yet here's the thing. You felt the tone of his expressions through my senses. He openly supports His Satanic Majesty's policy of eternal damnation, and thinks the underworld has gone soft. I got the distinct impression Nettesheim believes in what we do and would love to see things become more…*stringent*, as would I."

"Pity there aren't any more like him, then. It'd make our jobs a damn sight easier."

I slowed my pace and lowered my voice. "There's more to what you say than you might realize. Nettesheim made light of being able to neutralize a Dagger of Damocles, using, as he termed it, 'magic, sorcery, and hocus-pocus.' Something I didn't take seriously at the time. But now…?"

"Now that I *can* relate to," Gemini countered. "You've read my report regarding the raid on Chopin and Tesla's secondary home in Rue du Val de Harme. It was uncanny, the way Nettesheim knew Nimrod and I were in trouble—Champ and Yamato too, across in Niflheim—and like a knight in shining armor, he appeared from nowhere and didn't raise a sweat, freeing us from the time dialysis traps."

Gemini got a faraway look in her eyes. "It made me think about what you said to me, regarding the way our distinctive abilities are harnessed and elevated once we're inaugurated into the Hell Hounds. For all that we've been magnified by the Bãlefire, Nettesheim is powerful in ways we can't even imagine. He could have fucked us over six ways from Sinday, but never entertained the notion." She smiled, "It didn't stop me trying to zap him though. A somewhat infuriating experience, as his mumbo-jumbo spell casting stopped me dead in my tracks. And do you know what he said after he'd done it...?"

This time, it was Gemini's turn to link to me.

The corridor about us faded, and the next thing I knew, I could see a darkened basement, filled almost end to end with tables and racks of neatly stacked tools. To my right, Nimrod stood like a life-sized statue, frozen in mid step, at the moment the ambush activated. On my left, Nettesheim was talking to me/us...

"...like I said, I'm not your enemy. As events proceed apace, those with the right inclinations need to stand firm together against what's coming."

"And what is coming?"

"Insanity and chaos. Although new to the higher echelons of Hellonian society, you're far from naïve. You know that Chopin and Tesla are just the tip of the iceberg. There are angels and demigods involved. Mystics and morons alike. And while each might have a hidden agenda, they are all intent on releasing a plague of woe upon us to achieve their aims..."

The extract ended, and I discovered we'd both come to a standstill.

"Makes you think, eh?" Gemini remarked, starting forward once more.

"And then some. When we first bagged Nettesheim at the Brass Steel, Nimrod mentioned we ought to exploit his skills and get him on the team."

That reminder of my old friend's advice raised a valid issue. Nimrod had been a man of few words, and I'd always been able to rely on his judgment. For him to have suggested such a thing, even in passing, carried a lot of weight.

And if I hadn't been so preoccupied by other things at the time, I might have followed up on it sooner. Aloud, I ventured, "Would you trust Nettesheim?"

"Trust him?" Gemini refused to be swayed by sentiment. "Daemon, I don't know the guy from Dante. He's a maverick...then again; I suppose you could have said that about me before you decided to take a chance on a free-spirited girl with her own evil agenda. Of course, I didn't know at the time the process of ordination reveals your deepest, darkest secrets, warts and all."

Gemini stopped and turned toward me. "As I've already mention, Nettesheim caught us with our pants down a number of times, and didn't think twice about helping out on each occasion. My gut tells me we ought to give him a chance. If he's not on the level, the Bãlefire will reveal all and you'll be able to end his scheming in an instant. Thankfully, I'm not the one having to say yea or nay," then she tapped me on the chest, "so, it looks like you have a decision to make..." and winked, "it doesn't stop you being cautious in the meantime though, does it? Like you said, he *is* an unknown factor."

And one who could make a hell of a difference. I came to a decision.

"Gem, until I know for sure which way things are going to pan out, I want you to shoot up to the security center and put everyone on alert. No fuss. Do it quietly. Get the Pack to double their patrols and casually slot officers into place on all the exit and entry points. Once everybody is ready, activate the Den's shields. We have one of the richest sources of Bãle-fire in the entire underverse. Mystic or not, Nettesheim won't be going anywhere."

"I'm on it." Pulling my head toward her, Gemini gave me a quick peck on the cheek before sprinting for the stairs. I was treated to an all too brief glimpse of her finely tone ass cheeks, flexing from side to side like two ripe apples, and then she'd rounded the first landing and was gone.

With a sigh, I struggled to concentrate on the task at hand.

Okay, let's see what the Hell Data Net has to say about the elusive Mister Nettesheim?

I'd incorporated interface ports at strategic locations throughout the castle decades ago. However, due to the nature of our duties here, I'd upgraded the Pentatron Fleshware system with the very latest Dhell Uninspiron UTHD hands free telepathic units only last year. They were just the thing for people like us who were always on the go.

Having entered Nettesheim's basic details, I didn't have to wait long to get a hit. After all, it wasn't like I was search-ing for someone with a surname like Smith, Li, or García.

Selecting *psychic print*, I transferred the info-bundle di-rectly to my brain and waited for the semitransparent overlay to settle across my eyes. Resuming my journey, I opened the file, to be greeted with the main header.

Heinrich Cornelius Agrippa von Nettesheim

DOB: Sept 14 1486—Cologne, Germany

DOD: Feb 18 1535—Grenoble, France

DOR: Feb 22 1535—New Hell. #189594MS:ADT12229

Confirming this was indeed my man, I started with the main précis:

Heinrich Cornelius Agrippa von Nettesheim.

Born near Cologne to a family of middle nobility, Nettesheim was a polymath, whose thirst for knowledge and subsequent expertise in a wide variety of subjects led to him becoming an authority as an occultist, theologian, astrologer, magician, alchemist, physician, legal expert and soldier.

"Bugger me, talk about the perfect C.V. Stuff the outline, I want to know more. And seeing as he was quite happy to walk into the lion's den and wait while we finished up down here, a few minutes more won't hurt. Let's see what his full record has to say about him?"

Coming to a standstill, I skimmed and then highlighted the relevant pages of interest, spread them out, and took my time to digest their contents...

It says here that, not content at earning a Magister Artum from the University of Cologne in 1502, Nettesheim began travelling to broaden his experience and understanding. His keen interest in the occult led him to Paris where he first became involved with a number of secret societies. Whilst there, he was drawn to the adventure offered by military life, and during his subsequent exploits in Valencia, Sardinia and Naples, worked his way up to become a mercenary captain serving in the army of Maximilian I, the Holy Roman Emperor. Maximilian recognized Nettesheim's talents and went on to award him the title of Ritter, or as we would say, knight.

Upon his release from service, Nettesheim's focus re-
turned to academia. In 1509, he received the patronage of the
Governor of Franche-Comté, Margaret of Austria, whereup-
on he was offered the opportunity to lecture at the University
of Dôle, France, an incredible forum for religious cannon
and civil tort. Nettesheim so impressed the authorities with
his agile mind and grasp of ethics that he was awarded a fur-
ther doctorate in theology and law. However, his continued
love affair of all things arcane led to his denouncement by
some members of the clergy as a heretic.

Undeterred, Nettesheim merely packed his bags, re-
turned to Germany, and endeavored to refine the length and
depth of his occult knowledge. Satisfied, he then travelled to
the Netherlands where, once again, he was able to secure
employment as a mercenary in the service of Maximilian I,
who later sent him to England as a special envoy.

Such was his political and legal acumen, that Net-
tesheim's service continued under the next Holy Roman Em-
peror, Charles V...

I'd seen enough, and resumed my journey in earnest.

"God Almighty," I cussed aloud, "is there nothing this
guy can't turn his hand to?"

Ignoring the distant rumble of thunder and invasive trem-
ors rippling through the flagstones, I flipped to an appendix
to study the full list of Nettesheim's accomplishments. Examining each one carefully left no doubt in my mind that
Nettesheim would have excelled as one of the world's most
accomplished and illuminated minds, if not for his preoccu-
pation with what would become his true calling: Arcana. Or
as others called it, the mastery of all hidden secrets.

This revelation both thrilled and disturbed me.

"The thing is, there are only a handful of damned souls
who know of the anagogic byproduct spawned during those

final moments before the wells of God's Grace that had been sealed on this side of the Veil began to change into something darker, something cabalistic. And though it's common knowledge that Satan went to great lengths to hide the truth of those times behind a many layered smokescreen of threats, deceit and prohibition, even I don't understand the full extent of his reasons, for I hadn't come to power then."

I read through the prodigy's record for a second time. *Being the type of man he is, it doesn't surprise me in the least that Nettesheim was able to cut through all the bullshit and tap into the inherent dominion remaining from the Time of Sundering.*

By now, I'd reached the subbasement area leading up to the Black Tower. Wanting more time to ponder on what I'd learned, I decided to ride the elevator instead of taking the stairs. The doors were already open. Sidling inside the six-foot by six-foot compartment, I pressed the button for the ground level area and, as the car began to ascend, started to reason on what I did know.

"I'm one of a tiny minority in existence who can wield both God's Grace and the Bãlefire. Even Samael and his butt-buddies can't do that, and just as well. The two elements are antithetically destructive. Even I'm careful about employing them too close together...?"

I thought about that detail in more depth.

"Apart from that time in the cellars of the Brass Steel when I combined their dominion to overcome what Nettesheim had done to a Dagger of Damocles, I don't think I've ever dared to mix the two. And that's peculiar, seeing as how they're from a common source and I've mastered both mediums. So, why do I have such an aversion...?" Then it hit me. "Unless, I've been conditioned to think that way? What if I'm capable of more?"

There's only one way to find out....

Summoning my potential, I first made sure to create a defensive sphere in which to work, then cautiously and methodically generated two balls of divergent energy within the palm of each hand—one red, one silver. *Right, let's see what happens.* With the utmost care, I brought Bālefire and God's Grace together.

Initially, the feeling was akin to pressing two magnets carrying the same polarity toward one another: difficult. It also induced an alternating cadence that set my teeth on edge and which also gave off increasing amounts of heat. Undeterred, I continued applying pressure, and imagined molding the two fireballs into a united whole.

Whatever conflict was taking place at the subatomic level continued to escalate, higher and higher; hotter and hotter. Strengthening the integrity of my shield, I prepared for the worst. The rhythm of the pulsations increased, faster and faster. I screwed my eyes shut and braced myself...

...and suddenly, all signs of resistance simply melted away. An electric shock coursed along my arms, leaving a strange hollow numbness behind that evidently signified the success of my efforts.

Did I...? Opening my fingers, I peeped inside and espied a small disc hovering in midair. Revolving round and around on its axis, I could see one face had retained an argent luster, while the other still reflected the ruby passion of the underworld's richest heritage. Even so, a theurgic piquancy, completely at odds to the normal environment, now laced the enclosed atmosphere of the lift. *That's what the Dagger of Damocles tasted like, neither damned nor celestial in nature... but something else entirely.*

Halting the rate of spin, I analyzed the source of the disparity and was amazed to discern a strange oscillating tone coming from the very edge of the amalgam. *Well I never, there really are more than two sides to a coin. And in this case, the smallest area reveals much more than is at first apparent.*

Delving into the aberration's molecular composition, I could see a lustrous green haze, shot through with innumerable dazzling white micro-filaments filling the ether. *What are they? They seem to be negating whatever opposing current flows their way in a perpetual, creative-cum-destructive loop...Hey, I've seen this kind of stuff before?*

In moments, I'd experienced a flashback to my last visit to the Bunker of England.

"The Chancellor of Coin, Philip Whitehead, had a similar setup powering the code key within the Rotunda. He must have used the latency created by the proximity of hell's equivalent of matter and antimatter to gain entrance into the wyrm chamber. So *this* is what protected the way to the repository? And what did Whitehead say about that wyrm chamber?"

"...It's a specially fabricated rupture beyond the Sheol-space continuum, a place in-between that exists outside of the normal laws of physics, metaphysics and whatever other ysics you care to mention. Your abilities won't work here..."

"And when I asked him how such a thing had been created, he replied..."

"...I haven't the faintest idea, old chap. All I do know is that it took His Infernal Majesty and his entire coterie of fallen angels some considerable time and effort to anchor the schism here. To reach any part of the main vault or the repository itself, you must now pass through this eye of nothingness. If you don't possess the right key, you'll be marooned here until the platform fades and you end up falling into... badness knows what..."

I stared in wonder at the complexity of the third element's makeup. "Look at that. It's ubiquitous in character and threads its way through everything else. The air I'm breathing; the metal in the floor beneath my feet; it's even hidden away within the substance of the Bālefire in my bloodstream. And though it tends to negate both primary sources, its symbiogenic, and constantly fluctuates across the line between existence and obliteration."

Is that how you attune to it? I had a sneaking suspicion I was on the right track. *Talk about experiencing a Daniel moment. This will require a leap of faith.*

Summoning my courage, I homed in on the constant humming that sounded like a swarm of wasps with metal wings had learned to tap-dance, and soon distinguished the modulation of its unique pattern. Blending to it, I felt as if I'd been impaled by millions of superheated acupuncture needles, then my perceptions expanded. On impulse, I snapped my fingers, igniting a shower of iridescent emerald sparks that rocked the car from side to side.

Ice-cold nails scraped down my spine. *What in the...? Thank purgatory I remembered to erect a shield. That would have vaporized the elevator?*

The lift came to a stop, the doors opened, and I was greeted by the smiling face of my unexpected guest. "Daemon Grim," Nettesheim extended his hand, "I felt that from out in the hallway. If I may say so, you have the look of someone who realizes he's not in Kansas anymore. Welcome to the club."

Chapter 10: Best Laid Plans

Carryall in hand, Yamato descended the main staircase of his home for the past couple of days, and cast his gaze across the abundant—and somewhat sumptuous—fixtures and fittings that typified the interior décor. *I'll say this for Chopin and Tesla, they don't believe in slumming it.*

The five story townhouse in Place Venôme had once belonged to the dynamic duo, until the fateful day they'd been forced to flee a raid led by Daemon Grim and their former comrade, Nimrod. For some reason, the eloquent residence had remained vacant ever since. A shame, as far as Yamato was concerned, for it contained some of the finest works of dark art he'd ever seen. *Ah,* Massacre of the Innocents, *by Rubens. A superb interpretation of one of the most blessed times in history. And one of Champ's favorites;* Anatomical Pieces, *by Géricault, a composition that always makes him feel hungry....And the series of wood blocks over there in the cabinet? Are they Holbein originals? Where in Hades did they get them?*

Reaching the first floor landing, Yamato lingered to study a superb copy of Wolgemut's, *The Dance of Death.* It took him a moment to realize it was one of a pair following the same theme, for a similar painting, *The Triumph of Death*, by

Pieter Brueghel the Elder, hung from the wall on the far side of a small cupboard.

Odd, that I would miss something so esteemed? It touches on my favored subject and each rendering is rather soulful. He glanced between the pictures again, only to find his attention skipping away to a nearby set of figurines depicting the famous episode from William Bouguereau's, *Dante and Virgil in Hell*, where the heretical alchemist, Capocchio, is bitten on the neck during a fight with Gianni Schicchi, a con artist responsible for stealing a dead man's inheritance. *Oh yes, the infamous scene that spawned many a vampire legend and mis....wait a minute? I know what this is?*

Steeling his resolve, Yamato closed his eyes, stepped forward, seized the door handle leading into the closet and yanked it open. No sooner had he done so, than the weight of compunction to ignore this niche completely, lessened considerably.

"I was right," Yamato breathed, "it's the wormhole that Daemon mentioned previously. And from the feel of it, the damned thing retains quite a bit of clout. Strange, we've been here since the day before yesterday, and although I knew it was here, I never —?"

"Hey!" Champ's hail made Yamato jump, "Is that the void doohickey we were all told about?"

"One and the same. I'd meant to investigate it as soon as we arrived, and of course, completely neglected to do anything about it....which I suppose is the point." He beckoned his partner closer, "come and see."

Both Hounds peered inside, and Yamato was surprised to find an empty cavern waiting beyond the sill. The walls were comprised of stone, each brick of which had been embedded with numerous small rocks that glowed warmly with the radiance of a long-forgotten sun. Something about the chamber irritated his throat and nose, and it wasn't long before Yamato felt tears running down his cheeks."

"Now *that* is shit off a shovel, cool." Champ's voice betrayed his awe. "No wonder Pascal wants to commandeer this joint as an office and residence complex for his GDSI operatives. Can you imagine where he'll be insistin' they take their coffee breaks?" Champ grunted, loudly, "though they'll have to leave the door ajar, or no one will ever find the fewkin' thing."

"Seeing as how they're about to appoint Pascal as the new Deputy Director of Intelligence, I think he'll have a trick or two up his sleeves to make things...? What are you doing?"

"Just checkin' somethin' out." Champ poked his head across the threshold and inhaled deeply, setting off a bout of sneezing and coughing. Using the back of his hands to wipe his nose, he marveled, "weird to think that's an entirely different world in there."

"And it's permanently open, too."

"Is it even in our underverse?"

"I haven't got a clue," Yamato admitted. "There are no visible exits that we can discern, and nobody seems inclined to investigate. That's why Pascal sent across to New Hell for a team of specialist, Fiendish Bureau of Investigation examiners. They'll be wearing the very latest hazmat suits, and have been tasked to see what they can do to neutralize the compulsive element."

"I thought the impulse was supposed to have been switched off?" Champ leaned even further into the smoldering interior, risking another hacking fit.

"It has, Daemon negated its power when he breached the wards. *This*," Yamato gestured at the doorframe, "is just a little reminder of the potency we're dealing with. The esoteric spoor saturating these environs still retains enough strength to manipulate our desires."

Champ fell silent, and Yamato could see by the way his colleague's head kept bobbing from side to side he was mulling something over. Yamato let it go for a couple of minutes, then was forced to concede, "C'mon. Out with it."

"I was just supposin'....Is *this* why we've found diddly-squat of Chopin and Tesla?" Champ rapped his knuckles against the lintel. "If those bozos know how to create holes through time and space and how to protect 'em with all their fancy mind gimmicks, what's to stop 'em doing it on a larger scale with their new home? If we want to find the scumbags, we need to isolate the frequency these things operate on."

"A sound idea, my friend, but how do you propose we narrow the field?"

Champ chewed on his bottom lip for a moment and spat on the Tabriz carpet without a second thought about its value. "Chopin and Tesla may be crafty, and wilier than a skunk up a tree, but their shit still stinks."

"I'm sorry?" Yamato wasn't quite sure he'd heard his partner right.

"What I mean is, they might be smart an all, but think about how we've been trackin' 'em so far. The hell-rats managed to sniff 'em out, so why don't we get Gemini to do her stuff? If she's as good as we think she is, it won't take a lot for her to spread the word among all the critters in the other circles. That way, we get the varmints to do the legwork...or should I say, nosework for us, and we can move in with the heavy stuff once we have a general location."

Yamato was speechless. *Kuso Kurae! He's right. We've been concentrating on Perish for so long, we didn't think to expand our net to other realms. That...that's brilliant.* Aloud, he muttered, "Have you been eating brains?"

Champ sucked through his teeth and threw Yamato a dirty look. "Just cause I ain't cultured and speak with a plumb up my ass don't mean to say I'm stupid. Besides, if Gemini can get us in close, there ain't no way they're gonna get away. Only one person in hell is better at trackin' than I am. I tell you, brother. I've got a good feelin' about this."

"So do I." Yamato was already formulating a plan. Snatching up his bag, he made for the stairs, "Follow me. We'll shoot across to Pascal's office and get him ask his FBI contacts to choose the most likely place for us to start. Once we have the best location, I'll task Gemini to join us, and the hunt will be on."

*

Magnified by proximity and atmospherics, the surface of Kesh—one of Jahannam's greater moons—loomed larger than usual as it broke free of the horizon. From Garôk's perspective, it made the bowl of the Paradân valley look as if it was dissolving in a celestial vat of acidic fumes, creating a sense of peace, despite the urgency of the situation.

Standing slightly higher up, next to the restraining collars of the methân portal, First Fist Jotûn watched as more than four thousand sweat-soaked slaves labored in the sultry heat of flame-down's fifth hour. Glistening like well-oiled sithen serpents, their emaciated bodies toiled to shore up the trenches and strengthen the bulwarks from which the Incendia Blade of the Left-Hand Path would soon rage in open hostility.

Silhouetted against the pale amber glow of a predawn sky, Jotûn's stance revealed his agitation. Eager to see if her actions had curried favor, Garôk moved closer, and whispered, "Will this be sufficient, do you think?"

The First Fist didn't reply immediately. Instead, he contented himself by running a professional eye across the wide extent of the fortifications, before kneeling to examine the calodes themselves.

This close to the esoteric lodestones, Garôk could feel their influence upon the eternal flame burning within her, and was glad the soul of an Al-Jinn was made of sturdier stuff than that of the human cattle she oversaw. She glanced off across the open plain, where the bodies of those lesser mortals who had already succumbed to the pull of the calodes lie burning, their pyres offering eternal testimony to the harshness of existence in this, one of the oldest realms in existence.

"*Shân!*" Jotûn cursed aloud. Standing, he brushed the dust from his cuisse, and complained, "By this time the day after tomorrow, I judge the flow of aha'del will have dried up completely. You did well, Garôk. Your initiative has saved precious time and allowed preparations to proceed unhindered."

Relieved by the compliment, Garôk replied, "How do you think Nishôgh will take the news?"

"Badly." Jotûn's visage crackled and his form billowed like a storm cloud as he struggled to bring his temper under control. "He's old school, remember. To his way of thinking, anyone not of heaven or the Al-Jinn is inferior, and all the more so if they form the dregs of humanity cast into hell...irrespective that the creator of those latterday circles is a fallen cherub himself."

"So you feel it will escalate?"

"Undoubtedly. I've already ordered the Chains from Sáeer, Ladthâa, and Saqar to join us here. With a full Weld already in formation by the time our Gauntlet arrives, it will at least give him time to focus on the task at hand before he acts..." he turned toward her, and Garôk caught the full force of his gaze. A frightening experience. "At least this cycle's quota of El-aha'del lamps has been fulfilled. As you pointed out, the mere fact we have sufficient essence to please the king's court for several months ahead may be sufficient reason to stay Nishôgh's wrath. But..."

"But?"

"But I doubt it."

"It's war then?" Garôk didn't know whether to be elated by that prospect or not.

"What do *you* think? Lucifer and his fallen choir won't take the theft of their reanimating chattel lightly. And though I relish the thought of full on combat after so long, the deceiver can be a tricky fenôme when he wants to be."

Garôk had been waiting for the right moment to remind the First Fist of her other proposal. Now was the perfect opportunity. "Then you'll give credence to my strategy regarding the slaves?"

"That we promise them their freedom if they acquit themselves in battle on our behalf?" Jotûn's bark of laughter was cruelly devoid of all humor. "A truly excellent idea. These fools will jump at any chance for liberty, not realizing for one moment it will be their death that grants them the release they so desperately crave."

"Yes, it *is* odd that they don't appreciate how being away from the influence of New Hell negates any chance of their ever being recycled," she ground her tusks and chuckled, "though, if I may be so bold, I would allow one or two to survive? Can you imagine the enhancement in productivity it will engender, once all this is over, if they think there's a way out from their drudgery. We can always send such ones away to the capital with tales that they will live out the rest of their lives at ease...no matter how short that might prove to be?"

Jotûn was stunned to silence. Then he grinned in return and placed a calloused claw upon her shoulder. "Such thinking indicates you have a bright future ahead of you, Garôk... *if* you don't lose your head to ambition."

*

Under cover of the protection afforded by the *Sword of Seraphim Speed*, Chopin completed a final circuit of the environs surrounding the Statue of Lost Liberty and decided to call it a day. *Events couldn't have unfolded better had we tried.*

The enforcers had stuck only forty-eight hours previously. Not understanding the nature of the contagions used by the Fourth of Seven as he did, Chopin realized most people were probably under the impression that Lost Liberty Island was still a no-go area, and for that, he'd be eternally grateful. *Such a belief will increase the likelihood of our little hideaway remaining undiscovered until we are ready to depart, or it is too late to prevent our victory. Either way, that's music to my ears.*

Thanks to the jewel affixed to the sword's hilt, Chopin was able to return to the final staging area within a disused storage silo beneath Fort Blood, faster than the human eye could follow. He found Tesla hard at work, completing their final inventory and equipment check.

"It looks as if we're still in business," Tesla stated without preamble, "the psychic dampening field managed to hold them off, and the chameleon shield held."

"And the artifacts?"

"Look for yourself."

Accepting his friend's offer, Chopin set the *Sword of Seraphim Speed* to one side, and strolled across to inspect their ill-gotten gains.

The Scroll of Divergent Union sat within an open box, thrumming softly. Next to it, a fragment from the Key of Sighs rested, its radiance swallowed by the greater glory of the Golden Fleece which shone like the sun. On the far side of the room, hovering in midair, Grislington's wings took pride of place. Ruffling gently as if still attached to an angel preparing for flight, their feathers gave the impression they'd been dusted in diamonds, for every movement they made cast pearlescent shadows about the chamber that relaxed the mind as much as it soothed the heart.

Perfect. "And everything else?"

"The orbs, temporal pyramid, Dagger of Damocles and Mermaid's Pin are intact and remain fully operational. We were lucky, Frédéric. Very lucky,"

"I agree. We were also fortunate it was the Fourth and Fifth who carried out the attack. Of all the Seven, they are more intent on generating casualties as they audit, as opposed to wanton destruction. Had the First or Seventh been tasked, the outcome might have been very different."

Tesla shrugged. "That's why we chose these lower levels. Even before Grislington ran amok, they have lain abandoned. And in all truth, the Sibitti show little interest in relics of power, and more in those who crave them. In a way, circumstance has worked in our favor, for the Sibitti rarely strike twice in the same place."

"There is that," Chopin acknowledged. "So now...?"

"So now, all we need do is sit back and relax. Obviously, that'll be easier said than done, especially after we move in here over the last three days before the Soulstice. However, while the living arrangements are somewhat basic, at least there'll be plenty of food, drink and reading material to help pass the time. And of course, we have the added benefit of being close enough to New Hell Harbor to be entertained by the lights and music coming from the RSS Titanic every evening."

That aspect intrigued Chopin more than he cared to admit. "If the locals are still loath to set foot here when we do make the move, I think I might take advantage of the binocular stands along the eastern shoreline to watch the nightly dunking up close. I hear the fools try to put on a bit of a show by cross-dressing? That'll be a sight to see."

"As indeed are the Madhatten and New Heresy skylines. Sea mist or not, I'm told they're rather spectacular."

"I can't believe were just a hop, skip and a jump away from fulfilling our destinies, Nikola. After all this time..." Chopin was gripped by a sudden sense of anticlimax. "Is there anything left for us to do?"

"Not really. I should have finished molding the medusanite casket to hold the wings within the next day or two. Once it's finished, I'll run a few tests to check the seals, and if all is in order, it'll be safe to transfer our seraphinite stash to this location without fear of unwanted flashovers." Tesla then gestured toward a group of four signet rings sitting on a fold-out camping table. "I've not long finished priming the bands so that they link to the appropriate soul sapphires. Each pair will activate automatically should we meet an unfortunate end, and redirect our essences to the desired destination."

"What configuration did you eventually decide upon?"

"I chose not to complicate things and stuck to the original plan. Kí-gal remains our primary fallback site. We won't use the secondary location unless we run afoul of dire calamity."

"Well then..." Chopin strode purposefully across to a nearby ice bucket in which a magnum of Cristal Brute sat chilling. Lifting the expensive vintage free, he declared, "I think *this* would be an appropriate time for a little toast."

Removing a vicious looking flick knife from his jacket pocket, he extended the blade and snapped the neck of the bottle free, cork and all, before pouring two frothing servings into a couple of ordinary mugs. Offering one to his companion, Chopin tapped the rims together, and said, "To best laid plans…and dreams come true."

Chapter 11: Hell Hound

We'd been talking for three hours now. Three long and exhausting hours, during which I'd grilled Nettesheim about his life as a human, what he'd really been up to in the nearly five hundred years since his damnation, and the size and composition of his balls for walking into the one place in hell he might never walk out of again.

It had made compulsive listening, for I'd learned things not contained in executive records.

Keeping to form, no sooner had he been reanimated and released from the Mortuary, Nettesheim had set out to continue his pursuit of the one thing that had driven his entire life: the amassing of arcane wisdom. His quest led him to Melgaróth, demon lord of Angár, from who he'd gained the secrets of speaking in tongues, elemental manipulation and shape shifting. Next, he'd risked unlife and limb by journeying to the S'gãth homeworld, Gãresh, to acquire those skills needed for extracting memories from the minds of sleeping individuals. Whilst there, had also learned the art of shadow hunting under the teutalage of Dread-Master Ashéd of Kõlesh Prime. Nettesheim had also hinted that, from Gãresh, he'd gone on to study the disciplines of astral hexing and blessings, divination, and the comprehension of multiple reality schisms, at the feet of Isla, the Oracle of Rû.

Having achieved what he felt were the basics, Nettesheim subsequently decided to travel extensively to foster an in-depth knowledge on such diverse subject as, geophysical design and function of the elder circles of hell; the expanding underverse theorem; uncivil tort—application and procedure—as practiced by advocates of Satan's Blue Suits; astrological dogma; and the impact of diabolical excesses on the inhuman psyche.

Thereafter, Nettesheim turned his hand to his other passion: soldiering.

Serving first under Bertran de Born, Nettesheim soon made a name for himself as an accomplished commander and strategist who became instrumental in some of his mentor's greatest victories. In later years, his acumen helped him gain positions of prestige within the Devo Pact, the Devil's Dogs, and the Democratic Resistance Freedom Fighters, where he was known to lead from the front—whilst strangely—shunning any form of prestige or publicity for his achievements.

Recent years had seen a change, though, for Nettesheim turned into something of a recluse. A hermit wandering through all the levels of the underverse, learning of an enigmatic *third way*, whilst offering his services—here and there—as a jack of all trades to those who needed to get things done, quietly and efficiently. Needless to say, his reputation amongst the criminal fraternity and white market racketeers rapidly became legendary.

At this moment in time, I was sat opposite the legend himself, in front of a roaring fire in my office, and we were each nursing a glass of Diabhalvulin 18.

Breaking the silence, I offered an observation. "It seems to me you get bored easily?"

The flames from the hearth reflected back from Nettesheim's eyes, and just for a second, appeared to blaze brighter. "From the outside looking in, I suppose many might see it that way. I'll give you that, Reaper. But you have to understand, although I eschew the limelight, I'm the type of man who needs to feel as if he's making a real contribution." He pursed his lips and shook his head. "I just haven't found the right outlet, yet, that special avenue through which my talents can be expressed in a way that keeps me *stimulated*. Does that make sense?"

"In a way. Though it disappoints me you think self-expression would be important to anyone here in underworld?"

Nettesheim appeared surprised by my comment. "Why? Damned or not, being true to yourself is one of the wisest things an individual can do. After all, the highest wall is only as strong as the stones that go into its making. Just one lose bolder, one weak link, can weaken the entire edifice and cause it to crumble, affecting everyone. I want to be the kind of person who weeds out those who would bring everything crashing down on us and what our dark father has built."

"And you feel you're the type of man who would make a difference?"

"I do."

Part of an earlier conversation with Nettesheim, back at the Brass Steel, came to mind. "Because hell has been established for a reason, yes?"

"Indeed. I've always believed in hell's principles. They need to be upheld and strengthened, not undermined by disgruntled morons incapable of seeing the bigger picture."

"Which is?" I set my glass on the table and leaned forward.

"That even the strongest of us are merely pawns in a

monumental game of three-dimensional chess. Heaven, hell, humanity. We're all part of the same team, except that we exist on different levels of the board. If only more would recognize their place in the grand scheme and do their bit to play their part, well...everything would progress far more smoothly than it does." Nettesheim placed his own drink down, and his demeanor hardened. "Those who foment treason and attempt to destabilize all that is precious? Now, *they* need to be crushed without mercy."

They do indeed.

The passion in his voice was tangible; his candor refreshing. Such evident zeal helped make up my mind.

"I find your enthusiasm for Satan's system uplifting, and if you don't mind my saying, gratifying. I could help you fulfill such desires more comprehensively, *if* you were so inclined?"

"You could?"

"Oh yes. But here's the thing you need to understand. If you agree to what I propose, there's no going back. The level of commitment expected is rather...imposing."

"Imposing?"

"Some might say it's *eternal* in nature." *Until some fuckwit of a fallen angel with his own agenda tries to stab you in the back.*

Nettesheim remained silent, content to study me closely, so I thought it might be a good idea to emphasize a little detail that would appeal to him. "Believe me when I say, it would facilitate your quest for further hidden knowledge."

The light of comprehension flicked on and his pupils dilated. "You want me to work for you, don't you?"

"Using your own analogy, I want you to work for something greater, something that would checkmate the opposition forever. Interested?"

That light became more intense, this time animating his entire face.

Pushing away from my chair, I manifested my power and drew my primary sword from its sheath. The tattoos adorning my body blazed bright as hell's grace infused me in majesty. In seconds, the welcoming stench of sulfur had completely overpowered the smell of the log fire.

Raising my weapon, I pointed it toward Nettesheim. "If you'd really like to make a statement, one that counts, place both of your hands on the blade."

Nettesheim's gaze fell on the razored medusanite edge before him and worked its way up and down, drinking in every detail that had gone into its forging. Then the soldier in him won through. Surging to his feet, he strode forward and didn't hesitate to grasp the tip as tightly as he could. Ruby vitality welled from between his fingers, only to evaporate instantly, in a cloud of hissing carmine-colored steam.

Channeling my might into a steady flow, I began the transfer of power.

Engirded within a web of silver and purple dominion, Nettesheim tensed, rose up onto his toes, and kept levitating until he was hovering more than a foot off the floor.

Now, let's see what the Bālefire makes of you?

"Heinrich Cornelius Agrippa von Nettesheim. You are about to be anointed into the Ancient Disorder of Hell Hounds, a fraternity whose history is as malevolent as it is abominable. Know this. Few are considered and even less get chosen. Do you understand the gravitas of what you now face?"

"I do," he breathed, "please continue."

"And do you gravely swear that you will unfaithfully adhere to the debased tenets of our creed? That you will do your utmost to be guided by the Laws of Lucifer, and protect and defend the most despicable of the Doctrines of the Devil? Will you endeavor to pursue all enemies of the state throughout the length and breadth of the Sheolspace continuum, and do your damndest to execute both them and your duty without fear of favor, or hope of reprieve?"

"I, Heinrich Cornelius Agrippa von Nettesheim, do so swear."

As he spoke, Nettesheim ran his hands along the blade for a second time. His cuts opened up and blood flowed again. On this occasion, the Bãlefire licked along the length of his wounds, measuring his DNHA in a flash of bright crimson light.

Absorbing his genetic key, I reverted to ancient Hellanese.

"*Mar-sin troh a' lùthse ain mi sealbġh etom an a' Satanas ainim* (Then by the power invested in me and in the name of Satan), *thu ar thoir* ŭghdrash *do ruaig feadháte uile a' ríghachdes measg ilfrinn* (you are empowered to hunt throughout all the realms of hell)."

The tenor of my voice drew forth the full authority within the Bãlefire's constitution. Nettesheim's skeleton became visible as his flesh momentarily lost substance. I waited for his tissue to rematerialize, and then placed my free hand on the crown of his head. "*Fritheille a-nise etom gu suthain. Cho cobhair mi, Drôch-Fhear báirig* (Serve now and forevermore. So says the everlasting Dark Lord)."

For a final time I exerted my will, and the radiance encompassing Nettesheim from top to bottom bloomed with gold and scarlet mastery. Gradually, the halo began to pulse and shrink, infusing his skin in concentric waves of xanthous potential as it lowered him toward the floor.

He blinked. "So, what happens now?"

"Now? Even for someone as accomplished as yourself, it's going to be an interesting twelve hours as the Bãlefire bonds to your spirit and triggers a metamorphosis of your occult skills and abilities. I can appreciate why you, of all people, might think you've gained a degree of competency in the secret and obscure," I laughed out loud, "but believe me when I say, you haven't seen anything yet."

Nettesheim still seemed a little distracted, and looked as if he was already scanning deep within himself for any perceived changes. "That should be a fascinating experience," he murmured.

I headed for the exit. "Yes, I'm sure you'll enjoy the process. And if you survive the trials tomorrow, you'll find the changes will mature and endure. I'll make sure some of the other Hounds give you a run-through of what to expect."

"Why, aren't you going to be here to take part?"

Impressive. He didn't react to my inference of personal danger? "Me? There's something I need to do. In fact, it's a pity you weren't recruited sooner; I think you may have proved of value in sorting it out. As it is, I'll just have to go it alone...

"...ah, I nearly forgot." Pausing in the doorway, I turned to face him, raised my hand, and spoke a single word in the divine language, "*Bráthon* (Brother)."

Nettesheim jumped as if he'd been stung.

"Don't worry, that's just an esoteric encryption. You'll need it to walk around the environs of the castle unhindered. If you're still standing after the assessment, it'll bond permanently to your soul and you'll truly be one of us. In any event, I have to get going. Stay here and I'll send Gemini to come and get you and show you around. I sincerely hope to see you when I get back. Bad luck."

As I closed the latch, I heard Nettesheim chuckle, and growl, "Oh, I'll be here alright. And luck will have nothing to do with it."

*

In contrast to the silent footfalls of the woman next to him, Nettesheim's steps thumped off along the corridor, announcing his presence to any who might be unsure a Hound in the making stalked these desecrated halls. Not that Nettesheim was in the least bit concerned with being stealthy, for the tingling sensation emanating from deep inside his guts and the droning voice of his companion made it difficult to concentrate.

Fortunately, his eidetic memory came to the rescue, for it was able to compensate for such distractions by absorbing stimuli from his surroundings as he walked along.

Beside him, the Lady Gemini came to a stop. "Well, that's about it for the castle grounds and basic rundown of Inquisitor and Hell Hound duties. Is there anything you would like to know or any specific place you'd like to see?"

Another hot flush surged through Nettesheim's body, causing him to break out in a cold sweat. *C'mon, Heinrich. Get a grip.* "Actually, I'd appreciate a heads-up as to where the trials actually take place. And if it's possible, can you tell me a bit about what to expect?"

"Sure." Gemini spun on the spot and headed back the way they had just come. "Follow me, we'll take the elevator and head down to the maze, or as we call it, the Jumbles, a topsy-turvy web of traps and shifting floors and walls. We carry out most of the appraisals down there as the wards have been fortified to prevent stray emanations frying anyone to a cinder."

"And has that ever happened?"

"Once or twice, so I'm told. The tests release a great deal of energy, you see, as they're administered via a series of themed modules. The first challenge you'll encounter is elemental, involving each of the primary forces of nature. It's been designed to stretch you and reveal how well you can adapt to sudden changes in the environment. If you manage to get through that, you'll roll straight into the mental evaluation segment, which factors in how you react when coming face to face with circumstances that might trip you up at an inopportune moment; things like your worst fears, avarice, ethical and moral dilemmas or doubts. That phase really does send your senses reeling. So, if you survive and have managed to keep your wits about you, we'll immediately shoot next door into the kill pit and start working up a bit of a sweat."

Kill pit? Nettesheim was understandably taken aback by Gemini's casual allusion to such a thing. "What? Are you inferring you want to see me actually execute someone? I assure you, having fought in one form of military conflict or another for many decades, that won't present any difficulty."

Now it was Gemini's turn to look perplexed. "Oh, I'm sorry. I didn't really make that clear, did I? No, what I meant to say is, the kill pit is a specially designed arena where Yamato, Champ and I will arm ourselves to the teeth before surrounding you, and doing our level best to take your head."

At first, Nettesheim thought his guide was joking. But a quick glance Gemini's way soon reinforced the fact she was stating a simple truth. "Unholy shit! You're serious, aren't you?"

"Of course, think about it from our perspective. You are aspiring to join, what is, the most prestigious and unconventional team in all the underverse. We need to know we can rely on you under all circumstances, and particularly when you're under stress. What better way to measure a person's worth than by putting you in genuine fear of your unlife? Needless to say, if you end up on Slab A, you've failed and you're out. Forever. Your memories will be erased, and once you've been reassigned, you'll never hear from us again."

Something I can't allow. "You *do* know I've been a soldier many times? What if I hurt someone defending myself?"

"That's the point. While we're doing our best to snuff you out—and I really can't emphasize that enough. We *will* take you down if we can—you have to demonstrate technical finesse, and avoid landing a lethal blow. Bummer, eh?"

Nettesheim was aghast. "*Scheisse*! And just how am I supposed to do that? Use harsh language or sparkling humor?"

"I doubt that would work," Gemini replied lightheartedly, "though I think Champ would adore the sentiment. No, you have to disqualify us from the contest—or as we say, dump us—by knocking us on our assess, or better still, out cold."

"Fantastic," Nettesheim complained, "a walk in the park, then."

"For someone with your skill set, yes, I should think so."

So my reputation comes back to haunt me for once. "And if I survive all that, *then* do I get to be a Hell Hound?"

"Almost, but not quite." Gemini wagged her finger and smiled, "if you do make it that far, there'll be one final hurdle."

"Another one?"

"Call it the signature test. Having demonstrated your flexibility and stamina, your mastery of the environment and of yourself, you then have to exemplify that you can do what you aspire to be: a Hell Hound who can hunt.

"You'll be provided with a current list of our top thirteen fugitives from injustice, along with the latest intelligence package covering each one. Once you've picked a target of your choice, you'll have six hours to track, bag, and tag them."

"Six hours? From scratch?"

"I know." Gemini's smile widened into a broad grin, "just when you think you've made it, Bam! We knock the wind out of your sales." Then she patted him on the shoulder. "But think of the benefits. Daemon likes us to work in pairs. If you make it, you'll probably get to work with little old *me* every day."

Taking stock of his situation, Nettesheim came to a realization. *I keep forgetting. By the time I'm required to do all this, I'll have undergone the change. Once manifested, I'll be stronger, faster, and far more adept than I already am...?* He caught his breath and thought back to a clandestine conversation recently exchanged within the High Church of Lucifer, in Cullogne. *How providential. As close as my shadows are to Chopin and Tesla, they are bound to be on that list and won't be prepared to deal with my enhancements.*

Nettesheim turned to his de facto mentor, "I take it the actual methods I use to stalk my victims and reel them in will be left to me?"

"Victims, as in plural?" Gemini giggled, "It sounds as if you intend to make a statement? That's the spirit...But I digress. To answer your question, yes. The *however* and *wherever* is entirely down to you."

Perfect. "Then I hope to entertain you all with a stunning display of trivial pursuit in the near future."

Especially as all I'll have to do is make it look as if I've lowered my guard a little. Guiteau and Corday won't be able to resist. They'll come to me, and their sacrifice will ensure I'm in the perfect position to direct events as the game enters the final quarter.

Chapter 12: Guess Who's Coming to Dinner

Following Nettesheim's elevation, I'd made my way directly to New Hell and the Mortuary, to prepare for my mission into the Dead Zone—if not knowing what the fuck I was going to do once I actually got through to the other side could in any way be construed as, *preparation*.

As usual, I'd been greeted by the ever cordial Buttkiss. However, instead of directing me to the Undertaker, Buttkiss had led me to the Mortuary's chief ass-kisser in residence, Gorgonous, a clear indicator that the asshole himself was not only busy, but had left strict instructions not to be disturbed.

After detailing the reason for my visit and reminding Gorgonous what usually happened to those stupid enough to impede my enquiries, he'd switched on pretty quickly and had escorted me to where I'd wanted to be anyway. Not one minute ago, I'd arrived at the Hub only to discover every orthodontist's worst torment was hard at work, surrounded by a gaggle of white-coated flunkies, and conducting badness knows what experiments on the sealed incursion site.

A whole host of different machines, gizmos and other contraptions had been grouped around, perched on boxes beneath, or pointed toward the aperture, and those minions who weren't essentially operating anything, either took notes, sketched diagrams, or listed results on myriad recording devices.

Still dressed as a tartan halfwit, and sporting a new beret that was large enough to land jumbo jets on, the Undertaker provided me with the perfect opportunity to poke fun at his expense. Nevertheless, the mere fact he seemed to be working his socks off trying to remedy the problems this rogue anomaly had caused, earned him a degree of grudging respect in my book, so I decided to cut him some slack. Waiting patiently just inside the doorway, I whiled away the time by examining the Hub itself.

It was with a sense of relief that I noted one of hell's greatest sanctums had regained something of its former glory. Not only had the vibrant bands that segregated the orb into different zones of agitated deviltry recouped much of their deep, rich consistency, but there were considerably more of the darkened hurricanes swirling across its surface layers. *Now this is a cause for celebration. If sin is returning, that must mean —?*

"Ah, Reaper. My apologies, I didn't realize you were here." The Undertaker was in a far happier mood than the last time we'd met. "I was just confirming some of my latest findings before sending a brief memo to our dark father. Now he's been made aware of the crisis, he's keen on regular updates."

"Good news, I take it?"

"Excellent news. As you've no doubt noticed, your forbidding has worked wonders. I've just this second confirmed the flow of tincture into the unsanctioned rift has all but ceased."

"And how did the Boss react to your original report?"

"As you previously intimated, because we had already identified and isolated the problem, he withheld his wrath.

And now that problem's been negated..." the Undertaker exhaled in obvious satisfaction and struck a pose. It was like standing in the back draft of a farting contest between two camels suffering from a severe case of gastroenteritis, "well, I'm sure he'll be delighted by our progress."

Blinking back the tears, I remained sufficiently compos mentis to catch the way the Undertaker had casually been able to spread the blame for his security breach onto me. Neither did I miss the way he'd included himself as one of the heroes of the hour. *Our progress?* "We're not out of the woods yet," I warned. "It's when Satan holds his temper he's at his most dangerous. If I were you, I'd add a little addendum to your account."

"An addendum?"

"Yes, to emphasize to His Infernal Majesty that, not only has the threat been neutralized at this end, but that the Reaper is personally journeying through into the Dead Zone to ensure the upstarts on the other side are under no illusions as to the consequences of their actions."

The Undertaker's jaw dropped. Then he glanced back and forth between me and the schism. "You mean to say you're going in there?"

"Yes."

"After the warning they so eloquently expressed?"

"Yes."

"Alone?"

"Unless you'd like to elevate yourself even further in Satan's eyes, by changing the *me* into *we* again in your report? I'm sure your appalling sense of fashion would prove a great distraction during the fighting that is bound to ensue? It'd cheer me up no end watching you in action?"

"But Reaper..." the Undertaker seemed unusually fearful of my safety and totally ignored my jibe, "you felt the weight of the statement these Blades of the Left-Hand Path made. Are you sure this is wise?"

"I have no doubts whatsoever." Opening my mind, I showed him a review of recent events: the arrest of Pea and Choke across in Perish; the subsequent capture of Bean by Nettesheim; Livingstone's questioning of the traitors and the discovery of the key sequence hidden away in their psyches; the revelation of the dreamscape it generated when recited.

Finally, I shared a mental transcript of the clue itself:

"Do not go gently into death,

For the valley of the shadow serves naught but a cup,

Filled to the brim in bitter tears of salt.

This perfect condiment to preserve your pain,

Sprinkled liberally upon open wounds

By those whose black hearts practice darker arts.

Existing in shadow and flame,

That gulf betwixt the silent spaces of now and then

They reap a windfall harvest of fallen Souls.

Tendrils of smoke, as fragile as a sudden intake of breath

Curl like lazy fingers around your heart,

Only to squeeze...and prevent what's left from saving you."

"Do you see the obvious reference to the Dead Zone?" I highlighted those parts of the passage relating to shadows and flame, the gulf, and especially the windfall harvest.

"Yes, I caught those references, but —?"

"The thing is, the vision this clue evoked also ties into the same place. It reminded me of a specific location, though I don't know how, because I've never been there before."

The Undertaker wouldn't be swayed. "Can you trust it though? This is Chopin and Tesla we're talking about, renegades and master manipulators."

"I appreciate the warning, but I've come to understand the way their riddles can be as helpful as they are misleading. It's essential to read between the lines as much as it is to look for what's missing. It's what they don't say that often counts. Satan knows what I'll find on the other side? Traps and snares; misdirection; false messages from a dead lover? Whatever it is, I'll take my time to defuse the bugs, and use whatever I can dig up against them."

"But the warning, Reaper. You felt its tone. Do you think you'll be able to handle these Blades? I got the distinct impression they're an army bent on domination."

"Somehow, I think I'll manage...even if it's only to carry out a little recce of the situation before hauling my ass back here to summon the choir and hell's armies to war." *And really, if it comes to that, when am I going to get another opportunity like this to make Samael's demise look like a tragic act of heroism?*

As I spoke, I walked further out onto the gantry and summoned the Phage.

The sheer force of the Bãlefire's potency charged the atmosphere within the chamber, cocooning me within an atramentous halation of glittering power. Purple and argent streamers glazed the edge of my aura in a glacial corona of stunning magnitude. A coronet of gold and magenta flames ignited around the crown of my head, triggering a convulsion of cosmic lightning that cascaded down my body-armor and off along the walkway. Metal warped, less resilient seals and exposed wiring started to bubble, and the Undertaker's skin began to redden and burn, causing him to step away quickly as his team of little helpers fled. This close to the Hub, my presence set off a two-way exchange of plasmic solar discharges. Even with my visor down, the eyepiece shone like the sun.

Glancing back toward the Undertaker, I said, "Something happened to me in recent months, something incredible." I clenched my fists and the molecules making up the gases in the air imploded, creating a high-pitched squealing sound. "I intend to use that advantage to impress upon our would-be antagonists the folly of their misassumption that Satan would ignore their incursion into his domain."

"And if they don't want to listen?"

I drew my ninjaken and charged them to full capacity. "Then I'll just have to make them listen. Stay alert for anything I might send your way."

Stepping toward the multidimensionhell rent in space, I broadcast a series of commands and the construct sealing the hex in place rippled to allow my passage. No sooner had I crossed the event horizon than it sealed behind me, and I was off, riding the breaker of a kaleidoscopic surge of energy that bowled me along at breakneck speed.

Certain aspects of the tunnel began to stand out. *This conduit doesn't appear to be suffering from the instability gripping the rest of the Sheolspace continuum. So how was it generated...and by who? Tesla? Does his technology now negate the flux, or was it the Blades themselves that caused it?* In the distance, an exit portico loomed ever closer. *I guess I'll soon find out.*

The nearer the terminus got, the denser my abstruse biological pattern became. *Does time move more slowly in this alien realm?* I reached out to examine the texture of the bore,

and as I did so, snatches of something I'd rather forget came
back to haunt me.

"Daaaaemon! Daaaaemon, heeelp meeeee."

*Well, it looks like I'm on the right track. I wonder what
else...oops! Watch out, here we go.*

Crossing the threshold, my lungs expanded as if it was
the first chance I'd had to take a breath in an age. My perspective also dilated, proliferating into the ether and allowing me to register a number of things simultaneously.

Gravity on this plane was definitely heavier, indicating it
was an older, deeper level of the underverse, comparable in
many respects to the Kigali homeworld. Its habitat was similar too: sparse, scorched plant life; baking hot topsoil that
rippled in the heat; mineral laced air that seared the lungs.
Unlike Kí-gal, this place reeked of a barely restrained violence that called to the basest ideals of my id.

The space immediately in front of me formed the apex
of a wide mound, dominated by two large stones which had
been fashioned into the shape of ornate miniature obelisks.
Lying on their sides a couple of yards apart, they were obviously the apparatus responsible for drawing the essence of
hell's citizenry here, for I felt their influence on my own dark
soul the closer I got.

Time to make a statement. Inverting each sword, I adjusted my grip to suit, dropped to one knee and put all my
strength into a simultaneous downward thrust. Both rocks
shattered into tiny fragments, releasing a blaze of amber and
green light, along with a piercing howl that made me suspect
they were somehow sentient. *Tough shit if they were.*

Only once that essential task was completed did I bother
to look beyond the hillock.

A desolate flatland yawned away on all sides, bordered
by mountains—dark and foreboding—to the north and

west. To the south and east, a molten sky fused into the horizon in shimmering waves, giving no indication as to how far this oven extended.

About a quarter of a mile in front of my position, an elaborate series of linked trenches and fortified bulwarks stretched off, left and right, manned by creatures I couldn't quite define...except for their predominant proclivity. That was one of open hostility.

But they were not my immediate concern. The five thousand shock troops much closer to home were, for that rabble was comprised of missing denizens of New Hell, with one or two interlopers from more exotic climbs thrown in. *So, the Blades are into inhuman trafficking? Another point of contention I'll have to remedy while I'm here.*

Casting my eye across the front column, I could see they were all armed to the teeth with strange serrated blades or gnarled cudgels, and hyped into the twilight zone on something that had them frothing at the mouth. Not that it would do them much good. None of them seemed capable of lifting such weapons for more than a minute or two without flagging, let alone wielding them for long enough to survive a battle.

They must be cannon fodder.

My hunch proved right. Obeying some unspoken command, the mob broke into a run. Shouting and screaming at the top of their lungs, they came right at me. *Is this supposed to slow me down? I think I'd better reinforce my last statement.*

Spinning both ninjaken, I reverted to a normal grip and leaped from the top of the hillock. Landing in a cloud of dust, I stamped forward and made a double pass in the air—inward, then out—across my body. The moment my gleaming blades came to a standstill on the return stroke, the entire charge collapsed into a tumbling mass of cloven flesh and fragmented bones that dissipated before they hit the ground.

Though pitifully scant, I channeled the sum of their remaining life-force back through the portal to where they belonged. *I'm sure the Undertaker will know what to do with what's left. If nothing else, he'll be able to increase his staff or boost the retinue at the Cirque du Freak. Not that...hello?*

A palpable shock ran through the ranks of my mystery hosts. *They probably didn't expect me to execute the whole damned lot of my* own *people. Suckers!* I decided to press that slight advantage. *Time to get blunt.*

Striding confidently out across the open ground, I slammed my swords into their back sheath and projected my voice mentally. "Who leads here? In particular, I'd like to know the cretin responsible for sending this ill-conceived warning: 'Intrude upon our sovereign affairs again, and you will face the wrath of the Blades of the Left-Hand Path.' Rather ironic, really, seeing as it's *you* who intruded upon Satan's sovereignty by poking your noses into his realm and stealing his subjects?"

A resounding silence met my rebuke.

Okay, I'll give them the benefit of the doubt. They might not comprehend the...? My recollection of the Blades' message induced a strange reaction from deep inside. Responding to that compulsion, I repeated the entire question, but reverted to their language—a language I had only ever heard once—to do it.

"*Min stakû aleh? El haûs, wê elhûd alnad atî set kô-me mesoôl* êl *serkhî her pfat'atâr ta-hadeê: 'Elmôh at fell janhîm rah e'ile,* âgus *cog to-gar nich set fêagk id set Ha'rthao id set Drig'vn Se-mol.' Neshîd er-hnêt, hel, seêl hedh indá* cog *areê elmêh at Shaiatâhn janhôme de kusâme coâg entî thêh ahî ahrnêm* âgus *tesslâh ahî el-nâha?* "

Where the fuck did that come from?

A rumbling challenge issued from the midst of the throng, easily carrying across the intervening gap, "And who are *you* that dares to speak the sacred tongue of the Al-Jinn?"

"The Jinn? I thought you lot were just a myth?" *So, they do understand Standard English.* "But, in reply to your question...I am Daemon Grim, Satan's Reaper of souls, guardian of all that is ungodly, and chief among those called Hell Hounds and Inquisitors. I ask again, who is it that speaks bravely while hidden away among a multitude?"

Movement throughout the lines massed opposite indicated my comments had struck a raw nerve. A low buzzing sound—part growl, part major chord—swelled in pitch, filling the stillness of the air with the promise of brutality fulfilled. The noise was joined by multiple sparking outbursts and miniature nebulas that swarmed and swirled like wheeling flocks of birds.

Look how they flow from one state to another. These Jinn must be shape shifters?

In amongst the seething horde, I caught glimpses of tusks and fangs, glowering orbs that pulsed like dying embers, and all manner of dark glittering swords, barbed chain flails and spiked clubs. My chest began to heave at the prospect of imminent battle.

*Now this...*this *is what I live for.*

I pushed further. "Do you feel no shame at remaining huddled like a sheep amongst your flock?"

"Why should I lower myself or walk into a possible trap when a score of other Blades march upon this location as we speak. No, you'll not bait us into acting rashly."

"Bait you? Why would I do that when your soldiers can sit safely behind your barricades?" Spreading my arms wide, I ambled forward as if enjoying an everyday stroll through the cemetery. "It's just *you* I'm interested in. Come, face me alone and we can settle this matter quickly...unless, of course, your army is led by a coward?"

My jibe did the trick. The background drone grew louder, and nightmarish apparitions leaped up from the fulgurous brume to glare at me, and howl in defiance. Their displeasure spurred my opponent to action, for as the crowd grew more boisterous, an eight-foot cyclopean horror detached itself from the press. Metamorphosing into a powerfully built, bearded troll wearing obsidian armor encrusted in gold, and possessing cruel spurs and curved horns that would put Aries to shame, he declared, "I am Nishôgh, Gauntlet of the Incendia Blade of Jahannam. You are about to..."

That was my cue. Letting the Bãlefire flow, I formed an additional blood-colored sheath around myself, and used its vivacity to alter my stature to match that of my opponent. Then I extended my arm toward him. *Gotcha!*

Nishôgh didn't realize what was coming, "...if you dare insinuate I am incapable —?"

From more than four hundred yards away, Nishôgh was yanked through the air like a lamb in the jaws of a lion. Less than two seconds later, I had the pleasure of feeling his throat between my fingers. Binding his shape so he couldn't shift into another form, I pulled him close, and snarled, "Hello, I don't believe we've been properly introduced? Let me help you understand what a Reaper actually does." Lifting him off the ground, I commenced the drain and felt the sinews of his neck brace against my grip.

It was quite a shock to experience the degree of incalescence radiating from Nishôgh's body. Fortunately, both Bãlefire and palladinium prevented that heat from becoming a problem. Unfortunately, the Gauntlet himself was no slouch, for he reacted instinctively with a double handed blow to the crook of my elbow and wrist that forced me to release him. By the time Nishôgh had gamboled to one side and regained his balance, the tip of his scimitar was already pointing at my jugular. Even so, something about his stance betrayed puzzlement, not anger. Refusing to get distracted by his odd behavior, I circled toward his weak side, drew my primary ninjatō, and stood ready.

Glancing across his shoulder, I saw that some within the Jinn ranks had reacted by breaking formation. Hooting and trumpeting, they hopped, skipped, or flew toward us, adopting all manner of hideous guises in gleeful anticipation of violence.

The pantomime didn't fool me. *I bet they're a distraction? It's the ones who've remained invisible I'll have to be especially wary of.*

Now I had a decision to make. *Bugger. Infernal security takes precedence over my own agenda. I'll have to end this fiasco quickly so I can make an orderly retreat toward the gate. As soon as I'm through, I'll get the Boss to dispatch Samael and the choir and we'll come back and hit them with everything we've got when they're least expecting it.* Peeved as I was by this development, one notion managed to brighten my day. *Who knows, Samael might have that unfortunate accident sooner, rather than later. . . Ah well, in for a penny, in for a...what's Nishôgh doing now?*

Even with backup on the way, the Gauntlet refrained from posturing or attacking further. In fact, the point of his sword dipped. "How is it you possess a tongue of the eternal flame within you?"

Nishôgh's statement caught me unawares.

"What did you say?"

Lowering his weapon completely, he edged toward me and reached out, tentatively. "This cannot be...?"

In response, I gathered my potential and searched his demeanor for the slightest sign of deception. Holding a killing blast at the ready, I waited, daring him to reveal his intent.

I sensed nothing except a keen desire to find answers.

This is getting weird...? His claw brushed lightly against my chest, taking the measure of my heartbeat. Without warning, the Bālefire empowering my core flared at his touch, as if recognizing a kindred spirit. Then it frittered away, taking the Phage with it.

I was stunned.

Evidently, I wasn't the only one. Recoiling, Nishôgh whirled to face his people, raised his fist, and bellowed, "*Kow-akîth* (Hold)!"

The charging mass of gargoyles hit an invisible brick wall and fell silent. Seeing discipline had been restored, the Gauntlet shouted for a second time. "*Jowtûn, alnad* îta (Jotûn, to me)."

Scanning the enemy for all I was worth, I tried my best to spot who Nishôgh had just signaled. And failed. Regardless, I didn't have to wait for long for my answer. A wisp of spoke curled up through a crack in the hard-baked soil not ten feet from where I was standing. Detaching from the ground, it coiled through the air and came to a stop right in front of us. Reality puckered, and an impressively endowed ogre appeared, clutching a finely wrought blade. He snapped to attention. "Gauntlet?"

"First Fist, I trust your shrewdness in this matter." Nishôgh hadn't stopped staring at me, "I fear my judgment is in error and we dare not proceed further until the truth has been determined. Test this dark warrior and tell me what you find."

The creature called Jotûn frowned and glared between his captain and me as if such a demand was unprecedented.

Slowly, reluctantly, he sheathed his saif, and approached me with the utmost caution. In a manner that mirrored his superior's movements, he then placed his talons against my sternum and fell still.

No sooner had he made full contact than he stumbled back in evident surprise. His eyes narrowed, studying my face, searching for secrets I didn't know existed. "Do we know you, fiery one?"

Fiery who? "Know me? What are you talking about?"

"You possess the Janīn within you. Were you once of Jahannam?"

"The Janīn?" *Jesus, I'm beginning to sound like an echo mic.*

"The revered flame that elevates the true people above all others...except for those of the heavenly host, of course. It is buried deep, deep within you. Nonetheless, it calls to us with a vengeance." Jotûn looked back toward his commander. "I lack your experience, yet I am certain of it. How is this possible?"

Nishôgh turned to face me once more. "Are there any others like you?"

I couldn't help but laugh. "You really are insane if you think I'd actually tell my enemies anything..." *Though come to think of it, I am unique. And the hole in my mind prevents me from remembering Jack Shit about my past...? My past!*

That thought reminded me of my recent discovery in Sentinel's Square and of the need to get back there as soon as possible. "I'm sorry, tender moment or not, I'm —"

"We are enemies no longer." Nishôgh brusquely cut in. "It is against our venerated tenets to raise arms against a brother. The error was ours. We did not realize distant kith existed in other Gates beyond those of Jahannam, and certainly not where humans reside..." He scrutinized me closely.

"You exhibit the facade of a mundane, but you are clearly not one of them. How do you stand it, living amongst such dregs?"

I really had no answer for that. "My task is to hunt them—not like them—and kill those who dare to transgress our laws. As to my appearance, I don't really care what I look like, so long as I can accomplish my purpose. Hell, I was without flesh or substance for the best part of a year at one stage. It made no difference to me."

"You see? Spoken like a hidden one." Nishôgh directed his comment toward his subordinate and ushered him closer, "Jotûn, send messengers to Shield Omniûs and her brigade. Tell her what has transpired here and that I would recommend a cessation of any further hostilities. The Jinn's sovereignty can be serviced by others less deserving of life. Until then..." Nishôgh spun back toward me, "would you care to dine with my fellow commanders at my pavilion? It is the least we can do before you journey home."

This is not *happening? A few minutes ago we were ready to tear each other limb from limb, and now he's inviting me for tea and crumpets?*

Then I remembered why else I'd made the effort to come here.

"Why not? As long as it's hot and spicy and screaming for mercy, I'll eat just about anything. It can't be any worse than the crap they dish up in Juxtapose."

Jotûn spluttered and expressed his mirth by baying like a hyena. More reserved, Nishôgh ground his tusks and hummed.

Seeing as how we were new best buddies, I thought I might also try my luck with a direct request. "Actually, there might be something you can do that would cement the bonds of friendship between us?"

I felt the weight of Nishôgh's gaze fall upon me. "And what might that be?"

Isolating the moment Pea, Choke, and Bean had harmonized their strange telepathic message within the sparring court at the Den, I replayed the entire incident aloud so the Gauntlet and his First Fist could experience the full effects themselves...

"Do not go gently into death..."

This time, however, instead of focusing on the words of the cipher, I concentrated on the image they invoked. Nishôgh and Jotûn didn't really need to know about specifics, but I did need their help as to location.

Sure enough, as the strange harmonies wove together and took hold, the plain about us faded into the background. Our outlook changed, so that now, it seemed as if we were hovering above a huge rent in the earth, a chasm of perpetual gloom haloed in shimmering mists and sparkling rainbows generated by the gargantuan volume of water spilling into the void below.

"...Only to squeeze...and prevent what's left from saving you."

As the song came to an end, I cut the link.

"The Gulf of Tears," Jotûn growled under his breath.

"You know this place?"

"We do. It is a sacrilegious blight on our lands. A zone of ill omen..."

Go figure. Where else would Chopin and Tesla send me?

"...and a beacon to all those apostates of the Right-Hand Path naïve enough to believe in miracles."

"Right-Hand Path? Miracles?" *I'm doing it again...*

"Yes. A major Soulstice approaches. We call it, the Ascendant, that one time in a hundred thousand cycles when the alignment of realms throughout all existence creates an astral resonance capable of piercing the veil between heaven and the lower planes. Those dedicated to the Right-Hand Path believe they can rise above their debasement and appeal directly to Ar-Rashid for mercy before the Last Day arrives."

"Really?" *So it's not just New Hell that's plagued with morons?*

"I'm afraid so. And there are more than you think. I'm surprised you don't have such a blight spreading its poison through your worlds?"

Chopin and Tesla...you sneaky sons of bitches. Bells pealed in my mind, and suddenly, a lot of disconnected things began to make sense. "Oh, we have our fair share of heretics, but all references to events likely to stir up sedition have been rigorously censored for millennia. Rebellions still occur, of course. Our citizens are damned, after all. My teams and I are there for those who persist in their disillusioned behavior. Needless to say, they don't last very long."

"Your kingdom must be remarkable indeed if you are able to control the masses so completely?" Nishôgh murmured, clearly impressed.

I decided it best not to burst his bubble. To divert his attention back toward my imminent mission, I reached out and placed my hand on his shoulder. "You mentioned earlier that those of the Janīn harbor no ill-will toward one another?"

Nishôgh flinched as I began to transfer energy back into him, then relaxed and bared his incisors as he recognized I was merely replacing his lost vitality...and more.

"You see?" he gloated, "Once again you follow the hidden principles of your heart. How odd that we should discover common ground under so strange a circumstance."

I seized my opening. "Indeed, I hope to use this occasion to foster better relations...with your assistance of course."

Catching the inflection in my voice, Nishôgh was eager to ask, "How so?"

"As I intimated, there was a secondary reason behind my visit here today. It concerns those heretics I mentioned. I have reason to believe a small group of them might have journeyed here to plant the seeds of further rebellion among the more unstable element of your society. From what you've just told me, those who worship the Right-Hand Path are just the kind of zealots they seek to recruit and manipulate. They need to be crushed. I wonder, could you tell me where the Gulf of Tears is, and how I can get there?"

It was encouraging to note Nishôgh gave my petition serious consideration. "The gulf is located within The Blaze, Haawiyah Gate. That's one level up from where we are now. As to *how* you'll get there...?" He whistled through his fangs. The sound reminded me of a broken pressure hose from a pneumatic drill, "Long lost brother or no, you are a stranger to our lands and our customs. The Shield will require that you be escorted at all times...at least until we know you can be trusted."

"Indeed, I would expect no less." Playing the initiative I had gained, I continued, "and in truth, I would welcome the company and the opportunity to discover more about the Janīn I possess. Perhaps we can discuss this further over that meal you promised?"

Nishôgh visibly brightened at the reminder. "Then come. Despite what first impressions you might have gained, we are a hospitable race to those deserving of respect. I'll introduce you to the rest of the Blade, and then I'll see what I can do about your appeal."

Chapter 13: Law of the Jungle

Since its establishment, Icepiccadilly Circus had become one of the major attractions throughout the many circles of hell, and not just because it was home to the underworld famous, Cirque du Freak.

Situated at the crossroads of four of Juxtapose's main thoroughfares connecting the boroughs of Westmonster and the Worst End, it was also the site of a major temporal conjunction, a scrambled tangle of different eras that had been thrown together in a frenzy of time-warping, mind-bending confusion. In the space of less than one half mile, it was possible for denizens to pass through pockets of Olde London Town in situations ranging from Roman settlements, right down to warped variations of the modern-day city itself, with everything in-between popping up at random.

While such disparity appealed to Nettesheim's adventurous spirit, that wasn't what had captivated his imagination. The mystic in him was drawn to the sheer volume and variety of arts and crafts on sale, for all of them had been shaped by the mutant hands of those misfits forming the circus' troupe. And their sophistication in such matters was breathtaking:

Iceflame candles, carved from the heart of the lava

caves of Upper Niflheim; tear leaves, as fragile as they were fleeting, pruned from the highest branches of Perdition's crystal weeping willows; Bumble Breeze, esoteric honey providers created by mixing the essence of Kigali fire opals with the zephyr's from Hades interior desert; bottled terrors, that when shaken like a snow globe, would induce transitory nightmares to freeze the soul until the last flake had stopped falling; life-sized and miniature representations of His Infernal Majesty's favorite rose, the Demonkracie, which legend told was originally produced from the still-beating heart of a phoenix; there were even droplets of cold sweat, captured at the moment of expression from the fevered brows of those experiencing the severest trepidation.

Nettesheim found himself at a makeshift stall constructed from upended trashcans, still overflowing with stinking refuse. Examining the items on offer, he noticed something he'd never seen before: a delicate clockwork masterpiece, called a cutterfly. Somehow, the toy had been fashioned from the blended strands of spider silk and razor wire, and looked like a misshapen cross between a praying mantis and a rose maple moth.

How do the malformed animate such marvels? From the resonance I'm getting, it feels as if they've somehow managed to tap into the third way without realizing it? Crazy, to think that such beauty can be found amongst such adversity. That observation brought forth an unexpected upwelling of emotion. "This is…*this* is why hell's principles must be defended and upheld, so that our inherent treasures can be nurtured and allowed to flourish."

The smell of human flesh, roasting over dung fires reminded Nettesheim he was famished. Breaking his reverie, he was drawn toward a line of food vendors. When he spotted one of them specialized in candies, his whole face lit up.

Treating himself to a mixed bag of snot-drops and earwax toffees, Nettesheim began meandering among the close-packed tents and lean-tos that made up the makeshift shantytown, otherwise known as, *Freakside*, and slowly made his way east, toward St Flames Park. To those looking on, he didn't seem to have a care in the world. Dressed in combat fatigues and sporting a number of fresh bruises, he appeared to be weaponless, and was obviously some form of hired thug or bodyguard enjoying a night out on the town. But such observers would be wrong in their assumption, for Nettesheim was far from relaxed…or off duty, come to that.

Only three hours previously, Nettesheim had concluded a deadly and grueling series of mental, physical and psychological tests. Tests so demanding and invasive, that he had been forced to call upon his centuries of experience and wisdom to beat the odds. But beat the odds he had, and now, he stood on the verge of becoming a full-fledged Hell Hound, *if* he successfully completed the final phase of selection: the hunt and capture of a category 'A' fugitive.

Though outwardly serene, he knew it was up to him to snare his prize—or in this case, prizes—and in that endeavor, he was certain of success, for his prey didn't realize they'd already been marked. How would they, when they believed that, for all the underworld, it was them doing the hunting?

Popping a sweet into his mouth, Nettesheim bit down and crunched on the morsel with evident delight before heading across the square toward a gathering of gypsy caravans parked in a lose knot around Anteros' fountain.

He lingered for a while, admiring the work that had gone into one of the most famous sculptures to be found, topside—as well as here in hell—for it represented the very epitome of what damnation meant: isolation.

Mistakenly known by almost everybody as Eros—the

god of love—the figure was, in fact, Eros' brother, Anteros. As the avenger of unrequited love, Anteros was a deity who constantly surveyed the multitudes passing below him for any signs of that one emotion that could never be tolerated… except, of course, for those privileged few who were wise enough to realize that even the closest of attachments would never be allowed to supersede their loyalty to Satan.

And so it should be, otherwise, what point eternal suffering? These fools have surrendered their every right to basic human needs and companionships. The sooner they're forced to realize that, the better.

Those sentiments reminded Nettesheim of the task at hand. Without any overt sign, he expanded his awareness and searched the surrounding mob for signs of pursuit.

Invisible to the naked eye, silent, and watchful, the Hell Hounds shadowed his every move from the edge of the rotunda, clearly intent on witnessing how their latest prospect would add to their fearsome reputation.

Closer in, two elusive and heavily armed assassins flitted from cover to cover, doing their best to remain inconspicuous within the bustling throng, and totally oblivious of their target's enhancements.

Nettesheim smiled, but that was as far as he would allow his satisfaction to show. His plan was working perfectly, and he wouldn't spoil things now by giving the game away. *Little do they appreciate the law of the jungle, where the hunter becomes the hunted at the drop of a hat? Speaking of which…?*

He scanned ahead and onto the opposite side of the river. *Ah, the perfect spot for a showdown. And fitting too, for it is a place synonymous to the aspirations of both sides.*

His strategy in place, Nettesheim set out with a fresh spring in his step, eager to put his new skills to use.

*

As adept as she was at dealing with would-be and actual assailants, Isabella Castile was having a hard time fighting off the advances of an endless parade of hawkers, peddlers and purveyors of every obscenity who insisted on forcing their wares upon her, whether she expressed an interest or not.

Offers and counteroffers rang out on every side.

"Armpit hair. Get yer lovely armpit hair. Tangled, free, braided and straight, we've got all colors and lengths available. Treat yerself to a full set fer only a tenner."

"Fart in a can. Flatulently fragrant, full flavored, and packed with calorie free pheromones. Omnivore, carnivore, herbivore; strained and unstrained. At half a blood bag, you'd be crazy to pass downwind of this chance to spoil your olfactory senses."

"Noses. Crunchy noses for sale. Take your pick of any fillin', deep fried and battered. Or try our double nostril blow-out. Startin' at only six diablos a box."

"Cruelty choker, dearie?" That from a wizened crone with the eyes and tongue of a toad. Holding a delicate, finely wrought chain between her fingers, festooned with human teeth and hummingbird skulls, she crooned, "just the thing to put around that pretty neck of yours, eh?"

*Oh, how I'd love to wrap something tighter around yours...*Isabella's hands twitched, though her bloodlust demanded more, much more. Instead, she had to content herself by scaring the hag away with a stone cold stare, frigid enough to freeze mercury.

Much less physical, it still did the trick.

Across the square, her partner, Charles Guiteau, was having a far easier time. Dressed in the plain outer garb of one of the Grey Friars, and with his cowl pulled forward, most people gave him a wide berth.

Isabella was grateful for small mercies, for the gap between her and Nettesheim had increased dramatically as she'd skirted the main marquee. Fortunately, her target had now stopped to consume the contents of a small bag of treats purchased only a minute previously, and at this moment, was admiring the fountain of Anteros.

Pushing and shoving for all she was worth, Isabella fought her way through a particularly dense cluster of revelers, only to watch her quarry abruptly set off toward the far side of Icepicaddilly Circus where the press was considerably thinner. *A thousand curses, I have got to start making headway.*

Reverting to the telepathic channel she shared with her partner, Isabella called, *Charles? Can you see him, heading toward the top end of Regret Street?*

Yes, don't worry, Guiteau replied, *he's a tall fellow and stands head and shoulders above everybody else who's out tonight. Just as well...hang on a tic.* It went quiet for a few seconds before Guiteau came back on the line. *Sorry, Nettesheim turned my way and I had to make it look as if I was offering devotions for a moment or two. He's off again now, and has stepped up the pace. From the look of it, he may be heading toward Saint Flames Park.*

The park?

Yes. If we can get out in front of him, it would be the perfect place for an ambush, especially at this time of night.

I agree. Isabella glanced from side to side. *But we can't afford to rush things and fall into a trap. This is Heinrich von Nettesheim we're talking about. We'll only get one chance for a clean kill, so we've got to get it right, first time. I'm going to take a little look to make sure we haven't picked up any tails. If the coast is clear, I'll catch up soon enough and we can make our move in tandem.*

Roger that.

You keep him in sight until I'm done. Just make sure you don't get spotted.

Will do, and don't worry. Isabella was treated to a brief flash of a laughing face. *I've got another clerical robe on under this one, and a Blue Suit's getup under that. There's no way he'll realize I'm on his tail. And don't forget, I'm quite adept at surprising people from behind. So, finish up soon, and haul ass sister.*

Ignoring that last vulgarity, Isabella cut the link and made a show of digging around in her purse for a while before removing a top-of-the-range Denizen Guileless mobile phone. After pretending to dial a number, she started to turn on the spot, all the time, gesticulating wildly as if enjoying an animated chat with a girlfriend. A master of her trade, Isabella managed to scour the faces of the crowd with the precision of an electron microscope.

Gremlins and bogglins abounded, as did harpies and griffins. Some folk possessed melted skin, mechanical embellishments or extra limbs. Others had perfectly natural heads or faces grafted to spiderlike bodies that sprayed foul-smelling ichor wherever they scuttled. Regardless, no matter how hard she tried, Isabella couldn't discern the slightest trace of surveillance.

Good, she thought to herself, *it's about time we had a stroke of luck in catching this bastard.* She relaxed a little and set off at a much faster pace. *He's tricky as hell, as evidenced by his escape from the Den of Iniquity. Gods, I imagined we'd lost him forever when he went inside that place. Why on earth he'd want to trust his luck on some harebrained scheme in there, hell knows. But it cost him. I'm betting his injuries are more extensive than they look...* Isabella smiled, and her features became clouded in menace. *Which will make things much easier for us when —?*

Hey, Isabella. Where are you? Guiteau's mental voice sounded anxious.

I've just entered Regret Street, why?

Get a move on. Nettesheim's just cut through an alley leading out onto Hearse Guards Road. If he sticks to the street, he'll have all sorts of last-second options, and we'll have to take the risk of getting much closer.

Cursing under her breath, Isabella broke into a flat-out run. Staying in character, she kept her phone pressed to her ear, and shouted, "I'm coming, dahling. Don't worry; your wardrobe will be fine. I'll be there as quickly as I can."

The urgent click of her heels suddenly turned to squelching as she passed into a temporal splinter wedged in medieval times. *Shit my best Christian Loubotamys.*

Kicking off her shoes, Isabella continued barefoot, and noted with satisfaction that the intervening department stores and apartment blocks didn't exist within this period, due to the vagaries of the time warp. Nettesheim was some four hundred yards ahead of her. Still relaxed, he seemed totally unaware he was being followed. *Perfect, we'll be on him before he reaches the end of the road.*

Fixing Guiteau's pattern in her mind's eye, she called, *where are you now?*

I'm in the park itself. It looks as if he might be heading toward Westmonster Bridge, so I want to be waiting at the bottom of Bird Rage Walk to cut him off.

Good thinking. I'm coming at full steam now, with my shields up, so he doesn't catch any stray emanations. Expect me in...?

The ether warped, and before she knew it, Isabella

found herself transposed into the Victorian era. Thick smog squeezed the life from the atmosphere, making the close-ranked buildings and dismal gas lamps almost nonexistent. *This is getting beyond a joke?*

The sound of metal scraping on stone nearby brought her to a complete standstill. Grumbling complaints—inaudible and heavy—oozed from the shadows, along with the overpowering stench of dried urine and stale sweat. Arm in arm, two vagrants staggered toward her, each waving a half-empty meth's bottle in their free hands.

Only at the last second did they spot the beautiful woman standing all alone, right in front of them in the gloom, whereupon they froze.

The bum to Isabella's right cackled, struggled to stand taller, and nudged his friend in the ribs. "Well, lookee 'ere, Harry," he slurred, exposing a crooked row of broken, stained teeth, "we've gorn and got us a —?"

He never finished his sentence. Nor did Harry get the opportunity to reply, for a heartbeat later, both hobos were face down on the cobbles, gasping and gurgling into a widening pool of ruby impotence.

Isabella, where the fuck are you? Guiteau's frustration was evident.

Sorry, I was delayed. She sent a stark image of what had just happened hurtling his way. *As you can see, I had to take action.*

Why now? Guiteau snarled. Isabella could tell his anger was directed as much toward himself as it was to the circumstances that had gotten in their way. He was getting desperate. *We're going to be too late to stop Nettesheim before he gets to the bridge. Do you want me to try and take him? I have rip-bullets?*

No, don't do that. He is beyond either of us when acting

alone...hang on a second. Composing herself, Isabella projected her senses along the far banks of the River Tombs. What she saw caused her to express a huge sigh of relief. *Try not to fret. We'll bide our time and follow him across. Lambsdeath is even more topsy-turvy that the Worst End, and still retains much of the damage caused by the lava tsunami and hellquakes of last year. If we're patient, I'm sure we'll get our chance before the night is through.*

Disgruntled resignation radiated back, indicating Guiteau would do as suggested.

Isabella looked to the dissipating remains of her would-be aggressors, and to herself, added, "And these dear boys have given me an idea."

*

Are you seein' this? Champ spluttered, his mental voice betraying the astonishment he so evidently felt.

Oh, we're seeing it alright, Yamato responded, his telepathic reply as soft as silk, *clear as day.*

They're goin' for it? Castile and Guiteau are actually allowin' themselves to be pulled in. When Nettesheim mentioned this job would be a walk in the park, I didn't realize he was bein' literal?

That's why he's allowed them to stay alive so long, Gemini postulated, *he knows they'll be easier to take and break.*

From their respective hideaways at Hearse Guards Palace and the Buried Treasury, Champ and Yamato only just managed to keep their thoughts shielded as they expressed their confusion in tandem. *What—What?*

Nettesheim of course, Gemini replied, as if the answer was obvious. *Remember? When I was chatting to him yesterday regarding what he'd be facing during the trials, he mentioned he wanted to end things with a bang by bagging two category 'A' prisoners instead of the usual one. I wondered at the time why he was so confident of success. Now I can see why.*

After a pregnant pause, indicating Gemini must be ruminating on the contents of that conversation, Yamato was forced to prod for further clarification. *And...?*

I've explained this to you both already? Gemini growled, the tone of her psychic overlay betraying her exasperation, *I knew you weren't listening properly. Grown men playing with their bloody knives like they were overstated dick substitutes for their dream—?*

Anyway?

Gemini bit her esoteric bottom lip. *Guiteau and Castile have been gunning for Nettesheim ever since he dared to help us escape the time traps back in Perish and Niflheim, yes? From what he intimated, the same tweaks the Undertaker applied to their profiles to increase their bloodlust also exacerbated their other base desires. In this case, they're pissed he dared interfere in their work—something nobody has ever managed to do before, by the way—and now, they're out for revenge. Plain and simple,*

How can you be so sure? Yamato didn't sound convinced.

Nettesheim told me. His mystic abilities have tipped him off to the fact that the more our deadly duo tries to fight against their compulsions, the stronger those impulses get.

Ah, so his windin' 'em up until they're fit to burst? Champ chuckled, *because irritated idiots make mistakes.*

Precisely. Gemini projected a feeling of appreciation toward the Hound's best tracker. *The trials proved how adept Nettesheim really is. He could have taken Guiteau and Castile, even before his elevation, but he understands there's more going on here than meets the eye. By stringing them along, Nettesheim hopes they'll become so frustrated, they'll inadvertently reveal more about what Chopin and Tesla have been up to...or where they might be.*

An admirable philosophy, Yamato conceded, *if somewhat naïve? Not five minutes ago we all witnessed how tactically aware Castile is. No matter how her cravings eat away at her resolve, I have a feeling we'll need to exercise caution. She remains ever wary and alert—?*

Maybe so, but Guiteau isn't. Gemini's punch line was perfectly timed. *I'm currently at the top of Little Ben and have eyes-on Guiteau as we speak. He's almost tripping over himself in his eagerness to engage Nettesheim, and to hell with the consequences. You know how finely attuned my empathic senses are. Castile's having a hard time reining him in.*

Where are our fledglings now in relation to you?

Nettesheim is two hundred yards away, and closing on me from the direction of Saint Flames Park. He'll be onto Westmonster Bridge in a couple of minutes. Guiteau is eighty to ninety feet behind him on the opposite side of the road, dressed as a deacon of the Fallen Saints. Castile looks to be closing on Guiteau, fast, though she's shed her coat...and her shoes too? Pity, I quite liked them.

Then we'd best get over to the east bank, and quickly. The tone of Yamato's orders became more commanding. *Champ, you take Jugular Underground Station. Gemini, you get your ass across to the junction of Lambsdeath Palace Road and Westmonster Bridge Road. I'll follow them in. We'll redeploy once we see which way Nettesheim is leading them...though I've got an idea where that might be. Remember, whatever happens, we are merely observers until the outcome is decided one way or another. When we go in, we go in hard, either to congratulate the latest addition to our pack, or to take down his killers. Understood?*

Yup.

Copy that.

As one, the highly trained team of predators moved off to take up their new positions, totally oblivious to the presence of Erra's foremost enforcer, the First of Seven, who had been studying their every move since the hunt began.

Chapter 14: The Gulf of Tears

I'd had to wait for the best part of a day for Shield Omniûs and her mighty host to arrive. While I'd initially chafed at such a delay, my frustrations had been mitigated, to some degree, by the drama of the occasion when they did, for the first time I'd noticed something might be occurring was when the horizon to the east had turned black.

That smudge had gradually distinguished itself into a thick line of advancing clouds. Low, dark, and Olympian in scope, they proved something of a contradiction, for the closer the weather front got, the more I was able to discern it brought no rain with it. Instead, a hurricane force storm had blasted great curtains of dust toward us at such speeds, that I'd been under no illusions that had anything else been moving out there, they wouldn't survive.

Then the tornados had appeared; churning, jumping, and writhing; vortices of such vehemence, that their passage scorched the earth and flensed the sky.

Those winds had died as abruptly as they'd started, and when they did, the massed ranks of the Blades of the Left-Hand Path stood revealed. Resplendent in ebony and gold, they'd waited silently. Disciplined, vital and masters of all they surveyed.

The Bãlefire had flared in salute as my heart leapt at the sight of them. And the reaction wasn't one way, either, for my ranging senses also drew a response. As the power of my gaze had swept across their lines, the ogres beat their chests and raised their fists high. A howling refrain followed that made me want to join in with a chorus of my own.

"They honor you," Nishôgh had explained, "for though I warned Omniûs of your presence, her troops can now sense for themselves the potency of the Janīn raging within you."

During the feasting that had followed, I'd been able to discover more about their civilization and way of life.

For one thing, the Al-Jinn were conscious of their sinful condition and of the need for bettering themselves. As such, they had become regimented as the years drifted by, with most members of their society either serving—or having served—in the military.

The army itself was well structured. Their equivalent of a lieutenant was called a *Palm*—the officer in charge of a troop strength unit—or as the Jinn preferred, a *Link*. The Palms reported to the *Fists*, company commanders under the oversight of the First Fist, their adjutant. The First Fist coordinated those companies—*Chains*—into one cohesive whole, and acted as second-in-command to the regimental colonel, their *Gauntlet*...or in this case, my new best friend, Nishôgh.

The proper name for an entire regiment was, a *Weld*. However, as the centuries passed and standards grew more stringent, the Welds became known by a term that exemplified what they were designed to do: *Blades*, for they would ruthlessly cut down invaders and anyone else that presented a threat to their way of life: an ideology that moved me to near raptures. Three Blades made up a brigade—*Scimitar*—under the banner of a *Shield*, a minor dignitary who also held the court rank of, baron—or in Omniûs' case—baroness.

After that it got a bit complicated, as the upper echelons of the Jinn's hierarchy were comprised of those who had shown bravery and merit in battle, the ability to lead efficiently, and had sufficient puissance to survive the heightened turbulence of greater Jahannam.

The realization they had courts and dukes, and even a king, had blown me away, for it revealed a level of erudition at odds to their openly aggressive nature toward strangers.

Most of this went over my head, though, for as I sat among them that evening—being made welcome and marveling at their strength and vitality—I'd felt more at home than I had, anywhere, for an age.

As fellow warriors, we'd drank and feasted and exaggerated our exploits late into the night—which didn't last long here—and I'd been introduced to a sparkling and rather intoxicating beverage called, *wyrmstongue.*

So potent were its ingredients that the first time I'd belched, I spouted real flames, just like a dragon. My surprise proved a source of great hilarity to my new comrades, who'd insisted I keep drinking until I'd experienced the more volatile reactions their insidious little brew could inspire. As I was sandwiched between Omniûs, Nishôgh, and several other Gauntlets at the time, I'd spent the rest of the festivities clenching my butt cheeks and praying to all that is unholy that I not sour the occasion—and the air—by committing a monumental internationhell faux pas.

I was glad to have made the effort, for come flame-up the following morning, Omniûs had given permission for my mission to continue unhindered. Even better, she had assigned First Fist Jotûn to accompany me, along with one of his Palms, Garôk, a feisty female Jinn (Jiniri) possessing a sharp mind and wit, and even sharper tongue.

No sooner had we prepared ourselves and checked our weapons, than we'd set off, out into the featureless plains of the Blaze. As we'd travelled, I'd spent those first hours making an effort to find out more about this strange new realm that kept itself so sequestered from anyone else.

The first thing I'd learned was that Jahannam was sentient; a living entity whose sole purpose was to ensure its subjects received the appropriate form of condemnation that was their due. And what Jahannam considered *appropriate*, made even the likes of Satan's Reaper wince in pained appreciation.

The lowest plane, Saqar, was reserved for the vilest and most reprehensible subjects: idolaters and hypocrites. Those cast into this level—or as the Jinn referred to them—Gates, were somehow linked together by red hot chains measuring seventy cubits in length. They were forced to wear clothes of burning pitch, and their faces were repeatedly set on fire. Of course, they were allowed to douse those flames, but had to use boiling water to do so, which then had to be ingested until their insides melted. No sooner had they regenerated, than the process would start all over again.

Above Saqar sat the binary Gate of Ladthâa and Sá-eer, in which the multidimensionhell rift had been located. As mentioned, this place was called *the Blaze*, and having walked that baked wasteland for hours on end, I could appreciate why. Apart from a withered form of bramble that seemed to thrive here, little else could. Enduring its heat was necessary, however, for we were journeying to the portal that would take us to the next circle: Haawiyâh. Known locally as, *the Abyss*, Haawiyâh was a world riven in two by a canyon deep and wide enough to swallow a small moon. A fitting tribute, if ever there was one, to the home of the Gulf of Tears.

I hadn't been able to find out much about the Gate beyond Haawiyâh, as both Jotûn and Garôk were loath to speak about a place that was held in reverential awe by their people. Named Hatamâh—that which breaks to pieces—was about all I could get out of them. And as neither of my guides volunteered further details, I'd decided not to press the issue.

Finally, the Jinn underworld rose to the blazing heights of Jaheêm and then Al-nâr, home of the king and his overlords, who ensured the subjects of Jahannam lived in a manner that not only supported the precepts of their living realm, but also fostered every opportunity for individuals to move onward and upward before the Last Day of judgment arrived.

It had made fascinating listening, and as we'd trekked across the endless leagues, I'd made mental notes of those areas where it might be possible to establish an official dialogue, and who we might trust with such a weighty responsibility.

I'd been struggling with that particular joy for the past three hours, and needless to say, had almost given up, for my thoughts were consumed by a rush of bad ideas and lost causes. Reluctantly, the blistering heat drew me back to the here and now, and the reality of my mission so far.

Ah shit!

No matter where I looked—up, down, left or right—the landscape was as bland and featureless as a disused sofa on a redneck's porch, and the prism of the air rippled under the relentless caress of invisible thermal fingers that seemed determined to worm their way in through the seals of my armor, just so they could leave their searing translucent signatures along the small of my back and crack of my ass.

The comfort of Nishôgh's pavilion seemed a distant fantasy sent to taunt me, and all too quickly, my mind reached out to wander the memories of that pleasant evening once again. *Ah yes, the dagger throwing contest. I was...?*

Some fool began tugging at my arm, spoiling my aim. "Reaper? C'mon little man, we're here."

"Eh?"

"Wake up, low pockets. I said we're here."

I blinked, and the simmering infertility of the Blaze came back to haunt me in all its radioactive splendor.

"Oh look," I remarked—dryly, of course, "we're still surrounded by sand that snaps like popcorn and...and what's that over there? Oh yeah, more nothing. Thanks a bunch, Garôk, I'll sweat all the better for knowing we're still in the middle of nowhere."

"What's the matter, Reaper?" Garôk retorted, "Afraid you'll singe the hair on your tiny balls?"

The First Palm had teased me mercilessly ever since I'd dropped my glamour and assumed my usual height. I still wasn't quite sure if this was a form of Jinn flirting or not, but I'd come to like her sense of humor. What's more, I knew if she ever met Gemini, they'd both get on like the proverbial house on fire. As such, I'd put up with her over familiarity with uncharacteristic patience.

"Despite what you think you understand about human anatomy from the measly bunch who served on your slave crews, I'll have you know my *physique* is heroically more spectacular than the wrinkled prunes and desiccated finger bananas you might have glimpsed so far."

Garôk removed a jeweled dagger from her belt and ran an impressive talon along the length of its blade, making it screech loudly. "Are you sure? Any time you want, all you have to do is say and I'll carry out a quick inspection, then use my Janbîya to make any *adjustments* you feel might be needed?"

Behind her, Jotûn's shoulders sagged, dejectedly, a gesture revealing his reluctant resignation to his subordinate's unruly behavior.

"Why thank you, First Palm," I replied, struggling to keep a straight face, "very kind. But I've become accustomed to the placement and proportions of my bits, and would prefer them to stay as they are."

She tsk'd loudly. "*Fenôm*! I could have done with a new set of center features on my favorite necklace —?"

"Okaaay." Fun as this little exchange was, I'd decided it had gone on long enough. "I thought you were trying to tell me something useful about our current location…?" I turned on the spot, "Wherever *here* is?"

The top of Garôk's lip curled back, revealing more of her ivory tusks. "Why, can't you detect anything peculiar about this place, Janīn bearer?"

Peculiar? I'd been so busy keeping score in our verbal table tennis match that I'd neglected to listen to the leadings of my natural inclinations. Coming to an abrupt stop, I cast my senses outward, and discerned the subtle background *hiss* present throughout all of the circles of the underverse. This one was definitely synced to Jahannam. *It's well hidden. Almost as if it's deliberately trying to conceal itself from the everyday perceptions of…of…? Like the Jinn themselves!*

Both ogres were watching my reaction closely. Playing along with their charade, I extended my hand and reverted to what I knew best. Alternative realm or not, this was still hell, and its ancient language would hold sway. "*Troh a'bitheó lasadh mi astig* (By the eternal flame within me), *bi comharr* (stand revealed)."

A loop of bright red light pulsed away from me, rampant with the essence of the Bãlefire. Where it passed, hoary flakes dropped from the facade of reality, exposing a sublayer beneath. In it, a small oasis bordered by tufted trees stood unveiled. Beyond those trees, an arch, fifty feet wide and more than three times that in height, stretched into the heavens.

I was momentarily lost for words, for while the bow's outer circumference looked to be made of a smooth, bronze-colored metal, its inside surface blazed with neon-bright stars and glowing nebulas shifting through the expanse of the cosmos.

The construct called to my soul somehow. *That is incredible. Such beauty and...?*

"Well done, Reaper," Jotûn enthused, "now we know you are truly of Jahannam, for these doors do not reveal themselves to just anyone."

If anything, I found the First Fist's comments slightly irritating. "Why couldn't we have teleported here in the first place and saved all that walking...and time?"

Jotûn appeared confused by my impatience. "This is Jahannam, Reaper. Jahannam determines who is worthy and when it wishes to bestow its gifts. It has taken until now to decide to disclose itself to you. Do you understand?"

Of course, the whole place is conscious "So you're saying such portals manifest at different times and in different places in answer to a need?"

"And if the aspirant is found worthy, yes."

Really? It's that aware? Unprecedented. I was flabbergasted. *Then why aren't the other latterday levels as responsive? And why would Jahannam respond to me when I've never been here? Or does it recognize Bãlefire in some way...?*

...Oh for fuck's sake, why does making a discovery always lead to a series of further questions?

Cogitating as I was, I obviously didn't respond straight away. Jotûn continued, "If you have finished seeking clarification, Reaper, you will find it necessary to refresh yourself before moving through the door. Other than stone and salt, there is little sustenance to be found in Haawiyâh. Come, join us."

He ushered me toward the oasis where I was gratified to recognize a number of date palms thrusting up from out of the middle of the foliage. It was easy to see why I had initially missed them, for they looked a lot like elongated pineapple plants. The palms themselves were crowned in razor sharp copper-blue leaves, and protected by sinewy bark that felt as hard as iron, yet was as flexible as bamboo. Clusters of dates grew from barblike fronds. Likewise adapted to extremes of the environment, the fruit was blessed with a tough outer membrane that reminded me of a scarab beetle's shell, and flesh that although juicy and black, tasted bitter beyond belief.

I noticed Jotûn and Garôk dipping their travel skins into the pool. Curious, I scooped up a handful of the lukewarm water and held it to my lips. Though pungent and possessing a definite alkaline tang, it was drinkable...barely. By the time I'd taken my fill, my companions were ready to go.

Jotûn led the way forward, and arranged us so that we stood in line within the width of the span. Employing the language of the Al-Jinn, he said, "*Wâ het Jowtûn, Hal Ûr*-mek *id set Insendûm Ha'rthâl id set Drig'vn Se-mol* (I am Jotûn, First Fist of the Incendia Blade of the Left-Hand Path). *Her kê La-dkthâa. El'ish Haâweghâ alnad* îta *ton* (This is Ladthâa. Open Haawiyâh to me now)."

What happened next reminded me of the effect you see in freshly poured carbonated drinks, except that in this case, the effervescent wash filtered downward from the top of the arch. Once the entire plane was filled with silver-gray exuberance, we stepped forward into the bubbles…and were someplace else.

I found it rather odd, for I'd felt nothing of the transition phenomenon usually experienced when jumping through hydraspace from one esophysical location to another. But reality quickly made up for it. Where Ladthâa was an oven, Haawiyâh could best be described as a giant pool table, covered in orange baize, devoid of any discernable features. If anything, it made this level look more desolate than where we'd just come from.

Please, no more French Foreign Legion crap…"Where to now?"

Jotûn jutted his chin toward a plume of mist in the far distance. "We need to go there, the moving mouth of the Abyss itself."

Motivated by the length of time it had taken to get here, I queried, "Can either of you fly, or do you need to assume an elemental form to negotiate such a distance quickly whilst retaining sensory integrity?"

"We usually prefer to travel as flame or smoke," Jotûn replied. "Failing that, aspects of the wind will suffice. However, when speed is a priority and we do not have to rely on the whim of Jahannam, we simply teleport. Why don't you do that now?"

"Because I want to catch the lie of the land before we get on site, and teleporting won't allow me to do that. If you have an aversion to taking to the air in physical form, don't worry. Neither of you can weigh more than five hundred pounds apiece, so I'll be able to carry both of you with ease."

"You can?" For a moment, I thought I might have impressed Garôk with my potential prowess. I should have known better. "But you're so small, and barely brawny enough to lift my sword?"

"Yeah," I shot back, grinning, "But as I mentioned earlier, my gonads are huge..." I used my hands to outline the shape of a basketball, "Gi-fucking-normous."

Before she had a chance to retort, I erected a protective sheath about us, then used my telekinesis to scoop them up and blasted us high into the sky. In doing so, I was immediately reminded of the dream sequence that accompanied the psychic cipher delivered by Chopin and Tesla's stooges, for the tabletop vista below yawned wide to reveal one of its two distinguishing features: a single river—devoid of tributaries—which forged toward us from the east.

The closer we got to the hazy cloud that Jotûn had indicated, the more that river narrowed, causing the waters within its constraining banks to surge and peak, as if boiled from below by the flames of Hades. Moisture laced the ether, brackish and rank, tainted from carrying the detritus of this foul plain over countless leagues.

Yes, but where there's moisture and humidity, there's...? Expanding my natural sight, I commenced an examination along the route of the watercourse in more detail for as far as the eye could see, eastward, but came up empty. *That's not right?*

Voicing my concerns aloud, I said, "I can't detect any signs of habitation or evidence that any civilization has ever lived here. Yet you say this Gate is overrun with heretics? Where are they?"

"Oh, they're here alright." Jotûn pointed toward our destination, looming rapidly now because of our speed, "but they tend to congregate within the Abyss. As you'll see, it's much more extensive that you realize when arriving here for the first time."

I immediately saw what he was alluding to. Beginning at a point directly beneath the vapor trail, a narrow couloir sloped into a bowl-shaped cenote mere yards from the edge of a sheer drop. Beyond that drop, a ravine extended to the west for several miles before widening out like the gaping jaws of a shark to form an immense canyon that stretched off toward the opposite horizon without any sign of diminishing."

"Screw me senseless…it's huge!"

"Yes," Jotûn growled, huskily, "not only do the head-waters of the arterial rush gouge a hole more than twenty leagues deep into Haawiyâh's heart, but the Abyss itself extends more than halfway around this world."

Garôk slapped me on the back and laughed, "Your balls don't seem so big now, do they?"

To say I was awestruck was an understatement. The sheer scope of what I was looking at refused to register and I completely forgot to breathe. "What caused this?"

"No one knows for sure," Jotûn murmured, his voice low and contemplative, "Shayātīn, perhaps, in a fit of rage at being cast from heaven? Jahannam, tearing itself apart in retribution for the conceit of its worst transgressors? Some believe it is a place of starfall, where angels spent themselves in battle, one against the other, before madness occluded all reason." He shrugged, and I could appreciate the depth of passion conveyed by that simple gesture, for I felt it too. "Whatever the convulsion that tore Haawiyâh in two, *this* is the result."

The First Fist's words and the emotions they evoked triggered memories I hadn't experienced for a while. Before I could prevent it, the flow of reality lost its authority over me, and an instant later, I found myself floating within a translucent fog as I returned to events from another time and place:

Something's changed…?

Struggling to break free of the brume, my stomach lurches. I pierce the clouds and majestic sunlight baptizes me in coronal radiance. Wind howls past my face and my insides heave again, but instead of puking, my perspective shifts and I somehow feel myself merge even deeper into the pages of a recurring and unwelcome episode of déjà vu.

I climb at a terrible rate, reckless of the consequence, but I care not, for I must answer the call of my true disposition: war. The thrill of imminent battle takes root in my heart. Nonetheless, I draw comfort from an object grasped tightly in my right hand. I glance to one side and see a huge red sword. It blazes with malice along the keen edges of its sunset sheen and encompasses me within a black and crimson aura that bonds the weapon to my flesh as it inures me against the terrible ascent.

My speed increases. Internal alarms trigger. As I scan the vicinity, something hurtles toward me across the vaulted sky and my sense of danger peaks, for it is plain this interloper would deny me my destiny. Instinctively, I stab out.

Glass chimes against glass and a shower of prismatic light and sparks glaze the heavens with glittering reflections of savage contradiction.

I clamp my hand around my adversary's sword wrist and squeeze as hard as I can. He returns the compliment, robbing us of momentum. Locked together, we tumble out of control, over and over. Vast ribbons of energy entwine us within a living tau field as we attempt to obliterate each other by sheer force of will alone.

Our exertions wreak terrible consequences, for we are evenly matched and parts of us are lost forever. Even so, we act instinctively, each determined to do whatever it takes to retain that spark of identity that will make the difference between life and extinction.

A terrible, soul destroying, epoch changing impact registers somewhere far, far away. We fade, and a suspended animation rush of impressions overwhelms us.

You will pay the penalty for your treachery.

No, I will not die; for I am willing to risk everything... see?

One spark dominates, subsuming the other within itself, but at a price.

I am adrift, bereft of...? No, there is a vessel in which I could take refuge...if I dare.

Conjunction. Metamorphosis.

A kernel of awareness remains, but it is a travesty of nature. Binate, it is overwhelmed and vacillates between light and dark.

Who am I? Who was I?

What am I? What was I?

Where do I belong?

Why can't I remember?

The weight of eons passing consumes me and antiquity swallows fragmented memories whole. But the lessons of history remain to taunt me, to remind me:

The terrible drop where I dare not release my grip...

Pain.

"Do you remember this?"

Skin, glowing white-hot from devastating friction...

Intense agony.

"Did you learn from your error?"

Primary flight feathers torn free by overwhelming drag...

Excruciating, prolonged torture.

"Has your resolve been tempered?"

A vast pit of malevolence rushing up from below...

Plunging.

"Have you cast off the dross?"

Light receding above...

Forever plummeting.

"And are you now stronger than before?"

A moment of clarity as the truth of my predicament finally registers.

I've pulled him too far. Now we will both suffer the same fate!

The endless spiral, down and down.

An overwhelming surge of heat as I pay the price...

Depravation.

The silence of eternal midnight...

Soul-crushing grief.

The inevitable pressure of all-consuming oblivion...

Anguish compounded a thousand-fold.

The familiarity of being taunted by the void—again.

"You are more than you appear to be...?"

Then why do I feel so emasculated?

"So much more. Do you not realize who you were...?"

Who I was?

"What you now are...?"

I am...I am changing?

"Better. Come, there is fresh vitality you must ingest if you wish to achieve permanent equilibrium. Fear not; let darkness show you the light—light—light..."

"Reaper?"

Other voices called to me, too remote to engender anything of consequence.

"Reaper? Janīn bearer, can you hear me?"

I must...wait a minute? Jotûn ?

"Daemon Grim. Lost brother found. Are you alright?"

My perceptions inverted and I felt the pull of actuality once more...along with Jotûn's grasp on my arm. At nearly eight-foot tall and built like a Minotaur, he was a strong lad.

The pain helped bring things back into focus. "Ow! What's with the Chinese burn?"

He released his grip and drifted free. "My apologies, but what in Iblīs name was that? Troubling images spilled from your mind that made us think the Last Day was about to overtake us."

"I'm the one who should be apologizing. I get—I don't know—flashbacks from time to time? They're like splinters of someone else's memories that push their way into my thoughts. As you've just witnessed, they can be a bit over-powering, so I'm sorry for any grief I've caused." Massaging the pins and needles from my bicep, I tried to keep things lighthearted, "Be thankful for small mercies though. Can you imagine what would have happened if I hadn't managed to keep us airborne?"

The incident must have left my new friends more shaken than they let on. For once, Garôk didn't seem to find the situation worthy of jest. Deciding it best to press on, I turned away to take in the scene below us and mark our progress, only to came up short. "Unholy shit!"

In all the commotion, no one had realized we had arrived at what could be construed as the source to our destination. And as sources went, it was mind-blowing.

In the dreamscape version of this place, the inlet to the Gulf of Tears was swallowed by a sinkhole that had cut its way like an aquatic blender through the intervening strata only thirty yards from the edge of a crag. Circling around to the other side, however, I could see there was so much more to the reality of the Gulf than my vision hadn't been able to capture.

For one thing, the far side of boiling cauldron had been fashioned in such a way that it channeled the mighty inundation of water toward the profile of a human face that had been rendered onto the inner aspect of the chasm, scant feet below the ridgeline. So skilled were the artisans who had managed this feat, that they had been able to ensure the torrent spewed forth from the eyes of that image in the ultimate expression of sorrow.

Look at that, it literally is a gulf of tears.

Even under the influence of gravity, the raging current fought itself as much as the shelves and boulders it bounced off on the way down. A roaring, hissing rebuke filled the air, completely at odds to the serenity induced by the sparkling veil of diamond-flecked spray now washing across my senses like the kiss of the ocean on a windy day.

I inhaled, and background reverberations filled my lungs with the harmonic of an overflowing resonance. A tune that called out to me from the froth filled depths, pitched at different frequencies due to the multitude of slender quartz spans crisscrossing the central bore. Though encrusted in a yellow-white residue, every single one of them had been worn smooth by the constant effusion from above.

Moving closer, certain details began to clarify. The weeping apostate sat at the top of a giant set of revolving cylindrical stones, set in a manner that reminded me of an immense Native American totem pole. Each segment had been engraved with what looked like the branches of a sallow tree, and every so often, those branches would align, forming a pulmonary network of veins through which stray rivulets from the outflow could find purchase. When they did, the drums would spin faster and cut their way deeper into the slowly yielding headland in a never-ending battle of attrition that would take millennia to resolve.

So that's what Jotûn meant when he referred to the moving mouth of the Abyss? Impressive.

On either side of the waterfall, masked effigies covered in the most intricate runes I had ever seen, had been carved into the granite bluffs in tiered ranks that marched away from us along the broadening avenue of the defile. Somehow, their creators had encapsulated the raw fabric of the rock face into all manner of bruised and scowling expressions, so that it seemed the entire valley had united in brooding defiance against our presence.

"No wonder adherents of the right-Hand Path are drawn here," I mumbled aloud, "this place stirs your deepest desires. Moves and inspires you. No matter where you are in hell, *that* cannot be tolerated."

Retrieving the clue that had led us here, I displayed it anew so my guides could refresh their memory:

"Do not go gently into death,

For the valley of the shadow serves naught but a cup,

Filled to the brim in bitter tears of salt.

This perfect condiment to preserve your pain,

Sprinkled liberally upon open wounds

By those whose black hearts practice darker arts.

Existing in shadow and flame,

That gulf betwixt the silent spaces of now and then

They reap a windfall harvest of fallen Souls.

Tendrils of smoke, as fragile as a sudden intake of breath

Curl like lazy fingers around your heart,

Only to squeeze...and prevent what's left from saving you."

While they considered its contents, I scanned the tangled web of bridges below us. As thin as stretched warm taffy, those nearer the top had succumbed to the antagonistic pummeling of the cataract and fallen away, either in whole or in part. Those further down were still intact and seemed reluctant to share their secrets. Springing like stalagmite arrows from the gloom, they spent themselves in hopeless flight, for they were soon swallowed by the overhanging brows of the opposing cliff face. And there were plenty of them.

"So, what do you think?" I asked.

"There!" Garôk pointed to a cave mouth incorporated into the open jaws of one of the tribal masks, three levels down and about four hundred yards from our position. "Can you see?"

There were thousands of masks, and each of them had been decorated in different patterns and pictographs. Even so, they still managed to create a sense of uniformity that made it hard to tell them apart when viewing them as a composite whole. It wasn't until I peered closer that I caught on to what Garôk had spotted, for while everything else in this precipitous shaft was coated in glistening silver-blue dewdrops, that particular entrance was bone dry. *Aha?*

"Do you think we ought to start there?" she suggested.

"It's as good as place as any, "I was already maneuvering us lower through the blanketing haze, "and we didn't come all this way not to try."

Chapter 15: Fool Me Once

Thoughts of imminent butchery and sharing the experience of a slow and lingering death aroused Isabella Castile more than she'd care to admit. But that was a little thing she liked to keep to herself, for while most people believed it was the Undertaker's invasive psychological tinkering that had led to her becoming a bloodthirsty sociopath, the truth was far more disturbing.

Isabella had always enjoyed exercising control over the lives of others, a hankering that had first flowered during the religious reforms of the fifteenth century. Indeed, Isabella was not only responsible for reorganizing the entire governmental system in Spain, reducing crime and unburdening the kingdom of enormous debt, she was the main instigator of the *Reconquista*, during which, Muslim and Jewish subjects of her country were forcibly converted to the Roman Catholic faith on pain of banishment, or—under the grand auspices of the Spanish Inquisition—far worse.

Of course, what she did publicly was governed by the social constrains of her time. In private, however, Isabella's growing appetites led to an increasing compulsion to torture and maim and prolong the suffering of those unfortunates dragged into custody on the flimsiest of evidence.

Revered by her nation, statues and monuments had been erected in her honor. But Satan knew better, of course, and once Isabella I Queen of Castile had been condemned to hell...?

The Undertaker's healing hands only brought my true nature to the fore and allowed it to flourish. And who am I to deny my soul's calling?

Making an effort to control the fluttering in her stomach, Isabella used the reflection provided by the only remaining window of an abandoned car to check her appearance one last time. *A final touch or two should do it...* She lingered to smudge lipstick across the side of her face, then ripped her blouse so that her bra was now exposed. Satisfied, she stepped out of the alley and onto the sidewalk to resume her journey.

It had taken all of Isabella's considerable skill and speed to get ahead of her quarry, but it had been well worth the expense of adrenaline and energy. She was now only two hundred and fifty yards in front of Heinrich von Nettesheim, and staggering in the same direction as him along Lambsdeath Palace Road, a route which bordered the grounds of the abandoned St Thomas' Hospital. And, if she could judge the pace well enough, he would be very close indeed when her assailant jumped out to *surprise* her.

While most denizens of hell wouldn't bat an eyelid at her dilemma, Nettesheim had one defining quality in her opinion: he was a gentleman, and would rue the day a damsel in distress was attacked in front of him without some form of intervention on his part.

Scoping the street ahead of her, Isabella called out to her accomplice on the intimate mode they shared when communicating telepathically mid-mission. *Charles, are you ready?*

As ready as I'll ever be, Guiteau's mind whispered. *I'm a hundred feet from where you are now. Do you see the only streetlamp still working in that vicinity, the one right outside the main gates to the hospital?*

Yes.

I'm there, waiting behind the first pillar you'll come to.

Did you knock out the rest of the lights?

A visage possessed of intense blue eyes hovered before her. *Of course. We want to make sure my misdeeds take place in full view of our mystic friend back there. And really, what better way to ensure we grab his attention?*

Very good. Isabella's mind was racing. *And what other issues have you factored into your preparations?*

I have taken the liberty of trying to account for the speed at which our hero will try to rescue you. As such, I've concealed two shotguns under the dumpster just inside the entrance, and have a further pair behind a low wall at the first signpost we'll reach. If he's slow off the mark, don't worry. I have a number of silenced pistols strapped to my body under the cloak, so we can roll around a bit and you can scream to make it look like you're putting up a good fight while we get ready to pop him.

And if he manages to catch us flat-footed?

No problem! Reach up behind my neck as if you're trying to tear my ears off.

Why?

I've placed your blade there in a special sheath. I know you don't like being without it while you're playing hare, so when he pulls me off you, step in and sever his spine. But please, do it quickly.

How thoughtful. Grateful or not, Isabella wouldn't let her gratitude distract her from the matter at hand. *What about outsiders?*

From what I've been able to ascertain, there are a few groups of drunken bums scattered throughout the campus and in the main building itself, but nothing we need care about. Those that might have presented a problem have already been dealt with and are on the way to Slab A for reassignment as we speak.

Good, it sounds as if you've secured the area quite well in the limited time we had available. Isabella adjusted her speed to compensate for the sound of Nettesheim's footsteps. *Now keep a lid on things, we're less than a minute away from you, and I don't want your excitement tipping our target off at the last second.*

So what, he's unarmed?

And he's a bloody mystic, imbecile. You can never be sure what tricks he'll have tucked away up his sleeve.

Don't worry about me, Guiteau countered, *just make sure you* do enough to appeal to his caveman instincts, or we'll have to go down all guns blazing anyway.

Oh, it won't come to that, Isabella retorted, *you'll see. Here I come...*

A solitary bulb flickered from a shattered lamp. Though pitifully dim, it still managed to cast a dismal cone onto the pavement and environs around the entrance to the derelict site. From her position only thirty feet away, Isabella could see a double chain-link gate hanging crookedly from broken hinges. Fastened at the midpoint by an old rusty lock, the frames creaked loudly in the still night air, as if announcing the danger that lay hidden within. For a moment, Isabella was reminded of an alien abduction scene from a film she'd watched several months ago, and had to suppress an involuntary shiver.

Playing to that movement, Isabella slowed her pace even more and allowed her torn blouse to swing free. For good affect, she started to sob. Then she leaned against the wall and made a point of limping heavily to one side, before whimpering, "Why me? I...I've never done anything to hurt anyone. I ke– I keep to myself and—ouch!" she stumbled, almost falling to her knees. "Doesn't anyone in this godforsaken place have the guts to help?"

In the distance, thunder rumbled. Behind her, the echo of approaching steps paused, only to resume an instant later at a much faster pace.

And he takes the bait. Now for an Oscar-winning performance.

Risking a quick glance behind, Isabella caught sight of an indistinct silhouette striding purposefully toward her. *Shit! He's only fifteen yards away.* Reacting as if she'd seen the specter of all her woes, she threw her hand to her face, and wailed, "No, not again. Why can't you just leave me alone?"

Isabella turned and broke into a floundering run, only to trip on a discarded tin can.

The shadows boiled, and a cloaked figure detached itself from cover. Isabella felt someone grab her by the hair, and a harsh voice snarled, "Not a night for bitches to be out on their own."

Before she could find her feet, Isabella was hauled backward and in through a gap between the gates. Once inside the darkened precincts of the hospital, the pressure eased slightly.

"Are you sure you don't want me to hold back?" Guiteau hissed.

"Of course I am," Isabella spat, "now get on with it...and for badness sake, make it look like you mean it."

Stars exploded behind her eyes.

"It's your funeral..."

*

As Nettesheim tracked Isabella Castile along Lambs-death Palace Road, his outward demeanor was one of self-absorbed distraction and carefree abandon. But like her, his current deportment was all for show, for while he appeared outwardly relaxed, his rarified senses swept the area about him like a diaphanous radar beam.

He noted with interest how the Hell Hounds had moved closer in anticipation of the finale. Yamato Takeru had taken up position close to the northern entrance of St Thomas' in Westmonster Bridge Road, while his partner, Champ Ferguson, lingered on the Embankment side of the hospital, adjacent to the river. His enhancements notwithstanding, it took Nettesheim some considerable effort to locate the Lady Gemini, hidden away as she was in the belfry of St Thomas' clock tower, overlooking the only remaining courtyard still standing.

Nettesheim didn't bother calling out or acknowledging their presence. His future brothers and sister were there to observe him in action, or witness his defeat if he had sorely underestimated the capabilities of his paired quarry.

Not that such an outcome was likely.

A superb tactician, Nettesheim could see only one street-light along this stretch of road actually worked. He comprehended immediately what Castile and Guiteau had done. *So, they've set the scene and highlighted the stage on which their play will be enacted?* That's *where they'll try to lure me in off the street.*

While there was still time, Nettesheim briefly reviewed what he knew of this area.

St Thomas' was ancient by the time a mixed group of Augustinian monks and nuns established their hospice back in

1215. Originally set up to provide shelter to the poor and sick, it's riddled with disused tunnels and bunkers, some of which are thought to extend back under the River Tombs and into the Worst End. Those passages were constructed in a forlorn attempt to avoid the effects of the Black Death that raged through Europe, topside, in the fourteenth century. All they did was provide the perfect breeding ground to break quarantine and spread further disease and infection. No wonder Satan thought to transpose the entire network into Juxtapose, it reminds us all of the insidious nature of his reach. Nowhere is safe from his influence. Though I'm betting Castile and Guiteau are grateful for that and have their escape route all prepared...if I let them get that far.

Nettesheim thought about the warren running under his feet and risked a little more power in order to scan the grounds more thoroughly.

One or two of the dilapidated buildings still retained a trace of the lustrous red brickwork and contrasting fascia cornicing that had made St Thomas' such a landmark in its heyday. Now, it was a graveyard of mostly empty shells and ramshackle ruins left open to the elements; a one-stop shop for vagrants, rodents, and other kinds of vermin who preferred to conduct their business well away from everyday folk. While Nettesheim couldn't discern any concealed openings, he knew they'd be there.

Hmmm. Most probably within the basement area, close to where the old furnaces are located. Hello...?

Up ahead, Castile was putting her heart and soul into the performance of an unlifetime. Her usually impeccable attire was torn and disheveled, her hair was a mess, and she stumbled—most proficiently in his opinion—in a clear effort designed to elicit sympathy, even calling out, "Doesn't anyone in this godforsaken place have the guts to help?"

Ignoring the rumble of thunder growling down from the heavily laden skies overhead, Nettesheim endeavored to capitalize on the scant illumination provided by his locale and summoned his potential in a gentle trickle that wouldn't arouse suspicion. A tiny fissure through into the third way formed at his fingertips. Probing inside that opening, he felt for his weapons and activated the wex that would bring them flying from their place of concealment within a pocket of hydraspace and into his hands in the blink of an eye.

In readiness for the confrontation, he'd forgone his usual preference for bow and arrow and long hunting knife, in favor of two gladius-style short swords. Blades that would afford greater flexibility in a close quarter battle environment, especially as these ethereally powered weapons could do much more than simply slice and dice.

He grinned, then swiftly wiped the smile from his face. *Now, now, Heinrich. The lady's plight is no laughing matter, and we wouldn't want her to think I was anything other than fully committed to her safety.*

As he quickened his pace, Castile caught sight of him and reacted as if startled by his *unexpected* presence, yelling, "No, not again. Why can't you just leave me alone?"

Oh, I say...That's very good. If I were your average Joe, I'd be completely taken in by the witch.

Castile drew level with the entrance to the hospital and somehow tripped over an item of refuse that skittered off toward the gutter. Movement erupted from the shadows as someone dressed in a black habit and cowl, cinched about the waist by a blood-red cord, capitalized on the distraction and grabbed Castile by the hair, only to begin hauling her toward the gates.

A gruff voice declared, "Not a night for bitches to be out on their own."

Charles Guiteau. I was wondering when he'd make his entrance. Nettesheim silently applauded his performance. *Said with feeling, and just the right amount of menace.*

Nettesheim slowed to a near stop. Glancing around the gatepost, he watched as Guiteau struck Castile a ringing blow to the side of the head that sent her sprawling toward an overturned dumpster.

Ouch! Nettesheim winced in genuine sympathy. *That must have hurt. I wonder how far he'd go if I let him?*

Playing with that idea, Nettesheim hesitated at the threshold and made a show of patting himself down, as if searching for weapons or something to protect himself with. Then he took his time, surveying his immediate vicinity.

Espying a broken pipe jutting from the wall, he worked it backward and forward until it came loose, then hefted it between his hands, testing its weight. *This will create the right impression. A valiant protagonist arms himself with what's available and rushes to the lady's defense against a sinister attacker, only to discover at the last moment they're both heavily armed with an arsenal that would put a small army to shame...I think not?*

Nettesheim's train of thought was disturbed by a great deal of shouting as the ruckus took on a new dimension. Castile had just kneed Guiteau in the groin to break free of his clutches, only to catch her toe on a nearby low wall. Landing in a heap on the far side, she rolled, and bumped into something that made a distinctive clanging noise. *Have they stashed weapons on the other side?*

Cursing, and groaning in authentic pain, Guiteau limped after his victim.

Watching the charade closely, Nettesheim edged through the meshing and erected a defensive screen about his physical form. On this occasion, he didn't mind that his invocation was tangible. They knew he was a mystic and would be expecting some form of a reaction. However, when he didn't immediately rush to her aid, Castile surged to her feet and made a break for the portico leading into the ruins of the main ward complex, screaming blue murder as she went and calling on the gods to provide a miracle to deliver her from calamity. After a moment's hesitation, Guiteau kept in character by setting off after her.

Nettesheim chuckled. "I'd better follow. If I don't start reacting more positively, they might suspect I'm onto them."

He advanced at a steady pace, wary of dead areas and blind corners, and alert for anything that looked out of the ordinary. By the time he'd entered the quadrangle, Castile and Guiteau were no longer in sight, though they'd though to ensure their continuing conflict was loud enough to leave him in no doubts as to their current location.

Main complex it is then. Considering his options, Nettesheim decided on a more direct approach. *It might be prudent to give them a show of my own.*

Conjuring an exact replica of himself—broken pipe and all—Nettesheim endowed it with a glowing green corona to make it more visible. Then he altered his perspective and engaged with its senses so he would be able to witness firsthand what it saw, felt and heard. Once prepared, he sent his double on its way to commence a methodical search of the foyer.

As soon as he stepped through the remains of the once proud doors, it was evident that time and neglect had taken their toll. The skeletons of high vaulted ceilings stretched away behind and on both sides of the welcome desk, and everything was covered in the accumulated detritus of rot and decay where the roof had fallen in a long, long time ago. Broken furniture and smashed floor tiles lay everywhere, covered in a green-white residue of moss and moldy bird shit.

Though it wasn't raining, water dripped from exposed rafters and ruptured tanks to form a collage of puddles across the floor, above which, marauding hell mosquitoes buzzed each other in lazy formations.

I see our taxes are being well spent? Despite the circumstances, Nettesheim had to struggle not to laugh. *Though I think the National Hellth Service is low on Satan's list of priorities this year?*

The atmosphere was thick and heavy. Long-established damp had eaten its way into the walls, creating a mottled gangrenous effect that caused bubbled plasterwork to hang in flaky patches in one place after another like melted skin. A notice board to one side of the reception teetered precariously on broken legs, the information it once displayed redundant now the paint had faded.

Not that Nettesheim needed much help; for no sooner had his simulacrum completed a cursory check of the layout than its presence was noted. A plaintive cry for help warbled out of the gloom, along the passage to his right. *My hosts are making this easy. They obviously want me to join them in the east wing? I'd best not disappoint them...*

With a miniscule exercise of power, Nettesheim cut the psychic link to his double and teleported into the lobby. Projecting his astral sight along the hallway where Castile and Guiteau lie in wait, he limited the strength of his scan to ensure they remained ignorant of his true capacity, and confirmed their precise coordinates. *Perfect, they've backed themselves into an abandoned office with only one exit.*

He blinked, and a single gladius appeared in his fist. Suitably equipped, Nettesheim sent his ethereal partner to scout ahead, but ensured to position it a few steps in front and on the far side of the corridor, where he was happy for it to announce its approach with an occasional lapse in concentration.

To him, every careless knock of the pipe or scuff of its boots sounded like a fatalistic fanfare to death. But his strategy worked like a charm.

Clack—Clack—Clack!

Three suppressed shots coughed into the night. Nettesheim's decoy slammed against the tiles and left a bloody trail in its wake as it slid slowly to the floor. Dark stains gradually spread across its neck and chest as it began to fade.

"That was easier than I expected?" Guiteau's relief sounded choked, "I thought this chap was supposed to be quite the soldier?"

"You can't relax yet," Castile warned, "check the residue to make sure it was him."

Hugging the wall on his side of the passage, Nettesheim crept toward the doorway, raised his sword high and went completely still.

The tip of a silenced barrel edged into view, trained squarely on Nettesheim's dissipating apparition. The rest of an automatic pistol quickly followed, along with the hand wielding it. This close, Nettesheim could see the extended finger was still white from the pressure being applied to the trigger. As the arm emerged, Nettesheim struck, and immediately jumped, tucked and gamboled high into the air, clearing the lintel with room to spare. Landing lightly on the far side of the entrance, Nettesheim repositioned himself for his next attack.

So keen was Nettesheim's blade that Guiteau didn't seem to register the loss of his limb until the weapon clattered to the linoleum. His gasp of shock quickly rose to a roar of outrage.

"Don't be a foo—?"

Too late. Ignoring Castile's admonition, Guiteau exploded from the office brandishing a second gun in his other hand. Firing blindly, he turned toward where he imagined his attacker would be standing, only to stiffen at the sword thrust that took him from behind. Skewered like a two hundred pound kebab, Guiteau was dragged backward and lifted into the air with ease.

"Bad move," Nettesheim's statement seemed blatantly obvious. "And by the way, I know all about your superlative regenerative powers. They won't save you today."

The mystic tensed his muscles, and delivered a venomous bolt of theurgy through his weapon, deep into Guiteau's core, incinerating the assassin on the spot. For the briefest moment, a skeleton hung by the ribs from a gleaming emerald blade, then it imploded, scattering ashy residue across Nettesheim's boots.

An expectant hush descended.

"You'll not find me so easy to take." Castile's voice flowed like silk from the darkened room; calm, calculating, predatory.

"I've no doubt about that, madam," Nettesheim replied, "nor would I presume to stab a lady in the back. Rest assured, you and I will fight..." Castile appeared in a blur of motion, knife in hand and eyes blazing, fueled by madness and hate. "...face to face?"

"A gentleman to the end," she crooned, "and blessed with a spine too. Such a shame we work for opposing factions."

If only you knew...

Professional enough not to labor the issue further, Nettesheim called his other gladius into play, dropped into a defensive crouch and made ready. A good thing too, for Castile burst toward him, greasing the air with inhuman speed and precision.

Fick mich!

Nettesheim's superior reflexes saved him, for as he pir-
ouetted to one side, he fell into an established pattern practiced over centuries of military service. Arresting his natural momentum, he stamped his foot down and twisted back
the other way, sweeping his sword high in a stunning riposte
that ran head-on into a follow-up assault sufficient to send a
numbing shockwave through his wrist. Capitalizing on his
bulk, Nettesheim used his opposite hand to deliver a devastating overhead strike, only to find himself on the receiving
end of another lightning-fast flurry.

My swords are too long. Circling his adversary, Nettesheim worked his arts to send a pulse of magic along each
blade. They trembled in his grasp, and in the space of several heartbeats, shortened to half their original length. *Much
better.*

Adjusting his style to suit, Nettesheim advanced anew,
and when Castile lashed out again, he was able to meet her
attack with a series of well-placed parries and counters of his
own. Back and forth they contested: high and low; spinning
and driving; beating and feinting; eluding and charging, in a
contest that braided the atmosphere in chiming sparks.

At some unspoken signal they disengaged and jumped
away from each other. Nettesheim seized the opportunity to
pay regard to his opponent's mettle. *My earlier assessment of
her was correct. She is formidable indeed. A shame her talent will go to waste.*

A cunning foe, Nettesheim hadn't yet resorted to his
enhancements. He commenced phasing them through in a
steady influx that boosted his speed, reactions and strength.
As the augmentation kicked in, a thrill rippled along his
spine. Castile must have realized something was happening,
for she slashed forward, unexpectedly. A wasted effort, for

her dirk only managed to slice the space where Nettesheim had been standing an instant before.

Slight though it was, Nettesheim registered a twinge of alarm in her eye, and decided to reward her concerns with a reverse fist to the back of the neck. His sense of satisfaction as the blow connected was immense.

Regardless, Castile was no slouch in a fight and used the force of the impact to roll away into space. Coming to her feet, she began a complex dance in which her knife wove to and fro in confusing patterns until she was close enough to initiate a driving charge, straight at Nettesheim's throat.

He ducked, redirecting her extended wrist across her body and up and over his own head. Now inside Castile's guard, Nettesheim stabbed upward into her exposed armpit and registered the tip of his dagger biting home. *Yes!*

To her credit, Castile didn't cry out. Blending to his thrust, she allowed herself to be hoisted into the air a little, where-upon, Nettesheim was startled to feel her foot press against the top of his thigh. Only when she back-flipped away from him did Nettesheim realize she had used his leg as a spring-board to free herself from his blade.

He couldn't help but nod in professional admiration. "Well played, madam. You are a worthy adversary."

Castile didn't acknowledge his praise. Calmly trans-ferring her dagger into her opposite hand, she came at him again.

Time took on a cadence all of its own. Nettesheim was fascinated to discover his supercharged acuity allowed him to anticipate Castile's next moves before they were enact-ed, simply by reading the play of her muscles, the shift in her posture, and every so often, by where she glanced as she spotted a potential opening.

Encouraged, he charged his reactions again, then stitched the air in a blur of motion that left Castile wide open to a killing stroke. When he struck, however, Nettesheim did so using the pommels of his knives.

Cartilage crunched and blood sprayed. Dropping her knife, Castile staggered backward clutching her nose. Pressing his advantage, Nettesheim followed, delivering a further bout of merciless blows that pummeled his rival senseless, before dumping her flat on her back. The sound of air whooshing from her lungs was just as loud as the rattle of metal skidding across the floor as Nettesheim kicked her discarded weapon away.

Dropping to one knee, Nettesheim switched grip so he could cross his blades beneath Castile's throat. She froze, and stared into his eyes without flinching.

Once again, Nettesheim found himself greatly impressed. *She begs for no quarter?* "From what I understand, you have been habituated to rebel by those who allow others to do their dirty work for them while remaining safe from the clutches of injustice. Though I don't confess to know how that must feel, I appreciate it must be rather disconcerting to be robbed of your sovereign will." He lowered his voice. "For what it's worth, I hope the Undertaker is inclined to take such circumstances into consideration when he deliberates your next reassignment...though I doubt it."

Leaning forward, he inhaled, and readied the necromantic blast that would decapitate the woman below him.

"Stay your hand!" Yamato materialized out of thin air beside him.

At either end of the corridor, Champ and Gemini took up their respective positions to ensure what was about to take place would continue undisturbed.

Easing back a little, Nettesheim expressed his confusion. "What, you want me to spare her after the mayhem she and her partner have caused?"

"No, I just need to ask the lady one or two things before sentence is carried out."

Nettesheim felt Castile relax. She positively beamed in Yamato's presence. "Prince Ōsu, a pleasure to meet you again...though I fear my joy will be all too brief."

"There is only one prince in hell, my lady." Yamato inclined his head and stooped down beside her. "But tell me. What do you *really* think of our little underworld?"

"I beg your pardon?"

The nature of the query had clearly caught her unprepared.

"It's a simple enough question," Yamato breezed on, as if he were chatting about an everyday occurrence, "I'd just like to know how *you*—Isabella Castile—feels about her condemnation? In as few words as possible, of course."

Nettesheim thought Castile might need a moment to formulate an appropriate response. He was mistaken, for the subject was obviously something dear to her heart. Almost immediately, she launched into her answer, "Though inundated with rabble, peasants and needless rules, I think it a wonderland of opportunity for those with the right motivation. A garden of cursed delights. A playground, for those wicked and depraved like me, who can indulge their dark hearts." She managed to shrug and make the action look graceful in spite of lying prone. "Why do you ask?"

Ignoring her last remark, Yamato continued, "And what of those who rebel? How do you view such ones?"

"I look on such ill-informed minions as fools who are only too ready to beat their heads against a wall for the sake of being stubborn. This is hell. We are here for all eternity.

What hope for revolution when such fantasy lies beyond their reach?"

"I see..."

A glimmer of comprehension flickered in Castile's eyes. "You refer, I'm sure, to the imbeciles who capitalized on my mental instability, and that of my former accomplice? Ha! Had you and yours not interfered in our affairs, Guiteau and I would have taken care of them eventually."

That's news? Nettesheim was astonished.

"Oh really?" Yamato was likewise taken aback.

"Yes. Really." Castile responded, firmly.

Yamato glanced toward Nettesheim himself. "Heinrich, how do you read her? I understand such skills are within your capabilities?"

"They are. A moment please..." After placing one of his daggers on the ground, Nettesheim pressed his free hand to Castile's forehead. Sorcerous potential gathered in the ether, granting him instant access to her thoughts. *Well I'll be...?* "She speaks truly."

"Of course I do," Castile snapped, "Damned I may be, but I am also a woman of quality."

Yamato hunkered closer. "Then perhaps you might like to tell us where these *imbeciles* are?"

The fire left Castile's eyes and her expression went blank. Nettesheim recognized the problem immediately. "Her conditioning has taken over. It's so deeply rooted, she will remain this way until she no longer makes any effort to recall what Chopin and Tesla might deem *harmful* as to their whereabouts or stratagem."

"A pity," Yamato stood back up, "though it might be a different story once we've broken their hold over her."

"Broken their hold? Yamato, that will require the Undertaker's assistance."

"Precisely." He gestured toward the still comatose prisoner, "If you'd be so kind as to send her on her way?"

"For Satan's sake, make up your —?"

Lulled into a false sense of security by the Lead Hound's behavior, Nettesheim had forgotten all about his other knife. But Castile hadn't. Before anyone could react, she scooped the blade up and plunged it deep into her own chest.

Straining to crane her neck, she gasped, "I vowed nobody would ever manage to take me alive. You see? I'm a woman of—of my wor..." Flopping back onto the floor, Castile went completely limp, then faded in a sizzling cloud of steam.

Retrieving his weapon, Nettesheim rose from his position and went to stand next to his new teammate. "Do you mind telling me what all this was about?"

"I'm just considering my options." Yamato turned away for a moment and whistled, drawing Champ and Gemini toward them. "You saw how competent she is without enhancements. Could you imagine what she might be like if her mind was unshackled?"

Nettesheim connected the dots. "You're going to offer her a job?"

"Possibly..." Yamato's demeanor became wistful. "Her obvious talents aside, there's something about her I find most appealing. And with the way things are going around here, well, I think we'll need all the help we can get. The decision isn't mine, but I'll certainly suggest it to Daemon." Then he sucked in through his teeth. "Of course, to do that, I need to be able to get hold of him."

Get hold of...? "Why, where is he? I haven't seen him since our chat, yesterday." Nettisheim glanced up and down the corridor. "In fact, I thought he'd be here to welcome me to the fold?"

"Usually, he would be. But he went through some damned portal on Reaper business. Evidently, the denizens of an obscure realm we've never heard of created a rift in the Sheol-space continuum that's been siphoning sin from our plane onto theirs. Satan knows why, exactly. Regardless, their intrusion appears to be the reason behind the latest spate of missing souls. Whatever they've been doing has screwed the reassignment process. Daemon's there now, sorting things out."

Privately, Nettesheim was horrified. Scheisse*! That's the last thing we need this close to the conjunction. I'd better report this as soon as I'm free.*

Chapter 16: Seraphinite

Graced with a lining speckled in black diamond flakes from the deepest mines of Diyu, the interior of the grotto was a tribute to monochromatic brilliance, an inverted bowl depicting the splendor of the faraway heavens in multifaceted phototropic glory.

A silver plinth had been erected in the center of the cavern, upon which, a pair of tiny but lustrous jewels had been positioned, side by side, in pride of place under a transparent dome. In the background, a metallic pyramid—slightly larger than a standard sized baseball—hummed quietly, its layered blue lights winking on and off in sequence, indicating it was busily engaged in whatever functions it had been designed to fulfill.

Two men loitered close by, their faces portraying the emotions each so evidently felt. While one was elated and clearly jubilant at the novelty of being in such close proximity to pure celestial power, the other was far more subdued.

Ever the scientist, Nikola Tesla's caution was well-founded. "Frédéric, I really don't think it's wise to transfer the seraphinite to our cache without conducting further tests."

"You underestimate yourself," Chopin replied, "I have every confidence in the integrity of your force fields. In any event, the cherub's wings will remain secured within the medusanite-lined case you made until the hour of reckoning is upon us."

"That's all well and good, but we're splicing sophisticated technology with the very essence of heaven and hell. A volatile mix at the best of times, let alone in the confined space we have available to us in the basement." Tesla shook his head, "No, the Sibitti's attentions reminded me how necessary it is to prepare for every eventuality. I won't relax until I've had a chance to measure how the different mediums react in close proximity..." *And perhaps added another layer to the shields as well?*

"A wise viewpoint, I suppose," Chopin conceded. Then his eyes widened. "Why don't we conduct a little test run now? Say, introduce one gem at a time so you can see for yourself how the presence of angelic tincture affects our current setup?"

At last, he's thinking objectively. "A splendid idea. I'll have a chance to recalibrate, and that way we avoid the risk of last minute mistakes. With everyone and his dog hunting for us, it wouldn't do for stray emissions to light up our hideaway like Lost Liberty's torch *this* close to the off."

"No it wouldn't, especially as the Reaper's been kind enough to take the bait."

That was news to Tesla. "He has? When?"

"According to my informant at the Bureau, he went through the portal sometime the day before yesterday. Chopin gestured to the vault around them. "I only found out myself an hour ago and was going to tell you after we'd finished here."

But...that's fantastic! So he won't... "So he won't be aware of just how severe Jahannam's temporal variances are, yet?"

"No." Chopin grinned and rubbed his hands with relish despite his obvious discomfort, "from Grim's perspective, time will be ticking along quite nicely. But here in the latter-day circles—and elsewhere, come to that—it'll..."

"...It'll be flying by so fast; it might as well migrate south for winter." Tesla completed his friend's sentence for him; "giving us the edge as the Soulstice manifests."

Not to be outdone, Chopin added the clincher, "Even better, Grim is bound to stumble into at least one of the vacant void chambers. Remember, the Gulf of Tears is riddled with them, so the odds are in our favor. And when he does, he'll be totally unprepared for the seraphinite induced high."

"Maybe so, but the effects will only be temporary."

"It won't matter. Any delay will be compounded by time dilation."

A stickler for details, Tesla refused to be swayed by premature victory celebrations. "And what happens if he enters a gallery already occupied by one of our suicidal heretic friends?"

Chopin shrugged. "Damned if I know, Nikola. And as long as it helps to slow him down, I don't really care. Soon, we'll be out of his reach...talking of which," he pointed at the gemstones on the dais, "are we going to run a little test, or not?"

*

Ever since Jotûn, Garôk and I had entered the cave system, I'd found it difficult to judge how long we'd been here. Not only were the fundamental laws of physics governing Haawiyâh at odds to the rest of Jahannam, but the initial entrance chamber had opened up into a warren of tunnels possessing a uniformity that was baffling.

By my estimation, we'd been working our way toward the heart of the Gulf's promontory for fifteen, maybe sixteen hours. And in all that time we hadn't seen a single soul. They were there, alright. We could hear their mournful descants above the constant drone of the wind. But no matter how far we trekked or how deep we penetrated, they never seemed to come any closer. My perceptions were oddly muted too, as if reluctant to intrude upon secrets that shouldn't be found, but Jotûn assured me that was probably a side-effect of being surrounded by the indomitable presence of the Abyss.

Light within the labyrinth was subdued, but bright enough to navigate by, thanks to an abundance of lambent crystals, threaded like veins through the substance of the many-hued strata. The thing was, there were no discernible gradients within those passages, and yet we were constantly working our way down, descending further and further toward the crypts we knew lie somewhere at the bottom. What's more, no matter which way the hallways kinked or turned, the breeze was always at our backs, something I took as a positive indication we were still on the right track.

As such, it hadn't bothered me when we'd negotiated the span of the Gulf on several different occasions, for every crossing had provided a welcome intermission from claustrophobic compression. Alas, such interludes were all too brief, and after each frenzied shower of stinging needles and acrobatic splash-back, the oppressive weight of countless tons of rock would swallow us whole, and we'd be lost to monotony once again.

Having been thus conditioned to the mind-numbing repetition of not much happening, it was with a sense of curious relief that we rounded the latest in a multitude of switchbacks, only to come up short. A four-way junction lay ahead—the first occasion we had seen such a thing—which had been fashioned in such a way that it created a small gallery. Recesses had been carved into the walls around it to form narrow benches, so that anyone who wanted to could observe the unfolding ritual taking place at the chamber's center.

An unconscious ogre had been suspended above the floor there in some arcane fashion. Dressed in a plain long white robe, he spiraled round and around on unseen eddies. I guessed he must be an acolyte of the Right-Hand Path, for his face bore a wealth of intricate tattoos, reminiscent of the totem masks outside, and a glyph of the All-Seeing Eye had been carved into the open palm of his right hand. Most mesmerizing of all, a hot ruby flame with a blue-white core cavorted across his forehead without burning his skin, and the longer we watched it dance, the more that flame waned.

"Do you know what's happening?" For some reason, I felt the need to speak softly.

Jotûn answered in a similar manner, "If memory serves correct, this aspirant's mind is being wiped of all the fears and transgressions accumulated during a lifetime of regret. Adherents of the Right-Hand Path think that once erased; their spirits will be refilled anew on the Last Day, a means by which salvation might be gained."

"You're serious?"

"No, but the heretics are."

"But that won't work, will it? No matter what version you end up in, this is eternal, inescapable, hell."

"I have no way of knowing. This will be the first Ascendant I have ever witnessed, and no records have been kept of events that took place the last time the veil between heaven and the lower realms thinned...or at least, that is what the king's council would have us all believe. Soon, the alignment of dimensions will create a—?"

"You might want to watch this?"

Though whispered, Garôk's warning cut the conversation dead. Glancing around, I could see that the tongue of fire on the comatose disciple's head was stuttering, as if on the verge of going out. The lower it got, the more a secondary resonance began to dominate. Eventually, the flame winked out. When it did, the force holding the ogre in place lost its purchase, and he curled slowly to the floor.

As he came to rest, his left hand flopped open and something rolled free, something that sparkled through all the colors of the rainbow with a sharpness that reminded me of sunlight on ice. *Seraphinite!*

The moment I saw it, my eyes filled with tears, my nose began to run, and for a heartbeat, my existence was consumed by a vision of overlapping vistas and contrasting vanities I'd experienced before. But once again, my actual perspective had changed:

Above me, celestial energies flared in a chaotic rush of polymorphic majesty that all but fried the heavens. Below, crimson expressions boiled within an unholy maelstrom of malevolence that threatened to shatter the very foundations of reality.

I stood upon a precipice, a dimorphic fulcrum upon which the future of creation itself might be decided.

So, it comes to this...at last.

A sense of self, hidden away for so very long, intruded.

Wait! How long has passed from...where...?

And then it was over, and the visualization shattered into myriad tinkling fragments that swept all comprehension away into a vortex of eclipsed sensibilities and otherworldly sensations. The tornado condensed, squeezing tighter and tighter, until the shards molded themselves like fresh neurons across the deepest contours of my mind.

Overhead, the heavens blazed bright in a chilling demonstration of omnipotent mastery. Below, the abyss beckoned, mocking the spectacle with an unrelenting display of might that left no doubt of its intentions. It hungered, and if left unchecked, such craving would consume everything that was pure and righteous.

I hovered between them both, sure once more; a living iris and conduit amidst opposing forces capable of eliminating all life in the universe.

Behold, the travesty of majesty runs to its inevitable completion. Who dares deny my destiny?

My challenge rang forth, and an equally vehement reply thundered across the expanse. Two blazing sword clashed. An anathema to each other's existence, light cancelled dark and evil the good. Galaxies trembled and stars were torn asunder. Arcane energies threaded the fabric of spacetime with plasmic eruptions. Insidious in nature, their potential swelled until the plane of reality fractured in a paroxysm of limitless might.

Engulfed within a storm of disparate rage, I-we felt the moment of death and rebirth, and became lost to the precipitous expanse that opened wide to swallow me-us whole.

Brother?

One moment I was-we were plummeting toward certain calamity; rending the earth in a cataclysmic upheaval that would forever destroy its substance; burning in frozen moments of eternity; screaming in rapture...

Brother, can you hear me?

...and the next I was but a single entity once more, aware that I was back inside the cave and that someone was shaking me.

Who?

Garôk's face loomed over me, "Brother, were you lost to another waking dream?"

"I'm afraid so. I seem to get an awful lot of them lately, and all triggered by different things." I nodded toward the iridescent jewel on the floor, "in this case, seraphinite, the tangible embodiment of an angel's quintessence."

"Angels?" Garôk appeared shocked by my statement.

As was Jotûn. "A son of God? Here? How?"

"That was going to be *my* next question to you, though one of your comments regarding the origins of the Abyss earlier today seems to carry more credence..." I gestured for a second time toward the gem, "in light of recent evidence? *That* can only come from one place."

"You speak of starfall?" Jotûn stared in disbelief at his comrade-at-arms, "so the legends must be true after all. How else could we explain...?" Then he kinked his head to one side. "Is somebody coming?"

A soft rustling sound, almost indistinguishable above the ambient background noise drew near. As one, we unsheathed our weapons and stepped closer together in order to better protect each other's backs. No sooner had we done so, than four ogres appeared, walking in single file from out of the corridor on the far side of the chamber. Noting our presence, they paused, and then carried on with their business as if we didn't exist.

Heretics.

Three were dressed in simple dark gray trousers and tunics, and wore rush sandals on their feet, while their companion—a female—was attired in a similar fashion to the unconscious disciple.

Two of the males bent to pluck their fellow worshipper from the floor, while the other stooped to retrieve the seraphinite. Having completed their task, the pair with the heavier burden shuffled off without a backward glance, while their friend approached the white-robed aspirant, bowed, and then transferred the gem into her outstretched hand.

The female took a moment to compose herself, then stepped into the center of the room. A brief flash—like a lightning bolt—dazzled everyone. By the time I could see clearly again, the new acolyte had already been transfixed, and was now hanging in midair with a vibrant ruby brand bobbing to and fro between her brows.

Out of the corner of one eye, I spotted the final ogre backing away from us. On impulse, I called out, "You there... wait!"

He seemed startled at being addressed directly, but did as he was told while keeping his gaze averted." My apologies, Great One," he murmured, "I did not mean to show disrespect."

Great One? "Disrespect? In what way?"

"It is not my place as one of the debased to share the presence of those better damned than I am, and especially one who possesses both eternal light and flame within. Nevertheless, once the ritual of cleansing has been started, the cycle cannot be interrupted without consequence, therefore I lingered only to fulfill my sacred duty."

"Then don't worry. I'm unaware of your customs and don't feel insulted. However, I would like to know why you called me, *Great One?*"

The apostate glanced up in surprise, caught himself, and dropped his head again. "You test me, yes? No matter. Our entire community felt your arrival, for it is clear you are a messenger, one who stands between both worlds. The opposing catalysts you carry within you sang to us the moment you entered Sanctuary." A look of hope broke like a wave upon his face. "Great One, are you here to lead us through the scourging embrace of the Shroud?"

"The Shroud?"

"Yes." He stepped forward, as eager as he was hesitant, "the silent expanse between what once was, and what will assuredly be?"

That phrase hit a nerve. *'...gulf betwixt the silent spaces of now and then...'*

It's part of the cipher Chopin and Tesla provided. But why? I considered for a moment some of the things I had learned since coming to Jahannam. *It doesn't make sense. If the separatists of the Right-Hand Path have stumbled on a way out of hell that might actually work, one that Chopin and Tesla have discovered, why would they draw my attention to it instead of just exploiting the unknown loophole? That pair have been waiting for decades for a chance like this, so it must involve something they don't like.*

I sniffed the air. The distinctive tang of seraphinite had been all but absorbed into the esoteric matrix draining the female disciple's psyche. *Hello?*

That roused my suspicions. Referring to her, I asked, "The process you seem so willing to undergo, is this part of the scourging? What actually happens to the memories and portions of her identity being removed?"

"What you see here is a preliminary requirement for the scourge. And as for her memories, they are sent to the only place in existence capable of destroying all trace of such offerings: Hatamâh, for only in that realm is there sufficient Wal to break things utterly.

"Wal? You mean dominion or might, correct?"

"That is correct."

"So, if I understand what you're saying, you hope to excise all trace of the sin accumulated during a lifetime—and unlifetime—of existence?"

"Exactly...but as you possess both light and flame, you must already know this?"

A cold hard shock ran through me. *What if this Hatamâh is somehow tied in to my past? I've had a hole in my mind for as long as I can remember?* Aloud, I asked the inevitable question. "Tell me, heretic. What must I do to journey there?"

"To Hatamâh? You are *Ayoôsh Nar-kûs*, a Fiery One, possessing both *El-elheêr Aûl* and Janīn. Only you can decide how to enter that which breaks to pieces. We mere mortals must assume a penitent position within the void and be willing to surrender our sanity."

"Reaper," Jotûn intervened, "remember, Hatamâh is sacred. For all that, this heretic speaks truthfully; the Janīn we bear is a tainted echo of that which once unified everything. If we are unwise to journey there, even the eternal flame will be subject to degradation. It would consume us."

"No it won't."

Jotûn and Garôk glared at me as if I'd lost my mind.

I continued, "You heard the acolyte. The Janīn *is* a corrupted form of God's Grace, and I have a special aspect of it flowing through my veins: the Bālefire. Gauntlet Nishôgh mentioned how the Blade seemed able to recognize it, empowering my soul, the moment you laid eyes on me. Even so, there's another facet to my nature that you've missed, one that sets me apart from just about anyone else in hell."

"And what's that?"

"The *El-elheêr Aûl*, this guy referred to, or as I would say, eternal flame. With it, I can do things like this..." Erecting my strongest shield, I stepped up to the floating disciple and clasped my hands around hers. The response was instantaneous. She tensed and her spine arched over, making it appear as if someone had just impaled her from behind. Then her eyes flared wide, and in a voice as absent and chill as midnight, she chanted:

"*I fall,*

Mocked by a sea of death's-head grins

Of those condemned, innocent and guilty alike.

I come to rest,

Amid a petrified forest of bleached white hands

That reach for the sky, pleading for mercy.

Lost,

I navigate the maze of a scarred and twisted mind

Only to be strangled by a philosophy of sweetest sin.

Choking,

I drown in a sea of crimson passion,

Tainted by poison and liquid vows of tainted possession.

Sinking,

I savor the sweetest embrace of pain and pleasure,

For they are served upon the dregs of my shattered dreams.

Burning,

I slumber upon a pillow of incendiary emotions laden by grief

Plumped upon a divan of carbonized dreams."

As the last line escaped her lips, she slumped forward and met my gaze. "I speak of you, World Walker. Do you see the solution to your conundrum hidden among the verse?"

As I considered the words of her song again, the answer presented itself. "I do."

"Then unlock the door. This is the time. This is the place."

The tones of her verbalization prompted some form of hidden impulse, for I responded with a set of phrases in the divine language which activated the seraphinite:

"*Zot ed yey ev-desh* (This is the time). *Zot ed yey ba-tesh* (This is the place). *Lan yey ga-del sha-veh tav eyl* (By the majesty invested in me), *a-zke eyl me-lah e-na yey he-met* (grant me access to the truth)."

The air turned to ice and a bubble of pristine glacial potential sprang away from me. As soon as it had expanded to fill all four corners of the gallery, it rebounded off the walls and contracted in a crackling rush that blotted out all comprehension and scooped everyone along with it.

A rapid series of incongruent sensations followed. Pulled in every direction at once, my ability to orient myself soon became scrambled. Thankfully, it wasn't long before I was slammed to the floor...only; I wasn't in the cave anymore.

Black skies thundered overhead in a supercell expanse that blotted out the heavens. Rain fell in loquacious waves, patterns that were as expressive as they were acidic, for the earth smoked under its relentless barrage.

From what I could ascertain, the ground itself was a crazy paving jumble of soil, rock, glass, vegetation and all manner of other things that had been melded together and allowed to coagulate under the orchestration of a deranged mind.

Two faces stared up at me from mass, forever frozen at the point of death. It was only at that moment that I realized the acolyte and her retainer had been fused into the substance of this strange new world like insects in amber. *How the fuck did —?*

"Brother, what have you done?" Jotûn spun on the spot, horrified by what he saw.

"I brought us where the elegy indicated we needed to be," I replied, unabashed by the bluntness of my actions, "welcome to Hatamâh."

Chapter 17: Decisions, Decisions

In the months since Marie-Anne Charlotte de Corday d'Armont—known simply as, the Lady Gemini—had become a Hell Hound, it had swiftly been established that she possessed tremendous resolve. When others gave way to panic, Gemini would remain an oasis of calm; a rock amidst the storm; someone able to make lightning-fast decisions at the drop of a hat to counter almost any obstacle she came across. Unless that obstacle happened to relate to preparing for important trips, that is. Then she would put Victor Hugo to shame, procrastinating as to what to pack, how much to pack and what to leave behind.

At least I don't have to strip naked to come to an eventual decision, she complained to herself, wryly, thinking of the author's patent remedy for dragging his feet, *though Hugo might have hit on a novel way to stave off indecision? I might give it a try?*

Two holdalls lay open on the bed before her. Still empty, they were surrounded by an archipelago of clothes, cleaning gear, weapons, various currencies, and all manner of other equipment, gathered together in their own neat piles.

I'll need to travel light during the first round of stops. In—make the offer—and out. It's the second circuit that will eat into my time. She glanced toward the little mound of specially prepared tokens, provided courtesy of the rat king of Perish. *And with the mementos from his majesty, that part of the negotiations should proceed much more smoothly. Brown-Tail's proposal to include a personal recommendation from their sovereign, expounding our credentials and trustworthiness, was a clever idea. I'm sure it won't take long for me to establish an expanding network of —?*

Ping!

An alarm sounded from her laptop.

Aha, hopefully that's the Fiendish Bureau of Investigation bringing me welcome news? Skipping lightly across to her desk, Gemini activated the computer and was greeted by the smiling hellcam image of Donna Nightshade. "Hi, Donna. Do you have anything for me?"

"Only that Chopin and Tesla remain as elusive as ever. Mind you, Bella's still wading through the latest intel reports, along with the most recent psychological profiles sent in by Doctor Livingstone, so, it'll be a matter of waiting to see if anything useful jumps out from all that raw data..." Donna's eyes glazed over for a moment and she glanced at something off screen. "Do you know when the worthy doctor will be finished with our three stooges?"

"Hard to say. I heard him chatting to Yamato after we got back from Nettesheim's final test last night and the inference seemed to point toward another day or two at least. The Doc can't rush for fear of reducing them to drooling imbeciles. Evidently, the more intact the gray matter, the more cohesive muscle memory will be on reanimation. If Livingstone can avoid reducing their temporal lobes to sludge, then the Undertaker will be able to get to work much more swiftly..." Gemini pondered some of the other factors affecting her mission. "Okay then, what about the Sibitti? Anything there to help me devise a sharper itinerary?"

"Well, they hit Dark Cairo recently, along with isolated pockets in Niflheim, Hades, Perdition and New Hell. Juxtapose will likely remain off their hit list because of the beating Daemon handed out the last time they dared to show their faces there..." To Gemini's mind, her intelligence counterpart appeared somewhat offhand. "The only place to escape their attention so far has been —"

"Perish!" Gemini couldn't help voicing her surprise.

"Precisely. Our Gallic friends seem to have lived a charmed unlife. You might have to ask Pascal what their secret is, we could all do with a large slice of that kind of luck."

"I agree. It's fortunate we've already flushed Chopin and Tesla out from that circle. Can you imagine, trying to run covert operations and having to look over your shoulder all the...?" Gemini's intuition started working overtime. "No way!" *Is that why the enforcers have ignored that part of the underworld?*

"What?"

"I've just had the damndest notion as to why Perish may have been spared." Gemini shook her head in denial. "Forget my rambling. It's too outlandish to even contemplate."

Donna's expression became serious. "Are you saying there's a link between Chopin and Tesla and the Sibitti?"

Fuck. I'm not that transparent am I? "It was just a thought, like I say..." *But you never know what a bit of digging might turn up?* "Even so, I might get on to Pascal and ask him to see what he thinks? It's his playground, and he might have local knowledge of stuff we don't know."

"You're busy, leave that to me." Before Gemini could argue, Donna cut the line and the screen went blank.

That was a little bit abrupt? Gemini shrugged, *I probably put her nose out of joint thinking of something she didn't.* She turned to face the contents of her closets and dressers once more, *Oh well, back to the serious business of...?*

Footsteps approached along the external corridor. Though light, their resonance filtered through the open door to her chambers. The most sensitive of all the Hounds, Gemini recognized the cadence of those steps. "Heinrich," she called out, "I don't suppose you'd care to join me on my whirlwind tour of the underverse?"

The newest addition to their ranks loped into her room without breaking stride and blocked the view of the passage outside. "I'd love to, but I have one or two personal matters to attend to that will take the best part of the week to finalize." He threw up his hands, apologetically, and waved a tablet he was carrying in her direction. "Sorry, my elevation *was* rather unexpected, and these loose ends need to be tied up—and quickly."

Gemini could see Nettesheim did look rather preoccupied and immediately felt sorry for imposing. "Anything I can help with?"

"Thank you, but no." The tall mystic smiled, warmly, "I have to do this in person, and I have to do it alone. I don't like unfinished business, and I'm determined to square things away promptly so I can devote myself properly to my new duties here. If all goes well, I'll be back sometime on Sinday. Sadly, you'll be long gone by then."

"Sinday you say? Well, that's no problem. I've allocated a two to three day window at each of the venues I need to visit, and New Hell is first on my list. I should be back across the water by the end of the weekend. We usually commandeer a suite at the Hexcaliber when we're over that way, so, if you do manage to get clear, you know where to find me. It'd be pleasant to have someone familiar with me as the Winter Soulstice rises."

"You know about the Soulstice, do you?" Nettesheim sounded surprised.

"Yes, I've followed the old ways for some time now. I think it'll be rather a nice little celebration, as its one of the few things denizens are allowed to get together for."

"Then I'll do my best to support you..." Nettesheim started backing into the hallway, "But no promises. Now, you'll have to excuse me, I really *do* need to get going."

As do I. After waving Nettesheim off, Gemini returned to the task that had eluded her all morning. *Where to start?*

Her gaze fell on the weapons and equipment pile:

"Knife rolls; assorted spare blades; travel orb; expandable shock baton; chameleon mesh; stun staff...ah, fuck it, I'll take the lot."

*

Deep and expansive, rich and profound, Erra's musings extended well beyond the extent of mortal minds to comprehend, for his imagination was utopian in scope. Self-absorbed, he sailed skies stripped of color; traversed continents laid waste; heaped vengeance and destruction on righteous and unrighteous alike; and best of all, he ravaged the latter-day levels of hell, cleansing them of the malady festering at their heart: incompetence.

One day, this vision will be a reality. I'll have legions of the damned dragged in chains before my throne and bathe in their blood as my auditors consume them, one by one. Erra took comfort in the emotions stirred by such convictions. *Now, if only the venerable saint would...?*

A steely thread of awareness intruded at the threshold of Erra's dreamscape. He peeped out to find the First of Seven waiting, proud, aloof, and as patient as ever. Premier among his weapons of fame, the First reeked of competence and death.

"You have something to report?" Erra's voice rumbled from the depths of his throne mound, setting the stones of Emeslam ringing and its chandeliers swinging.

"Excellent news, Sire. Grim can no longer be found within any of the infected realms governed by the upstart and his fallen choir."

"He can't?"

"No. An unforeseen emergency forced his hand, and Satan's Reaper was swift to respond to the threat...alone."

"Alone you say? Do we know where?"

"From what our own observations and informants tell us, one of the older circles. A place so remote, we ourselves have not yet graced it with an evaluation."

Will my commission ever end in this godforsaken pit? "That will occupy our time at a future date," Erra advised. "For now, I wish to know more of why you disturbed my meditations?"

"It's quite simple. Yamato Takeru now wields power in the Reaper's absence. He stretches his resources in a way that will work to our advantage."

Erra's mood darkened. "Yamato Takeru? Why do you rejoice? That creature dared to defy me. For all his sin, Takeru's spirit is indomitable, especially in its loyalty to Grim. He will be a most competent leader, do not underestimate him."

"We won't," the First seemed unperturbed by his god's admonition, "for he is not the focus of our attention. In line with Teresa's strategy, we have spread confusion far and wide as to our intentions, whilst keeping the true object of our desires under observation. Soon, circumstances will take a hand to ensure our target is isolated. It is then we will mount our attack."

At last. "And are you confident of success this time?"

"We are, for even if Grim returns in time to confront us, his aversion to harming those closest to him will act in our favor."

"And if he chooses to live up to his predatory nature?" Erra pressed.

"Then we will act in concert. Proficient as he is, it is doubtful Grim possesses the potency to withstand seven fighting unitedly as one. In the past, such has not been our way. Now, however, we possess the potential to destroy worlds, and Grim will feel the keen edge of our wrath."

"Then proceed. But ensure your brothers are on hand to deal with any backlash. No more random attacks until Grim has been crushed and lies broken at your feet."

The First bowed and folded from sight, leaving the god of plague and mayhem to contemplate his lot.

Erra's fingers drummed on the armrests of his divan, sending bone chips and teeth fragments flying. "Satan's system has proved nothing but a cesspit of frustration ever since we arrived. Once its guard dog is brought to heel, however, I think things may improve dramatically."

*

Turning his head slowly from side to side, Yamato's gaze roved across the stunning array of optical display units ranked in front of him. Some showed a series of contour lines ranging from blue through to red, while others were an amalgam of black, white and gray. Whatever their perspective, all portrayed a detailed view of a human cerebrum.

Behind him, Champ's snoring had reached new heights, drowning out the background hum of machinery and setting his teeth on edge. But ever since the new Chief Inquisitor had summoned the Lead Hound to his radiological diagnostics office to share a startling new discovery, Yamato had been expecting it. The only time Champ was ever interested in anything on a screen, was when the subject matter included, fucking, fighting or fishing—or cowboys and Indians—in that preferable order.

Doing his best to ignore the distraction, Yamato leaned closer to Livingstone, and murmured, "So what is it you need me to see?"

Livingstone stretched across the console, pressed a button, and set a three-dimensional image of one of the brains floating in the air. Pointing out two specific areas, he explained, "These are called the hippocampus and hypothalamus. They govern memory and autonomous functioning." Enlarging the space in between those two regions, Livingstone zoomed in on a dark spot, and continued, "Do you see that black area? It's necrotic, lacking even the residual sparking animus provided by hell's diabolical essence on reanimation. What's amazing is that whoever did this was able to obliterate the limbic nerve center without prejudice to overall cognizant functioning."

"Whatever you just said, it sounds complex and incredibly difficult to do?" Yamato hoped with all his heart the doctor would revert to plain English soon.

"It should be nigh on impossible." Livingstone tapped the side of his head. "Once any part of your gray matter is dead, that's it. It's dead. But watch what happens when I provide the appropriate stimulus..."

A bar graph at the bottom of the hologram registered the increase in power. Suddenly, the inanimate area of the brain blazed white, before sending out tendrils of golden energy.

Yamato sat back in his seat. "What was that?"

"*That*, my friend, is power. It's how Chopin and Tesla have been controlling their puppets so efficiently. Not only is each patient conditioned to obey a deep-seated set of behavioral responses, but this failsafe compulsion flares up every time the subject gets the urge to speak, or even think too deeply on the prohibited topic, whatever that might be. Ingenious, eh?"

"So who are we looking at?"

"This is a recording of the reactions displayed during the interrogation of Castor Bean. I've seen a similar result in all three agents. Stray where you shouldn't, and your questions induce a stroke-worthy surge of pressure that will all but fry their synapses. If they try to fight their habituation or you keep pressing them, it'll set off an embolism that will induce severe hemorrhaging, and a one-way trip to the Slab."

"And why did you bring this to my attention now?"

"Because there's something odd in the manner by which the behavioral modifications have been applied. From what I've been able to determine so far, the adaptations have been bonded to their personality at a molecular...no, at an esoteric level. If I'm right, we have a crisis brewing."

"Why? Just get the Undertaker to lobotomize them and stick them in the Cirque du Freak. Problem solved."

"That's just it, Yamato. I'm not only talking about our traitorous trio; I'm referring to others out there we don't know about. Even worse, what about Guiteau and Castile, denizens you have only recently dispatched? *They* are an entirely different level of shit.

Kuso! He's right. They're canny enough to hide their true temperament behind a façade of friendship. They could rampage within the Mortuary itself.

Thinking on his feet—or in this case, his ass —Yamato made an executive decision. "Doctor, send an urgent communiqué to the Undertaker, his eyes only. Tell him not to reactivate any part of either assassin until you've had a chance to examine this phenomenon further." Yamato beckoned the Inquisitor closer, "You'll find the Undertaker is a little *reticent* at receiving advice. Be friendly, but if he starts to throw a tantrum, you might like to remind him that—like it or not—*our* protocols take precedence, especially when there's a threat to Infernal Security. He is to put his staff on high alert and make damned sure his procedures can guarantee the quarantining and eradication of anything that might pose a danger. I'll ask Daemon to liaise with him with amended instructions on his return."

"I'll get onto that right away."

Livingstone turned to leave, but Yamato hadn't finished. "And David, once you've done that, get to work on Choke, Pea and Bean. In view of your revelation, they are now expendable..."

"They are?"

"Oh yes. I want you to take the top of their skulls off, if you have to. Dig, delve, poke and prod all you want. Do everything you can think of to find a solution...and fast.

Livingstone sighed. "It's going to be a busy day."

Yamato watched him go, and then leaned forward to cradle his head in his hands. *Daemon, where are you when we need you?*

Chapter 18: That Which Breaks to Pieces

Having arrived at Hatamâh by dubious means, I didn't want to piss off this sentient level of the underverse any more than I had to. Nevertheless, my needs were pressing, and so far, I'd done pretty well by pushing my luck.

Jotûn advised me it would be a good idea to try opening my mind to Jahannam and communicating directly with it, a suggestion I initially responded to with ill-concealed skepticism. I'd never been one for sharing my feelings, or sitting on a floor, cross-legged, om om-ing it for all I was worth and letting obscure vibrations take me where they would. The First Fist had merely shrugged, and assured me that letting Hatamâh assess my needs would save time in the long run. And as time was pressing, I decided to give it a go.

Selecting a flat area, situated on top of a small outcrop comprised of dull metamorphosed rock, I made myself comfortable and projected the events of the past year out across the barren plain, taking care to attune my thoughts to the distinctive resonance permeating the atmosphere.

Commencing with my earliest recollections, I began to apprise my role as Satan's Reaper; the privileges that went with such a position; my private life as a denizen of latterday hell; my struggle to come to terms with the lack of something

283

everybody else had: a past; the doubts and suspicions that plagued me because of that; and most of all, I went into great detail about the way things had changed over the past few years. To round things off, I also shared the latest clue, as sung by the female heretic that had led me to intrude on this, the Jinn's most sacred Gate.

It took a while, but as I finished, I had to admit, I was filled with a yearning sense of anticipation. The trouble was I didn't know what to expect, or how long I would have to wait. So, when nothing happened within the first several minutes, I started to feel like a complete dick.

I should have known it wouldn't...? My ears popped and a sense of increasing pressure built in the ether. *Did I speak too soon?*

Jotûn and Garôk had squatted down nearby. Turning to them, I murmured, "Guys, can you feel that?"

The shriek of rocks compressing together squealed up through the ground at my feet, drowning out their reply. Rising higher and higher, that sound built into a rumbling crescendo, making it impossible to stand upright.

"What the fuck is happening?" I yelled at the top of my lungs, "are we under attack, or is this some kind of reprisal for trespassing?"

Both ogres crawled toward me on their elbows and knees. "Fear not, Daemon Grim," I could only just make out what Jotûn was saying, "We are not in direct peril. You are merely experiencing the reality of Hatamâh. 'That which breaks to pieces' is living up to its name."

That which breaks...unholy shit!

A subliminal *snap* released all the pent-up kinetic energy at once, throwing us high into the air. Recovering quickly, I regained control, reached out to my companions and managed our descent with ease. Even so, the environment in which we landed was starkly different to what we had left behind.

The distant hills were still the same, but everything else appeared as disproportionate as they were familiar. By my reckoning, it looked as if a number of different locales down through the ages had been snatched away from London, top-side, and dumped here for my benefit.

To the west, the spire of Big Ben sprouted from wave battered cliffs. Seagulls nestled among the crenels of its lofty crown and squabbled for space along the length of its black iron hands, currently showing the time as three forty-five. Eastward, the MI6 building had been deposited on its side, right next to the dilapidated remains of the original Tower Bridge. Constructed centuries apart, both looked similarly weather-beaten and were covered in all manner of creeping vines and other invasive vegetation.

A pristine twentieth century "London Underground" sign canted precariously to one side, bowing in homage to the smattering of barnacle scarred, seaweed clad boulders, scattered like green-bearded islands in front of me. Slick with slime, every one of them had been stained brown by the murky, reed infested broth lapping gently at their roots.

It was an eerie sight, for the rocks formed a ravaged bou-levard leading toward the ruins of somewhere I knew well: the Victorian version of Paddington Tube Station.

Topside, latticed metal girders graced the curved roof of the Brunel-inspired edifice with a shining framework for all-over glazing. Here, only rusted shattered fragments of steel and glass remained, jutting upward like rigid fingers, forever locked in arthritic display.

Below them, fractured masonry and collapsed walls formed an assault course of sharp edges and treacherous cracks we would need to negotiate, if we wished to proceed further without testing the temperament of the crocodilian fiends peeping from beneath the surface of the swamp in all too many places at once.

By all that is cursed, what a marvelous place. This *is exactly what London could have looked like if it had been blitzkrieged into submission during World War Two. Sadly, our cockney friends were made of sterner stuff...* I studied the scene before me for a second time. *As am I. But where to go from here?*

My gaze came to rest of the immaculate subway sign again. To my mind, it seemed starkly out of place among such devastation. *Or is that the way it's supposed to look?* I began to laugh. *Could Jahannam be giving me a clue?*

Beside me, Garôk gnashed her tusks and scolded. "How do you find humor at a time like this? We have been abandoned to this freakish toilet of a place without recourse. Where are the deserts? Where is the blessed heat that helps us thrive?"

"They'll be back soon." I reached out to reassure her, and explained, "The reason I'm laughing is because I've only this moment realized what I have to do. The Gate has provided a source reference by which I can orient myself and navigate to where I need to go."

"What do you mean?"

"Well, if humans aren't quite sure of how to get someplace in London above, they'd hop on a train..." I nodded toward the half-submerged foundations before us, "but as we're in Hatamâh, we'll have to do with what's been provided. How are you both in water?"

"We are creatures of smoke and flame, Reaper," Jotûn interceded. Gesturing to the strange mixture of open sea and fens before us, he spat, "*that* is not our element of choice."

"Then don't worry, I'll keep your toes nice and dry."

Exercising my will, I created a tight sphere of energy about the three of us, then set us bobbing along the surface of the quagmire like a demented will-o'-the-wisp until I'd located the dark void marking the station's entrance. Altering trajectory, I strengthened the integrity of my shield and pressed us down into the mire.

It didn't take long for all sorts of inquisitive aquatic predators in all shapes and sizes to start checking us out. Not wanting to attract too much of the wrong attention, I raised my hand, extended my senses, and illuminated the way before us in ruddy brilliance.

That did the trick. A thousand and one shimmering wakes zigzagged away from us in panic, and in the space of a few heartbeats, we were all alone except for a waning web of lurid silver vortices.

True to memory, a white brick-lined tunnel snaked down into the unknown. We started to descend, and I quickly discovered Jahannam had simplified the underground network by providing only one main passage, at the end of which, a solitary platform awaited. I didn't mind in the least, for it removed the hassle of having to make choices, and I was a little distracted anyway, imagining what kind of conveyance would be provided to fit such a setting.

As before, the Gate was already anticipating my needs and adapting the environment to suit. Bubbles issued from grills spaced at regular intervals along the top and bottom of the walls. Rippling together, they grew in volume, forming a large pocket of air that billowed away from us in a shimmering halo toward the floor and ceiling.

A gurgling sound predominated, becoming more pronounced as the press of water decreased. In seconds, all three of us found ourselves standing on a bone-dry concourse that looked as if it had just been spring cleaned. Overhead, fluorescent strip lights flickered on. Reining back my power, I took the opportunity to look around.

Three yards in front of us, a pit containing an electrified track awaited my inspection. On the opposite side of that pit, adverts for all sorts of health drinks, hair products, and holiday destinations kept the eye entertained. In one poster, Lord Kitchener himself—whiskers a bristling—pointed directly at me, his slogan declaring how much my country still needed me. A point that struck home.

That's my problem. I don't know my country *of origin.* A spark of anger made me grimace, *and I won't rest until I find out who I truly am and why I was denied this knowledge in the first place.*

Down below, the rails began to hum. As the drone grew louder, the distinct skittering sound of metal vibrating distinguished itself, thrumming out from the blackness to our left. Peering into that tunnel, I discerned two amber coals glowing in the distance. Those coals drew closer, gradually clarifying into the lamps of a First Class Victorian carriage.

That thing must be from the eighteen sixties? On electric tracks? I grinned. *Who would have thought Hatamâh would be into steam punk?*

The coach pulled to a stop in front of us, glorious in burnished red walnut trim, gold paint and brass handles. A sign on the exterior panel said:

Everywhere 666

1st Class

Though the door was open, it was hard to distinguish what lay inside, for ambient light didn't seem to penetrate. Entering cautiously, we found a single occupant—an old style conductor—waiting patiently in the shadows by the first row of seats. Resplendent in a crisp navy-blue uniform and hat, starched white shirt and shiny shoes, he still managed to look distinctly inappropriate, for Hatamâh had elected to provide the simulacrum of a lilac-skinned Jinn ogre instead of a human being.

Even so, the Gate's ambassador was exceedingly polite. Tipping his cap, he addressed me directly. "And where will Sir be travelling to?"

"I'm sorry, I don't really know?" I turned toward Jotûn and Garôk, hoping they might have a suggestion, only to find them staring at me. Or more accurately, they were staring at the ogre and me in turn. Dismissing their unusual behavior; I asked our guide a direct question. "I'm not sure what I'm supposed to do. Are you allowed to help in any way?"

"Of course. Perhaps Sir would like to share the memories held by his blood? Or, if he feels reticent, he can explain the events that led him here, orally?"

Events that led...? The clue! "Of course, hang on a second." Concentrating, I brought the acolyte's song to mind and repeated it out loud:

"I fall,

Mocked by a sea of death's-head grins

Of those condemned, innocent and guilty alike.

I come to rest,

Amid a petrified forest of bleached white hands

That reach for the sky, pleading for mercy.

Lost,

I navigate the maze of a scarred and twisted mind

Only to be strangled by a philosophy of sweetest sin.

Choking,

I drown in a sea of crimson passion,

Tainted by poison and liquid vows of tainted possession.

Sinking,

I savor the sweetest embrace of pain and pleasure,

For they are served upon the dregs of my shattered dreams.

Burning,

I slumber upon a pillow of incendiary emotions laden by grief

Plumped upon a divan of carbonized dreams."

The conductor nodded appreciatively as I completed each line. I also noticed he didn't appear taxed in any way, giving me the impression he knew exactly what the disciple of the Right-Hand Path had meant all along.

When I'd finished, he stepped closer, and declared, "I'm thinking you'll all be needing safe passage to the Hall of Shattered Dreams. One moment..." he lifted the ticket machine slung about his neck and whirled the handle. Once—twice—three times.

A line of pink tokens appeared, jerking from the slot like the extended tongue of a petulant child. Tearing them free, he handed one to each of us. "There you go. Don't forget;

wait for the train to come to a standstill before exiting the carriage."

He saluted once more. "Good day," and disappeared in a flash of light and puff of purple smoke which rapidly condensed until it had been swallowed into the spout of a golden Aladdin-style lamp, partially hidden by one of the seat cushions.

Bloody hell, just like a gene? I almost verbalized my surprise, but managed to bite my lip at the last moment. *We're in Jahannam, dummy. What else would you expect in the land of the Al-Jinn? Hey, we're...?*

It was only at that moment that I realized we were moving, and that a fourfold cadence had been hurrying us along with absolutely no sense of motion. However, the inspector's departure had obviously initiated some form of braking sequence. Pneumatic pistons engaged and the clattering rhythm extended, drawing out into a decreasing tempo until it was clear we were slowing to a stop.

I frowned. "We can't be there already?"

Garôk's hand on my shoulder startled me. She giggled, sounding very much like a malfunctioning concrete mixer. "What? You get to converse with the living embodiment of our most sacred Gate as if it's an everyday occurrence; yet jump at a simple touch?" She shook her great head, "Little balls, you continue to amaze me, as does your lack of understanding. Of course we're here already. This is Hatamâh, remember? It breaks everything to pieces, including time. Once you gained Jahannam's approval, our journey was over before it even began."

A denizen of Juxtapose for millennia, I could grasp the theory behind paradoxical temporal conundrums with ease. That didn't make living with them any easier. Taking Garôk at her word, I grumbled, "I still don't know whether to be pleased or not. This was only supposed to be a two or three day mission. I dread to think how long has passed back home? In fact, you've given me an idea. It would be prudent for me to send a mess...?"

The doors clicked open and my thought was forgotten, for I stepped out into a wide expanse, filled with the ramblings of a demented mind that exemplified why people shouldn't abuse hallucinogenic drugs.

Here, overlaid limestone monoliths of varying heights had been arranged in such a way as to provide an undulating road, along which, 1930's gangsters in a white-walled Ford sedan were being pursued by a van full of cops. Gunfire was exchanged at regular intervals amid a backdrop of warbling two-tone sirens and squealing tires.

There, a luxuriant orchard, thick with fruit, basked under an azure sky. Except the trees were upside-down and their produce resembled human babies, plump and wriggling, hanging by their umbilical cords from the end of tentaclelike stigmas.

On my right, a waterfall spilled from the top of a red and white polka dot toadstool into a child's paddling pool, in which an armada of tiny pirate ships fought a pitched battle against flying saucers.

To my left, corpses littered a bloody battlefield pockmarked by steaming craters and mud filled trenches. A long whistle blast sounded, and soldiers on both sides broke off hostilities to enjoy a game of soccer while officers looked on, smoking pipes, twiddling mustaches, and enjoying afternoon tea and biscuits.

Jesus. If my mentality generated this, I'm *the one in need of medication.*

The train pulled away and trundled through a lone arch only a few yards wide that led nowhere. I wasn't in the least bit surprised when it didn't emerge from the other side. Nonetheless, I was rather put out when I spotted what lay beyond the occluding bulk of our carriage.

"Bugger me!" My jaw dropped, wide enough for cormorants to nest in.

Exclamations of alarm from behind me indicated Jotûn and Garôk had also caught sight of what I was looking at.

A crag towered above us: vertical, foreboding, and imposing. Shaped like the prow of a titanic icebreaker, its flanks were embellished with fantastical pinnacles, trellises and flying buttresses, adornments that swept the height and breadth of the bluff in a confusing rush of overlapping shapes and geometrical tracery.

But as mesmerizing as this sight was, it paled before the horn of the outcrop, for that had been sculpted as a gigantic figurehead depicting an angel's face.

Or it had, once.

At some unknown time in the distant past, the entire edifice had been split from top to bottom, as if rent in two by the stroke of a monstrous axe, exposing a cavernous chamber within that reminded me of the interior of a celestial temple. How I was so sure about that, I didn't know. In any event, this was no temple any mortal would ever set foot in.

Open to the sky, the main arcade was lined by a colonnade of intricately wrought pillars that stretched so far into the heavens, flocks of birds were able to soar and dip in gyroscopic swells throughout the framework of its eaves.

Behind those pillars, a library filled with ancient tomes lined the walls. Like everything else in this place, the repository had been designed to dwarf the senses, and stretched off, upward, in successive galleries until all detail was lost to imagination.

In the presence of such majesty, it was easy to imagine beings of power and antiquity, browsing volumes written in languages that no longer existed and contemplating long forgotten knowledge, while looking down from their lofty vantage point upon lesser creatures come to pay homage.

That part of the entrance porch situated closest to me was guarded by a lonely tree. Devoid of its canopy, it reminded me of an albino ash, for its boughs were smooth and free of the granulated pattern usually associated with bark. It stood out in stark contrast to everything else in my immediate vicinity, for there, the stones and paving slabs had somehow adopted the character of all the other rocks surrounding the exterior approaches. Bleak and gray, they pulsed with an icy rancor that exacerbated their dark and unforgiving aura. Testing the ether, it was a simple matter to discern how quickly the vitality of anyone entering the shrine unprepared, would by sucked from them in a matter of seconds.

Thankfully, the further in you went, the brighter it became, and as my gaze followed the line of the nave, it was treated to a subtle sunrise of color. Slate gave way to oyster; oyster to pearl, a precious mingling of the spectrum that shimmered through myriad hints and suggestions until it settled on palest ivory; ivory that blushed, infused to render its essence in luxuriant honeyed depths; depths that deepened to amber.

It was fascinating, witnessing how each tone blended to the other so effortlessly, for the overall effect only added to the atmosphere of all-pervading serenity.

In the far distance, a chantry as white as snow had been situated beneath a magnificent rose window, through which, a single shaft of solar brilliance streamed. Bathed in golden light, that altar blazed like the surface of the sun and created a focal point toward which I would have to work, for it called to my soul with a voice that was undeniably mine.

But how can that be? I...I've never been here before?

Whatever emotions were playing across my face must have been easy to read.

"Are you ready to do this?" Jotûn probed, his tenor betraying the awe he felt.

"As ready as I'll ever be," I replied, "though it seems a pointless question after what we've gone through to get here."

Jotûn cocked an eyebrow. "Neither Garôk or I have ever travelled to this Gate. Regardless, we know Hatamâh well. It will always remain steadfast to its purpose. I only wonder if it will break the illusion of who you think you are."

"I hope it does," I countered, "I'm sick of the pretenses I've had to live with over the centuries."

My ire prompted me forward, but I faltered after only a few steps. *Am I ready? Do I really want to know the truth? I've lived a life of privilege and power up until now. Will I lose all that?*

Now the moment had arrived, I found myself unexpectedly apprehensive as to the reality of my situation. *And will it tell me what I want to hear?*

Against my best intentions, a long suppressed fury commenced bubbling to the surface, fed by a storm of feelings at being kept in the dark for so long. Frustration, at being denied the knowledge of my origins or what I did before coming to hell; resentment that my own rank hadn't earned me the respect I deserved; bitterness at not being trusted enough to handle the truth; anger from the insult of being made to feel as inconsequential as all the other rabble in hell. *After all I've done and fought for...*

"No!" I declared aloud, as much for my benefit as to put Jahannam on notice, "Hatamâh mustn't tell me what I want to hear. But I do hope it reveals what I *need* to hear…No matter what the consequences."

"Then, if you're sure?" Jotûn stepped up beside me, as if forming an honor guard, and signaled to Garôk to do the same.

Clenching my fingers against the sweat now lining my palms, I swallowed down my rage, stilled my beating heart, sucked in a ragged breath, and growled, "Let's find out."

And with that, I stepped forward to claim my destiny.

Chapter 19: Dangerous Liaisons

"How someone hasn't said anything, I don't know. It's not as if..."

"...agree. If he had half a spine, she'd have been..."

"Well, I've demanded to see the bishop. If he doesn't do..."

Teresa Sánchez de Cepeda y Ahumada could hear the complaints of those standing nearby percolating away in the background, but she refused to let such bickering among the nuns spoil her meditation. "Lord, grant us simplicity of faith and a generosity of service that gives without counting cost. A life overflowing with..."

Rocking backward and forward on her knees, she was lost to a rhythm entirely of her own making, and timed her movements precisely to the passage of each bead through her fingertips. The cross decorating the end of the rosary dug into the flesh at the base of her thumb. Not that she could feel it, for her mantra now dominated her entire world.

"...everything, that we might show the power of love to a broken world, and share the truth from a living word. Lord, grant us simplicity of faith and a yearning to share it..."

Perspiration lined her brow. Her mumbling became urgent. The sound of those muttering from the sidelines grew more distant, as did the everyday noises of others sharing communion in this quaint little chapel situated next to the main monastery. Those aches and pains associated with sitting in one position for too long drained from cramped muscles, and as her perspective shifted, a bright light illuminated her face; from within or without Teresa didn't know. But she could guess. *It's happening again.*

In her mind's eye, Teresa could clearly see the smile spreading across her own lips as the vision took hold. Neither did she miss the disapproving scowls of those looking on. Teresa didn't care. Once again, she was experiencing a sense of stepping back out of herself. A superior vantage point from where she was able to watch her bowed form grow smaller as she sailed up through the roof of the chantry, high into the wide open expanse of the moon-filled night air, into the clouds...and beyond.

Blinding brilliance overwhelmed, and then gradually diminished about her. When it had passed, Teresa was able to discern she was someplace else, travelling an unseen road through milk white fields so translucent, it was impossible to see where the long grass ended and the path began.

Turning on the spot, Teresa couldn't distinguish the sun in the sky or any other direct form of illumination. Yet light persisted, pervading the environment with a surety that conveyed the impression that even the molecules of the most insignificant things were meant to shine here.

Tears blurred that image into one less achingly beautiful, but more sublime.

A familiar voice—soft, soothing, warm and inviting—warbled all around her, expressed from multiple places simultaneously. "You see it, don't you?"

"Is this heaven?"

"Almost, but not quite. These are the Fields of Tranquility surrounding the borders of Zion itself. The gates are not too far ahead. You'll see them soon, if you have the fortitude to withstand unadulterated rapture, that is."

Teresa found it difficult to speak. Her breath caught in her throat, and a thrill—sharp and clear—made the hairs on her arms and neck stand on end. "The...then I am privileged beyond compare."

"Why do you think that is?"

"Because I am devout?"

"That you are," the voice replied. Its source converged and deepened, solidifying to take on a more tangible form. "As are so many others. What makes *you* so special, do you think, that you are allowed to see such things and live?"

"Is it because I have an awareness of the true nature of sin and have striven to remain chaste in the face of temptation?"

"Maybe so, maybe not. We shall soon see. It is my function to test those who would dare such lofty aspirations in their endeavors to achieve a union with God."

Then you *are* and angel and not some figment of my imagination as others think?"

"You have doubts?" The gentle voice grew abruptly serious.

"Never. I was merely expressing the natural suspicions that beset all imperfect human creatures who stand alone in their convictions..." Teresa turned on her heels to better appreciate what she was now seeing, "and having witnessed such wonders firsthand, I know my faith can never be shaken."

An apparition manifested before her, haloed in a nimbus of refulgent flame; beautiful, serene, and altogether deadly. "Then you need not fear. I am happy to be here to fulfill the role for which I was sent," then more quietly, he added, "As are all God's servants."

Teresa was rendered mute. *As am I.*

Even so, the angel seemed capable of hearing her thoughts. "Then I ask you again, why are you capable of elevating your perceptions when so many others fail?"

"I...I don't know."

"Spoken with humility. I would expect no less."

Teresa glowed at the commendation. The angel continued, "In short, you are able to achieve communion with God because of the potential within you."

"Potential?"

"Yes. You are willing to make sacrifices; to suffer for righteousness sake."

"Suffer?" Teresa couldn't help her outburst.

"Of course, child. Was not the Lord Jesus Christ led into the wilderness for forty days and forty nights to be tempted by the devil? Forty days without food or drink or shelter, in a willing demonstration of his eagerness to prove Satan a liar. And are you not willing to do the same, to suffer any indignation to extol God's virtues?"

I must be strong. "Yes. Yes I am."

"Then prove it. Put aside your doubt. Ignore the spiteful accusation of narrow-minded bigots who say they love God, only to deny him by their conduct. Let your deeds attest as to your worthiness of the knowledge granted you."

"How?"

"You'll know when the time comes. Be strong, remember the apostle James who told us, 'faith without works is dead.' Prove yourself true."

"Gladly." Teresa felt her heart swell so much she thought it might burst. "But how will I...?"

All too soon, she felt herself slipping away. The ether dimmed as it solidified about her, reasserting the mundane and bringing with it the sting of continued accusations, half-heard above the song of those priests offering matins.

"...not right, I tell you. Who does she think she is, this mere slip of a girl? She's not fooling anyone by..."

"...must be unnatural. Did you see the way her face revealed...?"

"Well she doesn't fool me. She's in league with the devil. It's only a matter of time..."

Fools, Teresa thought to herself. *They don't understand the extent of my commitment. I may be a frail and sickly young woman, but my convictions have allowed me to attain the highest form of devotion. And once I prove to the angel I am willing to suffer –*

Teresa came fully awake with a jolt.

Drenched in sweat, her sheets had stuck to her flesh and twisted about her in a python's embrace, constricting her breathing until she'd been forced from the nightmare of past mistakes, prematurely.

She sat up and stared about the darkened chamber that had been her home for the past several months. "That was the day I began inflicting grievous harm upon myself, imagining I was proving my love for God." A self-depreciating smirk creased her delicate features. "So bright. So very beautiful. Did not the apostle Paul warn us that Lucifer could change himself into an angel of light? Caught by my own vanity, I was led like a lamb to my own spiritual slaughter."

Sighing, Teresa swung her feet out of bed and tip-toed across to the other side of the room to where her host had been kind enough to install a small kitchenette. Opening a modern-day fridge, she eyed the contents dubiously before selecting a carton of earwig juice. Of all the things she missed most about her former life; freshly squeezed oranges were high on the list, for the monastery at Ávila had been blessed with abundant orchards. Cracking the twist-lid, Teresa took several long disgusting gulps and smacked her lips in revulsion.

"Still, what's happened has happened. At least I'm now in a position to repay the arch deceiver in kind. My infection runs rampant. Denied the expression of their most basic human needs, denizens are becoming desperate and determined to claw some form of compensation back from the ashes of their lives, no matter what the cost. And so what if the majority fall to slaughter at Erra's hand? Is not any sacrifice worth the souls of those few who prove contrite?" A hint of fire flared in her eyes. "Although he didn't appreciate it at the time, Satan was right about one thing. 'Faith without works *is* dead.' And I will keep working until I've shown him just how strong love can be. In fact, I'll ram it right up...? But of course."

Inspired, Teresa hastened to change her sodden nightshirt before rushing to her work desk.

Oh yes. One or two little tweaks might allow my plague to propagate deeper and further than before. It's bound to intensify the rioting, but won't that help my dear friends to complete their audit all the quicker? Activating her computer, she waited for the screen to illuminate. When it did, a series of complex bio-chemical formulas and esoteric compounds were revealed, revolving slowly around each other. *I'll run some simulations first, and catch Erra in the morning. I'm sure he'll be most receptive to what I have in mind.*

*

Situated in a sublevel of the much larger Grand Church of Profanity of Cullogne, the Chapel of the Epistle of Judas Iscariot was a site seldom visited by anyone of consequence anymore.

That hadn't always been the case, of course. Only two thousand years ago, it had been *the* place to be seen, a hive of iniquity where devil worshippers could gather to celebrate the 'bad old days' when Christians were burnt at the stake, fed to the lions, or slaughtered in gladiatorial pageantry that stirred the soul as it appeased the bloodlust of the mob.

But, as the centuries passed and ever more denizens of note got to meet the man himself, everyone slowly came to realize that Jesus' betrayer was something of a two-faced toad. As such, interest waned, meeting attendance declined, and—as Shakespeare had so eloquently coined the phrase in one of his later productions about Judas and his third fall from grace—"the place to be, soon became the place *not* to be...without question."

Needless to say, the chapel had fallen into disarray not long after that, eventually being abandoned altogether until sixty years ago when it had been decreed the space could be put to better use to store unwanted scrolls and obscure artifacts.

Nettesheim had been delighted by this turn of events, for it played into his hands perfectly.

To maintain the charade of 'putting his affairs in order', it had been necessary for him to insist on meeting his contact for a second time in a row in the same city—something that was rarely done for fear of drawing unwanted attention to their activities.

However, as one of Cullogne's darkest sons, rumors had quickly circulated regarding his elevation to Hell Hound. Because of this, those in power were keen to milk his celebrity by making his acquaintance, instances Nettesheim had gone out of his way to stage, for he appreciated news of such incidents would most certainly work their way back to the Den.

While he was happy at the publicity his presence drew, he was equally as scrupulous in selecting a venue for his liaison that would be well away from prying eyes. And that was why Judas' chapel fit the bill so well. Not only was it isolated, but the Grand Church of Profanity was part of an *old school* diocese, which only opened to the public on Sindays. Ensuring to grant himself a one hour window in which no one would realize he was absent, Nettesheim had timed things meticulously.

Arriving not five minutes ago, he had easily evaded the half dozen or so deacons and disciples going about their duties in the cloisters above, and, under cover of an invisibility shroud, made his way through to the eastern arcade from where all the shrines to the epistles could be accessed.

Nettesheim had only ever been here once before—on his fact-finding mission—and still felt amazed at how this part of the church seemed set aside in an age all of its own. While the basilica above was an imposing edifice of high windows, vaulted beams, open spaces and clean lines, the catacombs seemed determined to pay tribute to a time when bricks were still made from mud and straw, and where worshippers were expected to congregate in all solemnity beneath hooded gowns to mask their identities.

The passage Nettesheim travelled at this very moment was a prime example of that, for not only was it claustrophobic, but he had to fight the constant urge to bow his head in penitence for misdeeds, committed and imagined.

At last, the entrance to his destination loomed from out of the shadows. Raising his hand, Nettesheim uttered a brief incantation and was rewarded with the sound of locks tripping and heavy bolts sliding back. Creaking, the door swung open.

He stepped into darkness. Fumbling along the wall to his left, Nettesheim located the switch and illuminated a chandelier hanging from the center of a domed ceiling. In moments, the interior was filled by a soft yellow radiance that spilled back out into the corridor.

Since its abandonment, the Chapel of Judas Iscariot had become something of a bric-a-brac treasure trove. Bookshelves filled the walls on either side, overflowing with sealed manuscripts and ponderous hidebound volumes. In the middle of the room, and assortment of tables bowed under the weight of all manner of stone chests, wooden boxes and leather-skinned cases, almost all of which were sealed by pulsing runes of power.

An arched window positioned within a sculpted tympanum was the strangest feature of all. Set into bare rock at the far end of the chamber, it somehow managed to look out onto the dusky view of a citrine colored valley beneath sandy skies filled with caramel clouds. And that, despite the fact it was more than two hundred feet underground.

The first to arrive, Nettesheim walked across to a stone fireplace set into a recess beside the casement and created a small ball of fire lightning. Igniting it, he adjusted its brilliance until the chill began to bleed from the air.

The slightest quiver in the ether gave him advanced warning of someone's approach.

"You think I require such comforts?" a cold voice enquired.

Nettesheim spun on the spot. A female dressed as a Priestess of the Precipice stood just inside the entrance. Tall and willowy, her sharp features and pale, blue-tinged skin presented a stark contrast to her blood red robe and the jet black hair that flowed out from the folds of her cowl to unfurl like liquid ebony about her shoulders.

Meeting her gaze squarely, Nettesheim stared into the abyss. "I didn't see you there?" he lied.

"Nor would you, until I deemed it necessary."

She's annoyed I made her meet up again so soon.

Nettesheim decided to get straight down to business. Pausing only to erect a barrier about the confines of the chapel, he began, "As you are no doubt aware, the initial part of my plan worked. That's why I suggested we liaise again here in Cullogne. It is essential people see me going about my business and putting my affairs in order before I take up my full duties as a Hell Hound..."

"And?" Her tone belied her impatience.

"It was also essential we have a chance to speak, face to face."

"Why?"

"You know how resilient I am when it comes to uncovering things that want to remain hidden. Well, it may not have escaped your notice that Daemon Grim is no longer within the confines of the latterday circles of hell...?" The slightest tightening of the priestess's jaw told Nettesheim he had hit the nail on the head. Though scant, the rest of her body language also suggested she knew why the Reaper was absent.

Interesting... "...and that his departure was ill-timed, emergency or not."

"So, what's your point?"

"My *point* is that we might be getting ourselves into a stew over nothing."

That got her.

Straightening, she narrowed her eyes and took a step closer. "Explain."

Nettesheim lowered his voice. "We live a privileged life, you and I. The circles we walk. The company we keep. The areas of hell we have right of admission to. And, without sounding presumptuous, isn't that only fitting? After all, we've earned our positions, yes? That's why we are also entrusted with secrets the Master would prefer never existed in the first place. Regardless, I recently learned his trust only extends so far..." he beckoned his contact closer. "Imagine my surprise, then, having been magnified beyond my wildest dreams by the process of becoming a Hell Hound, when I discovered my newfound abilities granted me access to knowledge previously withheld, even from the likes of you and I?" *Or perhaps, I was the only one excluded?*

The priestess's eyes blazed, "How did –?"

"It doesn't matter how I found out," Nettesheim cut the woman dead, "for I am loyal and without taint. The fact remains that I did."

"You speak again of Grim?"

Oh, so you did *know.*

"Yes, I do. Not only have I established where he is, but I now understand better the nature of what it is he seeks... *if* it has not yet been absorbed into Jahannam's all-consuming essence." Nettesheim spread his hands wide and took a bow. "You see, at last, why I insisted we meet again so soon, and here of all places. In demonstrating my integrity, I also wish to emphasize to the one we serve that even should Grim comes to a full realization of his past, I am positive he will not represent a threat to our unfolding plans or the continuing integrity of infernal security."

"What, you think the truth will endear him to us or to the Master? Are you insane, man?"

Nettesheim couldn't help but laugh, "Oh my badness, no. Of course not. If anything, he'll be more furious than he's ever been. Fortunately for us, the reestablishment of his strongest traits will guarantee he'll see his current mission through."

"Current mission? It's turned into a witch-hunt over his identity. How in damnation have you arrived at such a conclusion?"

"Because his actions have always spoken louder than words. Remember, his soul has been fractured a thousand times, yet that didn't prevent his core attributes from resurfacing. Once the other *factors* have been reintegrated into his psyche, his very motivation for living will drive him to feel duty...no, honor bound to fulfill the greater need. You'll see. For Azazel's sake, I even witnessed him breach the divide through into the third way. That would be impossible if he wasn't a balancing force of nature in the making."

"He managed that?" The priestess seemed astounded by Nettesheim's statement. But only for a moment. "Even if what you say is true, it may be too late. The Ascendant is upon us; already the Veil begins to lose integrity."

"Then report back with all haste. While certain contingencies must be put in place, I think I know of a way to reach our elusive Reaper. I established a rapport with him, brief though it was, so he'll respond to my hail. I'm sure of it. If I'm right, Grim will soon be in the perfect position to ensure nobody is able to exploit the Ascendant to escape."

"And afterward?"

"Afterward? Good lady, one thing at a time. Let's survive what's coming first, and we can worry about Grim's temper later."

Chapter 20: Of Shattered Dreams and Innocence

With Jotûn and Garôk at my back, I marched toward the solitary tree that marked the boundary between the Hall of Shattered Dreams and the rest of Hatamâh's insanity with eager determination. Until my stomach flipped, that was. I was more nervous than I realized and all sorts of emotions began stewing away inside the closer I got: hope, fear, anticipation, relief, concern. Why those feelings were there, exactly, I couldn't explain. They just *were*.

Part of me wanted to rush in, headlong, and peel back the layers of a past long denied me. More restrained, another part urged caution.

Erring on the side of prudence, I forced myself to take my time, and edged forward until I felt a tingling sensation that marked the extent of the Hall's domain. The temperature was considerably cooler on the other side of the threshold, which helped explain a few things.

I'd initially imagined the sentinel was some form of albino ash, or perhaps a silver birch that had been stripped of its foliage and smallest twigs. Stood beside it now, I could see it was, in fact, a seeping willow glazed in a fine rime of permafrost. Not only that, each of its slender limbs trembled as if shivering to stay warm, a process generating a constant trickle of musical notes that sounded like a dozen tiny tuneful tributaries, all flowing together quite happily, to produce a single crystalline score.

The moment I stepped through the divide, my fears evaporated, and as I looked up, my senses adjusted to the immensity of the edifice looming over me.

Though the archivolt and door lay in broken heaps across the steps, most of the exterior tower portal remained intact. This close, I could see how finely wrought the angel's features were, and how naturally they blended into the rugged outcrops on both sides of the entrance.

When I'd first arrived, I'd noticed the portico area had been stained gray by Hatamâh's dynamics to match the chromaticity of the transmuted plateau outside. But as I mounted the stairs and walked onto the first flagstones, I discerned reality inside the Hall was far more complex. Everything—even something as seemingly straightforward as color—possessed a many layered consistency that gave the impression it was meant to last.

It made me feel as if the master maestros who had crafted this place had managed to create the perfect monument to perpetuity. An effect only heightened the further I moved into the narthex, for even at this distance from the altar, the spandrels and balusters lining the outer aisles were intact, forming an effective barrier between the ruins and the library itself.

Regardless, Jahannam was a sentient Gate and never left anything to chance. When I moved closer to examine the condition of some of the volumes, I detected the presence of a powerful force field cunningly woven into the fabric of the air.

Hmm, these further layers of protection will ensure the knowledge this repository contains remains intact for future generations to discover. Which is odd, isn't this Gate sup-posed...? My own voice called out to me again from the far end of the sanctuary, sending chills down my spine. *Or is this all for me? Do these books contain a record of my history?*

Heart pounding, eyes alight with curiosity, I followed the line of the balconies along the length of the arcade. Then I craned my neck and projected my astral sight up into the expanse of the eaves above. *Yet how could that be, I haven't lived anywhere near long en...?*

Snap!

A sound from just ahead and to the left of our position caught my attention. Suspicions roused, I extended my stride and discovered an ornate cinquefoil window positioned within a small alcove along the western border of the nave. The scene within its cobalt and amethyst depths revealed a city under siege by a celestial being employing lightning bolts and storm winds as weapons. Keen to understand its meaning, I moved closer. A mistake, for the Bãlefire flowing through my veins flared unexpectedly, creating a pressure wave that shattered the whole pane.

The glass fell inward—against the flow of energy—and as each glittering shard struck the floor, they chimed, producing an increasing scale that refracted the light in such a way so as to produce a visible, written communication. Hovering in midair, it read:

This cruel arrow

Fired from the bow of exile enforced,

Invites you to feast on bitter bread

Sharper than any two-edged sword.

This tasteless path,

Shall leave you wanting,

For you are but a wolf in sheep's clothing,

Whose wrath cuts both ways.

"Do you understand what this passage refers to, brother?" Jotûn was clearly perplexed by the bizarre setting, "or how it may progress your search?"

"I think it's supposed to refer to me," I replied, equally as baffled. "But I've never been exiled from anywhere...Well, not that I remember. Hang on a second, let me think."

Reading the message again, my gaze lingered on two phrases in particular. *That reference to 'two-edged sword' and 'wrath that cuts both ways.' Does that relate to my ability to manipulate the Bãlefire and God's Grace? If so, it's nothing new. I've always been able to...to...wait a minute; this isn't the first instance I've been reminded of a vergence of disparate forces around me? Didn't I see this more clearly when...?*

Memory swells closed in, coalescing about me like a storm at sea. Before I could do anything about it, I'd been swept away and transported back to a stardust flecked cave where thunder raged and stalactites as big as boulders fell from the ceiling:

Grislington, he's gone!

Free of the restraints that had subdued its essence for an age, the *Sword of Celestial Arches* blazed, drawing a response from the opposite end of the cavern where a bone white archway ceased to exist. In its place, a portal into eternity beckoned, containing visions of such wonderment that for the first time in my long and lonely life I knew what it meant to be truly insignificant.

Oh my . . .

Scales dropped from my eyes.

Limitless potential waited within the nucleus of the smallest atom.

Past experiences, hidden within a vortex of uncertainty, tugged at the edge of comprehension.

Something significant clawed for air within the very core of my soul.

Remember—remember—remember…

Then, as I struggled with the turmoil created by such recollections, the multiverse took a breath and everything went silent.

When it happened, the overwhelming surge of incandescence blasting out of the heavenly gate shattered what remained of my broken husk and swept my shadow high into the air, out of the light and into the chaos beyond.

It was as if I'd never existed…a state of nonbeing I'd been forced to endure before.

What? Wait!

Without warning, my consciousness was yanked back into my body. No sooner had it slammed into place than I staggered, caught in an overlap between what was real and what was imaginary. Pain speared my head. My lungs felt consumed by the need to breathe. For some reason, I was inexplicably dizzy.

Staggering toward an ancillary pulpit that had been erected halfway along the nave; I quickly discovered the waking dream refused to give up its hold. Lingering images of Grislington sitting by a spring, running his hand through its water, kept pushing their way into my thoughts. Forced to lean against the rostrum for support, I let those impulses play out. *The Hall must be trying to help me reach an understanding?*

Grislinton looked exactly as I remembered him: a creature of unblemished purity that attracted light in all its subtle nuances. Reclined upon the low wall to a fountain, he

seemed fascinated by the texture of the outflow as it trickled through his slender fingers, and I could understand why.
Though removed from that moment by profane irregularity,
I could still taste its holy resonance as if I was there. I could
even perceive the gentle shower of ice flakes pattering down
against my skin, a feeling both alien and sublime.

But how does this help me?

And Hatamâh heard.

For a third time, my own voice called to me. On this occasion, however, the words were loud and clear, deep and
resonant, full of meaning:

"The tranquility of endless night resounds to an orchestration of soaring dominion. There, ripples of thought as in-
substantial as forgotten deeds impinge upon a long forgotten shore. But I am a creature whose cadence pulsates to the
heartbeat of the universe. I can sense those whose minds are
uncluttered by the dross of a self-centered gratitude. Are you
blinding yourself to the glories that remain hidden in plain
sight?"

His—whoever *he* really was—declaration struck a
chord. Even so, the meaning behind it continued to elude me,
a frustrating dilemma I wasn't prepared to accept.

"How do I see what is hidden?"

"Stand apart, take a breath, step back and put the rush on
hold. Open yourself to the noise around you. Only once to
stop being an extraneous factor to the riddle will you find the
solution."

"Solution?"

"We are miniscule, you and I, for all our power; frigid
temporary embers of stuttering consciousness lacking discernment or direction. If only we would make more effort to
recognize our purpose…well…"

"Well what?"

"You know. You've seen it: the glory of creation encapsulated within a speck of dust; the music that permeates all life captured by laughter; every hope for a better, brighter future shining in the eyes of an infant; accepting the clarity that only paradox can bring."

"The clarity of paradox?"

"Enter that place in which sound becomes silence. Taste the liquid transparency of indomitable might. Accept the limits of infinite choice, and simply tighten your grasp on letting go. Enjoy the certainty of taking a risk, of knowing the vast and endless is insignificant and miniscule. You've been there. You've embraced the incongruity of intricate simplicity to become what you are. Now wake up! The hour to navigate your course is at hand. Stop letting the answer slip through your fingers."

Somehow, everything I'd just heard made sense. Yet it only confused me more.

This is starting to piss me off. "If you've really got all the answers, stop beating about the bush and tell me plainly. How do I wake up? How do I know which path to take? *How* does this help me discover who I am?"

"Have you not been listening to a word I've said?" the mirrored voice conveyed a sense of patient restraint, "in this place, you gain symmetry by accepting contradictions. Is not 'that which breaks to pieces' preserving your history? Can you not wield power, both light and dark? You were made to do both...so *do* both. Did you not already break the seal to one side of your nature? To regain balance, you must repeat your accomplishment."

Whoa! Is he talking about what I just did to the –?

I never got to finish that thought. Momentarily dumbfounded, I was seized in the grip of an intense muscle spasm

that sent blue-white sparks leaping from my fingertips toward a second window, this one on the eastern side of the
chamber.

God's Grace? How the fuck did...? I just had time to register the fact that the corresponding frame also depicted an
angel—this one responsible for a devastating scene of carnage and destruction—before the entire casement burst from
its mount.

A dazzling mirage of silver and magenta glass chips cascaded down, each fragment creating a tonal resonance that
drew my attention like a siren's call. Captivated, my perceptions were enticed out of my own dimensional reference toward a place I had only recently come to appreciate seemed
intertwined with my fate: Sentinel's Square.

The Wyrd tree was still there, its rosy benevolence
shrouding my environs in warmth and hope. And so was the
mystery entity I'd encountered before. Once again I meshed
to the temporal thread and became part of its reality:

"Where...where am I?"

"Fear not," a deep and commanding voice intones, "we
found you, at last. All will be well again...eventually."

"Eventually?"

"Yes. You have suffered trauma sufficient to obliterate
even the strongest of us. Incredibly, you...survived. We need
to bend our arts to make you whole again."

"Whole?"

"You ended up far away. Somewhere beyond my reach,
a place that seemed to consume your remains as it preserved
them alive. It was disturbing to say the least."

"Then I might not endure?"

Trust me. You will be refashioned. Blended and forged
anew into something better."

"Better?"

"You'll see."

Hands turn me so that I face the light of the Wyrd tree squarely. Its leaves peal as they dance to the caress of an unfelt breeze. The sound of a distant choir recedes, while closer, a harsher chorus rises in unison. The weight of their song falls upon my neck, and the desire for slumber becomes irresistible.

I sag forward, exhausted, and my palms come to rest upon the hilts of two great swords of power. One steams, freezing to the touch in this environment, while the other burns, red-hot. "Who...whose are these?"

Murmurs of discontent and apprehension bruise the air in accusation on all sides.

The authoritative voice silences them, before replying, "Believe it or not, they both respond to your will, scant as it is."

"Both? How...?"

"No more questions. Sleep now. Though it takes an eternity, you will be restored to us, and you will be mine."

Heavy with exhaustion and sorrow, my lids drift shut. A shroud descends to filter out the glorious light still visible from on high. As it does so, a bane of stunning complexity is released that commences to weave itself through the very constitution of the plane about me. Detached, I am yet aware that seasons come and seasons go in a flickering cycle of baleful embers and somber darkness.

Memories from an age before fade.

Synchronicity marches on and new ones are introduced.

Eventually, everything, everywhere, is twisted into its most debased form.

As am I.

The viewing glass of my perspective jumps forward to an unknown reference. In it, a blood moon fills a cloudless sky.

Resonant with purpose, its sanguine purity focuses the night like a lens, and fills the now lush square with an expectant hush. It has snowed and a virgin glaze powders the garden, its crystal white cocoon stained red, yet still as cold and brittle as the heart that no longer beats within my obsidian chest.

From the edge of that sanctuary I maintain a silent vigil, waiting patiently, knowing that the day will come when I am ready to be released from my pupa. But for now, I wait...

The soft *crump* of feet upon icy flakes intrudes as a tall and imposing figure stalks the unblemished parchment of the path. Hooded in black, her footfall is light, and leaves an indented score along its length.

Without a word, she approaches and stands before me. Gnarled talons draw back the cowl, and burnished apricot hair that flares like a living flame cascades down around her shoulders. Livid scars denote her rank and prowess in battle, marks she bears proudly for all to see.

I feel as if should know her from somewhere, for this female bears a familiarity that is as appealing as it is instinctual. She has no need to climb the pedestal on which I stand, and leans across toward my ear.

Cupping her hands against tusks filed to razor points, she whispers, "I thought you were a wolf in sheep's clothing? The Soulstice is upon us and only you have the power to stand between both worlds. It's time to wake up—wake up—wake up..."

Garok?

"Daemon Grim, can you hear me?"

I reached out, blindly, accepting the strong hands that pulled me to my feet. "Yes, I'm here, I'm alright."

Except that I wasn't. I was suffering from a strange sense of temporal vertigo, and it wasn't until I'd taken a few deep breaths that its effects reduced to a level where I could ignore it sufficiently to stand unaided.

Even so, Jotûn and Garôk hovered close by, seemingly reticent to leave me alone. I didn't like being mollycoddled at the best of times, so when I cast a disgruntled look their way, Garok hastened to explain, "We mean no offence, Janīn bearer, but for a while there, we thought we'd lost you. It appeared as if the eternal flame had departed and left nothing but an empty husk behind. Yours was not the only unlife we feared for."

Shit, this is becoming a bit of a habit. What is happening to me? "Then there's no need to apologize. It seems reclaiming my identity is fraught with dangers I never anticipated." Stepping forward to give myself a bit of space, I turned to face my companions, and shrugged, "I suppose I'm to blame for that, though. I *did* ask Jahannam to show me what I needed to see in order to reclaim my life. And as you emphasized, each Gate will live up to its name. Hatamâh is just fulfilling my request in its own unique way…" I paused to rub my temples, "painful though that is."

"So, where does that leave us?" Jotûn inquired, his attitude as resolute as ever.

For a moment, I experienced a secondary flashback to that instant on Cog Isle where my whole existence fluttered on the edge of dissolution:

…I am the Bãlefire. Brimstone incarnate, made flesh.

I am also part of the Heavenly Light, celestial beauty eclipsed.

Perpetual discordance personified. At war with myself — within myself — because of myself, I am the very anathema of my own existence…

Yeah, a two-edged sword if ever there was one.

Glancing along the nave, I judged the distance between our current position and the high altar. "Simple answer? I'd say that leaves us with about two hundred yards to go. Whenever you're ready?"

*

Lingering in the shadows, Gemini sent her call again and waited patiently for a reply. Highly skilled at blending to her environment, she was, to all intent and purpose, invisible. Which was just as well, for this was one of the most dangerous locations in all the underverse, and not the kind of place for a woman—or anyone else for that matter—to be caught unawares, even if they were one of the fabled Hell Hounds.

Topside, the Khan el-Khalili was the main souk district of Cairo. Set in the city's most important economic zone, it was also an obvious tourist attraction, selling souvenirs, antiques and jewelry amongst other more traditional textiles, snacks and food.

What many people didn't realize was that this thriving quarter was also the site of a mausoleum known as, the *turbat az-za'faraan* (Saffron Tomb) which served as the burial site of the Fatimid Caliphs.

The mausoleum itself was part of the Fatimid Great Eastern Palace, a huge and intricately designed complex incorporating elements of both Coptic and Byzantine architectural features that stretched for miles in every direction. When the city's dark soul-shadow had been transplanted down into the latterday circles of hell, the crypt complex came with it, along with its multifarious system of tunnels.

Originally, those tunnels served as escape routes or white market highways, private roads by which the more powerful denizens of the criminal community could engage in their wheeling, murdering and dealing unmolested, and without hindrance from the regular magma flows or the many infernal law and disorder agencies operating throughout the length and breadth of the capital.

However, as District S16 continued to fill and the population of Sulforous Sands grew, so did its need for some form of sanitation. Needless to say, it wasn't long before the underground warren was turned into a makeshift sewer; a stinking, festering cesspit of putrefying bacteria and sludge so dense and so foul, it became responsible for the heavy pall that hung above the city like a shroud, and which ended up acting as an additional filter against the torpid rays of Paradise.

It went without saying that humans rarely ventured below ground in S16 anymore. At least, not those you would ever want to meet this side of a Slab A body bag. Regardless, this was hell, and nothing—not even space—was left to waste for long. Within weeks of being abandoned, the subterranean garbage dump became the new home of several of the most powerful hell-rat colonies in existence, and in their new domain tucked well away from humans, they thrived.

Or at least, they had been thriving at the beginning of the week when Gemini had last passed this way to make her offer.

On that occasion, the rat sultan and his nizams had been most welcoming to the stranger from Juxtapose who represented the elite of the elite of hellonian society, and who had not only treated them with courtesy and respect, but had brought gifts of food and bad tidings from fellow colonies in other circles. They had been especially entertained by the thought of establishing a relationship with the Reaper, and had asked her to return promptly to finalize the details of the proposed agreement.

Gemini had done just that, only to find the lowways and byways of the rodent community strangely deserted.

It's like they left in a hurry without bothering to take their belongings with them?

Noise filtering down from the newly rebuilt market above indicated she had reached the precincts of the Bab al-Ghouli catacombs, one of the lowest levels of Dark Cairo's souk region.

She sniffed and wrinkled her nose in distaste. *Like I need a mental map to tell me where I am?*

The reek of floating sewage and rotting animal carcasses—and worse—was so overwhelming, Gemini wouldn't have been surprised to see the ground above flexing like a bubble in an effort to put as much distance between itself and the source of a stench that even the Spouting Pyramids of Geyser couldn't burn away entirely.

Though the background resonance from the bazaars managed to infiltrate the gloom, the stillness within the passages surrounding Gemini was all pervading, and broken only by the sound of water and other, less savory fluids, trickling down from open toilets and broken cisterns.

Renown for her stealth, Gemini merged to those sounds perfectly, and to an outsider looking on, she would have been indistinguishable from the resonant gloaming that seemed to reach out in every direction, only to sink into every block and every brick, until nothing remained.

Reaching the terminus of a side duct, Gemini squatted down into the filth and considered her options.

This lot was far more outgoing than their counterparts in Perish and New Hell, and have adapted to the habits of their human neighbors remarkably well. So where are they? Half a million furry little bodies don't just disappear? She swore, to herself. *Damn Nettesheim for not being done with his... his...*whatever *he's doing. I could have done with his skills in helping me determine what's happened here.*

Adjusting her perceptions, Gemini checked the locale again.

Ahead of her, four major drains led into a junction that served as one of the hell-rats primary meeting halls. Known as Bab al'on, it was a place the sultan met with his nizams and other reeves from a number of nearby clans to hammer out local policies and settle disputes. On the previous occasion she'd been here, nearly eighty thousand subjects had crammed the vault with twinkling eyes and glistening whiskers. Now, stained rags, soiled clothing and rotting vegetables served as Gemini's only company, though, without anyone to sort through and consume the never-ending flow of detritus, a growing mound of trash had begun to form in the middle of the chamber, centered around the shattered remains of a plasma TV...and something else.

The faintest tang of an unfamiliar quality stained the ether.

That doesn't fit?

Refining her acuity even further, Gemini cast out her seekersense in pursuit of the elusive aura.

There, it's concentrated around the northern conduit.

She was just about to step forward when an abrupt silence folded itself across the hub. From Gemini's perspective, it felt as if the very stones lining the maze network had given up trying to hold the roof up while they too, paused to listen. A peculiar dampening of reality soaked into the atmosphere, an oppressive burden that clung to the lungs like deadweight.

Gemini pressed herself into the muck and drew one of her Bãlefire charged daggers. Keeping its quintessence suppressed, she selected a suitable posture, bunched her muscles, and then turned to stone, ready to pounce.

A shadowy helix unfolded from the blackness directly opposite her position and transformed into a shimmering wraith that swirled about the island of refuse like a flame of onyx malevolence. The more Gemini stared, the harder her target was to see, for its form ebbed and flowed in the most confusing manner.

*It looks to be fighting against its own substance in a constant war of...*the cold hard shock of recognition hit hard. *A Dread-Lock!* Then she amended her assessment, *No, it's too big.* That's *a Dread-Master, and a male to boot.*

Gemini had only ever seen these psychic vampires at a distance, but she'd read enough eyewitness reports to know the Hell Hounds and Daemon Grim himself had run into them on a number of occasions in the past.

It's important I stay calm. These fuckers kill to order and gain strength by feeding on negative emotions. The stronger the better. Now, Gemini could appreciate the signs of abandonment. *At least I know why this place is deserted. While the king wouldn't be bothered by the Sibitti, he daren't risk his subjects against this–?*

"Come out, come out, wherever you are—you are—you are..." As it spoke, the Dread-Master's spiraling dance intensified and slowed at irregular intervals.

It's scanning for something to latch onto.

"There's no need to be shy—shy—shy. Why hide when we can have so much more fun by simply playing—playing—playing...?"

So, you want to play do you? Pulling her secondary blade free, Gemini dropped all pretense at stealth and jumped to her feet with a loud splash.

The orbiting morass of malice solidified, and for the briefest instant, Gemini's mental defenses were assailed by splinters of fear and trepidation. She batted them away, disdainfully, and took several confident strides forward. "Foolish. Very foolish, especially when you don't know who it is you're dealing with."

"And just who might that be—be—be...?" the sparkling cloud challenged, condensing suddenly into a black well of terror.

Ignoring the posturing, Gemini bowed, theatrically, "I am the Lady Gemini, pack member of the Ancient Disorder of Hell Hounds...also known as the Angel of Assassination."

"A Hell Hound—Hound—Hound...?" The wraith's voice had dropped an octave or two, as if contemplating its next move.

"Indeed. While I normally respect other denizen's rights to exist as and where they can, I would inform you that your presence has impeded an official investigation. Tell me, are you here in order to fulfill the terms of a contract to which you are bound? If so, I might be able to accommodate your needs or even expedite its completion?"

"And if not—not—not...?"

"Then you need to tell me what has befallen the local residents. I hope for your sake the hell-rat colony that occupied this area hasn't been harmed?"

"Why? Do you feel secure about facing one of the S'gāth alone—alone—alone...?"

Gemini's response was swift and ruthless. Before her foe had time to react, she leaped forward and delivered a complex series of whiplike cuts that opened up several steaming wounds along the Dread-Master's torso, forcing it to back away. "Pretty secure, yes."

She spoke too soon. The Dread managed to shrug off its surprise to launch a stinging advance of its own, and Gemini was stunned to feel a barbed talon catch the ravaged side of her face. A timely lesson.

Idiot! Don't get cocky. I'm not Daemon Grim. Her cheek itched, a sure sign she'd been cut. Inclining her head, Gemini murmured, "Touché."

Without taking her eyes from her opponent, Gemini commenced dancing, skipping first one way and then the other, dodging and feinting, weaving her blades in intricate patterns that wove nondescript lies in the air. Sometimes her arms would snake out to deliver a viper's bite, at others; they recoiled to counter a deluge of lethal lunges or deflect killing blows.

It soon became apparent the S'gãth was slippery quick with lightning reflexes that would have easily overwhelmed a normal person. But Gemini was no ordinary anything. Keeping her mind fluid—yet focused on the sheer joy of conflict—she allowed her superlative skills to flow, and established an alternating cadence to her attack that made it difficult for her adversary to settle into its own rhythm.

A creature of cruel temperament, the Dread-Master refused to give quarter and over the next several minutes continued contesting for dominance at every turn. Even so, it was used to instilling panic in others and feeding off the fear that drained its victims as it strengthened its own resolve. The relentless exchange soon took its toll.

Gradually, the glittering facets adorning the wraith's epidermis started to dim. As the scales lost their luster, they peeled away from the Dread's form in such quantities that he actually began to shrink before Gemini's eyes.

From what I remember, they don't handle brute force well.

Gemini pressed the advantage, commencing an incessant fusillade of slashing engagements that immediately had the Dread-Master retreating. It shrieked and unbelievably, its defense became desperate, though far more erratic. Gemini replied by augmenting her speed to a whole different level, and a rapid swarm of blows soon found their mark.

The scrape of metal on armor increased, and a tinkling cascade of ruptured essence was answered by another yowl of pain. Gemini spotted several openings before realizing they weren't an insidious ploy to catch her off guard.

I've got to end this.

Choosing her moment, Gemini timed her assault perfectly. Leaping high into the air, she crashed down onto her opponent from above and plunged one of her daggers into the crown of his head. The Dread-Master stiffened and threw its arms wide. Capitalizing on her momentum, Gemini thrust her other blade deep into the exposed chest, piercing the cold heart within. Holding on tight, she next unleashed the potential of the Bālefire, and added her own might to the mix.

The result was inevitable.

The S'gãth's midnight mantle collapsed in on itself, a torn and ruined shroud that shriveled in short jerking contractions into a shapeless corpus that tightened and tightened until...

A final cry echoed into the night, its plea as helpless as it was potent. Then the remaining mass was gone, a loud *pop* the only fanfare to mark its passing as air rushed to fill the sudden vacuum.

An unexpected white noise receded. Gemini stood back, sheathed her weapons, and took a deep breath. Only then did she take the time to survey her surroundings once more, this

time taking care to search for tiny carcasses among the wa-
terborne castoffs.

What she found didn't raise as many concerns as did the
long-term repercussions. *I've got a good half dozen bodies,
but that could be down to simple attrition associated with
unlife in harsh conditions. I can only hope they haven't been
scared away...?*

The slightest pitter-patter of tiny feet on wet stone alerted her to approaching company. Falling still, Gemini made
haste to calm any stray sentiments she might be emitting
into ones of friendship, and waited for her mystery guests to
come to her.

Her attention was drawn to the ceiling, where a broken
section of pipe emerged from the base plate of a modern-day
flue. Two tiny noses clarified first, sniffing for all they were
worth and testing the air for unseen hazards. Age mottled fur
followed, along with broken whiskers, and though the button eyes that looked down on her were still keen, it was clear
they had lost some of their shine. *They sent old ones? Or perhaps they were left behind to keep an experienced watch on
how things went?*

Projecting feelings of security and protection, Gemini
spoke softly, "It's safe now; spread the word among the others if you want to." She opened her mind to present a record
of the events that had just taken place. "Tell your sultan the
danger has passed. Though this isn't the way I would have
planned it, it does emphasize why it's a wise strategy to make
our acquaintance. You'll be under our protection and won't
have any further problems from Dread-Locks or any other
form of itinerant perils that happen upon your lair."

A high-pitched squeak signaled her message had been
received and understood. The next time she blinked, the

hell-rats were gone. *Perhaps its better this way. They have a lot of important decisions to make...as have I.*

Gemini looked about one last time before heading toward the nearest tunnel that would take her directly to the surface. *This will bring me out by Wicca al-Qutn. A longer walk back to the hotel, but at least it will give me an opportunity to check the alleys and side streets. The more rodents I can meet on the way, the faster word will spread to all parts of the city that the Hell Hounds have acted on their behalf. Good for business and...?*

The peal of distant bells ached from out of a nearby passage. Gemini came up short and checked her wrist chronometer. "It's midnight already? Damn, but I've fallen behind. I'm supposed to be across in New Hell in twenty-four hours meeting up with Nettesheim...*if* he's sorted out his personal shit, that is."

That thought reminded her of the personal *developments* in her own life.

I wonder how Daemon's doing right now.

*

Moving forward, a strange sense of dislocation sent the butterflies in my stomach into a migratory frenzy. I wasn't surprised though, for each stage of my journey along the Hall of Shattered Dreams had proven something of an epiphany, and now we neared the altar, I knew the greatest revelation of all was finally approaching.

Below, the paving slabs gracing this portion of the nave were seamless and immaculate, primal and uncorrupted by something as mundane as the passage of time or simple wear and tear. Above, the ranked balconies leading up to the tritorium thrummed with potential as the spines of thousands upon thousands of encyclopedic volumes illuminated in an advancing fanfare of light and power. Even the main supporting pillars stretching up into the heavens—where far-off capitals lingered in cryptic obscurity—were imbued with latent majesty. Dominion laced the very atmosphere we breathed in an intoxicating mélange of omnipotence and omniscience.

From my perspective, it felt as if the entire structure was gradually awakening, charging like a cosmic dynamo that once empowered, would energize the heavens for all eternity.

I felt as exhilarated as I was nervous; especially as the solar spotlight streaming in through the huge rose window consecrated the entire transcript in an immaculate shaft of dawn's gentle embrace. But nowhere was that luminescence more glorious than the altar itself.

Constructed of an unknown material, it was as pale as alabaster and sparkled with a diamante sheen that made its surface appear viscous and protean. Set squarely within a finely crafted ciborium which captured the incoming wash and expanded it into a shimmering tau field, the framework warped the light, creating a flickering radiance through which the secrets of creation stood revealed.

One moment, I could see the power of a single atom being harnessed for the very first time and channeled into a demiurgic expression that would go on to form an expanding universe, and the next, reality was swallowed by an all-consuming blackness that turned the whole of existence inside out.

The drama accelerated: Stars were born to a sequence beyond my ken; galaxies slowly coalesced, lived and died; civilizations—above and below the Divide—existed within epochs of time reduced to an ecumenical instant before all history of them was lost forever. I even caught a glimpse of the celestial approaches where pearlescent clouds of heart-rending depth and clarity billowed in all-pervading serenity.

Enraptured, I mounted the steps leading to my destiny. Only once I'd reached the top step did I notice that the altar wasn't an elongated table stand at all. It was a sarcophagus.

Plain on all sides, the cover was nevertheless embellished in blazing runes so potent, so efficacious, that my eyes watered every time I tried to study the grain of the lid itself or read the glyphs inscribed upon it.

I know this place. I've seen it in my dreams.

The moment that fact registered, the inevitable ensued.

A loud retort resonated along the grand nave like the peal of a giant gong. The depiction within the window—that of two pairs of angelic creatures locked in combat—splintered in an extending fracture from top to bottom, whereupon the seals holding the pane in place ruptured, sending a shower of gold and red glass raining down on me.

As had happened on two previous occasions, the sound of fragments hitting the floor created a reverberating medium. That medium gained form and structure, a structure which became another visual and vocalized facet of my identity. Enchanted, I strode forward into the jingling cascade.

Listening to my own voice read those words aloud chilled me to the bone:

"The fourfold duality of the chimera's embrace

Enfolds you in frozen moments of forever,

A keeper of secrets,

You are granted tendrils of memory that have never truly been.

A fabrication

Is woven through your mind like a decoration,

There for you to look at and admire,

Beauteous but shallow.

Death has a new name,

Bound with a smile as cold as ice,

That constricts about those undeserving,

Until there's nowhere left to breathe."

Bugger me, if that isn't my story, I don't know what is. My whole life has been one long...correction. My unlife—*ever since my awakening in hell—has been a complete fabrication...or at least it feels that way. I've suffocated on lies, a charade that's kept me happily diverted from the truth about my past.*

I thought about that point for a moment. *But what kind of past was that? How can two be four? There has to be more to this* chimera *reference than meets the eye.*

Racking my brains, I juggled the pieces of the puzzle to make them fit the circumstances. *Chimera? In Greek mythology such a creature was a fire-breathing monster with a lion's head, goat's body and serpent's tail.* I dismissed such poppycock and tried again. *An illusion then? Something you long for, like a fantasy or mirage? Did Satan try and mold me into a likeness of his choosing?*

A much closer correlation, it still didn't sit quite right.

Hang on...there's also a biological reference to chimera involving the splicing of genetic material? The chill radiating along my spine got even colder. *What was it again? An organism containing the DNA of variant life, created by fusion, grafting or mutation?* "Fuck me, what am I?"

"Daemon Grim?" Jotûn's hand on my shoulder pulled me free of the mental carousel I'd been riding. "Are you any closer to establishing your true nature?"

The letters had begun to dim, but I was able to read them one last time before they disappeared. Though the beginning of the message made more sense now, it was the second line that held my attention. '...*Enfolds you in frozen moments of forever...?*'

"I think I am." Pointing that fading passage out to the First Fist, I explained, "There's only one place I know of where my visions have repeatedly shown me events frozen in time..."

"Where?"

"A secluded garden back in one of the latterday levels of hell. How would you like to join me on a little journey to check things out?"

"Unless Jahannam is willing, it will take considerable time to get from here to Ladthâa where the methân portal is situated. We will need to...?"

I waved him off, "Don't worry about that. I can take us there directly."

"Take us there?" Jotûn appeared a little confused, "Do you mean Ladthâa or are you speaking of your own realm?"

"My own realm, of course."

Now he was shocked. "You can do that from here?"

"Think of it as an inbuilt homing beacon. Once I've been somewhere, I can always find my way back..." *Home. If that's what it really is?*

"When would you envision leaving?"

"The sooner the bet –?"

A grating noise alerted me to the fact Garôk hadn't joined us. Spinning around, I saw that the First Palm had remained behind at the altar and had obviously decided to check what the sarcophagus contained. Fortunately for her, none of the runes appeared to be aggressive, for she was able to use her considerable strength to slide the cover to one side with relative ease and without consequence. Whatever was inside caused her to frown, shake her head, and look toward me in bewilderment.

"Garôk? What is it, what have you found?" Rushing forward, I leaned across the displaced lid and immediately caught my breath.

A huge, elongated amber colored gem more than six-feet in length and half that wide sat upon a purple velvet cushion. And while the structure of its many latticed depths glowered with the fire of a multitude of carnelians, that wasn't what caused my heart to skip a beat.

No, it was what lay within the crystal that made me challenge my sanity, for the sleeping form that lay in state undoubtedly belonged to Strawberry.

Chapter 21: A Little Digging

Chikushō! Yamato cursed and ducked as the blade flashed overhead, missing his ear by a whisker. Maintaining his momentum, he started rolling, only to arrest his sideways motion before sweeping an outstretched foot back in the opposite direction, hoping to catch his attacker off guard.

He did. Yamato's boot struck Champ's ankle just as his partner rushed in—and by his posture and momentum—it looked as if he'd intended to deliver an almighty kick to Yamato's midriff.

The movement upended Champ and dumped him to the floor. In moments, the two Hounds were a tangle of arms and legs as each tried to gain the advantage over the other. An arduous task, for while Yamato maintained control and was technically superior, Champ was a sledgehammer tough nut to crack, and more than made up for any deficiency with pure aggression and outstanding stamina.

"Ahem!" The unexpected cough was loud enough to interrupt their bout.

Tapping his partner sharply, twice on the arm—the signal to stop and disengage—Yamato glanced up from the mat to find the Chief Inquisitor waiting at the side of the sparring court. From his demeanor, Yamato could see the doctor appeared excited.

As Yamato stood and helped Champ to his feet, Livingstone strode forward, waving a portable holo-emitter in the air, "Sorry to disturb you both at practice, but you're going to want to see this."

"If its good news, doctor, feel free to disturb me any time you like." Yamato sheathed his tantō combat knife and started dusting himself down.

"Then you'll be pleased to hear I've almost cracked the behavioral conditioning instilled into the latest batch of prisoners. An uphill struggle, I might add, seeing as the modification has been incorporated into their psyches via an implanted DNHA encoded nanobot, which –?"

"I beg your pardon? A what?"

Livingstone was in his element. Yamato watched the doctor's entire face light up as he seized the opportunity to expand on a scientific topic. "A nanobot is a tiny biomimetic robot. This particular one is a most ingenious example that not only mimics brain matter, but also acts as a chemical bomb if the right—or, dependent upon your viewpoint—wrong circumstances arise."

Yamato was stunned. "How in Hades name did Tesla manage to fit something like that without leaving any form of evidence?"

"I'm still looking into it." Livingstone activated the emitter and a translucent 3D image of a human head appeared, complete with a digitized map of the brain. "This is a life-sized model of Castor Bean's skull. I checked all the usual insertion sites for a Trojan of this nature: ears; nasal cavity; cranial orbits; the eustracheal tube at the back of the throat. There was no form of scarring whatsoever."

"I take it you found the same absence with Pea and Choke?"

"I can't really say. Following up on your previous instructions, I was rather inventive and invasive where they were concerned." Livingstone grimaced, "You wanted results, and I was keen to get them. Unfortunately I pushed too far and triggered the failsafe. All that's left of their upper torsos is currently spread across the floor and walls of my laboratory..." he sniffed, and a faraway cast softened his gaze, "and one of the ceiling fans too. Quite a mess, but worth it."

Champ guffawed at the description of bloody mayhem. Shooting him a dirty look, Yamato prompted the doctor to continue, "You were talking of a breakthrough?"

Shaking his head, Livingstone swung back into the present and depressed a small button on the side of the projector. The picture within the holo-field expanded to show Bean's hippocampus and hypothalamus, with the mysterious dead area clearly defined between them. A tiny red spot illuminated within the dark zone. Referring to it, Livingstone explained, "The glowing dot is the bit I wanted to show you."

Adjusting the field's resolution, the dot expanded to show a strange filamentlike object with all the appearance of a deformed octopus made from gooey oatmeal. Gazing at it with obvious envy, Livingstone continued, "This is the nanobug I mentioned. I call it a *squiddy*. Avant-garde stuff. Futuristic, complex, and so advanced its way beyond any military spec shit we possess. It's simply, simply divine. I think it's an AI construct that somehow manages to..."

Yamato sighed as his colleague started getting carried away again. *I'd better keep him focused otherwise we'll be here all day.* "And your point, David?"

"Huh?" Livingstone blinked. "My point *is* that this bloody thing is what kills that area of the cerebrum in the first place. Then, from what I've been able to fathom, it lies dormant to its true purpose while replicating the host's brain functions. Along the way, it provides the necessary biochemical stimulus to keep them compliant. While it's in what I call its passive mode, squiddy remains totally undetectable to any of the scanning procedures we possess. Or it did until now."

"Until now?"

"I've managed to isolate the passive frequency it operates on." Livingstone held one finger in the air, "and before you ask, yes. I've already updated the Den's security protocols and passed it along the line to other infernal security agencies. Even so, I don't think we're out of the woods yet."

When are we ever? "What do you mean?"

"These squiddys operate on a restricted range of frequencies, part microwave, and part telepathic. While I've been able to zero in on the physics side of things, it's the psychic element that bothers me, because we won't be able to reprogram our subject until I've found out precisely how the squiddy receives its updates."

"Are you saying you might be able to break the conditioning factor?"

"If I play things right, I'll soon be able to compel dear Castor to—if you excuse the dreadful play on words—spill the beans *without* spilling his insides across what's left of the free space of my floors and ceiling. I'm becoming quite popular with our hell-ravens. Not a situation I want to continue, otherwise they'll be expecting nibbles all the time."

Ignoring the sounds of stifled mirth from his fellow Hound, Yamato asked, "What timeframe might we be looking at here?"

"I'm confident I should have a solution within three or four days. Elizabeth has offered to help. While some look on that offer as more of a hindrance, I've come to appreciate her alternate view of reality is a handy thing to have. If Daemon can rely on her insights, so will I."

"You raise a valid point." *Though I can't help feeling it's too little too late.* "Well done. I think it would be best if you crack on with your investigation, then. Though, I would ask you to keep the Undertaker in the loop? Now we know what we're looking for, he might be able to circumvent or neutralize the squiddy at source on reanimation."

"You're right. I'll get on that straight away."

As Livingstone breezed from the arena, Yamato couldn't help but compare their new compatriot to their former Chief Inquisitor. *Funny how karma seems to balance things out? Strawberry wouldn't have had a clue about half of the scientific stuff Livingstone manages to uncover. Yet, if what the worthy doctor says is true, we're sorely lacking her esoteric intuition right now. She'd have probably cracked this nest egg by coming in from the opposite side.* He smiled, sadly. *What the two of them could have done here, together? And if we'd gained this intelligence, what, just a week ago, it might have made all the difference and...?*

"Penny for 'em?" Champ's question caught Yamato off guard.

"Ah, just reminiscing, is all. We have some of the greatest minds, trackers and badass talent the underverse has to offer, and—I don't know—we always seem to be playing catch-up. I was hoping to have something more concrete on Chopin and Tesla's whereabouts by now to present to Daemon on his return."

Champ sucked in through his teeth. "I dunno. Seein' as how so much is always goin' on, we do alright. It's times like this I keep remindin' myself to follow Ferguson's Law."

That's a new one. "Ferguson's Law?"

"Yeah," Champ grinned, "I thought you'd like it. I named it after myself as it's a reminder to keep things nice n' simple."

Yamato had to bite his lip at the analogy. "Do explain before I beat it out of you."

"It was somethin' Daemon mentioned last year when we were all over at the Awful Tower huntin' down more of Chopin and Tesla's goons. When the world dumps on you from a great height, it's sometimes better to stop tryin' to avoid it so hard and just let things come to you. So, that's what I've attempted to do."

"You have?" Yamato was unashamedly stunned.

"Yep! It might be somethin' or it might be nothin' but..."

"Buuut?"

"I got to thinkin' about our raid over at the Unsûreté office the other day. I mean, in all the rush, Bean got the drop on us, didn't he?"

"He certainly did."

"Well, he was off the moment we busted in the doors. Nothin' to stop him. And of all the places in the underworld he could have gone, where did he wind up?"

Following Champ's line of reasoning, Yamato replied, "Nettesheim said he bagged him during the confusion generated by two of our enforcer friends over at Lost Liberty Island."

"Precisely. Have you ever stopped to ask yourself...*why* did Bean choose to hightail it over to New Hell? Think about it. There are all sorts of isolated little places in all sorts of far-away circles. But no, he bolted to one of the busiest there is."

"Hiding in plain sight," Yamato offered, "safety amongst all the other little fishes?"

"Maybe. Maybe not. I did a little diggin' and discovered Bean doesn't have any real friends or associates over that way. No women...or fellas come to that. No secret apartment.

So it got me wonderin'. What if he was conditioned to go there, you know, as if on an automatic pilot kinda thing?"

Not for the first time, Yamato was blown away by the clarity of Champ's uncomplicated logic. "Are you suggesting there might be a link between Chopin and Tesla's current location and Bean's behavior?"

"It's somethin' we gotta look into at least. If he's had one of those bugs in his head affectin' his behavior for some time, what's to say it didn't kick into gear the moment his adrenalin started to pump?"

Yamato felt a surge of optimism that lifted his spirits. "Champ, you ugly sonofabitch, I could fucking kiss you."

"I'd rather you didn't," the grizzled Hound protested, "You're not my type. Too skinny, an' all."

Resisting the urge to hug his partner, Yamato got down to business. "Do me a favor. Get your gear together and contact Nettesheim. Tell him to chivvy along and meet us over at the Hexcalibur Hotel as soon as possible, and by tomorrow at the latest. We'll get the team together and start checking your hunch out. I've got a good feeling about this that shouldn't go to waste."

"Sure thing...and Gemini?"

Yamato stopped to consider her current mission parameters.

"If she's not there already, she soon will be. I have a copy of her itinerary don't forget, so we'll give her a head-sked once we're in situ and ready to go."

"And if we have to wait for em?"

"Then how about we do a little mooching ourselves? Starting at Lost Liberty Island."

*

As she strolled along Tenth Avenue, Gemini had to admit, she rather liked the mood Hell's Kitchen generated in comparison to the claustrophobic press of Dark Cairo. The people here were as brazen as their city, but such an atmosphere fitted the vibe of the area perfectly.

The small park situated between West 47th and 48th Streets typified that ethos, for it had been decorated to reflect an 'in your face, buddy' attitude: spike tipped railings; gangland art deco outlining an ingenious number of ways to conduct a street execution; a combined razorblade court complete with hate board ramp obstacles to increase the chance of injury; lightning tree skeletons; hanging frames, from which locals could string up miscreants caught flouting local dielaws. Such attention to detail, and more, typified why Hell's Kitchen had become something of an unliving legend within one of the most abrasive circles of latterday hell.

Even better, citizens here seemed inured to the outlandish and bizarre, so Gemini's unusual demeanor drew hardly more than a second glance as she breezed along the sidewalk, waiting for the signal that would tell her the meeting was definitely on.

As she'd discovered on the first leg of her roundtrip, everything about Hell's Kitchen was gang and trust oriented. It influenced all aspects of life, whether you were an everyday denizen, a commercial wheeler and dealer, or vermin infesting the 'low-ways' beneath the city's streets. What's more, that trust had to be earned. Nonetheless, the gangs operated by a strict code, and if you ticked all the right boxes and the services you offered were deemed good for business, all sorts of doors—or in this case, manhole covers—would open.

The rat-president and his high table veterans had been intrigued by the testimony from the rat-king of Perish, and made no secret of the fact they were, for the most part, attracted to the idea of brokering a deal with the Reaper's coterie. Word had quickly spread to other chapters regarding what was on offer. In particular, the president had stressed the level of credence extended by the Hell Hounds regarding his subjects' ability to fulfill their end of the bargain. Initial feedback had been so positive that the president had assured Gemini that the proposal would be voted through without a hitch. He knew his people, and anything that gave them an edge in a cutthroat environment was always welcome, especially if that *anything* came with the Reaper's guarantee.

Gemini was itching to see how such assurances would transpose into action.

A high-pitched squeak drew Gemini's attention toward a type-C storm drain on the opposite side of the street. The cover had been lifted and dragged to one side, and Gemini just had time to make eye contact with a chubby, bristle-white face with a puckered scar running across one eye, before her rodent contact turned tail and disappeared belowground.

He's not hanging about? Mind you, I can't blame him. He'd most likely get eaten as much as simply shot. I'd better follow before he gets too far ahead.

Gemini crossed the road, and, without breaking stride, walked over the grate and stepped in. The inlet was rather narrow, and although the rungs were missing, she managed to control her descent by pressing her arms and feet against the side of the barrel shaft until she dropped out the other end into a much wider sewer pipe.

Having visited a half dozen different colonies around the underverse recently, trudging knee-deep in rank smelling, oily black sludge didn't bother her in the slightest. This latest channel was something of a revelation, however, for it reminded her of a subway tunnel more than an actual flush-away remedy for all the decomposing biomaterials that hell could muster in one place at the same time.

Large concrete blocks stretched off into the distance on either side of her, stained brown from use and age. A nev-er-ending stream of effluent trickled down a center trench, failing miserably to clear the small drifts of leaves, tin cans and animal bodies that had accumulated at the base of other inlets. Even more surreal, an agglomeration of strange lime scale deposits dripped from a large overhead grille. Looking like gray-green stalactites, they made Gemini feel as if she's been stranded within the bowels of a weird manmade cave system where she'd never see the light of Paradise again.

The splish-splash of tiny feet marked the way she was expected to go. Following swiftly, the noise of traffic gradu-ally receded, as did the meager offerings of illumination from other drains. When her guide turned away from the main pas-sage and into a side conduit, Gemini was forced to adjust her perceptions to compensate and then picked up the pace. Even so, the going was arduous and frustrating, as she was forced to slow down repeatedly to avoid housing cylinders, control valves and those additional pipes that began sprouting from the low ceiling in ever-increasing numbers.

Time dragged on, and as the sense of isolation grew, Gemini pondered the absence of hangers-on. In other colo-nies she'd visited, she had been surrounded by thousands of furry residents, all intent on being a part of something great-er. But here, the president ran a tighter ship and only allowed direct involvement from his veterans and tunnel captains di-rectly involved in one form of oversight or the other. Gem-ini felt inspired by such efficiency, and couldn't wait to get down to the nitty-gritty of finalizing the deal.

She didn't have to wait long.

Her guide steered her toward a short tiled corridor that branched away at a tangent from the culvert they'd been traversing for the last ten minutes. A faded sign on the wall said: *Sewage System Control.*

Five yards beyond it, a small office loomed out of the darkness. A lime-green door stood ajar, a plethora of markings indicating the bottom panel had been gnawed away by sharp teeth. Next to it, grimy widows obscured any chance of an early peek inside, though the faint chittering sounds emanating from within indicated a reception committee awaited her. Fighting down her excitement, Gemini resisted the urge to scan those occupants, and came to a standstill at the threshold. *Well, well, well. Who would have thought that someone would be so happy at the thought of working with my kind?*

Encouraged, Gemini edged through the entrance and peered in. The wall in front of her was taken up by a floor to ceiling monitoring station and an extended desk that ran the length of the room. Most of the space below each row of screens was filled with banks of buttons and dials. Covered in cobwebs and dust, it was obvious no human had set foot here for years.

The remaining space was occupied by a long, solid oak workbench, surrounded by more than a dozen brightly colored plastic chairs in various states of disrepair. A small cadre of well-groomed rats perched like acrobats upon the backs of thirteen of those chairs.

The president had positioned himself at the head of the table, closest to the top of a detailed carving of a skull and crossbones, below which, a short phrase had been carved into the fabric of the wood: *Hell's Kitchen M.C.—Muridae Canivorus.*

Examining the exquisite workmanship more closely, Gemini discerned the charter had been fashioned in minute detail by the skillful application of sharp incisors. *Would you look at that? Their dexterity is...?*

A stream of distinct cheeps and squeals rang out. Gemini's affinity to animals allowed her to translate the meaning of those sounds instantly.

"Lady Gemini, once again I'm happy to welcome you among us," the president began, "I know you are keen to foster closer ties, and the feeling is mutual. Regardless, I fear you may wish to cut this meeting short when you hear what I have to say?"

A jolt of alarm drained Gemini's *feel good* factor out through the soles of her boots. "Why? Have you run into problems I should know about?"

"Not as such. Think of it as more of a *development*." The president hopped onto the tabletop, stood up on his hind legs and uttered a shrill squeak.

While he waited for someone to respond, he continued, "Your last visit prompted much debate, debate that led to decisive action. Vermin we may be, but we are also a thriving, well organized society. A fraternity of likeminded individuals who are alert to what happens within our territory, and mindful of whom does what and where. Since the day of your departure, we endeavored to determine the whereabouts of those who might generate unwanted focus on our activities. To facilitate that, I had my tunnel captains distribute the fragments of cloth you provided throughout the various chapters of my own and bordering colonies. Though the scent of the humans was weak, our efforts were not in vain..."

It took a moment for the impact of what the president had just said to register. *Eh?* "Not in vain?"

The sound of approaching paws pattered along the hall-way outside, and the president replied, "We thought we'd do a little digging..."

Moments later, a concentrated swarm of dark brown fur-ry bodies burst into the room, carrying and dragging two ex-pensive and well-tailored jackets between them. Her senses being what they were, Gemini registered the fact that, while both items had recently been laundered, they still retained the slightest trace of Chopin and Tesla's spoor, along with a whiff of their respective colognes.

She tested the air. *Cursevoisier L'Eidolon and Infernity for Men, by Killvin Klein. That's our guys alright.* Then it hit her. "Hang on, these items are still...?"

"Still relatively clean? Yes, they would be. They were taken from their individual closets only recently. And as a sign of good faith, we share this find with you freely, though we have not yet officially sealed the deal."

"You have now!"

One moment Gemini stood rooted to the spot in shock, and the next, she was beside the bench, knife at the ready. Af-ter drawing the blade across the palm of her free hand, Gem-ini squeezed her fist and allowed a trickle of ruby vitality to drip onto the gang's logo. "By the power invested in me as one of Satan's Hell Hounds, I hereby honor our agreement."

The president responded by scuttling across the table to the same spot. Squatting down, he raised his tail until it was in front of his snout, and bit down. A dark scarlet drop formed at the tip which he added to Gemini's blood. "We ac-cept, and bind ourselves to that agreement," he concluded.

Chattering broke out among the veterans, which the pres-ident allowed to continue for a while before calling everyone to order.

Gemini couldn't contain her growing anticipation. Referring to the bundle on the floor, she asked, "When did you get these?"

"One of my teams brought them in late last night."

"You mentioned they were taken from actual closets? That must mean the address isn't far away?"

"It isn't. My captain said the apartment is situated on Eleventh Avenue, between Forty-Seventh and Forty-Eighth Streets."

Shit! That's only a block away from where I was walking? "Tell me, do you think your members would be willing to provide assistance on a raid? If you do, anything we don't take away as evidence will be yours to keep."

"Anything?" Unsolicited, chirps of agreement trilled out from around the table.

"That's the way it usually goes. Transgressors forfeit all rights to their property, be it real-estate or personal items. The address and its contents will be seized and is ours to do with as we see fit."

"So there will be no comebacks?"

"As long as you leave the apartment intact so we can use it, none whatsoever."

Those chirps became louder and more insistent. "Then count us in. What we can't eat or make use of directly can be kept for bartering and bribes at a later date. Thank you."

"No, *thank you*," Gemini stressed. Turning away, she opened her mind and gathered her potential to place a long-distance telepathic hail. "If I were you, I'd prepare your people for a busy twenty-four hours. Things are going to get rather hectic."

*

Frozen in the moment, I stared down at the sleeping form of the woman I'd loved for centuries and fought against the whirlwind of contradictory thoughts and emotions that refused to make sense: elation and despair; victory and crushing defeat; joy and sorrow; hope and fear. *This can't be happening. Hell doesn't work this way. It can't be real.*

The last time I'd seen a soul sapphire of these dimensions had been in the trúllefeng crèche on Kí-gal. An esomimetic crystalline construct, it was capable of imprinting on its host's DNHA in order to replicate them in their entirety. Chopin and Tesla had used these very things to duplicate themselves and had stashed their copies within the nursery itself, in the clear hope of evading the consequences of their actions once injustice eventually caught up with them.

But this? I never expected to see...

I couldn't comprehend what my senses were telling me, and tracing my fingers across the cool exterior of the gem didn't help make Garôk's incredible discovery any more tangible. *What's a soul sapphire doing here, of all places? And* how *did it get here?*

For what must have been the umpteenth time in less than a minute, I peered into the multifaceted depths before me. Apart from making my heart pound like a jackrabbit on heat, it didn't help one bit.

It looks like her, that's for sure. And the voices I heard sounded like her. Holding my breath, I scanned the cocooned mental emanations given off by the sleeping woman within. *And that's her signature alright. But is it Strawberry or some obscene copy?*

As usual, my questions only generated further questions, and I began verbalizing my inner conflict. "So who did I destroy back in the Den? Could it have been a doppelganger? If so, when did they copy her? After the original kidnapping in Olde London Town, or when she was reassigned following her execution by Grislington? After all, Chopin and Tesla still had access to part of the mortuary at that time. So this could be...? But that...? Ah fuck it!"

"Do you know this female?" Moved by the tone of my passion, Garôk's query was uncommonly gentle.

"Yes. She was my Chief Inquisitor, a special interrogator of the First Order of Shâitan, and someone who...she was my..." *Oh for Azazel's sake, what about Gemini?*

"You were mated?"

"We were until I..." *obliterated her. Or so I thought.* "It's complicated."

"I see."

"Believe me, no you don't," I countered. "There are two fugitives from injustice I have been hunting for a while now. They are unusually resourceful and have created a catalog of ambiguities that are wreaking untold havoc across the underverse."

Running my gaze along the length and breadth of the gem, I started searching for a catch or any form of indentation that might reveal a means of access to this paragon of confinement. The only thing I could find was a weak psychic trace concentrated in the top right-hand corner where six lattices came together.

There. That's *the source of the projections. She's been calling for help all this time...And I ignored her.* My guts twisted at the thought of Strawberry, alone, helpless, trapped. Blending to the residue, I received a momentary hit of confusion and frustration, a bewildered fugue of random periods of coherence strangled by fractured consciousness.

"She needs my help." Gathering my power, I raised my fist to strike. "I'll worry about her actual identity later."

Jotûn placed a cautionary hand on my arm. "Do you know what you're doing?"

"No, not really," realizing my gaffe, I stiffened, "but I can't just leave her here."

"Even so, I would advise caution. My own perceptions tell me the female is in some form of induced coma. It doesn't take a genius to appreciate waking her from such a state abruptly could prove detrimental."

My fist fell to my side and an irritating feeling of impotence squeezed at my balls. "I've got to do something, Jotûn. She was my...she's..."

"She's safe for now, yes?" he intervened, "surly the environment within the crystal will continue to protect her from Hatamâh's unfavorable conditions?"

"I guess I don't have much choice." Inside the sapphire, Strawberry stirred, making my inability to do anything all the more painful. "By all that's damned, it's so...so difficult just leaving her there."

"Then perhaps you need the assistance of those who have experience with such matters?"

The talle-bhést? And they owe me. "Perhaps you're right."

Jotûn bent close to my ear, "Our written histories tell us the Ascendant is a time for the fallen to rise. If this woman's soul is indeed transitory, or held in stasis, the resonance produced by the alignment of realms can be used to revive her. You cannot afford to jeopardize her future on sentimentality."

He's right. "Thank you, brother. I needed to hear that." Stepping away, I came to a decision. "If I left you alone, could you make your own way back and arrange for some kind of guard to be placed here to watch over her until my return?"

"Of course. I take it from your comments that you intend to seek the assistance I suggested?"

"I do. But first, there's some place I need to be. Understanding more about who I am and what my full potential can accomplish might swing this mess in my...*her* favor."

My thoughts turned to how Gemini would react to this latest development in the mire of my life. *Shit a sideways brick.* I sighed, "Anyway, I still have time, so I'd better get going. See you on the other side."

Chapter 22: Time to Roll a Hard Six

While Yamato found the efficiency of the people he worked with gratifying, it was occasions like this, when something big was about to go down, that he sometimes couldn't help feeling like a fifth wheel.

Setting up the raid had been surprisingly straightforward. Not only were the rodents of Hell's Kitchen remarkably well disciplined and highly organized, but by the time he had arrived in New Hell with Champ in tow, Gemini had not only obtained detailed floor plans of Chopin and Tesla's address, but she had also created an updated scale model of the apartment incorporating all sorts of additional useful details regarding the layout of furniture, comings-and-goings of fellow residents, and so forth, as obtained from those rats who had previously snuck inside.

It had quickly been established the elusive pair had gone out of their way to blend in. And while they had made use of a psychic fuzzer to prevent telepathic eavesdropping, that appeared to be the extent of their meddling. Like everyone else in the block, they relied on the buzz-key entrance and demon doorkeeper for security, as confirmed by Gemini, who had gone so far as to obtain hellectricity records for the property, which gave no indication of the excessive energy consumption indicative of extra concealed countermeasures.

Regardless, Yamato didn't intend to take any chances. Remembering their previous experiences in Perish and Niflheim, he fully expected Chopin and Tesla to have left a warm welcome for unexpected guests, and had arranged his forces accordingly.

An entire chapter of hell-rats had been dispatched to occupy the sewers, alleys and rooftops surrounding their objective, and each veteran in charge of smaller teams carried a tiny portable scanner set to probe the environs for unusual emanations. Further crews had been assigned to accompany the Hell Hounds as they stormed the building; Gemini doing so via the fire escape, Champ and Yamato through the front door. At the exact moment entry was effected, Pascal and his special units would activate atmospheric scramblers—thereby preventing teleportation by natural or mechanical means—while unmarked vans containing armed snatch squads moved into position on all approaches in a two-block radius.

Everyone had arrived on site fifteen minutes previously, and Yamato had allowed them the opportunity to get settled and carry out a final equipment check before deciding it was about time to see how deep the latest rabbit hole went.

Opening his mind to their covert channel, he called, "Everybody listen in. As per our briefing, this is a strike and retrieve mission. While it's doubtful our targets are here, they are the priority. If you see them, try and take them alive. If you perceive the slightest danger, dead will do just fine. Once the premises are secure, quarantine all prohibited articles for sulphorensic examination and stay clear until they have been passed as safe. You all know who you're dealing with, so stay sharp."

He paused to allow the weight of his words to sink in.

"Okay, stand-by..." Drawing his fabled weapon, the *Sword of the Gathering Clouds of Heaven*, he signaled to Champ, and they both sprinted up the final flight of stairs to find a party of rats waiting for them on the landing. Hoisting a Brimstone-Abaddon 6000 pump action shotgun to his shoulder, Champ leaned forward, took aim, and nodded.

"On my command," Yamato resumed, "three, two, one. Go—go—go!"

Yamato ran at the locked entrance, and a trio of deafening reports boomed out, obliterating one side of the doorjamb in three places. He raised his knee and delivered a savage kick to what was left, filling the foyer inside with wood splinters, and—a split-second later—a couple of stun grenades.

Two further detonations followed in quick succession, whereupon Yamato sent the hell-rats on their way to commence their search. As thirteen furry bodies flowed through the gap, the sound of a further explosion and tinkling glass alerted Yamato to the fact that Gemini's assault team had successfully gained access from the rear of the property.

Having worked together for centuries, neither Yamato nor Champ needed to speak, and automatically slipped into age-old drills that had seen them safely through countless trials. Champ curled through the opening and headed right. Yamato jinked left and found himself facing a large dining area adjacent to a well-proportioned kitchen. At first glance, everything looked neat and tidy, as if the occupants had just left for the day.

He paused at the room divide and inspected the integrity of the floors, walls and ceiling. *No pressure pads, infrared sensors...*then he adjusted the sensitivity of his assessment, *or esoteric traps that I can see.*

Such an absence made him all the more suspicions. "Champ, Gemini? This is too quiet and easy for my liking. Fight the urge to rush through. Hang back a little and let the locals do their job first."

Setting the example, Yamato lingered to observe as a small detail of *furballs*—as he'd come to think of them—tap-danced across work surfaces, scampered over furniture, climbed drapes and rummaged around in cupboards. Clearly more professional than they looked, some even stopped every few paces to stretch up on their hind legs to test the air or peer into hidden corners.

Â sô desu ka*! We need to put these little guys on a retainer. They're more astute than some of the people we have on the security details back at the Den.*

The sergeant-at-paws leading the contingent must have heard Yamato's musing, for he turned, gave a little wave and screeched once, before herding his merry band along the adjoining passage toward the main bathroom suite.

I think that means they'd be open to the proposal?

Swallowing down his amusement, Yamato got back to business and passed through the kitchen warily. Searching, tasting, and testing the ether for the slightest hint of anything that could be construed as out of place. By the time he'd emerged from the other side, the rest of his teams had started reporting in.

"The front aspect is clear," Champ hollered from somewhere down the hallway.

Likewise outside, Pascal added. *None of my mobile units have seen anything suspicious on any of the frequencies we're monitoring. Eyeball scans are also negative.*

Yamato went still, expecting Gemini to chip in right away. When she didn't, he allowed a few seconds to pass, before querying, "Gemini, are you still busy?"

You could say that, she answered, telepathically. *I'm outside the box room, the one next to the fire escape itself, and... Well, see what you think?*

She projected an image of an ordinary looking door, yet the moment Yamato's astral gaze fell on it, the urge to do something else incredibly important became overwhelming.

Gemini continued, *haven't you encountered the likes of this before?*

"I certainly have. Hang on, I'm on my way."

Hurrying along the corridor, Yamato took a sharp left and headed toward the rear of the property. He found Champ had already joined Gemini outside the room in question, along with a large gathering of hell-rats who were watching Gemini closely as she paced up and down with her head kinked over to one side in obvious concentration.

Joining the throng, Yamato allowed his ultrasenses to wash across the limits of the forbidding, and said, "I take it this is the first time you've encountered an active void room in the flesh?"

"Yes..." Gemini sounded distracted, "Yes it is. Talk about weird. Every time I fight against the compulsion and try to analyze its nature, my probe stretches and seems to sink into it until..."

"Until it fades from existence?"

"You got it in one. Weird, as I said."

Yamato clucked in sympathy. "That's exactly what happened to the rest of us at Place Venôme across in Perish. Though, from what I'm feeling, it was slightly different to the one we have here?"

"Different?"

"It's hard to explain." Yamato skimmed the esoteric threshold again, "This one is more refined? And smoother in some way, too?" He had an idea. "Let me try something. It probably won't work, but you never know?"

Grasping his sword, hilt upward in both hands, Yamato invoked the power of their order, "*Géill do mo úghdaresh* (Submit to my authority)."

A stuttering tremor shook the floorboards and rattled loose fixtures and fittings. Nevertheless, the door remained firmly shut.

Spinning his blade, Yamato placed cold steel against the lock, summoned the full reservoir of his strength, and tried a hex instead. "*An a' Satanas aínim, se thu* àithen *do anise* (In the name of Satan, I command you to open)."

Electrical discharges etched across the walls and ceiling; lights flickered on and off; the smell of ozone saturated the atmosphere. When it died down, nothing had changed.

Yamato shrugged. *Exactly as Daemon reported it. Where the fuck is he when we...?*

"Can I help?"

Gemini's offer seemed out of place. Gesturing toward the void, Yamato retorted, "You seriously think you could force your way through this?"

"I doubt I'd have any more luck than you did," she admitted, 'but why try forcing your way through when we could attempt something less drastic?"

"Less drastic?"

"Yes. When I was stuck playing escort to Nettesheim earlier this week, he shared several incantations with me that, in his words, 'should operate sufficiently well, seeing as the reactive agent incorporates traits of the Bãlefire which you all have running through your veins as a result of your ordination as Hell Hounds.'"

"What incantations?"

"One was for invisibility. Another related to the healing of personal wounds, and the final invocation is supposed to enhance an individual's capacity for more precise remote viewing. I hadn't mentioned anything as I haven't had an opportunity to try any of them out," she nodded toward the sealed room, "until now. I was thinking, why not try and take a peek instead of battering our way in?"

"*Urusai*! That could work. At least, it'll do until Daemon gets back and blows it wide open." Yamato felt unexpectedly encouraged. "What does it involve?"

Gemini pursed her lips. "For one thing, what I'm about to do is unnatural. So I'll be expending a lot of energy providing sufficient focus to filter through the static. *You'll* have to link to me and act as my eyes and ears."

"No problem. Let's do it."

Taking up a position directly in front of the door, Gemini reached forward and leaned her weight against the uppermost panels. Knowing that skin contact would be best; Yamato stood behind Gemini and placed his fingers to her temples. Then he relaxed.

A moment or two of severe disorientation followed as he adjusted to the world as experienced through Gemini's rarified perceptions. When things had resolved, a glittering curtain of luminescent wasps hovered before them, buzzing and sparking, and filling the abyss with flickering concentrations of light.

He felt a slow crawl of energy as Gemini gathered her potential and molded it to her purpose. Then her disembodied voice said: "Though what stands before me will remain both closed and dim, grant me the discernment Allsight brings, to behold what lies within."

Yamato thought the phrase a little ridiculous and started to grin. A sizzling *crack* wiped the smile from his face an instant later as his sensibilities were twisted out of sync by a sudden dropping sensation that caused his heart to leap into his mouth. *Unholy shit!*

Reality contracted and extended like an elastic band twanged in multiple different directions at once. Luckily, things soon snapped back into place. When they did, his acuity clarified into a restricted 'tunnel-vision lens view' of the room on the other side of the door. Except, it wasn't a room, it was a small cavern, the walls of which were lined in stones that glowered through subtle hues of red and blue, pink and green...and nothing else.

It's a cave—cave—cave... Yamato's mental deliberation resonated across an incomprehensible distance. *And it's been emptied of anything of value—value—value...*

Opposing energies clashed. Yamato became so lightheaded that he was forced to let go and took several steps backward. Fortunately, guiding hands prevented him from falling, and after a few quick breaths, the spots dancing across his vision faded away.

Champ clicked his fingers in front of Yamato's face and stared into his eyes. "Are you back with us buddy? I hope so, because I'm not the only one who'd like to know more about what you saw."

"An empty space is what I saw," Yamato snorted, "whatever Chopin and Tesla had stashed away in there is long gone...as I anticipated."

"Any ideas what we're gonna do next, then?"

"What we should have done a long time ago. Whatever our fugitives are up to must be into its final stages for them to have gone to ground so thoroughly. While we might not know where they are, we *do* know the location of one of their major insurance policies." He placed an arm around Champ's shoulders and hugged him closer. "I've wanted to resort to more drastic measures for some time now, so you and I are going to take a little side trip to Kí-gal."

"We are?" Champ's eyes lit up at the prospect.

"Yes, we are. I know Daemon was hoping to save the soul sapphires stashed away there for further examination, but he's not here. I am. We need to roll a hard six to regain the initiative; *do* something that will cause Chopin and Tesla to panic, or surprise them when they try and use their fallback option. Taking the crystals out of the equation might make that difference, so I won't rest easy until we've destroyed them."

"What about me?" Gemini had edged forward to join in on the conversation.

Yamato turned to face her squarely. "Gemini, you possess the most refined abilities of us all. After you've wound things down here, scoot across to Lost Liberty Island." He threw a quick glance Champ's way. "I've been led to believe there might be a reason Castor Bean made a beeline for that location after he fled Perish. If there is, I want *you* to find it."

*

Enjoying the solitude that evening brought, Frédéric Chopin faced into the stiff breeze streaming across from New Hell Harbor and breathed in the ambiance of the fetid night air. An acrid stench of rot and decay overpowered the salty tang of brine, though Chopin paid scant regard to either, distracted as he was by the sound of a waltz and the occasional *clink* of glass on glass wafting over from the soirée aboard the Royal Satanic Ship Titanic.

Approaching midnight, the party was in full swing.

From his vantage point on the lip of a small hatch cut into the base of Lost Liberty's torch, the gaily colored lights strung out across the balustrades and between the funnels of the forty-six thousand ton leviathan made it appear as if a fairytale castle was at anchor off the coast, waiting to disgorge its gossamer-winged hordes against the unsuspecting denizens of Madhatten at any moment.

"Odd, that I would find myself savoring the peace and solitude of a place I hate so much," he muttered to himself. "Soon, my love will be here to enjoy such dark delights with me, and then—free of the Undertaker's curse at last—we shall truly start to live, and I will rise to new heights as I release fresh works unhindered."

His daydreaming reminded him how fitting the site for initiating their daring escapade was. *In the world above, this monument is a beacon of hope and freedom. Well, by the time I'm finished, it will shine for all eternity as a reminder of Satan's incompetence to prevent my autonomy.*

Chopin glanced up at the raging inferno above him where a rubricated column of Bãlefire ascended more than a hundred yards into the heavens, searing the atmosphere in flames and menace. *Not long, my sweet Amanite. Not long...which reminds me, I'd better join Nikola. He'll be expecting me to help him with the final inventory.*

Easing the door shut, Chopin clambered down the forty-foot set of rungs fastened to the interior framework of Lost Liberty's arm, and made his way across to the nearest stairs leading up to the crown.

He found Tesla hard at work, tinkering with the settings to the interdimensionhell fuzzer and temporal mitigator interface. *That's so like him, not leaving anything to chance. Mind you, it is our main line of defense. Without it, we wouldn't be safe within our little pocket of warped reality and everyone and his dog would be out baying for our blood and the juicy reward that goes with handing us in.*

Tesla noticed his friend's arrival and looked up. "I'm glad you're here. I wanted to show you what I've prepared for when the Unveiling begins."

Leaving his current task unfinished, Tesla sauntered across toward the opposite side of the walkway where a number of foldout chairs had been neatly arranged in sequence. All of them contained one form of artifact or another. Referring to the nearest set, he began, "You'll see the first pairing involves a set of Damocles Daggers and signets. I took the liberty—excuse the oafish pun—of re-cutting the gem from the *Sword of Seraphim Speed* to ensure the rings now contain sufficient power to compensate for the time lag created by the field of distorted physics we'll be forced to operate in. The bonus being, once we're clear of the warp, they'll also help us stay one step ahead of the competition."

"As always, Nikola, I like the way you think."

"Aha, but there's more." Tesla indicated a bench, over which a dull, yellow colored animal pelt had been hung. He explained, "Don't worry; I've discovered the Golden Fleece lies dormant in the absence of soul energy. It'll manifest as soon as we approach it. I placed it there so we can both ensure to be free of our hell-induced maladies before proceeding further. A necessary precaution, I feel, especially as we not only have to use the wings, but *you* will need to enunciate the incantation contained within the Scroll of Divergent Union in a defined and orderly fashion. Only then will you be able to create the precise tonal reference to harness the power of the alignment."

"I agree. I have to drop the Veil at my first attempt; otherwise it'll blow our element of surprise."

Tesla gestured toward a sealed medusanite casket lying near the secondary stairs at the end of the gallery. "I must say, I long to see what the wings can actually do."

"I'd totally forgotten about that aspect," Chopin admitted, "did you manage to conduct further research on the matter?"

"I did. *The Sword of Uncovered Secrets* was quite explicit in regards to our circumstances. Evidently, all we have to do to harness their majesty is hold them close to our bodies and visualize our destination."

"That's it?" Chopin was genuinely shocked.

"That's it. Once invoked, their power translates us out from the underverse, across the Divide, through the remnants of the Veil and straight into the outer precincts of the heavenly approaches."

Chopin whistled. "Lucky that we've both had dreams about that, eh?"

"Indeed, otherwise we'd have been screwed at the last hurdle..." Tesla elbowed his companion in the ribs, "and you know how much I *love* being screwed over. Ask Edison." He chuckled to himself, briefly. "As it is, once we arrive, I'll only have to place the Key of Sigh's against Zion's gates, and they will literally fade away before our eyes."

"And we'll be in..." Trying his best not to let the lure of imminent success run away with him, Chopin turned to the matter of the hurdles they might encounter from within the holy city. "What major problems do you anticipate?"

"The heavenly host will react to our presence, of course. And when they come, they'll come fast and hard. Fortunately, I only require a few moments to obtain the frequency at which Zion's walls function. Once I have it, I'll be able to encode the mitigator to generate an appropriate field that not even the Reaper or the royal asswipe himself will be able to breach. Thankfully, our signets will keep us out of harm's way while I do that. No, *yours* is the more dangerous task,

Frédéric. Do you feel confident at being able to locate Miss Dupin's spirit promptly?"

Removing a small translation device from within his coat pocket, Chopin gloated, "Now you've incorporated a sample of Amantine's DNA into the orb's matrix, I'm certain it'll home in on her like a moth to a neon light."

"Just as well you were allowed to keep that pendant containing a photo and a lock of her hair then; otherwise I honestly don't know how you'd manage."

"Yes. For once, the Undertaker's cruelty backfired. I can remember his face, even now. The sneer, the curdling voice emphasizing how much I'd rue the day I'd been condemned. Forever separated from the one I loved, with nothing to remind me of her but a fading picture and few strands of hair wrapped in a bow. Ha! We'll see who has the last laugh now, won't we?"

"Indeed. Free of the curse, free of the strictures of condemnation, our unlives will truly begin. And not before time."

Time? Chopin glanced at his watch. *It's nearly midnight.* "If you don't mind, I'm going to watch the Titanic sink. Care to join me?"

Tesla looked back at the interface he'd been working on. "Thank you, but no. I want to make sure this thing is in tip-top condition. And of course, I still have to prepare our little, *going away present* for those who are bound to follow after we've left."

"Then I'll see you soon." Chopin grasped his friend by the hand and gave him an affectionate hug before starting his slow way back to the arm of the statue.

Climbing the steep stairs in such a restricted space set his joints to aching; reminding him of a thorn in the flesh he'd been forced to endure for over a hundred and fifty years.

Well, not for much long –? The sound of a distant siren alerted him to the fact that the witching hour had arrived. *Oops, I'd better hurry.*

Clambering painfully up the last half dozen rungs, Chopin emerged from the hatch just as a second blast from the same horn announced the finale had arrived.

Across the water, pyrotechnic bursts ignited the sky in red, silver, gold and green blooms, providing a brilliant retina-burning fanfare to escort partygoers on their way to a watery grave and imminent reassignment. Even at this distance, Chopin could see a frenzy of monstrous bubbles frothing and churning at the bow. Each spherule seemed eager, intent on eating its way through the hull plating to consume those denizens crowded within as quickly as possible. Sure enough, it only took a few seconds before the Titanic began to list. Then the nose dipped forward, whereupon a loud cheer erupted from those clinging to the railings along the upper decks.

Fools! Chopin thought them delusional. *I hope they feel sated, wasting what little opportunity they have on mindless charades at normalcy. Still, Satan must feel gratified his great conspiracy is hidden behind the veneer of a* live for the past—die for now—and live again later *pantomime. If only these morons realize they enslave themselves to...?*

The musical serenade screeched to a halt and, amid cries of alarm, was replaced by the nationhell anthem, *Nearer To Satan Than Thee.*

Just in time, for the stern of the great vessel rose up abruptly, lifting free of the water in a silver-white cascade that exposed three huge barnacle encrusted propellers to the world. But only for an instant.

The whole of the Madhatten skyline seemed to hold its breath, then the ship's lights went out, popping one by one as the prow of the liner knifed its way through an explosion of spray and steam into the inky depths.

In a matter of minutes, the surface of the bay was calm once more, with no trace that an oceangoing liner had ever existed.

Chopin felt the pomp and ceremony of the occasion a fitting conclusion to the day. "And *that's* how it will soon be for me, because once I'm gone, none here will ever see me again."

Chapter 23: Best Laid Plans

The rush of interdimensionhell travel receded, and Champ and Yamato stepped through the hydraspace terminus and onto a wide ledge cut into the side of a mountain. No sooner had they appeared than two Kigali sentries stood either side of the entrance to a decorative reception area snapped from relaxed wariness to full attention. Wings flared, quills erect, both stomped forward exuding aggressive competence. Once they'd registered who the intruders were, however, they returned to their posts without a word and resumed their watch. Even so, Yamato threw them a lazy salute before turning on his heel to take in the view.

Three thousand feet below, a wide open plain of simmering cinders and bubbling tar pits stretched away for as far as the eye could see. The ground shook beneath his feet as an adjacent volcano grumbled, belching sulfurous smoke and golden flames into a sky already overshadowed by a permanent ochre shroud.

By all that is unholy, I love this place, Yamato breathed, *I've really got to remember to press Daemon into negotiation a deal with Kur to allow us to vacation here from time to time.*

Beside him, Champ's reaction was the exact opposite. Coughing up phlegm from the soles of his boots and sneezing loudly, the former cowboy cursed, "Goddam soot and shite!" A layer of finely granulated ash had already started to coat them from head to foot. "Jumpin' Jehoshaphat, I'm glad we don't have to put up with this crap on a regular basis. It'd play havoc with my allergies."

"Allergies?" *That's a new one.* "Since when?"

Champ didn't miss a beat, "Ever since Him upstairs invented hugs and kisses, good deeds and warm sentiments… And kittens. I can't stand 'em. Cuddly little fuckers, makin' grown people act like retards, oohing and aahing and crashin' Hatebook with their endless video clips of utter drivel."

"We'd better get you safely underground then," Yamato snickered, "I can't have the meanest son of a bitch I've know for a hundred and seventy years reduced to a sniveling, tearful wreck because of a few specks of dust now, can I?"

Uncharacteristically silent, Champ stalked away, brushing himself off as he went. At first, Yamato was concerned his jibe might go unanswered. But he knew his partner well. As Champ crossed into the atrium leading to the caves, he flicked the finger and mumbled something under his breath. Yamato couldn't quite make out his words, but that didn't matter, for the telepathic picture Champ conjured in his mind—in which he invited the Lead Hound to engage in a spot of vigorous sexual gymnastics with himself—was graphically clear. *Ah, that's more like it.*

Moving to catch up, Yamato walked in silence and waited until they had passed the upper halls and completed several circuits of their spiraling descent, before taking out the hyperspatial translocation device.

"I was wonderin' when you'd start gettin' sensible," Champ teased, "this bein' an urgent mission and all. Why waste over an hour mincing down a subterranean helter-skelter when we could be there in an instant? We don't want our marks dyin' of boredom when *we* should be makin' their last moments as horrific as possible."

"I'm just being cautious, and respectful of our host's beliefs," Yamato hefted the orb up and down in one hand and peered along the passage in both directions, "and now we're far enough away, we can revert to our usual ignorant selves and get this show on the road."

Reaching out, Yamato grasped Champ by the shoulder and activated the generator. The world turned black, and then white. Wide granite blocks and regularly spaced torches gave way to a gloomy corridor comprised of blue-gray rock laced through with veins of glowing orange quartz that pulsed in time to the beat of the mountain's heart.

The hall before them now ended in an angled archway, bordered in ivory colored marble slabs. A lone character had been carved across the lintel: the Kigali word for peace—*Siothellnath*.

Side by side, the Hounds stepped through.

Yamato shivered, as the sensation always made him imagine what it must be like to be covered in a swarm of insects endowed with icicles for legs. Happily, the period of transition was brief, and the environment on the far side of the portal more than made up for any momentary discomfort.

On their left, the bulk of an impressive escarpment stretched up into infinite shadows. A narrow path threaded its meager way along the front of that wall, dropping away on its opposite side into a gaping chasm where the earth's blood spat and seethed as it spewed its way along, vomiting great gouts of liquid fire high into the air at irregular intervals. The heady perfume of brimstone soaked the ether in vibrant power.

Now this…this is more like it.

Two hundred yards away, a similar opening to the one through which they had arrived, beckoned. But Yamato knew they needed to adhere to protocol—protocol that came in the shape of living stone—or be forever lost in the warren of tunnels that lay beyond its innocent looking threshold.

A portion of the cliff face broke free at the midway point, creating a miniature landslide that spilled shale and pebbles across the track and into the thermometric pyre below. The slide clarified into an arm. Then a battering-ramlike head. A thick torso followed. Soon, a humanoid shape stood before them, devoid of hands, feet, or any discernable features and covered in thick plates that made it appear as if Victor Frankenstein had been let loose to spawn a new breed of crazy paving mutants.

Both Hounds waited for their escort to approach. It didn't take long, for the talle-bhést was able to move far more swiftly than its size or lumbering gait at first suggested. Once it was within a few steps of them, Yamato raised his voice to utter a single word, "Síothellnath." He followed it up with a brief psychic update as to why they were here.

The stone man halted its advance and seemed to consider the two Hounds in some unfathomable way. Whether it was communicating with anyone, Yamato couldn't discern, but the talle-bhést soon decided they were friends, for it turned on the spot and plodded off toward the exit.

In single file, Champ and Yamato followed, and having gained the labyrinth on the far side, began discussing what to do once they arrived at the crèche.

"If you want to send a message to all the other scumbags out there who might be contemplatin' treason, kill Chopin and Tesla's doubles outright," Champ snarled, his cheeks darkening to red at the thought of venting his special brand of injustice upon them. "Don't wake 'em up. Don't show 'em the slightest hint of mercy. Don't even let 'em speak."

"And what about intel?"

"What about it?"

"You know as well as I do what the soul sapphires are capable of. Gemini likened them to biometric flash drives that can create an exact copy of their physical hosts, memories and all. Just imagine the juicy morsels we might be able to squeeze from the dopplegangers before we send them on the way to the Slab…" He had a thought, "*If* they even get that far, being nonentities?"

"Are you kidding?" Champ scoffed, "do you think either of those bastards would have been that slack?"

"It's not a question of being slack, Champ, not where their own simulacrums are concerned. It *is* a question of being thorough. Think about it. If you were preparing a spare body for yourself, wouldn't you want it endowed with all your latest knowledge and insights and experiences?"

"Yeah, I suppose you're right," Champ murmured. He chewed on his lip and mulled things over, eventually brightening when he realized what Yamato's strategy would entail. "So, we get to torture the fuck outta them first, *then* we torture them some more as we slice n' dice 'em? Even better. Though I get first dibs on their finger and toe bones."

"I thought that might cheer you…?" *I don't recall this passageway?* "Hang on a second…"

Having visited the nursery on a number of occasions now, Yamato had always endeavored to remember large portions of their route through the maze, committing a little more to memory each time he passed the same way. The gallery they were currently traversing was completely different to anything he'd seen before.

Sneaky swines. Kur said it would take some time for the talle-bhést to relax about us, and it looks like he wasn't joking. They've never used –? "Shit! That was fast?"

Turning the latest corner, Yamato was shocked to discover they had already arrived at the outer precincts of the nursery. In the space of a score of steps, the ambient temperature of their environs rose considerably, a perplexing feeling, especially as the obsidian walls and flagstones did just the opposite, and gradually bleached whiter and whiter under the grip of an all-pervading hoarfrost.

How did we manage to cut more than thirty minutes off our journey? Have they been toying with us all along? Or does this mean we've gained a measure of trust?

As if hearing his thoughts, their escort picked up the pace and veered into a colonnaded corridor. Adorned with Cimmerian Teutonic sculptures and parametric symbols resonating with ungodly power, it terminated after fifty yards at a set of floor-to-ceiling double metal gates.

Two sentinels stood watch outside the entrance. Called talle-béth, they were attired in jet chain mail with matching helmets, and armed with jasper maces that appeared robust and long enough to hold up the roof should there be a cave-in. Not that the talle-béth would have any difficulty wielding their weapons in a fight, for they were more than twice the size of their smaller cousins.

Neither guardian gave the slightest indication they'd noticed the Hell Hounds presence. Nevertheless, the ponderous leaves barring entrance to the crèche swung open before Yamato's party had advanced more than half way along the arcade, exposing the reflective plane of the final barrier.

As they marched up to that foreboding, Yamato marveled at how completely it obscured any hint as to what might exist beyond its glassy sheen. *It never ceases to amaze me, the power some of the older tribes possess. His Satanic Majesty could learn a thing or two, if only he wasn't so averse to compromising and forming treaties with other rulers. The places we could protect with a shield like that...oh-oh, here we go.*

Champ and Yamato had been led to a halt between the talle-béth sentries. The giants reached out with their scepters to touch each Hell Hound lightly on their arms. For the third time that day, Yamato felt a chill worm its way along his spine. As it died, the invisible curtain barring their way shivered, then dropped to the floor, revealing the vast arena that was the trúllefeng crucible.

At more than half a mile across, the nursery gave the impression that an angel-hewn basilica had been carved out of bare rock to commemorate the perfect amalgamation of fire and ice. Its walls were carnelian warm, glass smooth and impossibly shiny, yet flecked through by bitter fragments in myriad frozen hues of blue and gray and silver. *Something this fragile shouldn't be able to exist in the roots of a volcano?*

Yamato was reminded of the evenings he had spent as a boy in first-century Japan, staring up at the bowl of a night sky so dusted in stars that it always made him feel as if the heavens might ignite at any moment.

High above, at the apex of the cavern, the point of a glowing inverted pyramid pierced the sanctuary like the beak of a prodigious great hawk, frozen at the moment it had skewered its prey. Ichor trickled from the wound in languid rivulets, bleeding the mountain's substance in a never-ending infusion of raw power.

Slowly, surely, a surfeit of translucent energies congealed at the tip of the monolith until they were large and heavy enough to form droplets of unadulterated vitality. Then they would fall—as silent tears of iridescent joy—adding their essence to the ever expanding crèche below.

Over the centuries, those drops had gradually accumulated into a mirror image fistula of hard surfaces and razor edges, a Nirvana setting of reflected light and rainbow prisms that vibrated to an inner symphony which set Yamato's eyes and gums to itching.

Set on an outcrop of dark volcanic rock, the nursery confounded the senses, for the mound sat in the middle of a membranous mass that stretched for the entire circumference of the vault, and which throbbed and pulsed and looked for all the world like a wildly palpitating heart.

The more he stared, the more Yamato perceived he was losing touch with reality, a sensation both disturbing and invigorating. *No wonder the Kigali and talle-bhést revere this place,* Yamato mused. *It's aware, a living kiln of primal beauty, powerful enough to educate even the darkest of souls.*

Beside him, Champ echoed the sentiment in his own sweet way. "Fuck me, brother. Who needs recreational drugs when you can sneak in here and enjoy burnin' your retinas to sloppy goo in less than five minutes?"

A timely bit of counsel. We need to be getting on with the business at hand.

A narrow viaduct extended from the gates and out toward the island. Yamato was relieved they didn't have to endure the full might of the mind-altering forge by hiking all the way to the far side.

Altering his perspective, he allowed his astral sight to sink down through the molecules of the bridge and glided along its length until he reached the pontoon supporting the central span. There, agents of the Cyber Ops Division of the GDSI—a unit Daemon trusted implicitly—huddled together, managing a bewildering array of monitoring equipment focused on two, coffin sized, lozenge shaped crystals attached to the underside of the arch.

Tucked well up into the overhanging recess, the soul sapphires were not only concealed from mundane sight, but had been secreted within a sensory asperity that masked them from all but the most resolute scans.

Extending his stride, Yamato led the way forward until they were directly above the anomaly, at which point he clambered up over the railing and dropped the twelve feet down onto the platform. Hot on his heels, Champ crowded close behind.

Addressing the officer in charge of the GDSI agents, Yamato said, "Sorry for the short notice, Alain, but I need you and your guys to pack up their gear. This site is being closed down."

A seasoned veteran, Alain took the news in his stride. "Another day, another Diablo. Any problems we need to know about?"

"No, just a change of our best laid plans...as usual. And it's something that needs implementing as soon as possible."

"Then we were never here." Quick on the uptake, Alain turned to his operatives and began issuing orders.

Thankfully, the surveillance system was of the very latest state-of-the-art integral modular design, so in no time at all, most of the apparatus had been unplugged and simply locked away within its own reinforced casing.

As the team completed their final inventory and prepared for departure, Yamato ushered Champ to one side. "How do you want to play this? Wake them both up at the same time and try to play one off against the other? Or disembowel the most resilient character and feed his intestines to the blabbermouth?"

Champ took his time to give the question sober consideration. He always did that when he was about to carry out an interrogation, for while he was one of the roughest individuals anyone would ever meet in hell, he was also a master of his art.

"If it were me," Champ ventured, "I'd bring 'em round together and paint the direst, most heinous picture I could regarding their lack of a future. After all, they're clones, so they don't officially exist. That means we can extend their sufferin' with no chance of 'em regeneratin' the body parts we hack off. And there'll surely be no escapin' to the Slab. You know the way it is when someone tries to tough it out. We pick that idiot, slice off his nose, ears, fingers and toes and start snackin' on 'em. Then, while he's bleeding out and screaming for a quick end, we turn the heat up on his buddy."

"So, a good cop—good cop, soft approach then?" Yamato met Champ's gaze squarely. They both burst out laughing at the same time.

By now, the GDSI agents had instigated the teleportation process. Having overheard the two Hounds conversation, the look on their faces as they disappeared betrayed a wide range of feelings, of which, revulsion predominated. Of course, that only caused the Hounds to laugh all the harder, and the sound of their jesting soon became entangled upon countless symmetrical corners and prisms, where it was amplified a thousandfold before being refracted onward. In moments, the entire chamber rang to a cacophony of mirth.

Yamato waited for the chiming ricochets to abate, and removed the *Sword of the Gathering Clouds of Heaven* from its scabbard. Peering up, he studied the two forms sleeping innocently within their amber cocoons, perfectly preserved and completely oblivious to what was about to befall them. *Except that they're* not *innocent. Not if they're exact copies of the two worst renegades we've ever had to deal with.* He smiled. *Of course, that only makes this all the more pleasurable.*

Adapting his probe, Yamato determined those points where the gems had been affixed to the bridge. Projecting those coordinates to his partner, he murmured, "Champ, why don't you see if you can't wake them up?"

The double *clack* of an explosive, solid shot slug being chambered gave Yamato the opportunity to step back a little. The shotgun barked, and then barked again, a total of four times in quick succession. Stone chips and crystal shards rained down, forcing Yamato to avert his eyes until the shower had passed. When he looked again, he was surprised to see both trúllefengs still clinging to the skirting of the arch as if glued in position. He was about to ask Champ to try his luck a second time, when the screeching protest of glass laboring under stress assailed his ears.

Both Hounds glanced at each other, and—barely in time—sprang apart as the soul sapphires let out a final shriek before dropping, nose first, onto the area they'd been occupying only a moment before. Already weakened, the stones shattered on impact, spilling their human cargo to the floor amid a tinkling wave of glittering surf—and surprisingly—snatches of frantic music.

Chopin and Tesla's doubles lay twitching on the floor, flopping from side to side and gasping for air like a freshly landed catch displayed on a fishmongers ice tray. A smell of chemicals and amniotic fluid predominated.

"Are they havin' a fit or somethin'?" Champ prodded Tesla's form with the toe of his boot, before squatting down beside the bewildered entity for a closer look.

"There must be a correct way of waking them properly," Yamato surmised, "Apparently, knocking on the door with an Abaddon 6000 isn't one of them."

"So how long do you think they're gonna stay like this?"

"I haven't a clue." Yamato sounded the immature psyches carefully. Their thoughts were chaotic, laced with jumbled memories of their accomplishments before death and all the opportunities they'd wasted after arriving in hell. Even better, those fragments also contained snippets of what they'd been plotting since teaming up to rebel against Satan's system. *Now that could be useful, if they ever manage to return to underearth's orbit.*

Their predicament gave him an idea. Nudging his colleague forward, Yamato suggested, "A little stimulus in the right area might help rouse them more fully?"

Champ didn't need asking twice. Placing his shotgun to one side, he stepped across the stricken scientist and straddled him. After making himself comfy, he reached into his pocket and removed a cruelly endowed pair of knuckledusters. Sliding them into place, Champ then leaned forward, supported himself on one arm, and drew back his fist.

Even so, before Champ could deliver his first blow, Tesla's sim somehow managed to gain an awareness of his surroundings. Sitting up, he grasped Champ by the shoulders, stared earnestly into his eyes, and said, "My good fellow, don't be a page torn from someone else's story…"

Yamato reacted. Surging forward, he raised his sword, ready to strike. *But is he actually awake or acting under a preprogrammed compulsion?*

Champ obviously didn't feel threatened. Signaling for his partner to hold back, he waited to see what would happen.

Tesla continued, "Have the courage to leave what you need to, behind. Like us, plan ahead and be eager to write that first passage in a brand new chapter to your life…" Beckoning Champ closer, Tesla whispered, "And for goodness sake, don't share any of your secrets with Edison. I mean it; he'll pretend to be your friend. Praise you. Push you. Encourage you. But in the end, he'll steal your sec...he'll try to..." The light of fickle comprehension went out. "Peter Piper picked a...he skipped and he dipped...this has all happened before, and it will all happen again."

Without warning, Tesla lunged at Champ. Grabbing him in a bear hug, the wayward scientist started sobbing. Yamato could see his friend trying to break free and stand up, but Tesla's grasp was so tight, there was no way Champ could prize his fingers apart.

Champ's face went white. Thunder congealed on his brow. So swiftly that Yamato didn't realize what was happening at first, Champ delivered a stunning head-butt that crushed the bridge of Tesla's nose and sent him sprawling. With his hands now free, Champ rolled to one side and flicked off his knuckledusters. Snatching up his shotgun, he came to his feet and unloaded it straight into Tesla's chest.

A scarlet streak followed Tesla's body as it slid along the floor, the surface of the pontoon clearly visible through the gaping hole where his heart and lungs used to be.

Ouch! Yamato breathed a sigh of resignation. "When I said, 'a little stimulus in the right area,' I didn't mean for you to...? Hang on, look at that." Yamato strode forward to stand beside his friend and pointed down at the doppelganger's remains, "he's not fading."

"Be careful what you wish for, cruel harbingers of death," a grieving voice intoned from behind them. Yamato spun on the spot to find Chopin's avatar had managed to stand erect. Despite its opening remarks, however, it seemed totally unaware of either Hound's existence and was instead facing out into the expanse of the crèche, as if delivering an oratory to an audience. "...the crimson tide you unleashed reveals how unsettled your dreams truly are. How will I savor that faltering cadence when your last breath was so violently wrenched from your mortal cup? My commiserations, stout fellow, for you were..."

"Fuck this." Champ cocked his weapon and brought it to bear.

Anticipating what his partner was about to do, Yamato restrained him with a single gesture. "Just remember, these guys can't dissipate. I don't know if that's because of where we are or what they are. You might want to take advantage of that?"

"Oh, I will," Champ growled in reply, "don't worry."

Slinging his gun, Champ whipped out his knife instead and crept forward with a definite spring in his step. Sidling up behind the still droning copycat, he picked his spot and brought the point of his elbow down on its neck.

Chopin folded like a deck of cards. As he collapsed, Champ caught him by the hair and bent him back across his thigh. The razor edge of his blade came to rest against an open and exposed throat. "Now you listen to me, you freaky stir-fried zombie. I don't know what rodeo your batshit insanity is wavin' its hat in, but I'm here to tell you plain as day, you're gonna die. It's up to you how quick you go. Quick n' easy, like your butt-buddy over there, or—my preference—nice n' slow so I get to cut pieces off you and eat 'em as you watch..." Champ paused to run the tip of his knife from one side of Chopin's throat to the other, opening a shallow cut all the way. "What's it gonna be?"

Yamato was impressed. *Now* that's *skillful. He managed to draw blood without going deep enough to sever anything vital.*

Notwithstanding the indignity of his posture, Chopin's deportment suggested he might take the threat seriously if asked the right question. That illusion was ruined the moment he opened his mouth. Tilting even further back so he could meet Champ's gaze, Chopin wailed, "You are a stubborn crown of thorns brandished against me in a storm racked sea. Gail ripped and besieged from all sides, I labor. Proud against attritions lash, I laugh as I spurn the advances of your abrasive kiss and the lack of…"

Champ's expression betrayed no emotion whatsoever as he swung his arm up high, and chopped down, neatly severing the clone's right ear. It made no difference; Chopin continued his diatribe as if nothing untoward had happened.

"…now aware, my passion resounds with the vigor granted to one born to contend through intolerance, oppression and bloody uprising…" The blade flashed again in a threefold arcing ribbon, and two complete nipples—with areolas intact—and another lobe fell to the floor. "…behold; I am tempered by the heat of contention. My fevered brow reaps sweat as you reap your enemies. Scything sinews and…"

Exasperated, Champ stepped back and turned to Yamato for guidance, "Buddy, he ain't respondin' to pain. Not even a little bit."

He's right. This is useless. There's an obvious process to follow to animate them fully. Without it, we may as well be interrogating a runny turd for daring to pose as a wet fart.

"End it," Yamato answered his friend's unasked query, "we might not have been able to get them to speak, but we'll still achieve what we came here to do."

Champ couldn't hide his disappointment, and vented it the only way he knew how: physically and violently.

Grasping his knife in both hands, the burly Hound bunched his muscles and put all his strength into a blow that buried his blade up to the hilt in Chopin's cranium. Not waiting to witness the results of such a devastating strike, he followed through immediately by driving a jackhammer knee into the side of Chopin's face, scattering blood and teeth like rice at a wedding. Maintaining momentum, Champ thrust forward and followed Chopin to the floor, using his weight and impetus to crush the fragile skull to a pulp beneath that same kneecap.

A sickening crack resounded throughout the length and breadth of the chamber.

Yamato could see the crown of Chopin's head had split, spilling gray matter and odd colored fragments across the paving slabs. Other bloody fluids seeped from his nose, mouth, and the stumps where his ears used to be. *If only this were real. Still, we're gradually working our way toward...?*

The body moved. "How in the blazes?"

Ahead of him, Champ swore and jumped back from the should-be corpse.

Chopin's eyes blinked open. Even at this distance, Yamato could see one of the pseudo-composer's pupils was wide and black, and focused on nothing but mysteries unanswered. Unbelievably, Chopin urged his executioners closer and struggled to sit up. He tried to speak, but his tongue and jaw refused to work properly.

Thinking his communiqué at them instead, he declared:

The skin you shed

Hides a perfect gift cast down.

An expression of yourself

I will employ for liberty and fire.

Malcontent,

I prepare the ultimate banquet here,

A dish, best served cold,

Knowing your last bite shall fog the vanity of misguided loyalty,

And your epitaph will be my crowning achievement.

Having remained alive for long enough to complete its task, the doppelganger fell limp, coughed once, and expired.

"What do you make of that?" Champ mumbled, clearly spooked by creatures that were almost a weird as he was, "Do you think their immunity to pain was deliberate, or a side effect of being off the reservation nuts?"

Yamato wasn't listening. Instead, he was busy; repeating certain passages from the poem Chopin had so heroically delivered:

"I will employ for liberty and fire…

"I prepare the ultimate banquet here…

"A dish best served cold…

"Knowing your last bite…

"And your epitaph will be my crowning achievement."

"Â *sô desu ka!* If I'm right…"

Champ read the concern etched across his partner's face. "What? What's wrong?"

Brandishing the travel orb, Yamato pulled Champ close-in beside him. "We need to get ourselves across to Lost Liberty Island. I think Gemini might be in danger."

*

Bringing her patrol to an end, Gemini ventured out to the terminus of the western pier and turned back to survey the extent of the isle, dimly seen in the florid glow cast by the Bãlefire's maleficent expression from Lost Liberty's torch, eight hundred feet away.

It'll survive, but the latest carnage means recovery is bound to be arduous and painfully slow.

Having been here for just under an hour, Gemini had determined to be as thorough as possible. As such, she'd refused to simply scan the island at a run, and had instead physically checked every inch of ground.

Evidence of the recent assault by two of Erra's auditors lay everywhere: wide fractures marred the perfect symmetry of the fort; gouge marks scoured the footpaths; ornamental walls and whole paving slabs had been ripped from their foundations; freshly refurbished gardens had been torn to shreds.

Those bushes and shrubs that had survived the trauma of the Fifth's attack still bore the scars of what the Fourth of Seven had accomplished. Gemini hadn't been able to spot a single leaf or branch that didn't bear some variety of rank pustule, mildew or other forms of obscene bacterial growth.

And the trees. Stripped of foliage, they now looked like reefs of petrified coral, wounded by claw marks and blighted by hardened secretions of scablike sap.

"I suppose we should be grateful for small mercies," Gemini murmured to herself in reflection, "the malignant stage of infection has passed. Everything will have a chance to heal…though it might take decades."

Content that she had gathered as much information as she could by mundane means, Gemini refined her acuity and initiated a fresh examination.

The ether thrummed with hidden augury, and what had been enfolded in anonymity jumped out in sparkling clarity. "Wow, the emerging Soulstice must be supercharging the atmosphere with excess energy? I'd better complete another walkthrough. If Yamato and Champ think there's a reason for Bean fleeing here, it won't stand out in the open waving at me to find it."

Strolling past abandoned pavilions, refreshment stalls and the ruined welcome center, Gemini ensured to cut out every distraction, and attuned herself with the vibe emanating from her surroundings.

"*Merde!* Supercharged is an understatement. It feels as if the very molecules in the air have been excited into exaggerated motion by…?" A probable reason for what she was witnessing occurred to her. "Ah, yes. I remember reading about it on the dark net. *This* conjunction is supposed to be special, something that only occurs every ten or hundred thousand years. They've given it a fancy name too. Ascent? Ascendency? Or something like that. I'm lucky to be around to share in it, especially if this is a taste of what's to come."

Upon reaching the main concourse leading to the sculpture display, Gemini began to dawdle and stare up into the night sky. The outer edges of the clouds appeared unusually bright, as if their mass had been infused with slumbering coals of argent purity.

"What a shame we don't have stars here, like they do, topside…" opening her arms wide, *l' ange de l'assassinat* started spinning on the spot, taking in the vista above and below, and basking in the chill of an all-pervading silver radiance, "it would make the moment all the more magical. Still, we have to make the most of what we've been…eh?"

Something deep underground snagged her attention. In a world full of shadows and silhouettes, Gemini wasn't quite sure if a fleeting afterimage wasn't playing tricks on her. Coming to a complete standstill, she homed in on the incongruity and scrutinized it more closely. "How odd, it's like a dead area. And it's been positioned about one of the old silos?"

Her discovery caused an uneasy alliance of caution and inquisitiveness to fester in the pit of her stomach. "But

Satan's armed forces haven't ever used this place for military purposes. And only the first few floors of the northwestern wing of the fort are open to visitors." She snorted. "No prizes for guessing who might have been snooping around down there, then. Okay, I'd better assess the extent of the problem right away."

Bursting into a flat-out run, Gemini circled the base of the statue several times in quick succession. Though littered with pockmarks and wide cracks, the structure of Fort Blood appeared intact. Gemini was grateful for that, as it would facilitate what she intended to do.

After skirting her target one last time, Gemini slowed her pace. Selecting the largest crevice she could find, she probed its depths, and found it just the thing to serve her needs. "Excellent, it leads directly into a disused section of the accommodation block. Once I'm inside, I'm sure I'll be able to work my way down to the sublevels without tripping any alarms, and a fast-scan will confirm if it's worth calling in the cavalry or not."

That thought reminded her of Nettesheim, and his promise to join her in New Hell. *I wonder what could have kept him. Having seen the way he works, it would have been nice to have his* special *kind help at my back. Oh well, at least he won't be slowing me down if I have to step things up a gear.*

Exhaling to make her frame slightly smaller, Gemini dropped—feet first—into the hole and began slithering between broken pipes, snapped steel cables and countless tons of crumbling concrete, whilst dexterously avoiding sharp edges as she went.

Less than a minute later, her legs wriggled free of the gap in the roof of the abandoned barrack room, whereupon, she dropped fourteen feet to the ground. Gemini found the air inside stale and those fabrics that hadn't rotted, threadbare and crawling with rockcoaches and a variety of other insects. *Now there's a surefire sign nobody's been in here for years. Good. Just the way I like it.*

Without a moment to waste, Gemini made her way to the swing doors, cracked them open, and peered out. To her right, part of the exterior corridor had fallen in, presumably as a result of the enforcer's attack. Fortunately, everything in the opposite direction remained obstacle free. She espied an emergency stairwell waiting in the gloom at the far end.

Activating her chameleon mesh and setting her psychic radar to an automatic, three second repeating pulse, Gemini became one with her environment and set off, skimming the ground and then the steps like a leaf blown on a gale.

Along the way, Gemini noticed how everything tended to confirm that this part of the fort had been decommissioned long ago. As such, she risked a little more power and extended her scans until the tang of something familiar, something alien, brushed across her receptors.

Whatever it is, it's isolated to one place.

Coming to a stop, Gemini stilled her suddenly thumping heart and tested the way again, on this occasion, taking her time to try and savor the full range of memories the exotic spoor triggered. *Goddam it, I know that signature from somewhere*, she chided herself. *C'mon, Gemini, wake up.*

Because she couldn't quite force those recollections through, she used the presence of her discovery as an impetus to greater efforts instead. Spinning down the remaining flights at breakneck speed, Gemini soon emerged at a wide bottom passage. Running the width of the edifice above, the tunnel was devoid of any discerning features, save for eight hangar doors, spaced at regular intervals, four along each side.

This whole area has been swallowed by the void... She reached out to run her fingers along tiles, yellowed with age, and allowed her perceptions to blend to the atoms making up their different elements. *Whatever generated it has long gone. But it must have used one hell of a power source; I can detect residual vibrations in one of the rooms that hint at... at...*

The zest of surplus celestial exuberance distinguished itself, lifting her reluctant recollections free of the quicksand that had threatened to stifle them. *That's it! I was at the Colonnade of Eternal Reflections at the Palace of Verse and Sighs. This same background frequency saturated the environs there after Daemon had destroyed Grislington. Fuck me. It can't be...can it?*

A snippet of the conversation she'd overheard between His Satanic Majesty and their leader rose to the fore. *Now how did it go? I can remember Satan looking rather upset about something Daemon had done. Then the devil raised a finger in the air, and said:*

"One thing troubles me, Daemon. Perhaps you can help?"

"Anything."

"Though succinct, your explanation was most informative. And while I would have preferred you kept my prized seat of power in one piece, I can understand now why it lies in ruins. Nonetheless, you mentioned that Grislington was able to reclaim his wings from the trap?"

"That's correct. Something about his essence caused the geodesic threshold of the glass to become malleable. He pulled them out before my eyes."

"And you're certain he didn't bond to them?"

"I'm no expert, you understand, but I'm positive he wasn't able to restore them to his being. I executed him before that happened."

Satan didn't seem to like that reply. It troubled him, and his next question threw Daemon for six:

"Most fortunate...Then perhaps you can tell me where they are?"

"I'm sorry?"

"The wings, Daemon. Where are they?"

"I don't know. The last time I saw either pair was just before Grislington got swatted to one side by the backlash from his sword's destruction. I didn't think to..."

Yes, that's when Satan went off on one about the fact Demon had been able to obliterate a Zion-forged blade so easily. We should have realized then, how apprehensive he was becoming of Daemon's growing power.

Gemini put the pieces together.

So, Chopin and Tesla must have been there. Somehow they got their hands on the missing wings. How else would heavenly tincture wind up down here?

Fully alert, Gemini drew her blades, ramped her sensitivity to maximum, and edged forward, alert for traps and hidden dangers. A wasted effort, as she discovered a couple of minutes later upon entering the abandoned silo, for she found it occupied by nothing but memories, dust, and the slightest sigh of wind generated by her own intrusion.

But the wings were here. I can taste it. And if Chopin and Tesla had them, they must intend to use them in some way during the alignment of realms. But how? Almost all knowl-edge of such things is prohibited, even to Hell Hounds.

Gemini decided it best to act prudently. *I'll worry about it later. The sooner this place is surrounded and crawling with investigators, the sooner we'll get some answers.*

A surge of indignation caused her anger to spark. *Chopin and Tesla might have been in New Hell all this time. Bastards. No wonder Bean tried to get his ass across this way; they're masters at hiding in plain sight...and making us look stupid.*

Strangling down her ire, Gemini gathered her thoughts into a précis of what she'd discovered, pictured the familiar faces of her fellow Hounds, and issued a blanket call.

Her message barely penetrated the roof above her head.

Mystified Gemini focused her attention more precisely and tried again. Then again. And a fourth time. *Shit, the mix of energies must be engaging with the convergence to create a dampening field. I'd better move to where there's less interference.*

As she reasoned on her course of action, Gemini absent-mindedly tested the extent of the void. It was only at that moment she discerned a subtle quality woven through the ether, so fine, so rarefied, that she'd originally missed it. *Hey, the amplitude produced by this Soulstice is a lot more concentrated than the infernet said it would be. And isn't it supposed to be spread out evenly across all the whole spectrum of spacetime? So what's causing...?* An SOS started repeating itself in the back of her mind. *I've got to get out of here...*

Throwing caution to the wind, Gemini sprinted from the room, back down the hall, and began mounting the stairs, five at a time. Fueled by a rising panic, she tore up the intervening distance and managed to settle into a steady rhythm until she reached a landing only a few storey's below her original point of entry. There, she cut across toward the other side of the citadel.

Her judgment proved sound, for the damage from the Fifth of Seven's attack was less pronounced on this level, and Gemini soon gained access to the World War II style blast doors leading outside. It didn't matter that she found the power had been cut. Locating the primary fuse box, Gemini flipped the lid, plunged both her daggers into the exposed mainline cables inside, and let rip with a devilish blast of theurgy.

A row of neon indicators arranged along the top of an adjacent panel flashed green. "Lights—camera—action." Depressing a large red plunger button, Gemini barely waited for the twenty-ton slabs of steel to inch apart wide enough for her to be able to squeeze through.

Charging outside, she adjusted her mental filters to compensate for the extent of the Soulstice's dominion, and cast her farsight high into the firmament.

What she saw rocked her to the core.

There's a vortex forming. And it's beginning to siphon cosmic energy down into one place...? The torch. They're here. Chopin and Tesla are in the torch and they're –?

A fanfare of light, sound and percussive agony rent the heavens, throwing Gemini to the floor. When she looked up again, she was stunned to see a pride of living weapons hanging in the night sky, gleaming like fangs and dripping with venom.

"The Sibitti?" Gemini was dumbfounded, "all seven of them? Have they been in on this from the beginning?"

One of the titans floated lower than the others. "Greeting little thing. I am the First of Seven, your end."

Moving into open space, Gemini charged her knives to full capacity and held them at the ready. "Change the cassette, why don't you? I'm not ashamed of the things I've done. And if there's one thing you should have learned by now, it's that Hell Hounds aren't so easy to take." She waved her blades, inviting them to partake of conflict and death, "Bring it on..."

Chapter 24: A Phoenix Rises

Nearing the interdimensionhell threshold separating Hatamâh from the latterday circles of hell, I experienced a gradual lessening of gravity. Once again, it reminded me how everything on this side of the rift seemed heavier, as if the perdurability of Jahannam's Gate system somehow managed to compress spacetime and force it to work differently.

Time. I almost choked imagining the rigors of eternity that still lay ahead of me. *Like any amount of time will ever be enough to work out a viable solution whereby somebody doesn't get hurt? If that is a replica of Strawberry, I'll have to destroy it. There's no way we'll ever be able to trust it, no matter how sweet and innocent it comes across. Not that Strawberry was ever sweet and innocent; of course, but…but if she's the real thing?*

Flickering images of the centuries Strawberry and I had spent together skipped through my mind. Certain times and places stood out more than others. None were more powerful or moving as the loyalty she'd shown after Satan had refused to restore my physical form. *She always supported me; was there when I needed her most.*

Then I thought of my new love, and my heart flipped. *I can't begin to imagine how Strawberry will take the news of what happened in her absence? Or the reasons behind it? Neither of them deserves the betrayal they'll feel if I'm forced to choose between them. I mean, I'm only with Gemini now because I thought Strawberry was gone forever. Nevertheless, now I've got to know Gemini, my feelings for her are real. I can't just switch them off like she'd never exist–?*

An abrupt release of pressure marked the moment I passed the event horizon between realms. Forced to take a deep breath, I viewed it as a timely reminder that I should be concentrating my efforts on the task at hand. *Hell and damnation. As if my life wasn't turbulent enough. Okay, let's sort out who I am first, then I can pick through the dilemma of my soap opera love life afterward.*

Casting my senses out into the photonic chaos of the Sheolspace continuum, I discerned I'd materialized right on top of one of the main coaxial foci's. Homing in on Juxtapose's hydraspace node, I interconnected with its distinctive parametric current and boosted myself along its rarified energy stream.

Such velocities were dangerous, for they created weird strobelight effects that often caused travelers to zone out, lose concentration and veer off course into the vast nothingness occupying the void between realities. I didn't know why, but I was confident that wouldn't happen to me. Focusing on the Perish district, I increased my speed and moments later, punched through the superfices in a discordant wash of fire and brimstone, surprising a nearby reaver patrol and throwing them into a state of disarray.

Their comfort was the last thing on my mind. Ignoring them completely, I turned around and was gratified to see the wide-open checkerboard landscape of the Palace of Verse and Sighs estate surrounding me on all sides. Even better, I'd landed only two yards away from the high walls of some-where I knew well. *Sentinels Square. Bang on target.*

I entered the square via the south gate, cut a sharp left and sprinted toward the southwest corner where my mystery quartet maintained their silent vigil, hands on swords, gaz-es fixed unwaveringly on the Wyrd tree occupying the exact center of the garden.

Standing on identical plinths, each statue came in at over seven feet tall and had been similarly fashioned from sin-gle pieces of glasslike stone. Armored, winged, hooded and looking as if the universal expanse had been encapsulated within their immeasurable depths, they were an enigma that had eluded my best efforts to understand them. Until now. For my last visit had revealed a minor—but crucial—dis-parity between them: elohgraphs, ancient celestial glyphs that were so old—even by heaven and hell's standards—that knowledge of their meaning had been lost...but fortunately, not forgotten by the fires burning within me.

As I came to a stop before the group, I noted how their corresponding characters somehow recognized my presence and blazed to life. The two on my left—*ꞵ* and *₵*—had been carved in an archaic form of Hellanese that flamed scarlet. Those on my right glowed so brightly blue, they were almost white. Rendered in a cryptic variety of the same dialect but with divine overtones, they said: *א‎ַ* and *ךֿ*.

Scanning them from left to right, I was able to translate with ease. Sèiadah *(storm),* cógath *(war),* eysh-éh *(burning flame),* shamár-as *(annihilation). Hmmm. Burning flame? That must be what Jotûn and Garôk were referring to when they called me,* Janīn bearer. *But how would they know?*

Questions. There were always more questions that need-ed answering. But not now. Refusing to get sidetracked, I glanced along the markings again, and read their meanings out loud. "Storm, war, burning flame and annihilation. So, how do these elohgraphs tie in with what I learned in the Hall of Shattered Dreams?"

It was only now I stood at the cusp of realizing who and what I was that I appreciated how nerve-wracking this whole business had been. My breath labored unexpectedly in my chest; my heart threatened to run away with itself; my knees felt weak; a strange sense of foreboding built inside, daring me to take the final step that would at last bring meaning to my life…and risk everything changing.

"I haven't come all this way for nothing," I snarled, suddenly angry. "And I'm sick to the back teeth of living in ignorance and being somebody else's pawn. It's time to change all that."

An icy disposition settled over me. *Good. No more distractions.*

"Right, let's review this, step by step.

"When that first window fell in, it told me something I already knew:"

This cruel arrow

Fired from the bow of exile enforced,

Invites you to feast on bitter bread

Sharper than any two-edged sword.

This tasteless path,

Shall leave you wanting,

For you are but a wolf in sheep's clothing,

Whose wrath cuts both ways.

"Yes, I am a wolf in sheep's clothing; a two-edged sword who can wield the might of the Bãlefire and God's Grace in tandem to literally, *cut* both ways. However, that bit at the beginning is a little confusing. Since when have I ever been an exile? I have a position of power and prestige. And this is hell. It's supposed to be cruel and bitter, something I wholeheartedly support. How can…?"

The symbols in front of each sword flared in unison, throwing out a nimbus of oscillating light so intense that I was momentarily blinded and stumbled back across the gravel path. Blinking my vision free of photonegative sunspots, I was amazed to discover I'd been regressed through time and into a completely different era; an age when the foundations of the square had only just been laid, and a place where desolation encircled me for miles in every direction.

The Wyrd tree was already here. A bastion against despair, its rose-gold radiance provided a source of reference by which I could orient myself.

A heated exchange behind me indicated I wasn't alone. An outsider looking in, I spun round to find Satan reasoning with members of his intimate choir. They appeared different, somehow. Bloodied. Weary. Excited, yet relieved and circumspect. As always, Samael was at the front of the largest group, making his presence known.

Strange? There seems to be more of them than I remember. Did he lose someone along the way?

Gathered in a cluster beneath a pair of sentinels—the only two, in fact, to have been set in position—the fallen coterie sounded as if they were divided over an issue that wouldn't be settled easily. What that issue was, exactly, I couldn't quite hear, as my attention kept straying to the imposing dark effigies towering over them like disapproving parents watching children squabble.

Wreathed in a glittering red and silver helix of stunning magnitude, the titans called to my soul. An affinity I couldn't deny. Before I'd realized what was happening, my spirit had been lured into the groping fringes of those eddies created by the spiraling vortex…and I was swept away, as helpless as I'd always been.

At first, my perceptions were dominated by nothing but g-forces and gut churning thermals. Eventually, however, the shimmering ascent slowed and all sense of motion ceased. When things had settled enough for my head to stop spinning, I found myself merged to the unfolding scene as if I'd been part of it all along:

"Where...where am I?"

"Fear not," a deep and commanding voice intones, "we found you, at last. All will be well again…eventually."

"Eventually?"

"Yes. You have suffered trauma sufficient to obliterate even the strongest of us. Incredibly, you survived. We need to bend our arts to make you whole again."

"Whole?"

"You ended up far away. Somewhere beyond my reach, a place that seemed to consume your remains as it preserved them alive. It was disturbing to say the least."

"Then I might not endure?"

Trust me. You will be refashioned. Blended and forged anew into something better."

"Better?"

"You'll see."

Hands turn me so that I face the light of the Wyrd tree squarely. Its leaves peal as they dance to the caress of an unfelt breeze. The sound of distant choristers recedes, while closer, a harsher refrain rises in unison. The weight of their song falls upon my neck, and the desire for slumber becomes irresistible.

I sag forward, exhausted, and my palms come to rest upon the hilts of two great swords of power. One steams, freezing to the touch in this environment, while the other burns, red-hot. "Who...whose are these?"

Murmurs of discontent and apprehension bruise the air on all sides with accusations.

The authoritative voice silences them, before replying, "Believe it or not, they both respond to your will, scant as it is at the moment."

"Both? How...?"

"No more questions. Sleep now. Though it takes an eternity, you will be restored to us, and you will be mine."

Heavy with fatigue and sorrow, my lids drift shut. Even so, the respite I crave eludes me, for I hear what now takes place below me, and it seems not all are content to let matters lie.

"My Lord Satan, I don't think this is wise," someone protests. "What you contemplate is unnatural and obscene, even by our standards."

"It is what we have become," Satan replies, revealing himself as the mystery benefactor offering kind counsel only moments ago, "though I am confused by your sudden reticence? Tell me, Samael, why do you shy away at this juncture? What we do here will send a clear message that we are not to be trifled with."

"But don't you think it excessive? Changing the attributes of someone into something counter to their natural inclinations?"

"Excess and depravity will be the foundations upon which our world is built, so why do you complain so loudly? You crave power and prestige where you had none before.

There you were as I, don't forget. A minion. One of countless myriads, no matter how glorious our station. Here, in this new order I am creating, we will rule as kings."

"You mean *you* will rule as king," Samael countered, "while we are expected to follow like sheep."

"One must always accept the burden of leadership..." Though weary, I didn't miss how Satan's voice took on a beguiling quality. "At least here you will lord it as princes over the chattel soon to be condemned in the wake of our rebellion. And now poor Gadré-el has fallen, who else can we rely on?"

"Fallen? You are massing our talents to keep what's left of him alive. Why?"

"Because without him, none of us would be here!" As he continued, Satan's voice softened, "his will to live is remarkable. Though how, exactly, his soul is able to inhabit the empty husk of Uriel's body is beyond me. The power it must have taken to achieve such a yoking is...well, it's something we must do what we can to exploit."

"Exploit?" Samael's disbelief was evident. "Are you mad? You're talking about one of the seraphim here, a bearer of the eternal flame incarnate. If this...this *thing* survives in its current condition, it will remain in a state of perpetual discord; repugnant of its own existence; crazed beyond belief by personality schisms and incongruent yearnings. Worst of all, it will represent an obvious danger to us."

"Then you had best help me do something to prevent such an eventuality from ever arising."

"How?"

"There are more than enough survivors to choose from. Prisoners too, if we're prepared to combine once more to overcome the will of their strongest."

Growing more distant by the second, the dread in Samael's tone was still tangible, "Are you suggesting that we betray…and risk the loss of…stalwarts?"

"How else do you…we gain the leverage we need to shackle our wolf into sheep's clothing and keep him there?"

"I appreciate the…do you know…will it work?"

"It should, if we choose champions from both sides. Those possessing…and whose temperaments most closely match…own would be best."

"We'd best proceed with all haste," Samael cautioned, "If a kernel of his own core identity emerges and takes root in the seraphim's body…only knows what…stoppable force of natu…of us here would be able to stand—"

And then they were gone, lost to an expanding shroud that envelops everything in a crucible of change, and completely unaware of creatures beyond the newly formed Veil, looking on from on high.

The pattern of what I once was unravels. Fading upon a loom of striking complexity, I am picked apart, only to be woven anew upon a weft of despicable design.

Slowly, surely, the entire scene bleeds into a haze-filled abyss that chills me to the bone. An eternity passes and a fresh breeze from a new dawn's rising shepherds the mists away. When they've dissipated, it doesn't surprise me in the least to find I am descending toward the garden I'd left behind in the present day…

My stomach lurched as I came awake. But there was no cause for alarm. Everything was as I'd left it, apart from the fact the sigils were now sizzling like hot rivulets of lava.

Hello?

Reading them with fresh eyes, I better understood their meaning.

Storm—war—burning flame—annihilation. "Bloody hell, it's like someone compiled a list of my four favorite pastimes. I've lost count of…? Wait a minute! Four?"

The insight I'd been granted by the specter of my own voice before the altar of the Hall of Shattered Dreams suddenly made sense. "That's right? When the huge rose window shattered, the entity uttered a declaration that's bugged me ever since I heard it:"

"…The fourfold duality of the chimera's embrace

Enfolds you in frozen moments of forever,

A keeper of secrets,

You are granted tendrils of memory that have never truly been.

A fabrication

Is woven through your mind like a decoration,

There for you to look at and admire,

Beauteous but shallow.

Death has a new name,

Bound with a smile as cold as ice,

That constricts about those undeserving,

Until there's nowhere left to breathe…"

"It *does* tell my life story. I'm nothing more than a tetrad of ruined personas, a mishmash sewn together into a patchwork quilt of…of…hang on?" The caution in Samael's voice near the end of my dream quest tweaked a nerve. "What was it he said again?"

" . . . *we'd best proceed with all haste. If a kernel of his own core identity emerges and takes root in the seraphim's body...only knows what...stoppable force of nat...of us here would be able to stand...*"

A Seraphim's *body?* "He was clearly concerned about the consequences of me gaining a degree of control." I thought back over the events of the last two years, and in particular, the way my power had grown exponentially. "It seems to co-incide with the scale of paranoia displayed by Samael and the rest of his cronies. And don't forget Satan himself? I've felt his distrust. He's wary of me now. Is that because I've become more than they expected? Has a nugget of my true individuality—whatever the hell that might be—started to emerge and triggered some form of cascade?" *And if it has, where will it lead?*

It was with a strange sense of elation I turned back to stare at the Sentinels. *There's only one way to find out.*

Opening my mind fully to the tenor generated by what I only now appreciated were the segregated constituents of those poor creatures who had been forced to supplement my own shattered psyche, I stepped to one side, and reached down.

Instinct guided me toward the outermost carving on my left. As my hand registered the heat radiating from the smol-dering elohgraph there, I said, "*Sèiadah* (storm). *Troh a' lùthse ain mi sealbġh, bi comharr* (By the power invested in me, stand revealed)."

An ethereal voice acknowledged my authority. "I am Anani'el, Angel of Storms, and a fragment of one who once fell from grace. Know then my fate:

"The anvil looms,

A thunderhead fist of charged potential

That roars its challenge

As it seeks my soul.

Photonic branches etch the sky,

Each trumpet clarion portends my doom,

Fulgurous intent and monochromic glory,

Striking, with the promise of rebirth.

Poisonous welts of molten fury

Leave steaming scars of wounded pride,

That fuses all hope into a fourfold cord...

How can this be?

Consumed, I am more beautiful than before, and more potent."

The instant Anani'el stopped speaking I felt a facet of my personality thrum like the strings of a violin being tuned. The vibrations expanded, permeating my soul, eliciting changes wherever their influence reached.

I feel...different, as if I'm gaining a depth of character I never possessed before?

Encouraged, I stepped to my far right and repeated the process, this time reverting to an idiolect of the divine Language. "*Shamár-as* (annihilation). *Lan khol yé zélah, a-mad ha-pâ-tah* (By all that is holy, stand revealed)."

For a second time, my demand was validated. The memory of another spirit replied, "I am Hasmêd, Angel of War, once a general of the heavenly host and now but a shade of what I once was. Savor the wisdom I bring in sharing my end:

"Intent,

Garnished in a musk of potent malice,

Licks my face in anticipation of the feast I know will come.

Faces,

As pale and as brittle as eggshells

Peer out from the shroud of imminent death.

Breath,

Caught in fear, and held within fragile cages,

Released to the rapture of the dread I bring.

Reproach,

Sighs across a marbled tombstone,

In remembrance of what I have become."

On this occasion, my consciousness rippled to unseen currents. Knowledge of places and events I'd once witnessed or taken part in filled my mind with substance. It was as if cataracts of blindness were being lasered from my cognitive functioning. Those changes were overwhelming at first, but as I blended to them and let them sweep over me, I found myself becoming anchored by a sense of belonging. Reflecting on those feelings, I almost missed the beginnings of an outward manifestation to my metamorphosis.

I don't believe it? It feels as if the Bālefire is superheating like a blast kiln. Enchanted, I held my arms out in front of me and wriggled my fingers. *My flesh is beginning shine, like that time I took on Al Catraz's goons within the Awful Tower?*

The sense of knowing increased.

"Anani'el and Hasmêd must be the champions Satan mentioned in passing? They were sacrificed to ensure the splicing took…no, that's wrong. I get the inference Gadré-el had already managed that alone. But he was badly injured in the process, his battle with Uriel having all but consumed him?" *Is that why Gadré-el took such a drastic course? The encounter cost him his own physical form, and he had nowhere else to go?*

Subconsciously, I empathized with him and saluted his tenacity. *Such a determination never to be denied. Just like… me, if it can be viewed as* me?

"So, Anani'el and Hasmêd's essences were used to stabilize the damage; to shore it up and boost the coalescing tincture so that a new hybrid mind was allowed to emerge. One that would eventually settle and mature…" *But who would dominate?*

Parting my hands, I looked down at the last two ciphers. "There's only one way to find out for sure."

DAEMON, we need your help. Where the fuck are you?

The telepathic plea for assistance was as crystal as it was clear.

"Yamato?" *Oh, you have got to be kidding? This is not the time to piss me off.*

After such an urgent appeal, the pause that followed was deafening. "Hello? Yamato? Are you still there?"

Yes I am. Relief flooded the ether, along with a puzzling aftertaste of ill-concealed shock. *I was a little thrown there. When you answered, it sounded as if you were standing right next to me…if only?*

"Why? Surely everything can't have gone tits-up in the few days I've been away?"

Few days? Daemon, you went into the dead zone nigh on a week ago.

"A week?" *I knew it. Time does flow differently in Jahannam.* "Well, I'm back now…in Sentinels Square to be precise. In fact, I'm a little tied up at the moment, sorting a few essential issues out."

Then I'm sorry to intrude, but we need you here with us, now.

And yet again my personal life is expected to take a back seat. "Why? What's the problem?"

Let's just say, the shit has well and truly hit a Sibitti-sized fan.

"The Sibitti?"

Daemon, I'm so sorry, they've got Gemini. We tried to get here as fast as we could but the Soulstice is generating some kind of dampening field around the site. That and the fucking Sibitti who see…

Yamato's thoughts faded into the background. Wrath: incandescent, pure and unrestrained surged up from the core of my soul. *They would dare?* "Where are you?"

No sooner had I asked, than my seekersense had locked onto Yamato's signal, and was homing in on him like a guided missile. *Gotcha!*

With the merest suggestion, I spun an upsilon field of enormous magnitude and finesse.

We're over in New Hell, at –?

"Lost Liberty Island," I cut him dead, surprising him again. "I know. I'm on my…"

*

As mesmerizing as the conflict outside was, Tesla's scientific discipline shone through. Mastering the urge to simply stop and stare, he continued to monitor the readout of his interdimensionhell fuzzer-mitigator hookup, and clucked with pleasure. "Well, well, well. For once, things *do* seem to be going our way."

The sound of hurried footsteps from behind indicated Chopin was approaching. "Have...have we been discovered?" the out of condition composer gasped, doubling over as he stopped to take several deep breaths.

"No. My initial misgivings were premature. While I do believe the female Hound was suspicious about something, the timely arrival of the Sibitti put an end to any further snooping...I hope."

"You don't think they'll detect us, then?"

"On the contrary," Tesla replied, warming to the logic of his reasoning, "while it *is* rather stressful having such creatures on our doorstep at such an inopportune time, we couldn't have asked for a better diversion. Do you know, in spite of her size, it took four enforcers working together to put the Lady Gemini down? Quite the...Oh, watch out?"

Both rebels crowded forward to the centermost window of the crown and pressed their faces to the glass.

"Is that the rest of the Hell Hounds?" Chopin hissed, instinctively ducking away, as if he'd be spotted at any moment.

"Yes...well, two of them, anyway. Yamato Takeru and Champ Ferguson, if I'm not mistaken."

"And their latest acquisition?"

"Don't know and don't care." Tesla glanced toward his friend before resuming his study of the standoff outside, "If Nettesheim was to show, I admit, I'd be worried. As it is, I think...? Oh look at that. The Sibitti seem to have changed their tactics and are...? Shit!"

On this occasion, Tesla was the one to shy away from the ledge.

"What?" Chopin's curiosity got the better of him. As he edged forward, Tesla grabbed him by the arm and pulled him down onto the floor, explaining, "The Reaper. He's here."

"What are we going to do?"

Think Nikola, think. Tesla went to check his electronic chronometer, only remembering at the last second he always took his jewelry off when working near sensitive equipment. Leaning toward his companion, he murmured, "Has the juxtaposition manifested yet?"

So nervous was he, that it took Chopin several attempts to remove his pocket watch from inside his jacket and flip the lid. "It's due to start in just over a minute's time; seventy-two seconds to be precise."

Close enough. "Then I suggest we collect our gear and begin. While the mitigator *is* holding, I don't want to push our luck. I have a feeling the Sibitti won't last long now Satan's slayer has arrived."

"Do you think Grim will spot us?"

"Not straight away. He's part of the reason I suggested we use Lost Liberty as our departure site. It's one of the few monuments in the underverse empowered—as our venerable Reaper is—by the Bālefire. As you yourself told me, Bālefire is a corrupted form of God's Grace. Anyone empowered by either source will already have noticed the resonance of the alignment, as it will be affecting them more acutely. If Grim picks up on any anomalous energy surges, he'll initially think it's down to the Soulstice, not us. By the time he investigates further, we'll be on our way."

Chopin's eyes were as wide as an owl's. "So we've done it? We've actually done it."

"Once we've activated the Golden Fleece, yes…though I would suggest we allow the wings to transport us well away from New Hell before you enact the Scroll of Divergent

Union. We wouldn't want any stray blasts causing a last minute hiccup."

Tesla and Chopin stared at each other, as if the moment
of truth belied its name and was too good to be true. Then the
statue rocked to its foundations.

*It seems things are getting frisky out there? Best not push
our luck.* Extending his hand, Tesla suggested, "If you please,
Frédéric. I think it's time for us to rise to the occasion."

*

"I know. I'm on my…"As I finished my sentence, a sonic
boom announced my arrival upon the eastern sector of Fort
Blood's roof. The accompanying shockwave that came with
it flattened everything in a widening swathe that propagated
out across the bay at over five hundred miles per hour. "…
way."

Bugger me! That was fast?

My augmented perceptions took less than a second to
register the details of my new surroundings.

The Statue of Lost Liberty was at my back, its keystone-
shaped tabula anasta looming over me like a copper-plated
slab. To my left and right, Champ and Yamato were scrambling to their feet, having been bowled over by the dynamics of my arrival. Before me, the silhouette of a pier played
in and out of the ripples cast by the cold waters of New Hell
Bay.

Everything around the statue's environs flickered with a
strange glowing phosphoresce that swirled up from somewhere underground and streamed off in a narrowing funnel into the firmament above. *I never realized the Soulstice
would produce a show like this?*

It was a surreal experience, watching the side effect of such a manifestation, for the Bãlefire issuing from Lost Liberty's torch was being sucked along an invisible conduit, making it look as if Hell's First Lady had just fired a flare gun into the clouds to warn of approaching danger.

An apt similitude, for further out across the bay to the east, the Sibitti hovered above the Madhatten skyline, their combined glory easily outshining the glitz of the sodium and neon highlighted backdrop.

Gemini hung limply in the arms of the foremost scumbag, the First of Seven. The moment I realized the extent of her injuries, an undeniable fury caused something new, something marvelous to germinate inside me. *Bastard, I should have executed you when I had the chance. Well...*

I blinked, and my ninjaken appeared in my hands so quickly, it was as if they had been there all along and had only now chosen to reveal themselves. My tattoos blazed, anointing me in a union of the diabolical and divine; a discordant clash, represented by ruby red and aquamarine violence that ran down my arms to ignite each corresponding blade in blinding brilliance.

The clangor of opposing forces set my senses ringing. And as my armor fused into place over my skin, I was gratified to see a palpable shock running through the sevenfold battle formation above me.

My voice thundered, "This time, you will die..." I swept the heat of my gaze across their ranks, lingering on each shining countenance for the briefest second, "all of you."

The small advantage gained by my kick-ass entrance didn't confuse them for long, and to be honest, I hadn't expected it to. The Sibitti were sons of heaven and earth, demigods, with egos to match the grandeur of their aspirations.

They were also bullies who felt a certain confidence in numbers, as their response demonstrated only too well.

"Oh, someone will meet their end this night," the First declared, his voice a grating irritation to my ears, "but it won't be us."

The forefinger of his gauntleted hand snaked out to tease a stray strand of hair free of a raw wound on Gemini's ravaged cheek. I was never more grateful for my cowl and visor than at that moment, for it prevented him from seeing my teeth grinding in frustration.

He seemed not to care about such trivialities. Referring to Gemini, the First continued, "This fragile creature, for instance. Such a bright and perilous predator in so diminutive a guise. Fortunately, we are now accustomed to such contradictions…" The rest of his brothers laughed, privy to what must have been a private joke. "And credit where it's due, she was a formidable opponent. For all her delicacy, she begged no favor and we gave no quarter. Alas, our being impressed won't save her…or you. Allow me to lay bare why we conspired to lure you here by such daring artifice."

Arranged in a perfect fighting circle, I expected the Sibitti to initiate their usual assault: one by one, and in order of designation. A strategy I'd often thought worked to their detriment.

Sometimes, I wished I could keep my mouth shut—or in this case—my thoughts, because it was as if the fuckers had read my mind. Behind their smug-faced leader, the six remaining enforcers flowed together to form three pairs.

The Second and Sixth attacked first. Swooping toward me, the Sixth clenched his fist, and countless tons of the Upper New Hell Bay rose high like a wall of gray-green filth, only to come crashing down like a battering-ram seconds later. As it struck, the Second smiled a beauteous smile and his eyes flashed, releasing a murderous bolt of energy that illuminated the crushing waters, turning them into a lethal brew of charged potential.

Caught flatfooted, I delayed my riposte and extended my personal shield to encompass Champ and Yamato. Thus protected, I returned my attention to our assailants, only to discover they had vanished, their place being taken by the Third and Seventh, who were almost upon us.

Through the mass of the still falling deluge, the Third appeared as a misshapen streak whose presence was warped by the shimmering penumbra of a thalassic lens. That didn't make him any less effective, however, for as he streamed past, he exhaled, transforming the torrent about us into a solid block of ice.

Unholy shit! That *is an outstanding change in tactics...* Behind the Third, the Seventh raised his blazing sword. *But the congratulatory back-patting will have to wait.*

Despite the presence of the intervening barrier, I could already feel the buildup of thermogenic potential. Not wanting to see where that might lead, I did the first thing that came to mind: I shouted, as loud as I could. "Azûra-él."

Amplified by confined pressure, the sonic wave my expression generated, shattered our frigid tomb and sent great algific chunks smashing into our would-be aggressors, swatting them from sight like the bothersome insects they were.

If this is the best they can do, then I don't...? The glint of light on metal down by the water's edge caught my attention. *The Fourth and the Fifth? You sly dogs.*

Using the previous sorties as cover, this elusive pair had landed on the northeastern shoreline and had already begun their incursion. The Fourth in particular was in his element. Having thrust his sword deep into the ground, he had called upon his unique talent and steaming welts were now worming their way toward us, blackening the soil, desiccating vegetation, and bursting the boles of every remaining tree.

Because of its sheer bulk, I thought Fort Blood might stymie such a strategy. I thought wrong.

As the plague storm hit, the constitution of the citadel's toughened walls degenerated into a collage of throbbing black, white and red pustules. Scanning inside, I was amazed to see the fungal outbreak had already breached the integrity of the shell's reinforced framework, and both steel and stone were being consumed at an alarming rate. *Bloody hell, talk about the ultimate concrete cancer. It's virulent enough to eat through just about anything.*

A glittering tumult of blades, vanes and razor-sharp edges, the Fifth chose that moment to strike. Already weakened by rot, the pedestal's foundations shuddered and crumbled away beneath my feet.

I thought it time to take a more direct form of action.

Champ, Yamato? This thing is going to collapse. You're more than capable of looking after yourselves, so I'm going to set us down on the deck. Work together, keep one or two of them busy, and I'll remove this infestation once and for all. Stay on your toes, I'm about to show you something new that will literally blow you—and them—away.

Two acknowledgments zinged back.

Go fuck 'em boss.

Understood.

We started moving. Distracted as I was by my charitable maneuver, I felt something test the quality of my defenses. Peering out, I spotted the Second and Third strafing us with lightning tipped icicles more than four feet in length. Behind them, the Fifth and Sixth had already begun a follow-up run.

Ah, I see what the plan is now. They're trying to keep me off balance by attacking in waves and rotating their pairings as they do so. While it's a clever idea to mix the elemental aspect, they should have known better. If it wasn't for the fact I was watching out for Champ and Yamato and...? I glimpsed Gemini, cradled in the First's arms. Then it hit me. *Oh, very good. They're obviously playing to the losses I've suffered in recent months and are banking on me not involving myself fully in favor of protecting my team.*

I knew what needed to be done. But the thing was, I did experience a tug on the heartstrings every time I was forced to look at Gemini's still unconscious form.

Imagining all sorts of scenarios in which things ended badly and Gemini was consigned to the reassignment process, I tried to reason things through. *Right, I've sealed the esoteric siphon that was draining sin through into Jahannam, so the Hub should be operating at close to one hundred percent efficiency. And both Nishôgh and Omniûs assure me the methân portal won't ever open again until some form of treaty has been established. If push comes to shove, Gemini's damned soul will end up on the Slab, complete and...and...*

Memories of what happened to Strawberry after her execution at the hands of Grislington returned to haunt me. Of course, that swiftly reminded me of the personal shitstorm from hell waiting back at the Hall of Shattered Dreams in Hatamâh.

Clenching my fists in frustration, I cursed my unexpected sentimentality. *Are the changes I'm experiencing causing this? Making me weak and indecisive? That kind of nightmare won't happen here. Gemini will be okay...*

Backed into a corner, I knew I was duty bound to act. For some unknown reason, that bothered me. *Yet, I must. It's who I am...isn't it?*

...but can I still do it so coldly?

Galvanized to action, I called out to the First, "Do you not realize I know what it is you hope to achieve by this posturing? If you were serious, Gemini would already be lost, consumed by the gluttony of your audit. Fools. All you have achieved by your duplicity is a guaranteed slow and painful end."

Sheathing my swords, I stepped forward to put as much extra space between Champ, Yamato and myself as possible. Satisfied they would be out of harm's way, I took a final look at Gemini. Completely out of it, she appeared relaxed and peaceful. I was glad of that, for it would be the last time I saw her for a while.

Then I kindled the new might at my disposal.

See you on the other –?

A coherent beam of sizzling light stabbed out from the darkness behind me. Roving across the First's heroic stature, it settled upon Gemini's body, intensified, and then pierced his wards as if they were nonexistent. Next moment, Gemini was gone, vaporized in a condensing cloud of emerald atoms.

I nearly lost it. Enraged, I turned on the spot, eager to destroy the entity that had dared to harm the woman I loved, only to find the latest recruit to our cause stepping down out of an unconventional hydraspace portal.

"Nettesheim," I roared, "what the fuck have you done?" The rapid flow of energy manifesting at my core signaled it was nearing its peak.

"Only what needed to be done." Nettesheim's gaze was apologetic, but unflinching. Hands raised, palms exposed, he approached slowly and continued, "I'm setting you free, Daemon Grim, for tonight you must fulfill your destiny."

"My destiny?"

"Did you think you walked your path alone without anyone to watch over you?" The cast in his eyes grew softer. "Though you were given the leeway to make your own choices, free of the bias of outside influence, you were never entirely alone, Daemon."

"Alone? Choices?" I was too angry to pay attention properly. Sparks danced across the surface of my armor. "Speak plainly, Nettesheim, or by Satan your next words will be your last."

Undeterred, Nettesheim paid scant heed to my threats or the relentless and continued barrage from Erra's minions. Walking straight up to me, he said, "You've suffered the pain of loss, too much of late. I set you free from that, as I said. In doing so, I prevented Gemini's soul from being audited. Have no fear; arrangements are in place to ensure her spirit arrives safely on the Slab. She will be returned to you, hale and whole...but not until you have fulfilled your purpose."

"Arrangements? My purpose?" Such repetitiveness was starting to annoy me. But not as much as my initial misgivings about this mysterious character who had so recently ingratiated himself into our unlives. "Who are you?"

"A friend, who—like you—wishes to see injustice served. Fortunately, I am also a fellow Hell Hound, sworn to service..." He motioned to one side and a star-studded gateway appeared right next to me, hitting me with an instant fix of the distinctive essence of Sentinels Square. "Now hurry, your destiny awaits. Only you have the wherewithal to prevent calamity befalling us all."

Sentinel's Square? How does he know about such things? Or my future, come to that? Bemused, I pointed to the encircling foe, and played for time, "But what about the Sibitti? You *do* realize you're surrounded?"

Nettesheim grinned and made a complicated series of gestures in the air. No sooner had his hands come to rest, than a huge window into the third way opened, one that was large enough to encompass the whole of Lost Liberty's pedestal.

"Indeed I do," he replied, seemingly without a care in the world, "but I'd have thought my little demonstration at the Brass Steel—and others since then—would have given you a hint of how skillfully I can counter celestial and other-worldly totems…?"

Of course, he completely negated the power of a Dagger of Damocles. And later, the temporal traps that ensnared my entire hunting pack. How…?

"These creatures have no comprehension of the dominion I can call upon. They may find they are unable to finish what they started, especially as I only have to hold them until more potent reinforcements arrive." Nettesheim's demeanor hardened and he nodded toward the mouth of the conduit for a second time. "Now, if you please? The Unveiling is upon us. I have fish to fry in your absence, and *you* must become what you were ordained to be."

He's right. There's only one way I'm gonna settle this and find all the answers.

I made eye contact with my Hounds, and an unspoken understanding passed between us. As one, all three banded together. Back to back, they drew fresh weapons and readied themselves to defend our realm against the invaders.

Stepping across the mystic threshold, I prepared to do the same. Though where my path might yet lead, I was still unsure.

Chapter 25: Endless Forms Most Beautiful

In my mind's eye, I stood alone upon the pinnacle of an alpine summit so high it punctured the clouds and reached up to threaten the sovereignty of the star laden sky above. Determined winds howled about my position, screaming in my face and nipping at my ankles; thrusting and probing again and again, until...

Plucked from my verglas coated podium, I tumbled over and over into the waiting void, a slave to gravity and the flickering cobalt blue and silver cavalcade that flashed past at breathtaking speed.

An explosion of light, pain and torn flesh marked the moment I glanced off a protruding lip of granite. Transmogrified into a tangle of spinning limbs and shifting priorities, my descent continued along a slightly different trajectory. All too soon, I found myself an unwilling passenger within a Reaper-sized snowball, one gaining a frightening amount of mass and speed with each passing second.

The ridgeline behind me shuddered, then shrugged its shoulders free of the hoary mantle that had adorned its frozen frame for an age. Within a heartbeat I was engulfed by boulder sized chunks of ice and dusted white flakes, and together, we formed a thundering, bounding procession, eager to see who could reach the bottom first.

Yup! That just about sums my life up at the moment. When something happens, it happens fast and it happens unexpectedly, sweeping my feet out from under me and hurtling me along with it, whether I'm ready or not. And it's gaining momentum too...speaking of which?

The hydraspace conduit Nettesheim had provided was unlike anything I'd ever ridden, and though not as powerful as my own last effort, it was nevertheless a marvel of abstract design. Turbulently tumultuous, devoid of any sign of Sibitti shenanigans, and totally lacking any of the usual 'fireworks display' reminiscent of the workings of a vast intergalactic brain, it was deceptively fast. I'd been travelling for less than twenty seconds, and already, I could feel my destination looming ever closer.

Nettesheim, when this is all over, you and I will be having the mother of all heart-to-heart's. If you survive Erra's playthings, of course.

My thoughts turned to the first time I'd ever met our elusive mystic. *From the moment I saw him, I knew he was an odd one. So much ability and knowledge and an uncanny knack for being in the right place at the right time. And this third way shit?* I couldn't help but glance at the lining of the tunnel as it sped by. *I'm one of the most powerful creatures in existence, and I'd never heard of it. Thank badness Nettesheim appears to be loyal to Satan's system. Whatever he's been doing behind my back only seems to have served the interests of injustice, too. And he's willing to stand against the Sibitti with his sworn brothers and sis...*

An involuntary image of Gemini's last moments flashed in front of me. I smothered such emotions instantly and chastised myself. *Suck it up, you idiot. This is hell and you're supposed to be its Reaper. Nettesheim did exactly what you should have done without hesitation. Fearing for her welfare was holding you back. Though from what, exactly, still remains to be seen.* Ahead of me, the terminus flared and morphed into an exit portico. *I'm sure I'll find out soon enough.*

Landing lightly, I found the tranquility afforded by the garden a stark contrast to the mayhem I'd left behind. Normally I'd have welcomed such a change, but at this moment it only served to remind me of the dangers my people still faced. *I hope my confidence in them isn't misplaced. Still, I'm in no position to do anything about it now.*

I'd materialized just beyond the low ornamental wall that marked the fringes of the Wyrd tree's roots. A roseate aura added a touch of warmth to the all-pervading peace, and gentle arboreal music trilled through the air in time to the play of wind on leaves. As soothing as this was to watch and listen to, it was the southwestern corner of the courtyard that held my attention, for there my fate waited beneath shadows cast by hooded avatars.

Striding toward them, I briefly reviewed aloud what I'd learned.

"Those entities that went into my making were involved in an epic battle during what must have been the Time of Sundering. Uriel and Gadré-el in particular were champions, and both sacrificed aspects of themselves during that conflict. Somehow, Gadré-el managed to fuse his consciousness to Uriel's mind to stay alive. But why do such a thing unless his own body was screwed and he had nowhere else to go?"

Part of me still identified with Gadré-el's predicament, and privately, I saluted his tenacity. *His will to survive, to endure and to win at all costs was undeniable. He wouldn't accept failure as an option. Just like me, really. Or should I say, us?*

Praises aside, some things about that whole arrangement still bugged me.

"While the inferences I've picked up do lean toward Gadré-el having gained dominance over Uriel, it's not clear what happened. Especially if Uriel was of the seraphim. I mean, how did Gadré-el manage that? Uriel's creative powers and persona should have been vastly superior? Unless, of course, Gadré-el was of a similar magnitude?"

Not for the first occasion were my suspicious roused by Satan's insistence that all records of the Time of Sundering be sequestered.

"Everyone knows Satan was of the cherubim before the fall. And there's a natural assumption that he was the strongest of the rebels. But what if he wasn't?"

A passing reference Satan had made in reply to Samael's protestations about rulership during my previous vision suddenly bore more weight.

"What did they say again...?"

"Here, in this new order I am creating, we will rule as kings."

Samael countered that statement. "You mean you *will rule as king, while we are expected to follow like sheep."*

"One must always accept the burden of leadership. At least here you will lord it as princes over the chattel soon to be condemned in the wake of our rebellion. And now poor Gadré-el has fallen, who else can we rely on?"

"Was Gadré-el another contender in the leadership stakes? Or a rival? Someone more powerful perhaps?" Doing what I could to balance the facts, I had to admit, it made a spooky kind of sense. "So, if Gadré-el *did* cancel Uriel's might out, was *that* the reason why Satan and his coterie had to go to all the bother of subsuming Anani'el and Hasmêd's essences? They needed that something extra to bind each champion's remaining pith in place?

"And don't forget, whatever it was they did, it took Satan and an extended choir considerable time and effort to achieve it. Were some of the fallen lost in the process? Is *that* why there are so few of them in comparison now? But what did they do, exactly, to create a perfect union? And which part of whom survived?"

The questions were starting to queue up again. And as always, the line at the answers aisle was devoid of customers. Except that, for me, another part of the mystery jigsaw that was Satan's recent behavior slipped into place.

"That grilling he gave me after I destroyed Grislington. Not only didn't he get to the point, but he was also trying not to show how put out he was over the ease by which I destroyed the sword and negated the power of the wings. Now I might know why."

The temptation to speculate was proving difficult to resist. Once again, I found it necessary to censure myself. *Stop being a dick. There isn't time. Just stick to what you know.*

"Okay then, what I *do* know is that it took the combined constitution of Anani'el and Hasmêd to create a stable template from which a new creation—*me*—could be fabricated. Then it went sideways, because having gone to all that trouble, you'd think they'd want me on board so I could be one of the team? But they didn't. They tried to hide what they'd done, creating division and mistrust. I need to know: am I a chimera, as the cryptic message in the Hall of Shattered Dreams suggested, or something more? I certainly don't *feel* like a mutation. And though I've always known there were gaps in my memory, I've never thought of myself as anything less than a whole person? What's more, I am unique in being able to wield the Bãlefire and God's Grace simultaneously...unless you count those like Nettesheim who can manipulate the energies of the space in between to achieve similar ends?"

Having traversed the length of the path, I came to a halt in front of the statues. As before, the elohgraphs welcomed me back, blazing brighter and buzzing excitedly, reminding me of my own strongest attributes: storm—war—burning flame—annihilation. Shielding my sight against their glare, I listened as the droning became louder and louder, and was surprised to hear the quadruplet hum modulate into a distinctive voice. My voice.

"Whilst convalescing,

This immortal cup flensed skin from bone upon a rack of utter ruination,

Quenching naught but the thirst of hope.

So I waited,

And as the centuries passed, devoid of thought and purpose,

I felt those changes within that made me less than before, yet more.

So what did I become?

A parade of endless forms most beautiful,

Or a phoenix reborn, burning to his own agenda?"

The closing words brought with them a cresting wave of power that lifted me off the walkway and sent me spinning through the air. As I dropped to the ground, my breath caught in my throat and I sensed my awareness inverting as it was pulled toward the waking expression of a drama I'd experienced so many times before:

Here we go again...

Reckless of the consequences, I pour forth my strength and gain altitude at a scalding velocity. Piercing a thick band of clouds, a tempestuous gale howls past my outline, covering me in skyborne dew. As I break free on the other side, majestic sunlight baptizes me in coronal radiance. But I care not, for I am here to answer the call of my true disposition: war.

The thrill of imminent battle takes root in my heart and momentary doubts assail me. Nonetheless, I draw comfort from an object grasped tightly in my right hand. I glance to one side and see a huge red sword. It blazes with malice along the keen edges of its sunset sheen and encompasses me within a black and crimson aura that bonds the weapon to my flesh as it inures me against the tumultuous pace.

Something hurtles toward me across the sky and my sense of danger spikes. Locking on, I spot my foe and prepare for battle. We close at speed and intuition takes over. Glass chimes against glass as we strike, and a shower of prismatic light and sparks glaze the heavens with glittering reflections of savage ferocity.

I clamp my hand around my adversary's sword wrist and my legs about his wings before squeezing as hard as I can. He returns the compliment, robbing us of momentum. Locked together, we tumble out of control. Vast ribbons of energy entwine us within a living tau field as we attempt to obliterate each other by sheer force of will alone.

Our exertions wreak terrible consequences, for we are evenly matched and parts of us are lost forever. Even so, we continue to act instinctively, each determined to do whatever it takes to retain that spark of identity that will make the difference between life and extinction.

A monumental, epoch changing impact somewhere far, far away barely registers. We fade in the face of a suspended animation rush of impressions that overwhelms us.

You will pay the penalty for your treachery, Uriel snarls, his outrage as plain as the contempt in my own eyes.

No, I will not die, I taunt, *for I am willing to risk everything...See?*

The flame eternal burns within us both. One pure, one tainted. But I am eager to dare a path that he is not. I take that leap of faith, and he recoils in horror.

My gambit works, but at a terrible price. *I...I am the victor, though adrift and bereft of...? No, there is a vessel in which I could take refuge if I dare anoint myself in the ultimate debasement for one of my kind.*

Conjunction. Metamorphosis.

A parody of nature, a binary star shines forth from the void. Unbalanced, it vacillates between light and dark, venting ruin and chaos at whim until others join together in harmony to prevent what remains of my soul from being totally overwhelmed.

Who am I? Who was I?
What am I? What was I?
Where do I belong?
Why can't I remember?

The weight of eternity passing consumes me and antiquity swallows fragmented memories whole. But the lessons of history remain to taunt me, to remind me:

The terrible drop where I dare not release my grip…

Pain.

"Do you remember this?"

Skin, glowing white-hot from devastating friction…

Intense agony.

"Did you learn from your error?"

Primary flight feathers torn free by overwhelming drag…

Excruciating, prolonged torture.

"Has your resolve been tempered?"

A vast pit of malevolence rushing up from below…

Plunging.

"Have you cast off the dross?"

Light receding above…

Forever plummeting.

"And are you not more than before?"

A moment of clarity as the truth of my predicament finally registers.

I've pulled him too far. Now we will both suffer the same fate!

"Yes, but you are stronger."

The endless spiral, down and down.

An overwhelming surge of heat as I face the consequence of arrogance…

Depravation.

The silence of eternal midnight…

Soul-crushing grief.

The inevitable pressure of all-consuming oblivion...

Anguish compounded a thousand-fold.

The familiarity of being taunted—again.

"You are more than you appear to be...?"

Then why do I feel so emasculated?

"Because of what it cost to make you..."

Cost?

"The outlay proved far more expensive than we realized it could ever be. But it was worth it, in the end..."

Are you sure?

"Sure? Do you not realize who you were...?"

Who I was?

"What you now are...?"

I am...I am changing?

"Better. But it sounds as if we'll need to rid you of the clutter that might slow your progress and make things more difficult in the future. Now come, there is fresh vitality you must ingest if you wish to achieve permanent equilibrium. Fear not. I will look after you. Relax, and let darkness show you the light..."

Recollections fade and my memory grows dim. However, other voices call to me from on high. So remote are they that it is only now—after eons have passed and my sensibilities have been amplified far beyond anything that I could have possibly imagined—that I am able to perceive their preserved existence.

Regardless, they remain at the very edge of my perceptions and I strain to hear what consequence they might bear.

"...remains intact. Most puis...holy influx to...and flame."

"...shall see. You retain...resilient of us all and...dormant within. Unbidden, clarity will...from the ruins shall rise again."

"Fear not this abomin…and his schemes. Is not…the stronger? Will…better days?"

"Most of…Remain true to…Prove yourself worthy… new name will manifest from the…and spring unbidden… lips—lips—lips—lips…"

As usual, a bile inducing, vertiginous attack welcomed my return to the land of the unliving. *Not now!*

Desperation gave me the strength I needed to cling on to those echoes for a vital few seconds longer. It worked. A lingering declaration oozed out from the annals of orphic history. "Know yourself—self—self—self…"

Losing my balance, I stumbled forward onto my hands and knees and was forced to brace my forehead against the cool stone of an intervening podium to prevent myself from keeling over entirely and eating dirt.

I chose to remain there until I'd gathered my wits.

The vision becomes clearer and more detailed every time it replays, that's for sure. Like a screening process filtering through what I need to know.

Notwithstanding my confusion, certain aspects of what I'd learned were quite encouraging. *If I understand what's happening correctly, it all seems to signify I am more than I once was. Better; enhanced; as if the process I've been forced to endure has magnified the sum of my parts.*

If so, it would go a long way to explaining why Satan found it necessary to mess with my memories. He obviously didn't account for such long-term side effects materializing and was fearful he might have created a rival instead of an ally. Samael certainly wouldn't like that. He's always seen himself as Satan's chief honcho and hates my favored position. Bloody idiots…the both of them.

For the first time I could ever recall, I gave serious consideration to what it must be like, having to rule and manage the insanity that were the latterday levels of hell.

The very idea repelled me. *Fuck that for a game of lobotomized soldiers!* More so, it made me feel dirty. *I wouldn't do it. Not even if they paid...if they...? I just wouldn't do it.*

The strength of my conviction only seemed to make more sense in the light of my most recent discovery. *I don't want any of that claptrap. Is* that *why I can perceive those others creatures reaching out to me now? Am I becoming what they foresaw...at last?*

Shaking my head clear, I pushed myself to my feet, dusted myself down, and looked at the waiting elohgraphs. The characters belonging to Anani'el and Hasmêd were more subdued. I received the distinct impression that, having served their purpose, they now held themselves ready for the end of a journey long in the making.

There's only one way to find out.

I lingered. Not for dramatic effect or anything like that. But now the moment had arrived, I felt strangely hollow. Numb almost. As if these events were part of a dream I'd wake up from at any moment and tell myself how silly I'd been, before resuming an entirely normal life.

But that's the stuff of fantasy and fairytales. My life is nothing but a major thread in a very real, very brutal nightmare.

"Know yourself—self—self—self..." an appropriate, if unearthly spectator echoed in the background.

Yes. It's about time I did just that.

Reaching down, I pressed my right palm against Uriel's sigil, and said, *"Eysh-éh* (Burning flame). *Lan khol yé zélah, a-mad ha-pâ-tah* (By all that is holy, stand revealed)."

A shade from the dawn of history acknowledged, "I am Uriel, the fiery one, former Seraphim of the Most High and bearer of the flame eternal who fell protecting purity's grace when the heavens were sundered. Know then, my tale, for what is everlasting can never be quenched. See how I live on within you:

"I burn with the fervor of a thousand suns,

Amid a starless expanse of midnight sky,

A champion fallen in an ocean of debris

Rising up once more from a storm-wracked sea.

Forged anew on an anvil of decay,

I feed upon the blood of the guilty and innocents alike,

Right or wrong, to me they're all the same,

All will fall, for I am free from blame.

Forever lost, forever changed,

Will I ever find myself again?

For I am Legion, a symphony of might

Devoted now to the majesty of night."

A segment of my mind seemed to unhinge, coming far enough apart to allow new thoughts and ideas to merge with my own. Within that mass of data, I saw raw passion being smothered by an all-encompassing blanket of darkness. Squeezed and compressed into a screaming nub of rage, it had all the appearance of a spent pulsar. Abandoned in the furthest reaches of interstellar space, it hung there, inert, awaiting the arrival of a power source with the might to recharge its once vibrant heart.

And I know just where to find it.

Leaning to my left, I placed my other hand against the last remaining glyph, and declared, "*Cógath* (War). *Troh a' lùthse ain mi sealbġh, bi comharr* (By the power invested in me, stand revealed)."

A deep and sonorous voice announced, "I am Gadré-el, fallen Seraphim of war and bearer of the flame eternal who spurned purity's embrace when the heavens were sundered. Know then, my fate, for I chose a path that would ensure my light would never be quenched. See how I live on within you:

"I was the supreme instrument of invincibility

And the ultimate vessel of violence.

Named anew, I am more beautiful than before,

A beast, caged for sacred duty.

Unleashed now as a prince of destruction

I vent my fury upon the masses already dead."

My blood ran cold. "This is describing who I am and what I do. I *am* a product of their making; an instrument of invincibility; the ultimate vessel of violence; a beast who vents injustice on the scum who have sinned and who now infest every circle of the underworld. I'm the Reaper. And what's more, I'm not just a damned soul who's been elevated. I'm a product of celestial origins."

In confirmation of my insight, recollections of my toughest battles as Satan's chief bounty hunter snapped by in quick succession. It took some considerable time to complete, for I'd existed in such a capacity for countless centuries. "No wonder I'm so hard to kill. I'm bound by the very fabric of heaven and hell. Both heritages run through my veins."

Enthralled by the unraveling revelation, I reviewed both Uriel and Gadré-el's pronouncements and tried to grasp the enormity of what it all meant. My attention kept returning to two phrases in particular: 'I am Legion' and 'named anew.'

"But I'm Daemon Grim. I've never been known by any other...?"

Something the wraithlike watchers from on high had alluded to during their disjointed discussion, teased me for a second time:

"...shall see. You retain...resilient of us all and...dormant within. Unbidden, clarity will...from the ruins shall rise again."

"Most of...Remain true to...Prove yourself worthy...new name will manifest from the...and spring unbidden...lips..."

"So, my new name—my *real* name—is supposed to lie dormant, and will only manifest once I've proven myself worthy. It'll arise, unbidden from –?"

And then the answer was there. *I wondered where that particular expression came from during the fight with the Sibitti?*

Scooping in a lungful of air, I threw back my head, squeezed my eyes tight shut and shouted at the top of my lungs. "Azûra-él."

My utterance mushroomed away from me like an atomic explosion. Gaining amplitude as it travelled, its dominion promulgated the length and breadth of the latterday levels of hell in less time that it took for a hell-eagle to beat its mighty wings twice. Reaching our borders, the shockwave kept going, out into the expanse between realms...and beyond.

*The third way too? That...*that *was exhilarating.*

When I lowered my head and opened my eyes, I could see why.

My entire form shone like a blue-white star about to go nova. The space above the crown of my head was filled by a maw of gold and silver flames. My slightest glance cast bolts of undulant lightning, until I thought to rein my power back to a less lethal intensity. Molten glassy stumps were all that remained of my guiding avatars and the wall behind them.

It's like a hyper-phage.

Raising my fist to the skies, I announced my presence to all creation.

"I am Azûra-él. I am Legion. And for the first time in history, I am whole."

Chapter 26: Find Another Way

"Stay sharp boys, the Third and Sixth have paired up again and are coming in fast." Nettesheim's warning induced Champ and Yamato to break off their individual maneuvering and move in closer behind him. Just in time.

Harder than steel, storm driven ice shards the size of whaling harpoons scourged the Hell Hounds position like a lash. Rebounding from a forbidding erected by Nettesheim's arts, the slivers bruised the integrity of his defenses a sickly yellow-blue color in multiple places all at once, before shattering into a million tiny pieces.

Beside him, Nettesheim felt Yamato grip his shoulder as the elemental champion moved to add his own dexterity to help counter the Third of Seven's strike. In seconds, the outer luster of the shield returned to its usual translucent sheen, and Nettesheim breathed a sigh of relief.

No sooner had he done so, however, than the turbulent surface of the bay erupted beneath them. Spiraling upward in an open-ended waterspout, the roaring maw of the funnel pursued the Hounds as they slalomed through the air, clearly intent on swallowing them whole.

We're too exposed here, Nettesheim thought. *Best to get back on dry land.*

"Gentlemen, if you please?" he suggested, casually gesturing toward the shoreline as if they weren't in danger of anything more hazardous than catching a chill or getting their toes wet, "it might be beneficial to get our feet back on terra-firma before the Second decides to join in and broil us alive?"

Yamato responded by providing a surge of additional energy that altered their trajectory toward the relative safety afforded by Lost Liberty Island. In doing so, they almost bowled straight into the Sixth of Seven.

The percussive report of Champ's Abaddon 6000 boomed twice in quick succession. Distracted, the auditor threw up his glittering sword to block the volley and veered away. Robbed of the malevolence driving it, the maelstrom lost cohesion and dropped back into the sable depths below, giving the Hounds the break they needed.

It had been like this for more than fifteen minutes now; fifteen frenzied fright-filled minutes, where the Hell Hounds wove ever more precipitous routes around one of the underworlds stateliest monuments with the Sibitti hot on their heels, pouring a continuous barrage of hate their way that never gave them a moment to rest or gather their strength.

Landing close to the memorial grove, Champ quickly began reloading his weapon while Yamato bent to the ground and commenced drawing nourishment from the environment itself.

Nettesheim stepped back a few paces to cover them, and watched their enemy closely. *The Sibitti seem rather frustrated by our tactics? Good. It must be somewhat trying to meet opponents who won't start panicking or simply roll over and die as soon as you turn up.* He reached up to massage his temples, *though I don't know how much longer I can keep this up? Remaining on the defensive is taking its toll...?*

Up above, the Seventh blazed like a solar flare and a river of fluidic fire spewed from the tip of his sword.

Reacting instantly, Nettesheim crossed his arms into an X configuration, and yelled, "*Air at mutádesh* (You are countered)."

Green and white eruptions sparked through the ether in an expanding wave. Though doused in molten fury, not one of the Hounds was touched by the heat of the inferno's wrath.

"About bloody time," Champ complained, "I was waitin' to see what kinda magically over endowed Wizard of Oz-shot you were. Up until now, it's the wicked witches who've been havin' all the fun. Why don't you drop another house on 'em so we can dish somethin' out instead of bendin' over with a sign on our asses sayin', '*Insert here,* ' all the time?"

Drop another house on them? Insert here? Nettesheim was confused by the reference.

Yamato must have caught the look on his face, for the next thing the mystic knew, the Lead Hound was giggling like a schoolgirl at a rock concert.

Recovering, Nettesheim countered, "Champ, I know I'm new to all this, but I'm not exactly naïve when it comes to walking the halls of power. These are Sibitti, you're talking about. You know better than I do what they're capable of, and what they'll do if they manage to nab us. I'm just keeping us out of the way until His Infernal Majesty and the choir gets here. You'll get the chance for a spot of payback once we have the superiority of strength and numbers, until then it'd be best if—*scheisse!*"

A stupendous burst of light and pressure engulfed them, casting shadows of flickering lunar intensity upon the water. Those shadows were tracked almost immediately by a peal of thunder that rolled across the bay and up onto the concrete and steel ramparts presented by Madhatten's tower blocks.

That must have been the Second taking a stab at us?
The screen about them dulled to a deep carmine color. "*Du
hurensohn.*" Nettesheim scanned the skyline surrounding
the island. *Where are you, Boss? Perhaps I ought to take a
leaf out of Champ's book and give them something to think
about? It might cool their ardor sufficiently to buy us some
time?*

Well used to the metaphysical complexity of the third
way, Nettesheim realized the unfurling Soulstice would am-
plify his potential many times over and make what he was
contemplating entirely feasible.

Unslinging his longbow, Nettesheim delved into the wex
and reached for the most pervasive, atavistic crux holding
the supernatural and mortal realms together. Scooping a
handful of its raw principle into his hands, he withdrew his
arm, and molded that essence into four separate shafts. Satisfied, he selected the first of his newly formed projectiles,
nocked it, took aim, and let fly at the nearest auditor.

The searing jade missile sparked and then exploded as it
cut a furrow across the Fourth of Seven's cheek, causing the
enforcer to wheel away in panic and his brothers to halt their
attack in shock.

"You pierced his wards as if they didn't exist," Yamato
gasped. "Please, feel free to do that again. Though I'd prefer
it if you inflicted a mortal wound this time?"

Nettesheim grinned. "If you can persuade them to stay
still for a second or two, I'll see what I can do."

A soldier in one capacity or another for more than ninety years, Nettesheim's drills in bringing his second arrow
to bear were smooth and unhurried. Forewarned by his actions, the Sibitti fell back to a safer distance. Spotting their
doubt, Nettesheim couldn't resist taking a little bow, though

he wasn't foolish enough to even contemplate lowering his weapon.

"Heinrich Cornelius Agrippa von Nettesheim at your service. While I may not lay claim to being a son of heaven and earth, I *am* someone who has studied at the distinguished feet of Melgaróth, the demon lord of Angár; Dread-Master Ashéd of Kõlesh Prime; and none other than the Isla, the Oracle of Rû herself. As you've just witnessed, if I wasn't so busy protecting my friends here, I'm thinking my craft would probably give you a run for your money and cost you more dearly than you're willing to pay?"

The silence that followed Nettesheim's announcement was disturbed only by the sound of Champ snorting back the contents of his nose, and then hawking the resultant gobbet out onto the concourse.

"You presume to mock us?" a venomous voice hissed. Englobed in a crackling auroral nimbus, the First of Seven moved closer. "Even Satan wasn't so foolish as to test us when we first met. What makes you think you won't suffer for such indignity as we feast upon your livers while you watch?"

Nettesheim waved his hand, dismissively, "Pah, my master has apprised us of the details of that meeting and your memories are plainly at fault. Or you confuse self-control for weakness? His Awful Majesty was merely extending a modicum of courtesy by not testing you in front of Kur, another—*rightful*—king of hell."

The goad that accompanied Nettesheim's reference to the Kigali monarch wasn't wasted. The Sibitti reacted by raising their swords and moving in for the kill.

Endosymbiotic in nature, the third way was unpredictable at the best of times as it constantly fluctuated between various states: pure, mundane and tainted; whole, partial and spent; existence, nonexistence and obliteration, a volatile synthesis creating a medium of creative self-annihilation. Calling on that nature, Nettesheim countered by unleashing the full augmented might at his disposal.

Streamers of iridescent emerald and silver disparity rent the heavens in two and rocked the island to its roots. As his vision cleared and the ringing in his ears subdued to a less painful level, Nettesheim was gratified to see the Sibitti advance had stalled. Even so, the effort had exhausted him and he fervently hoped the cost of his exertions didn't show on his face. Bravely, he declared, "Your temperament blinds you to the reality of failure...?"

A tingle behind his eyes alerted him to approaching power. Smoothly, he added "I'm rather relieved about that, as it's allowed my lord time to rally his forces...Behold."

An abrupt drop in temperature added weight to Nettesheim's pronouncement. Then snow in multifarious shades of yellow and green, brown and gray started falling in strengthening flumes from the blanketed vault overhead. Scudding across a no-man's-land of disputing currents, each putrid flake felt like a slap in the face, an insult that brought with it a cold so profound, so biting, that Niflheim itself would have been proud to call it friend.

A keening howl rent the night. Shrill and piercing, it grated along Nettesheim's senses like a set of monstrous claws raking the battlements of a beleaguered castle. In direct contention to the subtle, deeper resonance of the unfolding Soulstice, it was a welcome sound, nonetheless.

That's one way to make an entrance...and just in time, too.

Sinuous shadows materialized within the brume, along with the elongated cadence of feathers beating against the wind. The largest of those shades soared free, curling high into the sky in a graceful arc before tucking its wings back, tight against a scaled aquiline body.

Hurtling toward the Statue of Lost Liberty at an impulsive speed, that shape clarified into a scarlet dragon, a leviathan that roared again, belching fire and sulfur, and driving spiraling vortices of flame and frost before it.

Nettesheim was gratified to see the Seven begin circling around each other protectively. Even so, their weapons were held at the ready. With teeth bared and eyes flashing, it looked as if they were eager to contend with another foe that gave the impression it would stand and fight.

The dragon landed upon the statue's diadem and blared another challenge. Only then did it bother to change into the likeness of a beautiful, wide-winged titan of flawless appearance. Behind him, twelve smaller serpents hovered lower and followed suit. Transforming, they too appeared godlike in form. Nevertheless, each was marred by an inventory of open wounds and discolored bruising.

Ah, I see the strategy. Our Dark Lord is keen to remind the invaders of the foes his cabal successfully faced in escaping heaven. They would be wise to heed the warning.

In his guise of a beautiful angel, Satan spoke to Erra's cadre, his voice carrying easily across the intervening gap, "At the risk of repeating myself, it's a cold day in hell on one of the most important evenings in a long, long time. I'll be damned if I allow you any further leeway to stir things up. Now begone..." From somewhere, a glistening broadsword appeared, steaming with vitriol and venom, "or we'll settle this once and for all, here and now."

Around him, the twelve bared their own glowing blades and began to rise higher into the air, fanning out as they did so to surround the Sibitti.

Taking their cue from the choir, the Hell Hounds also advanced. Assessing the situation flawlessly, Nettesheim motioned to Champ and Yamato to tag along and headed directly for the Sixth of Seven.

Having read the personal files of each of his compatriots, Nettesheim was keenly aware that Champ and Yamato had fallen to a combined group of enforcers on one of their previous missions to Hades. Once captured, Erra had seen to it the Hounds were not only tortured, but hideously mutilated in the process. Thereafter, they had been left to rot in a cell under the watchful eye of the Sixth, who had kept them barely alive enough to prevent their reassignment to new bodies.

It had taken the direct intervention of the Reaper himself to free them from that misery, so Nettesheim was under no doubt that a brooding resentment must have lingered. Now would be the perfect occasion to settle old debts.

The Sixth saw them approaching. Making eye contact, Nettesheim winked, drew another verdant bolt from the troubled medium of the third way, and aimed its barbed tip straight at the demigod's heart. "Don't move," he snarled, "you've seen what I can do with one of these, and I won't miss from this distance. My friends here would like to get *reacquainted*. They never had a chance to thank you for your hospitality and the amenities lavished on them at Skull Island." Nettesheim glanced toward Satan, "That is, if His Infernal Majesty doesn't mind...?"

The devil smirked; the circumstances making his gesture appear one of the coldest and most ruthless deeds Nettesheim had ever seen. "By all means, faithful servant," Satan cooed, "Please, ram home to Erra's minions the consequences of taking liberties with my patience..."

"You would dare?" The First rasped, his voice rising to a choked-off squeak in disbelief and anger."

"Dare?" Satan bellowed, "In the realm I fashioned by my own might? Fools. Lackeys. You are gravely mistaken if you think I *dare* anything in this place. Stay then, and experience for yourselves why we were able to rival heaven's best."

Launching himself from Lost Liberty's crown, the devil raised his sword and stabbed forward. Lightning convulsed from the point, shredding the atmosphere and throwing back the gloom. As one, the fallen swooped to attack. Following their lead, Nettesheim fired.

Reality warped. One moment the Sibitti were there, and the next, they weren't.

"A pox on your filthy Babylonian balls!" Nettesheim cursed, as he was forced to watch his florid arrow sail through the space once occupied by the Sixth of Seven and out into the bay, where it disappeared beneath the frigid black waters with a resounding hiss.

Privately, he was shocked. *They withdrew? The Sibitti actually backed down? If I...?*

"You have done well, Yamato Takeru."

Eh?

Nettesheim pulled his thoughts together in time to find the Dark Lord addressing the Lead Hound from on high. "Were it not for your timely intervention, more ridicule would have been heaped upon my rule. Your tenure is off to a good start."

"Not good enough," Yamato complained, "we never seem to be able to get past playing catch-up. And when we *do* get a break, like today, there are never enough of us to deal with direct threats of this magnitude. If you hadn't turned up with the cavalry, we'd have had our asses handed to us on a plate."

"So what do you see as a workable solution?"

Yamato appeared surprised to be asked such a direct question. "That's easy. You either need to increase our ranks or grant us more power. Better still, allow us learn the skills Nettesheim obviously possesses. They proved rather effective in battle." Inclining his head, respectfully, Yamato concluded, "Of course, if it was up to me, a combination of all three would be preferable. Sadly, this is hell, and nothing is straightforward."

Bowing even further, Yamato floated away to rejoin his companions.

Satan looked thoughtful for a while, as if he were giving the new Lead Hound's recommendations serious consideration. Then something distracted his attention. Sniffing the air, he circled on the spot and eventually, his gaze came to rest on the statue below. "I see the thorns in my flesh have decided to take their little act of defiance to the next level?"

Abruptly, he turned to speak to Nettesheim directly. "And what of other matters?"

"As you have just surmised, Chopin and Tesla were here," Nettesheim replied. "Unfortunately, technology and circumstance combined once again to keep them from our clutches. Had the Sibitti not interfered, things might have been different."

"Then it is already too late?"

Nettesheim extended his senses into the ether, and beyond. "Alas, yes. The Soulstice is well underway and they are now beyond my reach."

"And mine..." Satan looked to be reliving memories of faraway places, "for they now traverse a region where I am no longer welcome." Then his resolve stiffened. "But tell me, what of the *other* topic?"

"Daemon Grim moves ever closer to fulfilling his destiny." Beside Nettesheim, both Champ and Yamato started, clearly puzzled by the turn of conversation. Ignoring them, he continued, "From what I saw, his core attributes and sense of duty have not been compromised by the transmutation thus far."

"And can you assess him from this distance? Warn him of our predicament so he has the opportunity to act in time?"

Nettesheim smiled and pointed to the east.

All heads turned. For a moment, the covering shroud thinned enough to grant the gathered powers of hell a rare glimpse of an expanse between realms. An expanse the fallen angels had fought tooth and nail to establish; an expanse the former humans had only ever heard of in whispered exchanges.

A blue-white comet rocketed upward from the ground at a terrible pace and Nettesheim's heart thrilled at the sight of it. "My Lord, it would appear Grim has achieved equipoise, and already moves to counter the threat. We stand at...?"

For some reason, the devil was now studying Nettesheim closely.

Satan signaled, and the twelve flexed their wings in unison, taking to the high heavens like the majestic princes they were. In seconds, they were nothing but blips on the horizon. Gliding even nearer, Satan continued to hold Nettesheim's gaze, and whispered, "You were always confident in Grim's resilience to weather the changes and emerge from the other side, weren't you?"

"For all his faults, his sense of duty is unmatched. That fact alone will make him our champion before a new day dawns. What happens after that, however, remains to be seen."

"So, we might yet prevail?"

"I don't think there's any doubt about it." Nettesheim peered eastward for a second time, but the fireball had already breached the mantle. "We'll find out, soon enough."

"If only we could witness the spectacle about to take place. What I'd give for one last..." Satan fell abruptly silent.

When Nettesheim looked back, he found their master had gone.

Champ and Yamato pounced immediately. As usual, Champ was the most vocal. "What the fuck was all that about? What's happenin' with Daemon? Is it anythin' to do with him bein' away so much lately?"

With no further need for pretense, Nettesheim huddled his friend together, and said, "Listen carefully. While I can't tell you everything, I'm going to share a tale that will..."

*

Thummm—thummm—thummm—thummm...

The meter of his journey along the banded, achromatic corridor never wavered, and Frédéric Chopin found its rhythmic inflection as hypnotic as it was soothing. Even so, his heart quivered so hard against his breastbone, he thought it might renovate into a drum roll heralding his demise at any moment.

For what must have been the hundredth time in the past few minutes, he glanced back along the gleaming hoops lining the interior of the tunnel and held his breath. *They're still not following? We did it.* Then aloud, "Nikola, can you detect any signs of pursuit?"

Thummm—thummm—thummm—thummm...

"No, my friend," Tesla murmured, "it appears we got the best of head starts. And I've no doubt *that's* due to the Sibitti's interference. Who would have credited, all seven of them coming together to work out their petty personal grievances with the Reaper's Hounds."

"Amazing, eh?"

"And providential. My calculations indicate we're fast approaching the limits of Satan's influence. He'd never reach us in time to stop us now."

That means his bloodthirsty henchman can't hurt us either. Subconsciously, Chopin tightened his grip on the pinioned paragon clutched against his chest. But really, there was no need for such an expression of anxiety, for under each wing's guidance, the redoubtable duo were traversing a cosmic conduit between realities with no more effort than it would have taken to cross a deserted street. Here, there was neither up nor down; left or right; in or out. Even mass, inertia and gravity didn't exist. Unfettered and unhindered, Chopin and Tesla were free to go wherever the wings were sanctioned to operate, at near instantaneous speeds.

Chopin wasn't really concerned with such aspects, however, for sheer relief brought with it a flood of other emotions. *We're home free. After all these years, his Royal Badass can't touch us anymore. And when this is all over, we'll be safely tucked away in a realm where his influence will no longer blight the quality of our unlives. Then, once we've had time to settle and prepare, we'll start to consolidate our position, and our power and fame will spread to...?*

Though daydreaming, Chopin wasn't so far lost in flights of fancy that he failed to espy a strange fogbank in the distance. With no defined limits, it flared like smoke, yet rippled to create the most amazingly precise symmetrical patterns. Circles and squares abounded, as did triangles and oblongs. But the closer he looked, the more Chopin realized he could see things like dodecahedrons, hexadecagons, icosahedrons, and every shape and configuration in between. What was more, the cloud was massive; a colossal nebula of pulsing, sparkling power that stretched for as far as was needed into the multiphasic reaches of time and space to ensure nothing remotely erroneous could pass...without the correct prerequisites, of course.

"It looks like we're just about there," Chopin called out, excitedly, tugging on Tesla's sleeve as he did so. "What would you say, sixty, seventy seconds?"

Thummm—thummm—thummm—thummm...

"Don't be fooled by appearances," Tesla advised, "I judge we have less than a minute. Remember, *that* is but a spot of window dressing to hide the real thing: a net of stunning power and lethal finesse. It will efface us from existence unless we're very careful. Now quickly, lest we get too close and trigger its defenses, open the Scroll of Divergent Union and utter the incantation."

Thankful of the cathartic effects of the Golden Fleece, Chopin reached over his shoulder without the slightest discomfort, and removed a four-foot long, rolled parchment from his back sling.

Gilded by an amber radiance, the totem was as light as a feather and seemed to mold to his grasp instantly. Not for the first time was he grateful for the absence of the hurricane force winds travelling at such speed under normal circumstances would have entailed, for it would have made his following tasks nigh on impossible.

Biting down with his teeth, Chopin snagged one end of a luxuriant jet-black ribbon, and pulled, loosening the volute manuscript and exposing a generous scarlet seal beneath.

"Nikola, if you please?" Chopin held the scroll out toward his companion.

Tesla responded by placing the jeweled pommel of the *Sword of Uncovered Secrets* against the inscribed stamp. The moment the two artifacts touched, a sigil hidden deep within the hallmarked wax gleamed bright.

Crack! The seal split in two, bubbled, and evaporated.

Holding the sacred scroll by its top border, Chopin shook it once. The entire sheet unraveled, revealing a twelve-lined sonnet arranged into three separate stanzas, embellished in glowing silver characters. As Chopin cast his eye down the page, the symbols flowed together and reformed into letters and expressions he could read and understand.

It must link to the mind of the entity holding it? How strange for something fashioned for seraph...? Then he frowned.

Motivated by his friend's reaction, Tesla enquired, "What? Is there something wrong?"

"I...I'm not sure," Chopin mumbled in reply. He scanned the verses for a second time, ensuring to say nothing out loud for fear of breaking the spell in some way, before turning it toward Tesla so his co-conspirator could better see himself. "Sorry if I scared you, but I was taken by surprise. As you'll note, the invocation looks a lot like an ancient prophecy or something of that nature. I don't know what to say, I certainly wasn't expecting it to be written like that?"

Thummm—thummm—thummm—thummm...

Waiting for Tesla to read the scroll's contents made Chopin feel as if he was slowly turning to stone. Eventually, he could stand no more and was forced to ask, "So, what do you think?"

"I think beggars can't be choosers. It doesn't really matter what the passage says so much as the acoustics each word generates..." Tesla pointed toward the end of the rapidly waning corridor, "Hurry, Frédéric, before it's too late."

Taking his friend's warning as a cue, Chopin lifted the parchment high, coughed to clear his throat, and in a firm voice, said:

"What was whole yet always divided,

A chasm yet riven before,

The space in between now presided,

In sorrows most bittersweet score.

One hundred thousand years we have waited,

For one who will bring fresh accord,

To empower again the benighted,

Once tainted, rewoven, restored.

From the ashes a phoenix awakens,

A champion twice fallen, arise

To replace what was lost and forsaken,

And envelop again sundered skies."

Chopin held his breath and looked up in expectation.

Thummm—thumm—thumz—thuuzz - thuzzz...

To Chopin's ear, it sounded as if a swarm of angry hornets had found their way inside the conduit.

Thuuzzz—thuuzzz– thuuzzz—thuuzzz...

The wall of the tunnel commenced falling away on all side. Widening—expanding—dissolving—fading. Until...

This time, Chopin really did think his heart would burst.

"Unholy shit, Nikola. Look at that!"

Chapter 27: Phoenix

My entire form shone like a blue-white star about to go nova. The space above the crown of my head was filled by a maw of gold and silver flames. My slightest glance cast bolts of undulant lightning, until I thought to rein my power back to a less lethal intensity. Molten glassy stumps were all that remained of my guiding avatars and the wall behind them.

It's like a hyper-phage.

Raising my fist to the skies, I announced my presence to all creation.

"I am Azûra-él. I am Legion. And for the first time in history, I am whole."

Through eyes forged anew, I spun slowly on the spot to survey the place of my rebirth, only to discover the rest of the sentinels had joined their compatriots by crumbling to a fine black dust. *They must have been connected in some way?*

My earlier suspicions regarding the missing members of Satan's coterie seemed less far-fetched than ever. *This whole quadrangle is one great sepulcher, a memorial to those who gave of their substance—unwillingly it would seem—to make me what I am.*

Turning full circle, I did the math. "All nine of them are gone. Add that to my boys over here, and that's a total of thirteen angels and fallen combined. A veritable legion if ever there was one."

Other things fell into place. *I was right. This went far beyond what Satan originally intended.*

Whistling in awe, I glanced up toward the hidden heavens. *And I've got a good idea who might have had a hand in running interference. But how did that actually come about? And more importantly, why?*

At that moment, it felt as if a new hidden impulse had been waiting in the wings to answer my every query, for an expanded reflection of the heavenly discussion I'd overheard during my previous vision started to repeat itself in my head:

"…we have no need to fear. Regardless of the grievance, the core principle of God's Grace remains intact. Most puissant of all majestic expressions, it will take but a spark, the merest pinch of holy influx to ensure the survival of both spirit and flame. Quickly, while there is still time, call to Uriel and those others of our brothers forced into this despicable act and remind them that all is not lost. Though and age must pass…"

A different voice called out.

"Hold fast, and you shall see. You retain enough…especially you, brave Uriel, most resilient of us all and…lie dormant within. Unbidden, clarity will...from the ruins shall rise again."

And another.

"Fear not the abomination Satan seeks to create from... The AllFather sees and moves to counter this fool and his schemes. Is not His will the stronger? Will He not intervene to ensure all is not…better days?"

Finally, the original spokesperson concluded the exchange.

"Most of all, never forget…Remain true to your heart, for there resides…Prove yourself worthy…before calamity befalls us all, your new name will manifest from the ashes of…and spring unbidden…lips—lips—lips—lips…"

Picking up on the content of the extended exchange, I was more convinced than ever of outside help. "Yes, there are definitely other things going on here that weren't initially apparent. And thankfully, I don't think the revelations have dried up yet."

Such a realization brought with it the satisfaction of knowing certain essential *tasks* would at last get the attention they deserved. *Just a little while longer, and the answers that have eluded me for so long will fall into my lap. And when they do, I'll enjoy a long overdue chat with His Nibs and find out* why *he felt all the smoke and mirrors were so necessary. After that, it'll be a quick side trip to the Pentagram where Samael will experience, firsthand, the consequences of pissing me off and causing the death of Nimrod.*

My smile grew into a self-satisfied grin. "Oh yeah. I'm going to enjoy…?"

A tinkling, musical serenade issued from the center of the garden. Looking toward the source of that music, I was relieved to see the Wyrd tree had survived the rigors of my transformation.

Sadly, such relief was short-lived.

Peering closer, I noticed a ruby carpet growing about the base of Wyrd tree's trunk. *Have I hurt it, or is this part of the process of my awakening?*

Like a requiem of fern fronded notes, a song began to emerge as the succession of falling leaves grew steadily heavier. Everything blended together into a melody I found both mournful and triumphant, for it was a lament containing promises able to lift my heart and transpose my soul:

"Azûra-él, you stand alone,

A sentinel cocooned within a web of fabricated dreams

Of what might have been.

Tears, astringent fragments of your spirit,

Spray like needles in outrage

Upon a sea of countless prisms.

Scattered through time,

Primordial thoughts of revenge consume you,

Held in abeyance until your duty is done.

Released at last, you must spend yourself

Before you stand upon the shore of absolution,

For your actions will determine the fate of all."

"My actions will determine the fate of all?"

True understanding hovered before me, tantalizingly still out of reach. Refusing to be swayed by impatience, I reasoned, "Well, any form of retribution will have to wait for a little while longer. I need to prioritize. First, I'll check in on the guys back at Lost Liberty Island to make sure they're okay. Second, I need to drop down to Kí-gal to ask the talle-bhést their advice regarding the activation of the larger soul sapphires. Once I have what I need, I'll shoot over to Jahannam and see what I can do about releasing the woman inside that gem."

I had a plan and it felt good. "Now the sentinels...*my* combined memories are slotting back into place, I'm sure it won't take long for something useful to turn up regarding this particular Soulstice as well. Once it does, I'll be able to use what I learn to open the trúllefeng stone and start getting to the bottom of another mystery.

"Strawberry or not, I'll have David subject her to rigorous testing in an isolation unit until we can better establish who, or *what*, we're dealing with. Then, once Gemini is back on her feet, we'll all decide—Hell Hounds and Inquisitors—on the best way forward for everyone involved. One way or another, I'm going to turn this nightmare to our advantage, or my name's not Daemon Grim...or Azûra-él? Shit, this could get confusing?"

There's a point. What should I call myself? I can't see things continuing the way they were before all this started. Satan's gonna squeeze off a prickly one when he realizes how powerful I've become. Will I still retain a position of prestige or will he try and...whoa!

I could see what was happening. The novelty of my situation was beginning to run away from me. Hamstringing such fruitless time-wasting before it built up a head of steam, I decided it might be a good idea to carry out a little test to see if my continuing evolution had enhanced me in ways I hadn't yet anticipated.

But what can I try?

Let's see...? Stepping into a clear space, I expanded my perceptions, just to see how far I could actually go. When I managed to pierce the barrier into an entirely different and mesmerizing level of actuality, I wasn't entirely surprised.

Previously unseen, radiant lines of lucent quiddity pulsed toward and away from my position, creating a vast network of energy connecting me to everyone and everything at the basest level. *Is it the same for all creatures of power, or just those at the top of the pecking order? I wonder? Does Satan still see at this level now he's debased? I'll have to...*

A nearby filament strummed several times in quick succession. To my ear, it sounded like the spasmodic twanging heard in the moments before a load-bearing cable snaps from being put under too much stress. Examining that filament closely, I could see the ectoplasmic streamers coursing along its outer structure shredding under the assault of an unseen influence. *Oh, that is not a good sign.*

My concerns were entirely warranted.

As I looked on, the thread continued to disintegrate, twining round and around and stretching as it darkened, spreading the blight to the strands on either side. Then the next lines along became infected. And the ones after that. Soon, a significant proportion of the gigantic web sounded as if it were being plucked by numb relentless fingers.

A sense of wrong pervaded the ether. In my current state, it took hardly any effort to broaden the scope of my awareness, and in an instant, I was able to grasp the full extent of the growing crisis.

"Chopin and Tesla? How in the...? No! The bloody fools are wielding the Scroll of Divergent Union. They'll drop the Veil, and in doing so, will shatter the restraints preventing heaven, hell and the mortal plane from overlapping."

I imagined the devastation such a scenario might produce, and balked. "It'll be pandemonium, and not just because so many disgruntled denizens of the underworld will seize the opportunity to jump ship, either."

A sense of outrage rekindled the fire in my heart, a fire that now raged with an intensity I would have never thought was possible. "I can't allow such a thing to happen. I'll have to...wait a minute? Is *that* what the Wyrd tree was trying to tell me? That I was fashioned to counter events like this, hazards that would threaten the safety of both the supernatural and mundane realms?"

It made a strange kind of sense, especially as I was the only one I knew of who could control both the Bãlefire and God's Grace, and travel freely between any of the levels of the underverse and earth.

And who knows where else I can go now?

The unexpectedly strong sense of indignation growing within me focused my conviction. *I will respond.*

Nerve endings blazing, I was moved to express my desire aloud. "I am Azûra-él, and I will answer this challenge."

My declaration was answered by a searing score of startling agony between my shoulder blades. The pain was so intense, it felt as if a Zion-forged blade had been dipped into the molten core of God Almighty's throne and rammed into my upper spine. Such anguish was indescribable. The joy, unimaginable. And as I sucked in a ragged breath to scream, I staggered beneath an additional weight that threatened to send me tumbling to the floor.

Adjusting my center of gravity to compensate, I was astonished to see a radiant pair of wings flare forward from behind me, forming a living halo in mother-of-pearl hues. Needless to say, I flinched, only to watch, incredulously, as the shimmering plumage shadowed my every subsequent move.

Then reality hit. "They...they're a part of me!"

In that moment, I knew from where they'd come.

That day in the Colonnade of Eternal Reflections? Not content with rubbing Grislington's loss in his face, Satan had to go the extra mile and display something even more valuable, something that reminded him of a seraphim's downfall. I wondered how Satan got his hands on two different pairs of wings. Now I know...

Instinct took over.

...and for once, I can't thank him enough for his boundless vanity.

Flexing my chest and back muscles, mighty pinions stretched wide. Full, proud, and erect, I held them there, trembling, ready for the down thrust that would mark my inaugural flight.

The slightest thought was all it took, and before I knew it, I was thundering into the higher firmament like a shooting star on a collision course with a place I'd never thought to see and live: the Veil.

Chapter 28: A Dish Best Served Cold

It was a peculiar sensation, travelling by means of sera-phim wings.

When I phased, I blended to and then skimmed through my surrounding environment as if I'd become part of it. Tele-portation was different, in that I'd negate the distance be-tween my departure and arrival points by jumping through hydraspace in hell, or hyperspace if carrying out assignments topside.

But the angels? They could travel anywhere, almost in-stantaneously, without any of the physical symptoms usually associated with moving at such breakneck velocities. There were no dizzying ascents or gut-churning, stomach-in-the-throat, descents. No, "I've had a stroke" facial contortions, induced by pulling thousands of g's in sharp turns. No organ squishing inertial trauma caused by instantaneous starts or stops.

I only had to will it, and my needs were translated into action. *Can Satan and the twelve still fly as freely as this, or was their range capped by the process of falling from grace? I don't suppose we'll ever know, seeing as such information has been proscribed?*

As intriguing as that notion was, I didn't have time to process it further. The signs of corrosion appeared to be spreading like wildfire, as different pockets of decay were breaking out like festering sores across the net in numerous places all at once.

Concern drove me to greater efforts. "C'mon, Daemon, move your ass. You're not going to stop this by dawdling. You've got to…idiot! What I've *got to* do is stop thinking small. Things are different now, and although I'm tugging at my bootstraps as I go along, I am operating on an entirely different level. So I need to act like it."

Slowing my pace, I took the time to examine the milieu about me more thoroughly.

To my mind, it felt as if I was fording an ever changing medium that had nevertheless been frozen into overlapping bands of power. On one hand, the visible quantum matrix flickered coldly, while right next to it, a neighboring efflux would glitter and flash in blinding concentrations of heat and light. The thing was, the longer you looked, the more each facet would change under the influence of unseen fluctuating energies.

Sometimes, the miasmalike strands were as thick as metal cables. At others, they were spider's silk thin. Together, they formed a permafrost and flame coated prism that braided the void and stretched off toward the edges of forever.

Forever? Then—just like that—I understood what I was experiencing.

"This *is* the Veil. I'm already there. Seeing it. Experiencing it…" *Switch on, Daemon.* "It doesn't occupy a single locale in the spacetime or Sheolspace continuum like the main gate to Misery Land. It's a utopian esomorphic construct existing everywhere and everywhen. How else could it stop anarchists hidden away in the deepest darkest caves of the underverse from plotting mayhem and unleashing nightmares on the mortal world? It's laced through the whole of infernity to prevent mischief. We've come to think of it as an actual location because…because *that's* what we were led to believe!" *The deception never stops.*

Such a realization was so profound—even to my fledgling new way of thinking—that I came to a full stop. *The Veil is omnipresent. So, that should mean…?*

I knew where I needed to be.

Curbing my excitement, I focused on that objective and envisioned a spot that would hopefully give me a tactical advantage. Then I watched, rapt with attention, as the latticed mists in front of me swirled briefly, only to solidify on a sight that sent a tingle of violent anticipation coursing along my spine.

Well, would you credit that? Down below in the non-distance, two little insects scampered about along the fringes of a growing cancer. Scanning the infection, I could see too many places where the Veil had almost rotted through. *And once it goes, it'll set off a chain reaction that will shatter the remaining links and unravel the whole thing. That simply mustn't happen.*

This time, I created an image of my being a mere ten yards behind my prey, and though I discerned no hint of movement whatsoever…I was instantly there. When I materialized, however, I did so to find Tesla waiting for me, a pyramidal-shaped device in one hand, the *Sword of Uncovered Secrets* in the other.

"Who the devil are…?" Out of sorts, Tesla frowned. His gaze jumped from my face to my wings and back again, clearly agitated by what he saw. "Reaper?"

"Yes, it's me," I replied, softly, allowing the weight of my presence to speak all the louder, "though with what I've been through, I think there's going to be a vacancy for my old job, real soon."

Upon hearing my voice, Chopin turned from what he'd been doing and recoiled in dismay. Leveling the *Sword of Seraphim Speed* at my heart, he hissed, "You? How did you manage…?" He too seemed mesmerized by the sight of my plumage. Glancing toward his counterpart, he urged, "don't just stand there, Nikola, use everything you've got. Kill him."

On the last occasion I'd faced this pair in the catacombs of Black Keep—the maximum security prison on the Isle of Cogs—neither Chopin nor Tesla had been keen to engage in any form of confrontation. Caught unawares and backed into a figurative corner, I had a feeling things would be different this time around.

All the same, when I raised one radiant finger into the air as a signal to parlay, my gesture stalled them long enough for them to listen to what I had to say.

"Gentlemen, you are making a grave error if you think any amount of artifice, artifacts, scientific devices or sheer bloody-mindedness will make a difference." I opened my arms and pinions wide and allowed my emerging identity to shine through. "Look at me. Compare *this* to what you once knew. Remember too, where we are. Surely, even fools as shortsighted as you are can see there have been a few changes?"

As I spoke, I ensured to glide steadily toward them at mundane speed, closing my distance and keeping an eye on the rapidly decomposing Veil. *Dare I resort to the Bãlefire this close to the barrier? What if I weaken it even further? I can't risk it. I'll have to play it safe.*

Two ninjaken appeared in my hands. I hadn't had to move a muscle. "You've tried this before, and failed. If the Cup of

Tartarus couldn't destroy me as I was then, what makes you think you'll have any chance now?"

Hyperenergized as I was, the rush of ill will coalescing in the minds of Chopin and Tesla tasted like ambrosia and served as a warning of their intent.

A tendril of rainbow brilliance lashed the rapidly dimming swathe about us as Tesla reacted first. A split second later, it was joined by an igneous sapphire bolt as Chopin brought the *Sword of Seraphim Speed* into play.

Dropping into a defensive posture, I used my gauntlets to absorb both blasts before augmenting their capacity and flinging their strikes straight back at them. Weakened by Chopin and Tesla's interference, the Veil chimed loudly and shimmered back and forth, like a wire mesh fence at a penitentiary overflowing with prisoners desperate to get out.

It's too brittle to take much more. Oh great. While I'll have to try and be as gentle as I can, these wankers will do their best to vent their spleens and fry me where—Unholy shit!

I was forced to duck as a ringing thunderclap narrowly missed rupturing my eardrums. *There you go, exactly as I thought. Right, let's keep them occupied and off balance while I think on how best to manage this mess.*

Thankfully, Chopin and Tesla were complete novices when it came to real combat, and their lack of experience showed. Thinking there was safety in numbers they had maneuvered closer together and combined the capacity of their Zion-forged blades to carry out their attack. While that strategy did work to increase the overall strength of their riposte, it provided me with an easy target.

Spinning my secondary ninjatō, I unloaded a supercharged pulse of energy toward their center of mass. Empowered by the crystal from the *Sword of Dauntless Strength*, my assault crackled with purple and lilac splendor. Held in reserve, my primary weapon throbbed with the bloody promise of death.

Iridescent potency collided. A ribbon of opposing authority formed, marked at its halfway point by a knot of sizzling radiation that grew bigger and brighter the longer the standoff continued.

Valuable seconds ticked by. Even though I was going easy on them for fear of speeding the demise of the Veil, I was still astounded by Chopin and Tesla's resilience. *They're certainly holding their own. While their glaives can wield a similar capacity to mine, it still takes tenacity to keep the flow coherent enough to be effective…?* Then I spotted a possible reason for such focus. *Aha, they each possess one of Grislington's wings.*

I was reminded of my final confrontation with the captive cherub, Gaz-árdiel, within the shattered throne room at the Colonnade of Eternal Reflections. Better known to the denizens of hell as the Angel Grislington, he had sought to reclaim his heavenly legacy from one of Satan's mirror cages and return to his celestial home. I had prevented that from happening at the last moment, much to his chagrin.

What was it he said again?

"…but I have my wings and can access the very crux of heaven. I am a cherub, of the Order of the Throne. You are…?"

That's right. Though he'd regained his heritage, he wasn't able to access their full potential. Like these goons here. And even if they could, it wouldn't matter. Grislington was a cherub, whereas I am blessed with the office of a seraph.

Meeting Chopin and Tesla's gazes across the top of the lurid glare cast by our photonic medley, I taunted, "Tough luck boys. You're fortunate I have to make sure something of you survives to face injustice, otherwise you'd experience the same fate as your doppelgangers back on Kí-gal."

Their eyes flared in shock.

"Yes, we knew about your little insurance policy."

I chose that moment to call forth the divine reserves at my disposal. Channeling the sovereignty of heaven down through my body, I unleashed it in a devastating surge which generated a spiraling vortex of destruction. Hammering my opponents from every side, I swiftly forced them to their knees.

As I thought. They've gone to all the trouble of collecting banned artifacts, but don't have the familiarity to wield their full might in battle.

The multicolored band electrifying the ether between us became ever more erratic. Flames licked along the Veil itself as lambent sparks thrown off by that streamer caught nearby strands, ignited them, and began spreading. *This has gone on long enough. I'll have to risk it.* Accessing the other side of my nature, I extended my primary weapon and brought the stygian scope of the Bãlefire to bear.

The culmination of such an addition—gradual though it was—became immediately apparent.

That part of the plasma strand closest to Chopin and Tesla flushed pink; salmon; and then rose. Gradually, it reddened to magenta. A lightning ball formed around the loop midway along the stream, creating a clear marker between both sets of antagonistic forces. That sphere darkened, and as it did so, it inched ever closer to my opponents.

I could see the panic on their faces as they realized that, after all their years of planning, it had finally come to this. They were fighting a losing battle.

Teeth bared, they struggled to hold their weapons steady. Sweat beaded their brows in fine rivulets of defeat. The cuffs

of their sleeves started to smoke; a sure sign the temperature
had risen beyond what they were capable of surviving. By the
time the blazing halation had reached the tip of their blades,
hell's most dynamic essence had exhausted their vitality.

With a grin, I stamped forward and delivered the final
insult; savage bolts of necromantic theurgy that latched onto
the fabric of the jewels adorning the hilts of each sword. Corrupted, the gems guttered, then winked opaque. Now black-
er than pitch, their cores ruptured, showering us in crystal
flecks and spawning a resounding shriek that tore the air, hurt
the ears and thrummed along the nerves.

Next moment, both weapons vanished, vaporized in a
psychedelic brume of imploding energies that left a static
charge in its wake powerful enough to swat Chopin and Tesla
aside like the insects they were. Stunned and mute, both men
floated free.

Seeing they were temporarily incapacitated, I seized the
opportunity to check on the integrity of the Veil. It wasn't
good. The entire edifice was riddled with fissures that continued to expand before my eyes like the ever hungry jaws of
miniature black holes. Wherever the putrefaction was most
virulent, the extremities of those rents would fizzle, releasing
a mélange of foul-smelling vapors.

Observing them at work, I was reminded of a science fic-
tion adventure I'd managed to catch during one of my mission's topside. In that film, space marines fought a virulent
life-form endowed with a unique defensive system. Not only
was the creature exceedingly difficult to kill, but anyone
standing nearby at the time ran the risk of being melted, as
the alien's blood was highly acidic. Capable of eating its way
through anything in its path, the blood remained a hazard to
everyone until oxidization robbed it of its potency.

"Yeah, except *this* stuff doesn't look as if it'll run out of steam anytime soon."

By far the largest gap yawned wide right in front of me, indicating where the ritual must have originally been enacted. Feeling completely out of my depth, I reached out with my senses and probed the interstices, checking for telltale markers that might help me fathom what to do.

Loose ends from a series of frayed cosmic strings indicated those spots where major conjunctions of the Veil had once been anchored. "Most of them are still active. I need to find something suitably potent to kick off the regenerat –?"

"You bastard! You're not going to get away with this."

Spinning about, I found Chopin had recovered sufficiently to arm himself with another shining blade. Advancing toward me, he waved it in a threatening manner.

A Dagger of Damocles.

Desperation gave him courage I didn't know he possessed. As his face contorted into a mask of rage, he snarled, "It took me years to work out a strategy that would reunite me with my long lost love. Decades, in fact. Everything I've done, everything I've worked so hard to accomplish was geared to achieving that one goal. I won't allow you to ruin it, not now, when I can almost smell the scent of her."

The forthright passion of Chopin's declaration was so clear, so bright, that even the occluding brume of hell wouldn't have dulled its sincerity. What's more, the earnestness of his voice stung my receptors like the lash of a whip.

He's telling the truth?

Recalling some of the evidence we'd recovered over the past eighteen months from various addresses belonging to Chopin, I knew a woman—one Amantine Lucile Aurore Dupin—had been instrumental in his desire to be free of Satan's influence once and for all. But I'd never realized until now that the hope of rekindling that earthly relationship had been Chopin's sole motivating factor.

So, he's put himself through all this; all these trials and tribulations; risking my wrath and life and limb countless times, for a woman's love? Part of me identified with the depth of his devotion. *How far am I prepared to go, to give Strawberry—or whatever that thing is—a chance at a second lease of unlife? One way or another, I have to try and see if I can make something work. Her loyalty alone over the centuries has earned her that much. But Chopin?*

Chopin was still crawling toward me, only now he'd been joined by Tesla, who had managed to retain his grip on the pyramid.

That must be one of the temporal mitigators the guys mentioned in their reports. A nasty bit of kit. But this place operates outside the usual laws of the spacetime and Sheol-space continuums, so what are they hoping it will do?

"Was that pity I saw marring the frosty sterility of your countenance, Reaper?" Tesla's question caught me off guard. "Empathy, perhaps? Surely the coldest killer ever to walk the desecrated halls of the underworld wasn't about to feel a shred of sorrow for one of his latest victims?"

Brandishing his device seemed to give Tesla confidence. In a harsher tone, he breezed on, "It's a pity you've never thought to show such considerations before, eh? Had you made the effort, you'd have realized no long-term harm would have been caused, other than to allow two irrelevant individuals greater leeway to stir things up in a place that—let's face it—is supposed to exist to serve the tenets of endless turmoil. But oh no, you had to interfere. So we upped the ante. And here we all are, with everything falling apart around us."

Then his mood seemed to switch, and Tesla cradled the mitigator like a child or some other precious thing that held the answers to all his problems. "Still, all is not lost. The Veil unravels as we speak, and my associate and I stand but a hairsbreadth from claiming our prize. Of course, to do that we need to get past you. Normally, I'd not fancy our chances. As you've just demonstrated, you're rather a dab hand at fighting. However, I doubt your prowess extends to technology?"

Activating the device, Tesla threw it directly at me. I did what anyone blessed with telekinesis would do under such circumstances, and batted it back toward him before the damned thing got anywhere near me.

Chopin and Tesla shied and threw up their arms, then abruptly froze in place as a glistening bubble encompassed them in sparkling light.

"Seriously? What the fuck else did he think I was going to do. Catch it and pass critical comments on its aesthetics and color until...*Oh shit! It's a trap?*"

Fording toward them through the ensuing gravitational surf, I lingered near the edge of the pyramid's active range to take the measure of its depth and consistency. "Seeing as time doesn't flow here as it does elsewhere, Tesla must have adjusted this particular unit to generate a limited field in which to operate..." I glanced behind me at the continuing desolation, "not that I'm complaining. I can zap these two to a frazzled cinder without further ado, and get on with saving the Veil." *Yeah...and just how am I gonna do that?*

Both my ninjaken were already fully charged. Pointing them at my unmoving and blissfully silent adversaries, I couldn't help but feel a little melancholy. *Strange, now I'm about to reassign their asses—at long last—I thought I'd be jumping through hoops? Oh well, I suppose* that *will come later when I've seen how ingenious the Undertaker gets with their...?*

My gaze came to rest of Chopin's weapon.

"Hang on a second. I recall Grislington prattled on regarding the nature of those daggers the day we met in Black Keep."

Casting my mind back, I started to piece together the events of that day in more detail.

"That's it. Nimrod and I had just arrived to find Chopin and Tesla in the middle of a heated exchange with Doctor Thomas Neill Cream. It seems the unworthy doctor had tried to screw them over, and despite the presence of a captive angel, things quickly turned ugly. This pair went to attack him, and Cream defended himself by pulling one of these beauties from beneath his jacket. What was it Grislington said...?"

With the utmost care, I relived the conversation all over again:

...Hang on! Cream's got his own agenda. Will he try to use the Sword of Damocles to counter Chopin and —

A *sword of Damocles*, Grislington's condescending mental voice interrupted. He seemed amused by my apparent faux pas, and I could sense his hunger increasing by the second. His eyes smoldered brighter, and his chest heaved beneath his shimmery gown.

The angel gestured toward Cream's weapon, and resorted to verbal speech to educate me:

"Only a hundred and forty-four thousand of those blades were ever made, one for each attendant who formed the echelons squiring the Chosen in battle. Such treasures reveal a heritage, both hinted and richly evoked. For they disclose a hidden purpose that He Who Causes To Become would have preferred remain secret."

Try as I might, I couldn't concentrate on everything at once. Grislington's words carried a profound weight of truth I found hard to ignore. I snapped a mental order toward Nimrod. *Watch what those clowns are doing!* Then I interposed myself between Grislington and his entertainment.

"What the fuck are you dithering on about?"

"My apologies," Grislington replied, his attention now fully on me. "Although at times I might act without convention, you must remember, I have been disassociated from reality for far too long. I am talking of the true purpose of the Damocles Daggers, and what Satan has striven to do with them ever since."

"True purpose?"

"Cousin, He Who Causes To Become couldn't have his holy angels and Vidium Swords falling into the wrong hands without *something* to counter them, could he? He was at war, after all, and a bloody war at that. He had to ensure an appropriate countermeasure was on hand to take away their edge, so to speak; you know, the danger they represented. Of course, bright Lucifer saw potential in that provision, and set out to vitiate his Creator's intent from the word go—go—go—go..."

My gaze locked on the dagger in Chopin's hand. "Yes, I remember now. Although of divine origin, these things were designed to counter heavenly power. So..."

I stared up at the extent of the task ahead of me. *While I haven't got a clue how to go about clearing this mess up, I am becoming something of a wiz at interpreting the character of different energies. What if I use the dagger's template to help me analyze which frequencies might stop the degradation and which will regenerate the Veil? After all, it's not like I'm going to run out of power. I have the mother lodes of two realms I can rely on.*

At that moment, I thought of another source I could turn to if all else failed.

Nettesheim, you crafty bugger. Were you put in place to ensure I'd start digging and unlock a whole new playground, just to prepare me for...for this? I looked back toward my imminent victims. *There's only one way to find out, I suppose. But how about I experiment a little, just to see how much of a Reaper I still am?*

Thrusting my blades forward, I stabbed into the dilation field and commenced feeding on its warped vitality. Though it tasted unusual, my gambit worked, and I found it a fascinating experience, following the bubble as it collapsed in on itself. In less than a minute, its radius had reduced far enough to allow me to extract the Dagger of Damocles from Chopin's frigid grasp.

That milestone achieved, I decided to have some fun. "Perchance the occasion won't be as disappointing as I first thought, especially as I've already caught my fish in an appropriate net. Now all I've got to do is fry them."

Leaving my primary weapon in place so I could continue the drain, I extracted the one empowered by the crystal from the *Sword of Dauntless Strength* and used its redundancy to create a highly charged bioelectrical field.

It didn't take long to uncover Chopin and Tesla's limbs in their entirety. Once I had, I ramped up the current to the secondary field and watched with satisfaction as their feet began kicking and their fingers clutching at the void in desperation. Exposed flesh reddened, blistered and cracked, revealing fresh raw tissue beneath.

I reveled in their distress. "Now this, *this* is more like it."

Doubling the torrent, I thrilled as their clothes burst into flames. Veins swelled then popped, spraying sweet coppery delight into the firmament. Finally, after their arms and legs had been cooked enough to shrivel, the pitifully sparse strips of meat that remained crusted over like the flaky skin on top of lava. Chopin and Tesla's constant wriggling caused those flakes to fall, like blackened autumnal leaves from skeletal branches.

I savored the moment, for inhaling their spoor was like breathing in the heady scent of a funeral pyre. "Right, time to end this, once and for all."

Absorbing what remained of the dilation field, my senses were immediately assailed by a garbled verbal and telepathic tirade of woe. The obscenities spilling from Chopin and Tesla's minds quickly disclosed that the time-bending effects of the pyramid had prolonged the vehemence of their suffering—from their perspective—for more than an hour; an hour in which neither man had been able to move properly or do anything to reduce the horror of their torture. Needless to say, both had been driven to the edge of delirium, as evidenced by the volume of blood saturating their chins from where they had bitten through their lips and tongues in an effort to appease their anguish.

A fast scan of their mutilated limbs reveled where any remaining pain receptors were located. Targeting those nerves, I destroyed each and every single one. As I sheathed my swords, both rebels experienced an instant high. Blinking rapidly, they gulped for air and cast mad, fervid glances from side to side as if expecting the misery to start again at any second from an unknown quarter.

I allowed them a few moments grace, and then wreathed myself in binate majesty. Two faces turned toward me.

"Ah, I have your undivided attention. Good. I'm sure there's no need to tell you, my removing your capacity to feel pain has nothing to do with mercy. I merely wanted to make

sure you were fully aware of what's about to happen, and
who it is that's doing it to you."

Gesturing to one side, I employed the nature of hell,
and said, "*Dorash! Mi dreósgadh anise* (Portal! Open to me
now). Faid thun úgháth (Behold your future)."

The plane of reality sagged and puckered inward, as if
someone had just removed the plug from a bath of water. Moments later, a whirlpool swirled into being, creating a lurid
dappled void between dimensions. Astral lightning played
along the inner edge of a boiling corona. Stabbing out, those
tendrils probed the walls of the conduit in sizzling discharges that sent sparks dancing through my prisoners' hair and
across the surface of their charred clothing. Chopin and Tesla
were drawn by an irresistible tide toward the mouth of the
maelstrom. As they drifted, I spoke for a second time.

"Nikola Tesla. Frédéric François Chopin. Your crimes
against His Infernal Majesty are many, and have been duly
noted over a protracted number of years. I am therefore authorized by His Dark Highness to reap your eternally damned
souls and sentence you to reassignment with extreme prejudice. Punishment is to be carried out immediately. Are there
any last words you'd like to say…or in your case, seeing as
how you have no tongues, think?"

To his credit, Tesla didn't beg or complain once.
Tears—be they of resignation, repentance or sheer frustration, I didn't know or care which—filled his eyes and trickled down his cheek. But from his mind, not a single thought
was spilt.

Chopin, on the other hand, was a fountain of regret. One
name in particular was foremost in a cascade of complaint.
*Amantine, no! Oh my love, I'll keep on fighting, I promise
you. One day, sweet Amantine, we will be together. Nothing
will keep us apart–*

And then they were gone, swallowed whole as they broached the event horizon in a wash of thick sulfurous fumes.

Left alone to contemplate my lot, I knew I still faced the greatest dilemma of all. I turned back to the Veil and was shocked to see how badly it was faring. Hardly any of the geometric grid remained uncorrupted, and of those links that were still visible, all had tarnished. Even so, a misty, mirrorlike soup still filled the spaces in-between. Liquescent prisms sparkled within their depths, providing multifaceted glimpses of another world filled with myriad angels and endless light.

I felt dwarfed. "Look at it. Look how far its spread. I've been a Reaper for countless millennia. A killer. A destroyer and taker of life. What do I know about *this*, or being anyone's savior?"

It was just as well I was alone, as I would have found it highly embarrassing if anyone had been able to witness how badly I was floundering. *I've never felt so out of my depth. All I've got to go on is a hunch. How is that going to translate into anything positive?*

"Know yourself—self—self—self—self..."

Ah, my spectral spectators. Why can't they be more forthcoming for once? A nice set of instructions, 'Cosmic Veils: Maintenance & Construction—One on One' would come in might handy right now. But oh no, they've got me on the hook and keep baiting me with ever more questions and guesswork. I shook my head in disgust. *I've only just found out what I am. How am I supposed to know who...?*

Stewing over my predicament reminded me of certain characteristics Anani'el, Hasmêd, Gadré-el and Uriel had revealed about their inherent personalities. Using that as a starting point, I fought down the urge to rush, and stared off into the multifarious tides still stirring the remains of the Veil into an agitated broth. The ebb and flow of those surges soon cleared my mind and helped me relax.

"If I think about this objectively, I *do* know who I am. My whole life's course has been one prolonged exhibition of Anani'el, Hasmêd, Gadré-el and Uriel's personified attributes: storm, annihilation, war and fire. But I'm more than that. I'm both sides of each coin. While I have a fiery temper, my zeal and ardor make me fiercely loyal. I am the calm before a storm to my friends and a safe harbor in which they can take shelter. I don't just annihilate things; I can create and breathe new life and substance when the need arises, as evidenced by my restoration of the far side of the River Tombs after the Sibitti attack in Olde London Town. And though I revel in bloodshed, I'm a stickler for law and disorder. I really do believe prevention is better than cure, and I'm willing to sacrifice myself for the greater good…or evil, come to that…" *as were those who contributed to my making, I think? All thirteen of them.*

"Know yourself—self—self—self…" my otherworldly guides whispered again.

"It all comes back to Sentinels Square. That's where everything started to fall into place. The dreams. The memories. And now I come to think about it, the Wyrd tree has been there from the very beginning." *The tree is the root of…?*

An image of the Wyrd tree as it was now overlaid itself across my mind. Stripped of its leaves, its purpose fulfilled, my arborous enigma revealed it wasn't yet finished playing a part in my destiny. As I looked on, its silver trunk and bare branches started to shine with an inner radiance. The brighter that light got, the more the covering bark became diaphanous, flowing together into a visualization of an old, bow handled jailers key hovering next to a solitary lock that somehow managed to exude a sense of mystery. In my mind's eye, I plucked the key from the air, inserted it into the keyhole, and turned...

"Know yourself—self—self—self..."

"Okay then, I'll take another look. What did the Wyrd tree actually say about me that might help in this situation?"

Recalling that occasion in detail, I considered the message for a second time:

"Azûra-él, you stand alone,

A sentinel cocooned within a web of fabricated dreams

Of what might have been.

Tears, astringent fragments of your spirit,

Spray like needles in outrage

Upon a sea of countless prisms.

Scattered through time,

Primordial thoughts of revenge consume you,

Held in abeyance until your duty is done.

Released at last, you must spend yourself

Before you stand upon the shore of absolution,

For your actions will determine the fate of all."

Now things began to make more sense.

"For once, someone was being literal. In revealing my name, the Wyrd tree showed my actions will literally determine the fate of all. Here I am, standing alone in a web, an incorporeal sea of countless prisms that were scattered outside of time. And even though certain affairs have been fulfilled, other aspects of those same events still are, for nothing is linear. Probability is reflected off through many facets into elsewhere and elsewhen. It's my duty to gain—as it says—a release of some sort by *spending* myself. That's the only way everyone else survives." *And there it is. The unavoidable cost…as always.*

The inevitability of what I faced finally bore down upon me and I felt my heart quail under the weight of responsibility.

The watchers must have sensed what I felt. "Know yourself. You stand upon the shore—shore—shore—shore…"

The shore? "Of course, *that's* why I've always been able to access the crux of both realms. Only I have the capacity to identify and adopt the corresponding value of what's required to balance the scales." *What's more, I've got to follow my gut to do it.*

Behind me, the last vestiges of the barrier began to seethe, spraying abstruse froth and spume every which way at once. *And there's no time to lose.*

Standing tall, I reasoned things through. "So, if this were left solely to me, I'd keep things nice and simple and infuse the Dagger of Damocles with sufficient dominion to undo what Chopin and Tesla started. Of course, to do that, I need to recant the ritual…?"

Twin laser beams scoured the vault of the inter heavens. I located what I needed floating nearly half a million miles away. *Wow! Tidal shearing must be far worse that I realized.*

A moment's deliberation caused the atramentous foundation of null-space to shiver, and the Scroll of Divergent Union peeled out of thin air before me. From my perspective, it appeared much like an ultrafine sheet of molten copper, though its luster seemed dull and lacking in some way. *Hmmm. It's probably depleted of energy. Let's see what I can do about that.*

Holding the scroll carefully by one end, I commenced rolling it gently round and around the blade of the heavenly dirk, taking care not to wind it too tightly for fear of rupturing the integrity of its unfathomable texture. That done, I stepped sideways into the induction zone between realms.

Not being a natural resident of Zion, I'd expected some form of reaction. Sure enough, a layer of bone-chilling ice began coating the right-hand side of my body from head to foot. Regardless, the clash of divergent energies wasn't as harsh as I'd expected, and I could see why. Robbed of their forbidding, the substance of each realm was already bleeding into the other at the subatomic level, forming a broth of conflicting eddies in which I was being pushed and pulled in all directions at once.

Drawing those currents, I blended them together and started binding them within a frenzied helix empowered by the augury of the third way. As had happened before when dealing with polar and dimensional opposites, my summoning created an alternating current that fought back against my efforts. Undeterred, I transformed my mind into an indomitable living conduit through which my will would be accomplished and continued to press and to mold and to squeeze, until…

…the essence of all three realms bonded together into an articulate whole. *Yes!*

Inspired, I then added the entirety of that invocation to the Dagger of Damocles.

A metallic chime pealed loud in my ears and a thrill skittered along the surface of my skin. Instead of fading, that tone built into a ringing echo. Analyzing the timbre of its resonance, I quickly established a corresponding frequency to enhance its value, and then spliced everything together, myself included.

It was like plugging a light bulb directly into the nation-hell grid. Now in triumvirate union with the dagger and the scroll, I blazed like a sun rising across a shrouded valley. My consciousness expanded, and in that instant, I could see... everything.

"Stay true to yourself—self—self—self..."

A timely reminder from my ever-present observers. Even so, it took all my strength to stay focused on the task at hand. As quickly as I could, I fumbled for the scroll and unfurled it to its full length. What I saw was a great help, for my jaw dropped in astonishment.

Not only were the contents of the parchment written in the same language as the Sentinel glyphs, but as my eyes grazed the elohgraphic message, I felt as if I was reading an ancient prophecy portraying the events that had, and were just about to take place.

I was too stunned to do anything but grunt. *Hindsight's a wonderful thing when it sneaks up and bites you on the ass. This thing doesn't just drop the Veil, it was prepared as a contingency to respond to such a situation ever arising. Bugger me! I can honestly say, I don't think anything will ever surprise me again...* Then cold hard reality set in. *Not that it makes what I've got to do any easier.*

Checking to ensure the influx of heavenly, hellish and mundane potential was more or less steady, I took a deep breath, gathered the entire sum of my ever replenishing life-force together, and said:

"What was whole yet always divided,

A chasm yet riven before,

The space in between now presided,

In sorrows most bittersweet score.

From the ashes a phoenix awakens,

A champion twice fallen, arise

To replace what was lost and forsaken,

And envelop again sundered skies.

One hundred thousand years I have waited,

To act and to bring fresh accord,

And empower again the benighted,

Once tainted, rewoven, restored."

A monstrous python must have slithered from the bowels of hell to wrap itself around my chest, for no sooner had I finished speaking, than it felt as if the marrow was being squeezed from me by a level of mastery that demonstrated how insignificant I truly was.

This must be a precursor for the new gravitational template?

It was. And I was smack bang in the middle of it. Splinters of pain gouged upon my every constricted inhalation. Spots flickered before my eyes. It took me an eternity of instants to realize the trimorphic medium had started to glow in an escalating cosmic standoff: heavenly light; devilish malignancy; mundane stolidity. And there—far below, on the fringes of the mortal realm—dappled hues of blue and white and gold reminded me of what was really at stake.

Without warning, the foundations of life shifted, becoming something ravenous, rapacious, voracious, and insatiable.

That jump was followed by banshee winds, a cyclonic din that howled out of the depths, promising both death and resurrection. Rising swiftly, the gales formed a giant tornado that poured itself over me, into me, around me and out of me, an aerial bore that pummeled my soul with razor-edged cliffs of veracity, before grinding what was left of my sanity to a pulp.

Silence ensued, and in the oscillating halls of forever, I could feel myself changing.

Whispers tickled their way along a DNA möbius whorl of new beginnings.

"Ashes to ashes."

Embers flared in the void. Here, there, everywhere at once and off across the universal expanse, sparking in a frenzied exchange of cataclysmic urgency. Those embers were then engulfed by a staggering confluence of contrary eruptions: ebon and argent; sapphire and scarlet; gold and blue. Etched in darkness and despair, the boundless legacy of those reflections enfolded me and used my psyche as a fulcrum upon which to balance their creative matrix anew.

"Dust to dust."

Unadulterated might rushed along my spine, expanding as a sentient amalgam that saturated my waking dreams in promises and muddled metaphors of what still might be should I fail. Anointed with infinite possibilities, I bled tears of joy and ruptured hope. Exhilarated beyond measure, my immortality asserted its dominance and I burst into astral flame.

Burning undiminished, I held onto that potency and accessed a deeper understanding of life.

"I have waited since the dawn of time for this moment. Eternal, I was made flesh to experience weakness and frailty. Thus tempered, I pass the test. The Bālefire and God's Grace mark me as a paradox of contradictions, a creature who, with one word, can save or damn. Yet hope remains, for I embrace the heritage that was mine all along."

The transformation within me gained pace and my exuberance adjusted to a different equilibrium. *It's happening... as it has before.*

My palladinium armor—the hardest know substance in the underworld—sloughed from my form like plates of desiccated turtle shell. My skin shone translucent, a skeletal network of pulsing brilliance beneath, rendering my flesh and organs inconsequential.

Only the sigils that had once adorned my frame remained. They flared white in an Arcadian display that induced the most excruciating pain I had ever experienced.

There it is...I knew it would to come to pass. Though, I fear it's not over yet.

A spasm rent my spirit in two and ichor flowed, severing my multiversal connection. I screamed, releasing a coruscating novalike convulsion that radiated away from me and took the entire sum of my potential with it. Where the shockwave passed, vestigial roots were reenergized and new primary strands started to bud. Sizzling and snapping, frizzling and cracking, each main root condensed and immediately began acting as achromatic lodestones that absorbed all light, and which drew the remaining superfluity into a fretwork of unsullied orbital tethers.

Solidifying, those tethers waxed molten and adopted a unique paradoxical resonance that shimmered in and out of reality. As they tightened, the knots formed new links, attracting trillions upon trillions of incongruent matter streams. Both fluidic and intangible in nature, they eventually settled into a quasi-corporeal state of flux, only to explode forth in a second wave of energy that seeded the ether with an embryonic template of growth and nascent viscera that matured exponentially.

By now, I'd been carried far, far away from the spectacle. Endless sleep beckoned. Nonetheless, when an intonation of purest pitch and clarity rang out, I dragged my reluctant awareness back into the here and now and looked down. The fabric of the newly restored Veil shimmered below me. It pulsed once, and a trellised window into eternity beckoned.

My nonexistent heart swelled at the sight of it.

Fancy that. I actually did it?

I knew what was coming, for though this was the first time I'd ever faced true extinction, I'd been here before.

Oh my . . .

The universe peeled away.

Limitless potential waited within the nucleus of the smallest atom.

Memories, hidden within a maelstrom of confusion, tugged at the edge of comprehension.

Something significant clawed for air within the very core of my soul.

"Azûra-él, your time is at an end."

Who the voice belonged to, I didn't know. Neither did I care.

Well, go figure…

Part of me remained aware, conscious of the fact that I was slowly fading. And when the blackness came, I felt more at home than I had done in my entire life.

A final poignant thought intruded.

I wonder, what happens next?

Chapter 29: Unlikely Associates

The unknown entity floating within a stupefying sea, ascended slowly toward the surface and full wakefulness. Nevertheless, the restrictive fugue was slow to abate, and enfolded him in an oppressive, clinging sense of confinement. *Where am I—I—I—I...?*

Though he hadn't expressed himself aloud, the entity's concerns resonated with a vibrant quality that chimed over and over until their echoes faded sufficiently to drift away.

Eyelids fluttering, he tried to move, but found himself held almost entirely motionless by an all-encompassing amber mellifluence that inclined his attention along multiple octahedral pathways. *What the dickens is this place? Have I been incarcerated in some new fiendish hellhole—hole—hole—hole...?*

Once again, the entity's thoughts reverberated within multifaceted reflections that rose in pitch and amplitude until it sounded as if a cavern had been filled with a treasure-trove of teasing tympanic titters.

An ache in his chest caused the entity to suck in hungrily. Only then did he appreciate he was desperate for air. The rasp of his breath caught on adjacent lattices and was augmented into one prolonged hiss. *Why am I restrained in…in whatever this damned thing is—is—is—is…?*

A splintering sound intruded, and the entity perceived a shift of alignment. From his perspective, it sounded and felt as if he'd been dropped onto the center of a wide sheet of glass too fragile to bear his weight for long. He could almost visualize the frenzied zigzag dance of cracks, radiating away toward the edge of his imaginary pane.

Subtle vibrations amplified the experience. They were swiftly followed by an audible, *snap!*

An explosion of light, sound and sensation brought with it a hectic storm of last-second prismatic impressions:

Heat, devastating and relentless; hungry, burning, consuming, destroying. Absolute defeat; humbling, overwhelming, subjugating, enslaving. Loss, so profound and so painful, he thought his heart would break; and finally, comprehension.

Hell's bells. It worked!

Frédéric Chopin sat bolt upright in the midst of a pile of tinkling shattered gem shards. Ignoring the fact it was now stifling and he was as naked as a newborn babe, Chopin endeavored to fight down his discomfort and take stock of his situation.

He was on an exposed hillside somewhere, hidden away from line of sight beneath the overhang of a large boulder within a granite outcrop. The spot afforded a panoramic view of a wide-open span, a stark plain of rock and dust that stretched for leagues in every direction.

"Sá-eer," he mumbled, "I remember now. This is Sá-eer Gate within what the Jinn call, the Blaze."

An apt analogy, for when Chopin peered into the distance, rippling waves of thermal savagery soldered the desert to a Cimmerian overhead expanse, effectively masking the point where land and sky met. Zephyrs, as scorching and as dry as the exhalation of a blast furnace, scourged the wilderness with grit and shingle, marking it forever as a place no living thing had a right to be.

"Thank goodness we had the sense to position everything on the leeward side, away from the prevailing winds. I dread to think how badly we'd have been…? Wait a minute, this is Jahannam, not…?" Twisting to look along the ledge behind him, Chopin cried out in pain as a crystal fragment pierced his buttocks, "Ow!"

"Careful how you go there," Tesla's clone chided, "we wouldn't want to start damaging our new bodies before we've had a chance to enjoy them or cause some mischief now, would we?"

"I think the damage has already been done," Chopin complained. Extricating himself carefully from the jumbled nest of glassy splinters, he paused to ease an inch-long tawny sliver from his right butt cheek, much to Tesla's amusement. "I'm serious, Nikola. Think about it. The replicants here were an additional tier of insurance and would only have been activated if all else had failed."

Tesla's brow furrowed, his frown indicating he'd caught the inference behind his partner's statement. "So, not only were we stopped from achieving our goal, but it seems our primary avatars back on Kí-gal must have been taken out of the picture as well? That sucks."

"It does indeed, my friend. But the question remains, how long has passed since…?" Chopin espied a military style kit bag wedged deep within a crevice further along the shelf. "Aha, provisions. We should find a timepiece within and further instructions to help us decide what to do. I tell you what. I'll get ready first while you keep watch, then we'll swap places."

Both men had known each other long enough not to be bothered by the other's nudity. Even so, as Chopin caught sight of Tesla's nakedness, he couldn't help but stare. *There are absolutely no marks on him, nor any signs of the brutal wear and tear living in hell incurs?*

Thrilled, Chopin gave himself the once-over and held his hands out high, flexing his fingers and making fists a good dozen times before the truth finally sunk in. *There's hardly any discomfort? So, Jahannam's environment has countered Satan's influence? How providential, especially as it will help facilitate a prompt response to our setback.*

Scooting across to the holdall, Chopin opened it to find it contained several sets of freshly laundered desert fatigues—goggles included, food and drink, a hyperspatial translocation device, two Hell-Brass 6.66 Magnums, and one of the very latest Denizen Guileless H8-U cell phones.

Chopin dressed quickly, and then selected a bottle of water. Though tepid, his drink brought a welcome respite from the sandpaper texture in the back of his throat. Feeling somewhat refreshed, he activated the mobile phone and hunkered down against the rock face while Tesla went about his business. Chopin was surprised to see the deck registered as fully charged. What was more, a front screen icon indicated they had two waiting voicemails.

"You might want to pay attention to this as you go," he called out. Scrolling through the menu, Chopin swiftly located the appropriate page, selected the first message, turned up the volume for Tesla's benefit, and pressed, *play.*

"Nikola, Frédéric," his own voice began, "If you're listening to this, it means our best laid plans have been brought to nothing. For whatever reason, we failed and our previous bodies were eradicated in order to trigger the reassignment process. However, the mere fact that *you* have been animated suggests that your counterparts on the Kigali homeworld have either been destroyed or neutralized.

"The starter pack contains all you need to get on the right track. Besides protection, a set of clothing and basic refreshments, you need only really concern yourselves with the travel orb at this stage, as it will allow you to get to safety. As to *where* that safety is, however, you will have to listen to a series of questions in the following voicemail. While we appreciate this will be a somewhat frustrating diversion, it is necessary given your state of affairs. Thankfully, your minds will have retained all you need: an intimate history of your former lives. As you'll see, being able to recall times, dates, places and events will not just allow you to answer those queries, but your appropriate responses will provide clues toward a precise set of geophysical coordinates within this world. There, you will find a brief intelligence package from which you will be able to establish which of our remaining sites are still active. Only then will you be able to secure fresh identities and the funds already set aside in a number of bogus bank accounts. Most importantly, you will also acquire knowledge of equipment and weapons caches that will enable you to continue the fight.

"Remember, as perfect copies, nobody will realize you exist. While your flesh might be new, the souls activating them aren't. You *are* us now."

The voice changed, with the original Tesla replacing Chopin as narrator.

"For your convenience, we synchronized the Denizen Guileless unit to your particular trúllefeng stones, as well as Gehenna Mean Time—Juxtapose. This should help determine how long has passed between the Soulstice—the event that no doubt led to our executions—and your current situation. To access that information, simply follow the clock option within the main menu. Having done that, I'm sure you'll be keen to proceed to the following message where the listed questions will help you ascertain your first port of call.

"Bad luck to you both. We have every confidence in your tenacity. And if you manage nothing else, give 'em hell.'"

The recording finished, and Chopin turned to look at his associate. "How do you feel?"

"Given what we've been through, better than I thought I would. It must be because we were spared the trauma of our demise." He shook himself vigorously as if suddenly cold, "though I have to admit, I did experience an odd rush of emotions just before I awoke."

"So did I," Chopin confided, "There must have been a residual feedback loop as our essences homed in on the crystals? It makes you wonder if we suffered, doesn't it?"

"While I have no doubt we have the Reaper or any one of his henchmen and women to thank for that, does it really matter? Dead is dead. Or not, as the case may be. We've found a way around reassignment, and need to be swift incorporating such a strategy into our future planning. And all the more so if we can adapt it to alter our physical appearance."

"You're right, of course," Chopin agreed, "and as it transpires, unerringly wise. Some might even say, *vatic*, in your preparations? Your insistence that we omit any reference to our remaining hideaways in the preceding downloads, for example. Pure genius. If our doubles on Kí-gal *were* discovered, as we suspect, it's saved us from a whole litany of woe."

Tesla didn't look in the least bit concerned. "While I appreciate the sentiment, Frédéric, don't forget, soul sapphires of this size and capacity are also encoded to the psyches of their subjects as an added safeguard. Without the proper activation sequence, our dear twin brothers would have emerged as drooling imbeciles."

"Oh, I hadn't forgotten. I just wish we could have been there to witness our enemies trying to wake them. Can you imagine it? The whooping and the hollering; the self-congratulatory pats on the back; imagining they were so clever; thinking they'd done so well. Then the grand reveal—and shocking realization—that all their interference had guaranteed, was the resurrection of a pair of retards blessed with the IQ of a Hell Hound."

"Touché."

Both men chuckled, happy for a while—however brief—to be free of the stress of constant pursuit, and relieved that their strategy for redemption had actually worked, albeit in a roundabout way.

All too soon though, it was time to move on.

"So, once we've finished puzzling out where we need to go, what next?" Tesla ventured, "Do we dive straight back into the main current of our little misadventure, or take a well-earned break and get established in our new home first?"

Chopin was just about to suggest that the latter option might serve them better, when a subliminal message hidden deep within his newly emerging consciousness demanded to be heard.

Accessing the information it contained, Chopin's eyes flared in surprise. *Well, well, well. What a devious duo we are. And such delicious implications if we play things right?*

Then he smiled. "If you don't mind, Nikola, I think it best to stop off somewhere along the way. Our circumstances notwithstanding, it might be wise to increase our indemnity against such mishaps ever occurring again."

"Indemnity?"

"Oh yes, you'll see what I mean when we get there."

*

A warrior for untold millennia, Jotûn, a First Fist of the Blades of the Left-Hand Path, wasn't afraid to acknowledge beauty when he found it, especially is said beauty hinted at hidden strength. And the balusters, spandrels and capitals adorning the support columns along the main arcade of the Hall of Shattered Dreams were certainly that, for each decorative feature glowed with an aura that reeked of mayhem, age and permanence. Entranced by their splendor, he reached out and ran a razor-sharp talon along the surface of a nearby pedestal.

Made of a material he'd never seen before entering the temple, it looked as coarse as unpolished granite, yet felt as slick as wet marble. "Would you credit that? I can put my claws through toughened armor if I have to, but I can't even scratch this stuff."

Every so often, the First Fist made sure to stamp his feet as he walked along the nave, sending blunt shockwaves thudding through his ankles and resonant protests ringing off along the aisles. "And whatever force was needed to break these paving slabs must have been impressive indeed. My spurs don't make the slightest indentation."

Reaching the eastward facing window that had shattered in response to Daemon Grim's presence, Jotûn stooped to retrieve a long silver and magenta colored shard of glass from the floor. *I wonder?* On a whim, he bent his muscles to the task and was surprised to find it took all his strength to snap it.

He smiled.

In this simple representation lies the majesty of Hatamâh made manifest. While lesser creatures fail in the face of such latent dominion, there is nothing that it cannot break to pieces with ease.

Throwing the sliver aside, Jotûn slowly made his way back toward the transcript where his lieutenant, First Palm Garôk, still loitered, deep in study.

What he saw made him chuckle, for Garôk had eased herself across the lip of the sarcophagus to reach inside, and her backside was sticking high into the air. Rhythmic chimes indicated she was still at work, conducting whatever tests her inquisitive mind deemed necessary to help better understand the strange crystal and its contents that had so disturbed their newfound brother.

"Anything?" he enquired.

"Nothing," Garôk spat back, "not even the sweat from a sandgorgon's tongue. Of course, I daren't try too hard in case I do something that might harm our sleeping beauty. Nevertheless, I've learned that jewel is at least as hard as diamond, and it's resistant to any of the tools and blades I have to hand."

"I'm not surprised." Jotûn motioned toward the profundity of extremes evident in their surroundings, "Only the most resilient things can hope to survive the rigors that Hatamâh can invoke, for any length of time."

"That's exactly the thing I've been mulling over," the First Palm sneered, her expression conveying the fact she had something on her mind.

"What do you mean?"

"I've been contemplating how well this woman would fare, were it not for the protection afforded by the gem? I mean, look at her, Jotûn. She's all soft and smooth and shiny. We've witnessed the aptitude of the Janīn bearer personally. There's no doubt as to his power. But…?"

"Buuut?"

"I find it perplexing, trying to imagine what Daemon Grim would see in such a delicate flower? She doesn't possess any tusks that I can discern. No tough hide. No visible spurs or talons. She looks like all the other slaves we managed to capture from Shayātīn's realm before the ban was imposed: fragile, and incapable of withstanding the rigors of hardship. I can't imagine anyone like that being sufficient for him."

Jotûn scrutinized the golden haired, athletically formed goddess lying in state for a few moments, and replied, "The mere fact she is—or was—Daemon Grim's mate should tell you something of the female's fortitude. He only spoke briefly about her, but I remember he referred to her as his former Chief Inquisitor, and a special interrogator of the First Order of Shayātīn. Or as they say, Shâitan. To my mind, such titles denote dedication, application, prowess and hard-won achievement. No, like the bound volumes lining the walls of this sanctuary, do not be swayed by her covering. I suspect her potency is beyond…what?"

While Jotûn was speaking, Garôk had fallen abruptly still, her paw coming to rest upon the hilt of her scimitar. At this moment, she was staring across the First Fist's shoulder at something behind him.

Has our brother returned already? Spinning about, Jotûn's gaze came to rest on two individuals standing only fifteen yards further along the aisle. Startled, he skipped a few steps away from his comrade to give himself room to maneuver. *Odd, I didn't catch any indication of their presence? And it's not like Garôk to allow anyone to sneak up so close on us either?*

Both figures were small in comparison to the Jinn ogres and dressed as ones well used to the severity of Jahannam's environment. Though their heads and upper torsos were wrapped tightly within wind shawls, the rest of their clothing hung free, and Jotûn couldn't detect any overt sign of weapons.

"Hail, First Fist," the shorter of the new arrivals raised one hand to his heart in a formal gesture, "may your house find honor in battle. Can I ask, to which Weld are you linked by service?"

He is familiar with our ways?

"Greetings," Jotûn replied, warily. After mirroring the salute, his own paw fell to hover scant inches from his saif. "And may your blade always stay sharp. You seem to be acquainted with my kindred and the courtesies we expect? There, you have me at a disadvantage, for you are unknown to me. Who should I address?"

The strangers threw back their hoods to reveal themselves as two human males. Humans, who confounded his senses, for while they possessed an outward appearance of maturity and carried themselves with the bearing of seasoned travelers, both exuded an air of innocent naivety. What's more, the deeper he scanned the men, the greater the impression that everything they experienced was new and fresh to them. *Yet that cannot be, for very few outside of Jahannam are even aware this series of Gates are a reality?*

Stepping forward, Jotûn decided to extend a modicum of courtesy. "Trust must be earned. Allow me. I am Jotûn, First Fist of the Incendia Blade of Jahannam under Gauntlet Nishôgh. And this…" he turned to introduce his compatriot who dropped into a fighting crouch as he watched, "is First Palm –?"

Boom!

Garôk's face exploded in an emulsion of blood, bone and gore. A fine green mist saturated the ether beyond, marking the trajectory of the magnum round that had killed her.

For a frozen moment, Garôk's body remained stock still, as if too stunned to do anything except stand proudly in defiance of its appalling injuries. Then her legs folded, and a headless corpse crashed onto the pristine flagstones below.

Jotûn rolled to one side. Drawing his saif as he moved, he called on the sacred flame that would transform him into a fiery apparition.

Too slow.

Thunder pealed, several times in quick succession.

A moving target, Jotûn proved a harder mark to hit than his lieutenant. But not an impossible one. And the humans were uncannily accurate. What felt like the molten fangs of a pyroviper bit deep into his thigh, chest and shoulder, throwing him like a deadweight onto the cold, unforgiving floor and sending his sword clattering along the aisle.

It was only at that moment that Jotûn realized his adversaries had flicked aside their cloaks to reveal they both carried strange, steel colored weapons with short handles and long snouts, from which smoke now curled in lazy spirals toward the rafters.

Incensed, he cussed, "Who are you that would dare the wrath of the Blades of the Left-Hand Path?"

The charlatan who had originally greeted him so warmly spoke up. "Why, my name is Frédéric Chopin, and that of my ignoble companion, Nikola Tesla. And not to be rude, but you and your confederates are the least of our worries, for we dare the wrath of a much greater foe." He paused to sniff, loudly, and for a fleeting second, got a faraway look in his eyes. "That, however, is not your concern, for we are here to retrieve the most unlikely of associates from her resting place."

Chopin glanced toward his colleague and nodded.

As the one called Tesla sprinted toward the altar, Chopin raised the long-barreled device in his hand, pointed it directly at Jotûn , and sounded completely genuine in expressing his regret, "I really do apologize for this, First Fist Jotûn. Despite your stern appearance, I perceive you are a creature of quality, refinement and manners, which—believe me—is rare in those cast down…" Chopin sighed, as if contemplating a heavy burden. "Alas, we can't afford to let anyone know we exist, you see, because as far as the entire underworld is concerned, we're just like you. Dead."

On this occasion, Jotûn only had time to glimpse a bright flash from the muzzle of Chopin's weapon, and then the glory of his flame was extinguished.

Chapter 30: Remain True

"So, what are we going to do with you now the moment has arrived?"

Who the...? Unexpected, the query caused every fiber of my being to recoil, sending me into a spiraling, stomach-turning nosedive of apoplectic shock.

What the fucking hell is happening? My mind screamed, at the top of its ever dysfunctional lungs.

"Hell?" the disconcertingly familiar, commanding voice intoned, "Oh, this has nothing whatsoever to do with hell. Quite the opposite, in fact."

The opposite? I discerned the weight of ages surrounding me.

"Ah, I see the problem. You're still a little wonky after your trip down no-memory lane. Understandable, I suppose, seeing as how..."

A chill frosted the outer layers of my consciousness. *Are you saying I'm finally dead?*

"Not in the fullest sense. You're just a little upside-down is all. Here, let me help you on your way."

Almost immediately, my tumbling descent slowed to a much less threatening pace. As I decelerated, fleeting images continued to speed by, one after the other: an expanse, rolling forever in every direction at once; golden fields and silver forests; wide, snow lined valleys and unfathomable, heaving green oceans; endless skies and countless stars; burnished nebulas and wheeling galaxies.

And there, high above everything else and yet all around me at the same time, a glimpse of eternity bound within complete and seamless white; towering heights and majestic depths; shining walkways and Olympian edifices of translucent light. All presided over by an elusive but constant presence seen only from the corner of the eye, a personification of all that was bright and beautiful, if I could only lay my eyes upon it.

In many ways, I was reminded of the disappointment experienced when waking—smiling and content—from the most incredible dream, only to then lie impotently by as the details immediately started slipping away.

And will I retain any recollection of this?

Rain, as clean and fresh as morning dew pattered down on my face, drenching my hair and making my skin tingle, filling my nose and lungs with the aroma of wet grass and ozone.

It's like the aftermath of a thunderstorm when...? Hang on a second, how am I feeling this? Do I still have a body?

"Of course you have," the same intangible voice announced. "Here, anything is possible if the heart is pure and the will strong enough. And it seems your will—especially to live—is stronger than all others, Azûra-él."

Needless to say, I found such a statement totally confusing.

The last thing I could remember before falling into the endless well of nothingness was the dreadful feeling of my corporeal form and ethereal nucleus shredding away as they were forfeited to the genesis of the new Veil. That being said,

I wasn't about to refute the possibility that a higher power had intervened on my behalf.

So, I'm still alive then?

"Not in the strictest sense of the term. Think of it as a kind of limbo while certain *issues* are decided."

The inflection behind the entity's assertion was rich and deep and full of meaning. Suspicions roused, I asked, *Are you...are you Him?*

"As good as. I am He Who Is Like God. Otherwise known as Michael, Firstborn, Arch Angel and the Word, King of Kings and Angel of the Abyss. As highest of my brethren, I stand at the right-hand of He Who Causes To Become, and speak with His authority."

I take it I didn't qualify for an intimate face-to-face with the Supreme Being?

"Correct, for He is holiness in its cleanest and most absolute form, and does not deign to consort with any creature enveloped by sin."

Of course. And as Satan's Reaper, I was most sinful of all.

"Honest and forthright." Michael sounded pleased. "Remarkable, considering the battlefield of your origins. But in this regard you are mistaken. The wages sin pays is death, and though the blood of billions stained your hands red, your passing settled accounts. By His reckoning, you are now a slate washed clean, Azûra-él, a soul with the potential for a new beginning."

Hang on a moment. I thought you said I wasn't dead?

"You aren't...*now.*"

So I did die! A dread foreboding wormed its way along my spine. *But why would He forgive me? How come I wasn't reassigned? I know I wasn't condemned to hell like everyone else, but as the devil's bounty hunter, I thought my deeds would have spoken loudly as to my fate?*

"That fate is not reserved for one such as you. The true death obliterates all thought and devising, all tangible sense of self-awareness and personality. For a while, Azûra-él, your thread floated free of the grand tapestry."

It was humbling to think that, after all I'd done, all the power I'd accrued, the godlike foes I'd fought, the amount of times I'd faced annihilation and wheedled out of it, the ultimate omega had finally caught up with me in the end.

I suppose it's only fitting that the Reaper personally tastes what he's dispensed so often to so many, I mused to myself, *though I never realized my work had reached such a tally. Did he say, billions?*

My previous suspicions bounded back with a vengeance. *So, why am I here?*

"Your time is at an end, Azûra-él. That hasn't changed. It's what comes next that should concern you."

"Your time is at an end?" I knew I'd heard his voice before. *That was you?*

"Yes. I was there. Watching, waiting, seeing how you would fare and if you had the mettle to pass the final test. Suffice to say, your actions have earned you an opportunity rarely granted since the dawn of time. A choice, you might say, as to the course along which your future will develop. However, before the road you will travel can be determined, you need to be apprised of certain facts."

Such as?

"In short, though you spent most of your sentient existence as a servant of the Resister, you were also an agent of the Most High, put in place to safeguard hope."

I'd already gathered that much in cracking the ciphers governing the history of Anani'el, Hasmêd, Gadré-el and Uriel. But why all the subterfuge?

"It was necessary. What you won't know is that the Veil was only made possible by the quick thinking and voluntary life offering of Rian-él, one of the Seraphim Chosen, who allowed himself to be infected by sin's dark blight in order to better understand our enemy's intent. But Rian-él's might wasn't the only factor in allowing He Who Causes To Become to fashion the barrier. It was also down to Rian-él's motivation. He appreciated the mark of sin would disbar him from the AllFather's presence. Nevertheless, his heart remained true and his gesture allowed the generation of a reactive interdimensional forbidding that perfectly blended the tincture of the Holy Spirit with what went on to become its mirror image, the Bãlefire, for the seeds of both were present within him.

"He was one of a kind, and in seeking to protect the heavens from what had befallen him, Rian-él made a remarkable discovery. A third way, neither blessed nor damned, one that was as mutually antagonistic of its own milieu as it was of others, and one that was able to invoke the nature of the mortal domain and bind it into an additional layer within the filter. Thus, the threefold charge of the Veil was made manifest, a denying champion that kept discord from spreading throughout the whole of creation.

"Omniscient, He Who Causes To Become saw ahead to a time when someone would be needed who could call on the codex of all three realms again. That someone was you, forged in Rian-él's image from the embers of both Fallen and Faithful at the Time of Sundering, creatures whose spirits would most closely resemble the essence of what was lost. Of course, Satan sought to manipulate this opening so that you would serve his interests, and set about recruiting instruments of his own who might better understand this strange new source from which power could be accessed. I believe you've met such a rare talent?"

Nettesheim?

"Precisely. Sufficeth to say, though the mystic's—and those few others like him—influence was limited and went in some small way to serving the greater good, steps were taken to ensure you would retain that vital ingredient in the secret place of your heart, that catalyst, which would keep you a viable hope: free will."

So it was never certain I would succeed?

"Nothing is ever certain, Azûra-él, except God's love. But the odds were always in your favor because of who you are, inside."

I can't see Satan being pleased by that.

"Oh, he wasn't. Regardless, he was forced to cooperate or run the risk of losing face, along with everything else he had fought so hard to achieve since his rebellion.

Wow. Talk about keeping your friends close, and enemies closer still. That couldn't have been comfortable for anyone.

A tenebrous presence manifested. Insidious, iniquitous and foul, it reeked of attar and burning coals.

Satan?

"Was someone speaking my name in vain?" the dark lord sneered. "I'm here, lurking in the shadows, as always."

So this isn't heaven?

"Oh badness me, no," he replied, his relief and repulsion clearly evident in equal measure, "I'm standing right where I belong, while golden balls over there is fluttering about on his own side of the Veil."

Aha! That means I'm where I should be too, then. Smack bang in the middle.

"Yes, but you must understand, things cannot remain this way," The Arch Angel's tone made it evident he was addressing me, "for the dust must be allowed to settle."

I take it you're referring to that choice *you mentioned earlier?*

"I am."

The inevitable catch, I thought to myself. *Heaven or hell, it's always the same.* Then aloud, *Okay, let's stop beating around the bush. What do you actually want of me?*

"A decision," Michael was equally forthright, "one that will affect your eternal future."

So, I do have a future then?

"You do. As to where that will be, exactly—up or down—remains to be seen."

Only at that moment did I fully understand what Michael had been alluding to all along. *You mean I get to…? I'll be allowed to…? I can…?* Heaven? *Me?*

"You are a chimera, Azûra-él, as much divine as you are damned. If you decide on ascendancy, sufficient excellence will be ascribed you to allow your birth-name to grow to maturity, thereby allowing you to adopt the full dignity of your celestial station, free of taint."

"Be careful of such temptations, Daemon," the devil hissed, interrupting my thoughts, "as they may reap consequences you are not yet aware of."

Consequences?

"Daemon, once you decide upon your next path, there's no going back. You will wholly belong to one ethereal sphere or the other."

Michael?

The Arch Angel was quick to respond. "For sure, the Slanderer speaks truthfully."

What would someone like me do in heaven?

"In my Father's abode, there are many halls and chambers. Each serves a purpose. All are transcendent. And every one represents an opportunity to sample treasures beyond compare."

I've no doubt. But you didn't answer my question. What would I do there?

"Live. Grow. Become who and what you were destined to be among the multitude serving before God's throne as you provide living testimony to the power of his loving benevolence."

You mean I'd be a poster boy?

It was a strange experience, listening to the Firstborn of all creation laughing heartily at my expense. "In a sense, that's a rather apt analogy, for your acceptance would have far-reaching implication that all the sons of God would applaud. But the call of the sublime goes far beyond mere worship and devotions. To be succinct, it would entail…"

As Michael expounded the virtues of heavenly life, my heart didn't just lift, it swelled and expanded and filled with a yearning to be part of such a wondrous macrocosm.

Nonetheless, something worried me. Eventually, I had to express what that was.

I hear what you say, Michael, I really do. But there are myriads and myriads of angels in heaven and they all seem geared toward one united purpose: God's glory. Don't I run the risk of losing my individuality in such an environment? I mean, who would I be?

"A nobody," Satan was quick to interject, his tone accusing. "While you might have forgotten, I certainly haven't. I was a cherub, a high-ranking spirit blessed with my own station within the court of He Who Cannot Be Named. Yet for all my splendor, I was just one of a vast, immeasurable crowd consigned to endless servitude and singing hosannas.

How boring and droll. I found it a pointless, dull existence. At least if you stay with me you will have power and prestige. And things would never be monotonous."

Power and...? I was stunned. *After what you've put me through by keeping me in the dark? You don't think I'd opt for the underworld and allow myself to be conscripted to you again, do you? My station was higher in many respects than –?*

"You would have no say in the matter, Azûra-él." This time, it was Michael's turn to interpose, "for in determining where you wish to live in perpetuity, you will also—by default—decide who you will be in subjection to. Hell belongs to Satan."

So I'll lose everything I was?

"You already have. Remember, in spawning the Veil you were stripped entirely of the magnitude that made you what you were. That's why—I'm sure—the Adversary so casually glossed over the impact of naturalization, for you will become vassal to the sovereign of the realm you choose and the binding tenets by which it is governed."

Something about Michael's statement carried a deeper meaning than was first apparent. Fortunately, I surmised what it was almost immediately.

Are you saying that if I chose to remain a denizen of hell, I'd no longer be capable of employing the might of God's Grace by rote?

"Yes, that's right."

"And what about my ability to walk amongst mortals, topside?"

"Once a true denizen of the underverse, there you would stay. Such are the decrees by which the Canon of Sundering was established."

At last, I finally understood why it was I could walk between worlds so easily and call upon the powers at my disposal. *I was never an actual citizen of hell or…?*

A thought intruded. Taking my line of reasoning one step further, I asked, *Michael, if I'd ever been inclined to try, could I have encroached upon heaven's borders?*

"Though I would have dispatched angels to prevent you from progressing further, your heritage would have granted you such authority, yes."

Dumbfounded, I spent some considerable time looking between the pair vying for my eternal soul. A scintillate concentration of blinding light, truth and serenity on one side, a pulsing maelstrom of insatiable selfish craving and hunger on the other.

I knew who I could trust, that was for sure. Yet, even with the offer of a second chance of eternal life on the table, it still felt as if my guts were being twisted, for either way, it was going to cost me.

I've no experience of the divine environment or what ministering to the Most High would be like, despite Michael's lucid explanation. Can I make a sound judgment based on so many unknown factors? Can I risk losing who I am to blissful quietude, day in—day out? Wouldn't that be boring as Satan intimated?

But what's the alternative? Knowing what I do. Knowing what I was and how the devil held me back all those years to protect himself and his little clique of power. Such a hurdle might prove insurmountable?

Remnant echoes of my past, present and future came to the rescue. "If in doubt, remain true to yourself—self—self—self—self…"

They're right. It doesn't matter where or what I am so much, as who *I am.*

Picturing myself in different guises, I took the time to examine what I might become: an angel of light, or a creature similar to what I'd been before, for countless centuries; someone bright, resplendent, clean and wholesome, or a killer, dark and perilous, without remorse or pity.

"And loyal friend, don't forget—get—get—get—get..."

Now there's a point. No matter what I've done, I've always been dependable and steadfast to those who've earned my trust. That would never change, would it?

No matter how hard I tried, I couldn't imagine angels having recourse to rely on me. They were so powerful, so complete. Everything in their world was perfect.

When would they ever have occasion to lean on anyone like me for support? And in light of that, would adding one more to their ranks really make a difference?

Then I pondered that same issue from the perspective of Satan's Reaper.

There's always something different happening or someone to track down. It's an ever bubbling pot of contention, strife and discord, with unrest and adversity aplenty. And of course, there's a constant need to dispense Injustice. Unlife is a challenge, true, but at least you get a sense of achievement by staying on top of things and surviving from day to day.

What about Gemini? My fellow Hell Hounds and Inquisitors? Then there are my new brothers and sisters of the Left-Hand Path to consider. Treaties to be brokered. New territories to discover and conquer.

The only major downside I could see returning to hell involved was the fact I'd be back under Satan's thumb. Only this time, it'd be for real and there'd be nothing I could do about it.

The Arch Angel obviously felt I'd had long enough to deliberate the issue. "Have you reached a verdict?"

My apologies, Michael, I haven't. His aura darkened, so I quickly explained, *I'm not trying to drag my feet, it's just that I honestly don't think I'd do any good or make much difference if I made the change and stepped over to the other side.*

"You actually prefer the prospect of eternal damnation?"

Prefer? Of course not. But the colloquialism, 'better the devil you know' springs to mind. I don't know anything else. And I'm more than certain that I'd probably make a better contribution to the overall pattern of that tapestry you mentioned earlier by staying where I am. Do you understand?

"So, it's settled then?"

Er, actually, no its not. I'm sorry to have to admit this—as it sounds as if pride is getting in the way—but my main issue revolves around the fact that I can't stand the thought of submitting myself to Satan again since I discovered the depth of his mistrust and betrayal.

"Azûra-él." Michael's manner became softer, almost fatherly in its inflection, "What else would you expect from the Arch Deceiver other than self-serving treachery? Hubris was the main cause of his banishment. Do you think he will ever change?"

To say I was tongue-tied was an understatement. So overwhelmed was I, so daunted by the immensity of the decision I had to make that I had no real way of expressing the tangle of emotions that now knotted my ability to express myself clearly.

Thankfully, Michael seemed to sense my inner turmoil and offered an unexpected solution. "What if your memories could be...*altered* to accommodate?"

Altered?

"Something with which you are familiar, yes? It would be a simple matter to modify your emergent awareness at this stage, to fit agreed upon parameters."

What parameters?

"Simply? You would awaken, restored as hell's Reaper, cognizant of most of the facts leading up to the regeneration of the Veil. However, as far as you will be aware, the heritage granted to you to achieve such a feat was temporary and part of a greater collaboration between the powers of heaven and hell to ensure the sanctity of life was protected, and good and proper order maintained. You stepped into the matrix and freely surrendered your life-essence, fully aware that, if successful, the process would strip you of your heavenly and earthly attributes entirely. A costly venture, to be sure. Regardless, your spirit and sense of honor and justice are renown throughout the underverse. It will not surprise anyone to hear that you made such a sacrifice willingly."

I didn't know what to think. Michael's plan was as simple as it was perfect. It fitted the circumstances. It felt right.

He continued, "Of course, the precise intricacies will be more involved, especially among those few who might have a more intimate knowledge of the events leading up to your augmentation. But as we three here are the only ones party to this proposal, it should be enough to allay your immediate fears and prevent unwanted questions from other quarters until we have a framework in place to deal with the longer term consequences."

So, in a nutshell, I'll wake up thinking everything went according to plan?

"Yes."

And I'll have no recollection this conversation ever took place?

"No."

Or that either of you were in on this little arrangement?

"That's right. You will awaken, sore and bruised, following a long and strenuous task. Resigned to the cost of your victory, you will nevertheless feel relief at being alive and will no doubt be eager to return to work and the company of those with whom you find –?"

"If you don't mind, there's something I'd like to add to your little party of two?" As ever, Satan felt the need to stick his nose in, "after all, you seem to be making plans that involve me."

"I find it hard to believe you might have objections?" The Arch Angel rounded on the devil, "when you consider the value of Azûra-él's service and what he's saved you."

"That's all well and good," Satan leered, "but hell is my domain and mine alone. It rankles me to think someone I've sponsored and guided for so long would display such disloyalty the moment he gets a chance to cut and run."

Disloyalty? I bridled. *Cut and run? Why you –*

"Are you rejecting Azûra-él's offer?" Michael spoke over my outburst, drowning it out entirely, "and if so, what do you propose?"

"Oh, I accept the offer," Satan countered, "there's no way I'm going to lose my right-hand man on the street. After all, it's the fear of what I'll unleash through him that keeps the massed rabble in line. But now I've seen his true colors—so to speak—I think there needs to be a little adjustment in his attitude before I'm ready to take him back."

"An adjustment?"

"Yes, call it compensation, if you will."

"And what would this *compensation* involve?"

Satan made a show of pondering the issue deeply, even though it was evident he merely wanted to be the center of attention. After he'd pouted and postured for what he felt was an appropriate length of time, he announced, "I think it only fair that my Reaper be made to deal with the pain of loss and disappointment, as I have."

"Do not try my patience, Slanderer." The ether crackled for the merest instant. That's all it took to glimpse the terrifying might of the Angel of the Abyss made manifest. "Clarify what you mean, and be quick about it."

Satan hid his fear well. "Up until now, Daemon has been able to act as Reaper with impunity and without pity or remorse. That's going to change. While I want no lessening of his effectiveness or commitment to duty, I *do* insist that he be reassigned as one cursed with a quality I noted reared its ugly head more and more as his seraphim side became dominant: empathy."

"You're serious?"

"About something that will earn my gracious accord? Of course. Think how insidious it will be as the underworld learns that Satan's executioner now shows an understanding of each victim's battle to simply live by the rules. The problems they face. The uphill struggles they contend with that will never end. Imagine their surprise when they see compassion for their plight in the Reaper's eyes. Imagine the hope that might engender. That desperate need for someone in authority to understand what they're going through. And though such expressions on the Reaper's behalf will be genuine, though he'll feel real sympathy for their predicament, it won't make a shred of difference, for he will be obligated to take their heads. And take them he will."

"He has always taken heads."

"True, but now…? Ah, he'll feel it, intimately, each and every time he ends a life. Isn't that simply delicious?"

I thought he might be done, but no sooner had Satan finished, than his previous statement seemed to give him inspiration for another way to twist the knife. "And speaking of feeling things…I also demand he be inflicted with the occasional physical reminder regarding the loss of his wings. Nothing major, mind you. I don't want him remembering any of this, and I'd certainly hate for his prowess to be inadvertently reduced in any way. But an infrequent twinge, here and there, should keep me happy?"

A heavy silence hung in the air.

In due course, Michael turned to address me, personally. "Do you accept the devil's terms for reanimation?"

Though it grieved me more than life itself to think I would have to abide by Satan's petty self-aggrandizing rules for the rest of infernity, too much was at stake for me to put my own desires first. My friends and the denizens of hell needed me now, more than ever. And in the end, that's what influenced my answer.

I do.

"To think such delectable fare has been laid before me at so little cost." Cackling laughter, cruel and sharp, faded in the background.

Ignoring the devil's jibe, Michael passed sentence: "Then Azûra-él, know your time is at an end. That of Daemon Grim, Reaper, Left Fist of Satan, will continue. Know also, that as bright Rian-él's incentive to uphold the greater good was held in high regard, your motivation this day will not be forgotten."

Infinite black yawned wide.

I fell, knowing that, for the first time in my long and event-filled existence, part of me would never return.

Epilogue

Stood upon the ledge of one of the casement windows in my bedroom, with my nose pressed to the glass, I was afforded commanding views of the southern bank of the River Tombs. But that wasn't surprising, as my suite was situated at the top of Black Tower itself, the tallest, most imposing structure within the Den of Iniquity.

Across the castle wall, Olde London Town brooded in a perpetual twilight. At this distance, her soot-stained rooftops looked for all the world like the blackened gums of an old crone from which modern-day high-rises jutted skyward in the manner of broken fangs. Towering monstrosities of steel, glass and neon strip-lighting, they lay bared, threatening all comers, including the integrity of the perpetually smog-laden brume.

Closer to hand, the languid waters of the Tombs perfectly complemented the overcast expanse. Thick, dark and mysterious, the river undulated, no more than an oil slick, a black artery that only grudgingly acknowledged the presence of the concrete jungle and those denizens working and living along its banks.

Down below, hell hounds of the K13 variety ran free, roaming the precincts of the entire inner ward. Though vocal, their growls failed to stifle the piercing shrieks and constant weeping of those far underground, being questioned by my Inquisitors.

Vents placed at regular intervals around the base of the fortifications gave those screams a warbling resonance, pleasing to the ear. Even so, such protestations pierced my soul like a stiletto, as each stab represented a plea for aid that never would be answered.

Those fools languish, incarcerated, forever condemned. Here in hell, the damned all stand guilty. All deserve the very worst we have to offer, with no hope of parole.

As usual, a conspiracy of hell-ravens roosting among the buttresses and crenels squawked and hooted in unkindest reply. To them, the sinners serenade represented a call to lunch—and breakfast and dinner too, come to that—along with any other snack you'd care to mention, where tasty tortured tidbits and bloody morsels were in plentiful supply and going spare.

Home.

I felt glad to be back after such a long and laborious assignment. But now that the Ascendant had passed, it would be another hundred thousand years before such an alignment of realms could jeopardize creation that way once again. *And hopefully, by then, Satan and Those Upstairs will have found a more permanent solution to keep everyone safe.*

A pity it cost me so much.

Jumping down from my perch, I made my way toward the full-length mirror on the room's far side. As I walked, my perceptions sank down to where a spark of the divine once resided.

Still smarting from a sense of loss, I attempted to call forth the heartrending splendor of God's Grace. *Nothing.*

I'd expected as much. As a consequence of victory, such a blessing had been stripped from me, along with the priceless ability to walk freely among the living. Of course, without the willing sacrifice of such majesty, forming the Veil anew would not have been possible. Even so, that didn't make acceptance of the unspeakable loss any easier to bear.

At least I've managed to retain access to the one thing that matters . . .

Catching sight of my reflection, I was gratified to note the jade green lightning that played in the depths of my eyes. This new facet of my making intrigued as well as excited me. Then the tattoos adorning my body flushed. In the next second, I found myself wreathed by a cocoon of gold and scarlet astral flames as the Bãlefire answered my call.

Tears of joy blurred my vision. *Now this! This is* my *heaven*. I inhaled, and the heady scent of brimstone and myrrh filled my lungs, soothing my concerns.

Yes, it's good to be back, even if my actions did induce some rather unusual side effects I hadn't expected.

One of those side effects related to my temperament. Somehow, my emotions—always so controlled and precise—had become off-the-charts hypersensitive. A condition I'd initially been concerned would aggravate the fuck out of His Satanic Majesty. But I needn't have worried. Ever since I'd awakened, the devil had evinced a particularly good mood, not only removing my need to regenerate among hell's most tainted essence, but enhancing my features as well.

Most concerned about fulfilling the duties of my office, I'd never bothered about my appearance. Even stripped of mortal flesh for months on end hadn't unduly worried me, for I'd been able to act as Reaper unhindered, due to a wondrous gift from my dark father: A set of polymorphic palladinium armor fitted around my skeleton, a synthesized second skin through which I could still feel sensations.

And now I felt privileged beyond compare, for Satan had refashioned me in his celestial image.

During the several weeks of this most recent recovery, I hadn't ventured beyond the castle's environs. Nevertheless, I heard the unabashed thoughts of passersby, and the whispers of my Hell Hounds and Inquisitors when they stopped by to visit.

"Beautiful."

"Amazing."

"Stunning."

"Angelic."

Even Gemini, newly returned from the Slab, had been rendered speechless when gazing upon my countenance for the first time. A strange affair, and reactions I didn't encourage, for I knew that if my compatriots reacted in this manner, then hell's miscreants would most certainly misunderstand.

"They'll look upon me, thinking my godly form promises benevolence, restraint and mercy." I grimaced, and my likeness in the mirror scowled like an obscene Adonis. "If they think this beatific façade represents anything more than a guarantee of unjust desserts, well…more fool them. Hopefully this 'heart on my sleeve' crap is but a temporary hiccup, manifesting only till my new complexus settles down and I get my mojo back.

"And if it isn't, I'll just have to do what I can to turn this glitch to my advant–?"

Daemon? thundered a telepathic hail in my head, its insidious mind-tone clarifying instantly who summoned me.

"Boss?"

If you'd care to leave off admiring your new look for a moment? That's m' boy. Join me in the drawing room across in the adjacent tower where I've just this minute finished going over your proposals for a treaty with Jahannam.

"And?"

And with a few refinements, I think we're onto a winner. I particularly like the way your pitch ties in their agreement to provide military aid and support as part compensation against damned souls lost through their little backdoor into and out of my realm. That *could provide substantive opportunity in the future. Well done, you're quite the politician in the making.*

I shuddered at the compliment. "I'm glad you like it. But please, don't bandy such ideas about, Boss. I prefer to let my blades do the talking."

As well you should, —a menacing chuckle grated through the ether— *especially as other matters demand your immediate attention?*

"Other matters?"

Why, Daemon, have you forgotten all the other things that happened while you were off on your grand adventure? There's revenge to plot against Erra and his Sibitti. Moles within our desecrated ranks to catch. Panic to spread amongst the rioting masses. Bloody murder to unleash at will and random. I'm sure your teams are itching to get their leader back after your little hiatus?

Are they ever!

I gestured, and two gleaming ninjaken flew across the room and slammed into my hands. Sheathing them, I ran for the door and gathered the power to phase.

"I'm on my way."

www.ingramcontent.com/pod-product-compliance
Lightning Source LLC
Chambersburg PA
CBHW032257020726
47495CB00001B/138